ROYAL FLASH

What happened to Flashman, the caddish bully of *Tom Brown's Schooldays*, after he was expelled in drunken disgrace from Rugby School in the late 1830s? What kind of man grew out of the foul-mouthed, swaggering, cowardly toady who roasted fags for fun and howled when he was beaten himself?

For more than a century the fate of history's most notorious schoolboy remained a mystery – until, in 1966, George MacDonald Fraser decided to discover a vast collection of unpublished manuscripts in a Midlands saleroom. Since then the scandalous saga of Flashman, Victorian hero and scoundrel, has emerged in a series of bestselling memoirs in which the arch-cad reviews, from the safety of old age, his exploits in bed and battle.

George MacDonald Fraser served in a Highland Regiment in India and the Middle East, worked on newspapers in Britain and Canada, and in addition to nine other Flashman novels, has also written many other bestselling novels, the latest of which is *Black Ajax*. Thousands of readers around the world have also been delighted by the three volumes of stories about Private McAuslan, thoughtfully described as "the biggest walking disaster to hit the British Army since Ancient Pistol". He has also written numerous films, most notably *The Three Musketeers*, *The Four Musketeers* and the James Bond film, *Octopussy*.

Also by George MacDonald Fraser

The Flashman Papers
(in chronological order)

Flashman
Royal Flash
Flashman's Lady
Flashman and the Mountain of Light
Flash for Freedom!
Flashman and the Redskins
Flashman at the Charge
Flashman in the Great Game
Flashman and the Angel of the Lord
Flashman and the Dragon
Flashman on the March
Flashman and the Tiger

★

Mr American
The Pyrates
The Candlemass Road
Black Ajax

★

Short Stories

The General Danced at Dawn
McAuslan in the Rough
The Sheikh and the Dustbin

★

History

The Steel Bonnets:
The Story of the Anglo-Scottish Border Reivers

★

Autobiography

Quartered Safe Out Here
The Light's on at Signpost

★

The Hollywood History of the World

ROYAL FLASH

From *The Flashman Papers*,
1842–43 and 1847–48

Edited and Arranged by
GEORGE MacDONALD FRASER

TED SMART

For Kath, again, and for

Ronald Coleman,
Douglas Fairbanks, jun.,
Errol Flynn,
Basil Rathbone,
Louis Hayward,
Tyrone Power,

and all the rest of them

HarperCollins*Publishers*
77–85 Fulham Palace Road,
Hammersmith, London W6 8JB

www.harpercollins.co.uk

This edition produced for The Book People Ltd,
Hall Wood Avenue, Haydock, St Helens WA11 9UL

This paperback edition 1999

Previous paperback edition 1993
Reprinted three times
Previously published in paperback by Fontana 1989
Reprinted three times

First published in Great Britain by
Barrie & Jenkins Ltd 1970
Reissued by Collins 1981

Copyright © George MacDonald Fraser 1970

George MacDonald Fraser asserts the moral right to
be identified as the author of this work

ISBN 0 00 775052 8

Set in Bembo

Printed and bound in Great Britain by
Clays Ltd, St Ives plc

Explanatory Note

The second packet of the Flashman Papers—that great collection of manuscript discovered in a saleroom in Leicestershire in 1965—continues the career of the author, Harry Flashman, from the point where the first instalment ended in the autumn of 1842. The first packet described his expulsion from Rugby School in 1839 (as previously referred to in Thomas Hughes' *Tom Brown's Schooldays*) and followed his subsequent military career in England, India, and Afghanistan; the second packet covers two separate periods of several months in 1842-43 and 1847-48. There is an intriguing four-year gap which the author seems to indicate he has covered elsewhere in his memoirs.

The present instalment is of historical importance insofar as it describes Flashman's encounters with several persons of international celebrity—including one most eminent statesman whose character and actions may now be subjected to some reappraisal by historians. It also establishes a point of some literary interest, for there can be no doubt that a link exists between Flashman's German adventure and one of the best-selling novels in the Victorian period.

As with the first packet (entrusted to me by Mr Paget Morrison, the owner of the Flashman Papers) I have confined myself to correcting the author's occasional lapses in spelling. Where Flashman touches on known history he is remarkably accurate, especially when one considers that he was writing in his eighties; wherever he appears to make a minor slip I have left it uncorrected in the text (as, for example, where he describes the pugilist Nick Ward as "the Champion" in 1842, when in fact Ward had lost his title the previous year), but I have added such notes and comments as seemed appropriate.

Like most memorialists, Flashman is vague about exact dates; where these can be established I have entered them in the notes.

G.M.F.

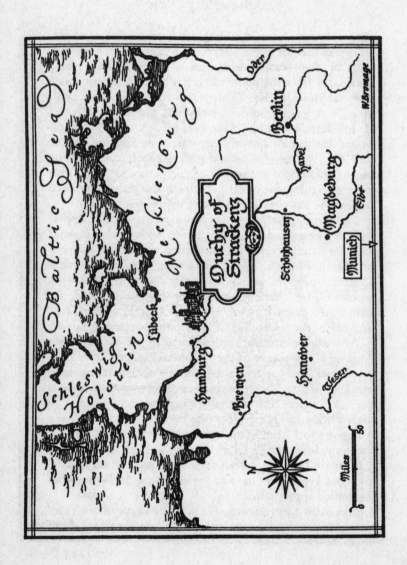

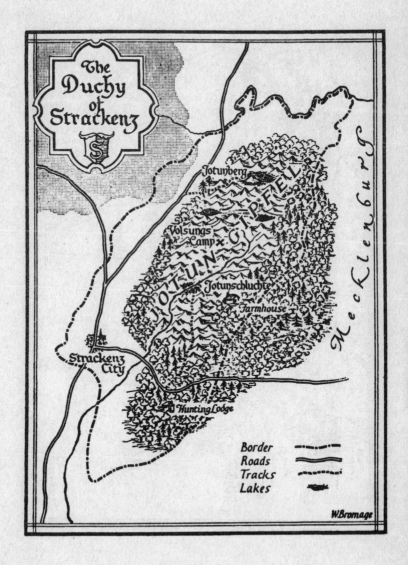

If I had been the hero everyone thought I was, or even a half-decent soldier, Lee would have won the battle of Gettysburg and probably captured Washington. That is another story, which I shall set down in its proper place if brandy and old age don't carry me off first, but I mention the fact here because it shows how great events are decided by trifles.

Scholars, of course, won't have it so. Policies, they say, and the subtly laid schemes of statesmen, are what influence the destinies of nations; the opinions of intellectuals, the writings of philosophers, settle the fate of mankind. Well, they may do their share, but in my experience the course of history is as often settled by someone's having a belly-ache, or not sleeping well, or a sailor getting drunk, or some aristocratic harlot waggling her backside.

So when I say that my being rude to a certain foreigner altered the course of European history, it is a considered judgement. If I had dreamed for a moment how important that man was going to be, I'd have been as civil as the devil to him, yes-me-lording and stroking his back. But in my youth and ignorance I imagined that he was one of those to whom I could be rude with impunity—servants, tarts, bagmen, shopkeepers, and foreigners—and so I gave my unpleasant tongue free rein. In the long run it nearly cost me my neck, quite apart from changing the map of the world.

It was in '42, when I was barely out of my 'teens, but already famous. I had taken a distinguished part in the fiasco known as the First Afghan War, emerged with a hero's laurels, been decorated by the Queen, and lionised all over London. The fact that I had gone through the campaign in a state of abject terror—lying, deceiving, bluffing, and running for dear life whenever possible—was known to no one but myself. If one or two suspected, they kept quiet. It wouldn't have been fashionable to throw dirt at the valiant Harry Flashman just then.

(If you have read the first packet of my memoirs, you will know all this. I mention it here in case the packets should get separated, so that you will know at once that this is the true story of a dishonest poltroon who takes a perverse pride in having attained to an honoured and admired old age, in spite of his many vices and entire lack of virtue—or possibly because of them.)

So there I was, in '42, big, bluff, handsome Harry, beloved of London society, admired at the Horse Guards (although I was only a captain), possessed of a beautiful wife, apparently affluent, seen in the best company, gushed at by the mamas, respected by the men as the perfect beau sabreur. The world was my oyster, and if it wasn't my sword that had opened it, no one was any the wiser.

They were golden days, those. The ideal time to be a hero is when the battle is over and the other fellows are dead, God rest 'em, and you take the credit.

Even the fact that Elspeth was cheating me made no real difference. You would never have thought, to see her angelic face, golden hair, and expression of idiotic innocence, that she was the biggest trollop that ever wore out a mattress. But I was certain, before I'd been home a month, that she was having it off with at least two others; at first I was furious and plotting revenge, but she had the money, you see, through that damned old Scotch moneybags of a father of hers, and if I had played the outraged husband I'd have been in Queer Street, without even a roof over my head. So I kept quiet, and paid her out by whoring to my heart's content. It was a strange situation; we both knew what was what (at least, I think she did, but she was such a fool you could never tell), but we pretended to be a happily married couple. We still bounced about in bed together from time to time, and enjoyed it.

But the real life was to be had outside; respectable society apart, I was in with the fast set, idling, gaming, drinking, and raking about the town. It was the end of the great days of the bucks and blades; we had a queen on the throne, and her cold white hand and her poker-backed husband's were already setting their grip on the nation's life, smothering the old wild ways in their come-to-Jesus hypocrisy. We were entering into what is now called the Victorian Age, when respectability was the thing; breeches were out and trousers came in; bosoms were being covered and eyes modestly lowered; politics was becoming sober, trade and industry were becoming fashionable, the odour of sanctity was replacing the happy reek of brandy, the age of the Corinthian, the plunger, and the dandy was giving way to that of the prig, the preacher, and the bore.

At least I was in at the death of that wicked era, and did my bit to make it die hard. You could still gamble in the hells about Hanover Square, carouse with the toughs in the Cyder Cellars or Leicester Fields, take your pick of the wenches in Piccadilly, set on the police at Whitehall and pinch their belts and hats, break windows and sing bawdy songs all the way home. Fortunes were still lost at cards and hazard, duels were fought (although I stayed well clear of that; my only duel, from which I emerged by fraud with tremendous credit, had taken place some years before, and I had no intention of risking another). Life could still be openly wild, if you cared for it. It has never been the same since; they tell me that young King Edward does what he can nowadays to lower the moral tone of the nation, but I doubt if he has the style for it. The man looks like a butcher.

One night my chum Speedicut, who had been with me at Rugby, and had come sucking round me since my rise to fame (he was well off) suggested we should go to a new haunt in St James—I think it was the Minor Club,

11

in fact.[1] We could try our luck at the tables first, and then
at the wenches upstairs, he said, and afterwards go to the
Cremorne and watch the fireworks, topping the night off
with devilled ham and a bowl of punch, and perhaps some
more girls. It sounded all right, so after collecting some
cash from Elspeth, who was going to Store Street to listen
to one Mr Wilson sing Scottish songs (my God), I set off
with Speed for St James.[2]

It was a frost from the start. On the way to the club
Speed was taken with the notion of boarding one of the
new buses; he wanted to argue with the cad about the fare
and provoke him into swearing: the bus cads were quite
famous for their filthy language, and Speed reckoned it
would be fun to have him get in a bate and horrify the
passengers.[3] But the cad was too clever for Speed; he just
turned us off without so much as a damn-your-eyes, and
the passengers tittered to see us made asses of, which did
nothing for our dignity or good temper.

And the club turned out to be a regular hell—the prices
even for arrack and cheroots were ruinous, and the faro
table was as crooked as a line of Russian infantry and a
damned sight harder to beat. It's always the same; the
more genteel the company, the fouler the play. In my time
I've played nap in the Australian diggings with gold-dust
stakes, held a blackjack bank on a South Sea trader, and
been in a poker game in a Dodge City livery stable with the
pistols down on the blanket—and I've met less sharping in
all of 'em put together than you'd find in one evening in a
London club.

We dropped a few guineas, and then Speed says:

"This ain't much fun. I know a better game."

I believed him, so we picked up two of the Cyprians
in the gaming-room and took them upstairs to play loo
for each others' clothes. I had my eye on the smaller of
the two, a pert little red-haired piece with dimples; thinks
I, if I can't get this one stripped for action in a dozen hands
then I've lost my talent for palming and dealing from the

12

bottom. But whether I'd taken too much drink—for we had punished a fair amount of arrack, dear as it was—or the tarts were cheating too, the upshot was that I was down to my shirt-tail before my little minx had removed more than her shoes and gloves.

She was trilling with laughter, and I was getting impatient, when a most unholy din broke out on the floor below. There was a pounding of feet, and shouting, whistles blowing and dogs barking, and then a voice yelled:

"Cut and run! It's the traps!"

"Christ!" says Speed, grabbing for his breeches. "It's a raid! Let's get out of this, Flash!"

The whores squeaked with panic, and I swore and struggled into my clothes. It's no joke trying to dress when the peelers are after you, but I had sense enough to know that there wasn't a hope of escaping unless we were fully clad—you can't run through St James on a fine evening with your trousers in your hand.

"Come on!" Speed was shouting. "They'll be on us in a moment!"

"What shall we do?" wails the red-haired slut.

"Do what you dam' well please," says I, slipping on my shoes. "Good-night, ladies." And Speed and I slipped out into the corridor.

The place was in uproar. It sounded like a battle royal down on the gaming-floor, with furniture smashing and the Cyprians screaming, and someone bawling: "In the Queen's name!" On our landing there were frightened whores peeping out of the doorways, and men in every stage of undress hopping about looking for somewhere to run to. One fat old rascal, stark naked, was beating on a door bawling:

"Hide me, Lucy!"

He beat in vain, and the last I saw of him he was trying to burrow under a sofa.

People nowadays don't realise that in the forties the law was devilish hot on gaming-hells. The police were forever trying to raid them, and the hell-owners used to keep guard-dogs and scouts to watch out for them. Most hells also had special hiding places for all gambling equipment, so that cards, dice, and boards could be swept out of sight in a moment, for the police had no right of search, and if they couldn't prove that gaming had been going on they could be sued for wrongful entry and trespass.[4]

Evidently they had caught the Minor St James Club napping with a vengeance, and it would be police court and newspaper scandal for us if we couldn't cut out pretty sharp. A whistle shrilled at the foot of the stairs, the trollops screamed and slammed their doors, and feet came pounding upwards.

"This way," says I to Speed, and we darted up the next flight. It was another empty landing—the top one—and we crouched by the bannisters, waiting to see what happened. They were hammering on the doors below, and presently someone came scampering up. He was a fair, chinless youth in a pink coat.

"Oh, my God!" says he, "what will mother say?" He stared wildly round. "Where can I hide?"

"In there," says I, thinking quickly, and pointed at a closed door.

"God bless you," says he. "But what will you do?"

"We'll hold 'em off," says I. "Get out of it, you fool."

He vanished inside, and I winked at Speed, whipped his handkerchief from his breast, and dropped it outside the closed door. Then we tip-toed to a room on the other side of the landing, and took cover behind its door, which I left wide open. From the lack of activity on this floor, and the dust-sheets in the room, it obviously wasn't in use.

Presently the peelers came crashing up, spotted the kerchief, gave a great view halloo, and dragged out the pink youth. But as I had calculated, they didn't bother with *our* room, seeing the door open and naturally supposing that no one could be hiding in it. We stood dead still while they tramped about the landing, shouting orders and telling the pink youth to hold his tongue, and presently they all trooped off below, where by the sound of things they were marshalling their prisoners, and being pretty rough about it. It wasn't often they raided a hell successfully, and had a chance to mistreat their betters.

"By George, Flashy," whispered Speed at last. "You're a foxy one, and no mistake. I thought we were done."

"When you've been chased by bloody Afghans," says I, "you learn all there is to know about lying low." But I was pleased at the way my trick had worked, just the same.

We found a skylight, and as luck had it there was a convenient flat roof close by over what proved to be an empty house. We prised up another skylight, crept down two flights of stairs, and got out of a back window into a lane. So far, excellent, but Speed thought it would be capital to go round the front and watch from a safe distance while the peelers removed their victims. I thought it would be fun, too, so we straightened our clothes and then sauntered round into the end of the street.

Sure enough, there was a crowd outside the Minor Club to see the sport. The bobbies were there in their high hats and belts, clustering round the steps while the prisoners were brought down to the closed carts, the men silent and shame-faced or damning their captors for all they were worth, and the trollops crying for the most part, although some had to be carried out kicking and scratching.

If we had been wise we would have kept well clear, but it was growing dusk, and we thought we'd have a closer look. We strolled up to the fringe of the crowd, and as bad luck had it, who should be brought out last, wailing and white-faced, but the youth in the pink coat. Speed guffawed at the woebegone look of him, and sang out to me:

"I say, Flashy, what will mother say?"

The youth must have heard; he twisted round and saw us, and the spiteful little hound gave a yelp and pointed in our direction.

"They were there, too!" he cries. "Those two, they were hiding as well!"

If we had stood fast we could have brazened it out, I dare say, but my instinct to run is too deep ingrained; I was off like a hare before the bobbies had even started towards us, and seeing us run they gave chase at once. We had a fair start, but not enough to be able to get out of view and duck into a doorway or area; St James is a damned bad district to fly from the police in—streets too broad and no convenient alleyways.

They were perhaps fifty yards behind for the first two streets, but then they began to gain—two of them, with their clubs out, yelling after us to stop. I could feel myself going lame in the leg I had broken earlier in the year at Jallalabad; the muscles were still stiff, and pains shot through my thigh at every stride.

Speed saw what was up and slackened his pace.

"Hallo, Flash," says he, "are you done for?"

"Leg's gone," says I. "I can't keep up any longer."

He glanced over his shoulder. In spite of the bad name Hughes gives him in *Tom Brown's Schooldays*, Speedicut was as game as a terrier and ready for a turn-up any time—not like me at all.[5]

"Oh, well, then," says he, "the deuce with this. Let's stand and have it out with 'em. There's only two—no, wait though, there are more behind, damn 'em. We'll just have to do the best we can, old son."

"It's no use," I gasped. "I'm in no state to fight."

"You leave 'em to me," cries he. "I'll hold 'em off while you get out of it. Don't stand there, man; don't you see it won't do for the hero of Afghanistan to be dragged in by the traps? Hellish scandal. Doesn't matter for me, though. Come on, you blue-bellied bastards!"

And he turned in the middle of the road, sparring away and daring them to come on.

I didn't hesitate. Anyone who is ass enough to sacrifice himself for Flashy deserves all he gets. Over my shoulder

I saw him stop one trap with a straight left, and close with the other. Then I was round the corner, hobbling away as fast as my game leg would carry me. It took me along that street and into the square beyond, and still no bobbies hove in view. I doubled round the central garden, and then my leg almost folded under me.

I rested, gasping, against the railings. Faintly behind me I could hear Speed still singing defiance, and then the nearer patter of feet. Looking round for somewhere to hide I saw a couple of carriages drawn up outside a house fronting onto the railed garden; they weren't far, and the two drivers were together, talking by the horses in the first one. They hadn't seen me; if I could hobble to the rear coach and crawl in, the peelers would pass me by.

Hopping quietly is difficult, but I got to the coach unseen by the drivers, opened the door and climbed in. I squatted down out of sight, heaving to get my breath back and listening for sounds of pursuit. But for several moments all was still; they must be off the scent, thinks I, and then I heard a new sound. Men's and women's voices were coming from the doorway of one of the houses; there was laughter and cries of goodnight, some chattering on the pavement and the sound of footsteps. I held my breath, my heart pounding, and then the carriage door opened, light came in, and I found myself staring into the surprised face of one of the loveliest girls I have ever seen in my life.

No—*the* loveliest. When I look back and review the beautiful women I have known, blonde and dark, slim and buxom, white and brown, hundreds of the creatures—still, I doubt if there was one to touch her. She was standing with one foot on the step, her hands holding back the skirts of her red satin gown, bending forward to display a splendid white bosom on which sparkled a row of brilliants matching the string in her jet-black hair. Dark blue eyes, very large, stared down at me, and her mouth, which was not wide but very full and red, opened in a little gasp.

17

"God save me!" exclaims she. "A man! What the devil are you doing, sir?"

It wasn't the kind of greeting you commonly heard from ladies in the young Queen's day, I may tell you. Any other would have screamed and swooned. Thinking quickly, I decided that for once truth would answer best.

"I'm hiding," says I.

"I can see that," says she smartly. She had a most lovely Irish lilt to her voice. "Who from, and why in my carriage, if you please?"

Before I could answer, a man loomed up at her elbow, and at sight of me he let out a foreign oath and started forward as though to protect her.

"Please, please, I mean no harm," I said urgently. "I'm being pursued . . . the police . . . no, I'm not a criminal, I assure you. I was in a club that was raided."

The man just stared at me, but the woman showed her teeth in a delightful smile and then threw her head back, chuckling. I smiled as ingratiatingly as I could, but for all the effect my charm had on her companion I might as well have been Quasimodo.

"Step out at once," snaps he, in a cold clipped voice. "At once, do you hear?"

I conceived an instant dislike for him. It was not only his manner and his words, but the look of him. He was big, as big as I was, slim-hipped and broad-shouldered, but he was also damned handsome. He had bright grey eyes and one of those clean-cut faces beneath fair hair that make you think of moral Norse gods, too splendid altogether to be in the company of the beauty beside him.

I started to say something, but he barked at me again, and then the woman came to my aid.

"Oh, let him be, Otto," says she. "Can't you see he's a gentleman?"

I would have thanked her gratefully, but at that moment there were heavy feet on the pavement, and a grave voice inquiring if the gentleman had seen anyone running through the square. The peelers were on the scent again, and this time I was cornered.

But before I could move or speak the lady had seated herself in the coach and hissed:

"Get up off the floor, you booby!"

I obeyed, in spite of my leg, and dropped gasping into the seat beside her. And then her companion, damn his eyes, was saying:

"Here is your man, constable. Arrest him, if you please."

A police sergeant poked his head in at the door, surveyed us, and said to the fair man, doubtfully:

"This gentleman, sir?"

"Of course. Who else?"

"Well . . ." The bobby was puzzled, seeing me sitting there large as life. "Are you sure, sir?"

The fair man rapped out another foreign oath, and said of course he was sure. He called the sergeant a fool.

"Oh, stop it, Otto," says the lady suddenly. "Really, sergeant, it's too bad of him; he's making game of you. This gentleman is with us."

"Rosanna!" The fair man looked outraged. "What are you thinking of? Sergeant, I—"

"Don't play the fool, Otto," says I, taking my cue, and delighted to have my hand squeezed by the lady. "Come on, man, get in and let's be off home. I'm tired."

He gave me a look of utter fury, and then a fine altercation broke out between him and the sergeant, which the lady Rosanna seemed to find vastly amusing. The coachee and another constable joined in, and then suddenly the sergeant, who had been frowning oddly in my direction while the argument raged, stuck his head into the coach again, and says:

"Wait a minnit. I know you, don't I? You're Cap'n Flashman, bigod!"

I admitted it, and he swore and slapped his fist.

"The 'ero of Julloolabad!" cries he.

19

I smiled modestly at Miss Rosanna, who was looking at me wide-eyed.

"The defender of Piper's Fort!" cries the sergeant.

"Well, well," says I, "it's all right, sergeant."

"The 'Ector of Afghanistan!" cries the sergeant, who evidently studied the press. "Damme! Well, 'ere's a go!"

He was beaming all over his face, which didn't suit my denouncer at all. Angrily he demanded that I be arrested.

"He is a fugitive," he declared. "He invaded our coach without permission."

"I don't give a dam' if 'e invaded Buckin'am Palace without permission," says the sergeant, turning back to me. "Corporal Webster, sir, Third Guards, under Major Macdonald at 'Ougoumont, sir."

"Honoured to know you, sergeant," says I, shaking his hand.

"Honour's mine, sir, 'deed it is. Now then, you, sir, let's 'ave no more of this. You're not English, are you?"

"I am a Prussian officer," says the man called Otto, "and I demand—"

"Cap'n Flashman is a British officer, so you don't demand nothink," says the sergeant. "Now, then! Let's 'ave no trouble." He touched his hat to us and gave me a broad wink. "Wish you good-night, sir, an' you, ma'am."

I thought the German would have an apoplexy, he looked so wild, and his temper was not helped by the lovely Rosanna's helpless laughter. He stood glaring at her for a moment, biting his lip, and then she controlled herself sufficiently to say:

"Oh, come along, Otto, get into the coach. Oh, dear, oh, dear," and she began laughing again.

"I am happy you are amused," says he. "You make a fool of me: it is of a piece with your conduct of this evening." He looked thoroughly vicious. "Very good, madam, perhaps you will regret it."

"Don't be so pompous, Otto," says she. "It's just a joke; come and—"

"I prefer choicer company," says he. "That of ladies, for example." And clapping on his hat he stepped back from the carriage door.

"Oh, the devil fly away with you then!" cried she, suddenly angry. "Whip up, driver!"

And then I had to open my mouth. Leaning across her, I called to him:

"How dare you talk so to a lady, damn you!" says I. "You're a foul-mouthed foreign dog!"

I believe if I had kept silent he would have forgotten me, for his temper was concentrated on her. But now he turned those cold eyes on me, and they seemed to bore like drills. For a moment I was frightened of the man; he had murder on his face.

"I shall remember you," says he. And then, oddly, I saw a look of curiosity come into his eyes, and he stepped a pace closer. Then it was gone, but he was memorising me, and hating me at the same time.

"I shall remember you," he said a second time, and the coach jerked forward and left him standing by the gutter.

In spite of the momentary fear he had awakened in me, I didn't give a button for his threats—the danger was past, I had recovered my breath, and I could devote my attention to the important question of the beauty alongside me. I had time to examine the splendour of her profile—the broad brow and raven-black hair, the small ever so slightly curved nose, the pouting red cupid's bow, the firm little chin, and the white round breasts pushing themselves impudently up from the red satin gown.

The scent of her perfume, the sidelong look of her dark blue eyes, and the wanton husky Irish voice, were all invitations. As anyone will tell you, put Harry Flashman next to a woman like that and one of two things is inevitable—there will either be screams and slaps, or the lady will surrender. Sometimes both. In this case, just from the look of her, I knew there would be no screaming

21

and slapping, and I was right. When I kissed her it was only a moment before her mouth opened under mine, and I promptly suggested that since my leg was still painful, a woman's touch on it would soothe the cramp out of my muscles. She complied, very teasingly, and with her free hand was remarkably skilful at fending off my advances until the coach reached her house, which was somewhere in Chelsea.

By this time I was in such a state of excitement that I could barely keep my hands still while she dismissed her maid and conducted me to her salon, talking gaily about anything and acting the cool minx. I soon put a stop to that by popping her breasts out the minute the door was closed, and bearing her down on to the settee. Her reaction was startling; in a moment she was grappling with me, digging her nails into me and twining her limbs round mine. The fury of her love-making was almost frightening—I've known eager women, plenty of them, but Miss Rosanna was like a wild animal.

The second time, later in the night, was even more feverish than the first. We were in bed by then, and I had no clothing to protect me from her biting and raking nails; I protested, but it was like talking to a mad woman. She even began to leather me with something hard and heavy—a hair-brush, I believe—and by the time she had stopped writhing and moaning I felt as though I had been coupling with a roll of barbed wire.[6] I was bruised, scratched, bitten, and stabbed from neck to backside.

In between, she was a different creature, gay, talkative, witty, and of a gentleness to match her voice and looks. I learned that she was Marie Elizabeth Rosanna James, no less, the wife of a fellow-officer who was conveniently out of town on garrison duty. Like myself, she was recently returned from India, where he had been stationed; she found life in London deadly dull; such friends as she knew were stiff and boring; there was hardly any of the bright life she craved; she wished she was back in India, or anywhere she might have some fun. That was why my appearance in her carriage had been so welcome; she had spent a preposterously dull evening with her husband's relatives, escorted by the German Otto, whom she found stuffy to a degree.

"Just the sight of a man who looked as though he had some—oh, some spunk in him—was enough for me," says she. "I wouldn't have turned you over to the police, my dear, not if you had been a murderer. And it was a chance to take down that conceited Prussian muff—would you believe that a man who looks so splendid could have ice and vinegar in his veins?"

"Who is he?" I asked.

"Otto? Oh, one of these Germans making the Grand Tour in reverse. Sometimes I think there's a bit of the devil in him, but he keeps it well hid; he behaves *so* properly because like all foreigners he likes to impress the English. Tonight, just to try and breathe some life into that collection of prigs, I offered to show them a Spanish dance—you would have thought I'd said something indecent. They didn't even say, 'Oh, my dear!' Just turned their heads to one side, the way these English women do, as though they were going to be sick." She tossed her head enchantingly, kneeling on the bed like a naked nymph. "But I saw the glitter in Otto's eyes, just for an instant. I'll be bound he's not so prim among the German wenches at Schonhausen, or wherever it is."

I thought there was too much of Otto, and said so.

"Oh, yes, are you jealous, then?" says she sticking out her lip at me. "You've made a bad enemy there, my dear. Or is the famous Captain Flashman careless of enemies?"

"They don't concern me, German, French, or nigger," says I. "I don't think much of your Otto at all."

"Well, you should," says she, teasing. "For he's going to be a great man some day—he told me so. 'I have a destiny', he said. 'What's that?' I asked him. 'To rule', says he. So I told him I had ambitions, too—to live as

I please, love as I please, and never grow old. He didn't think much of that, I fancy; he told me I was frivolous, and would be disappointed. Only the strong, he said, could afford ambitions. So I told him I had a *much* better motto than that."

"What was that?" says I, reaching out for her, but she caught my hands and held them apart, looking wicked.

" 'Courage—and shuffle the cards'," says she.

"Damned sight better motto than his," says I, pulling her down on top of me. "And I'm a greater man than he is, anyway."

"Prove it—again," said Miss Rosanna, biting at my chin. And, at the cost of more scratches and bruises, I did.

That was the beginning of our affair, and a wild, feverish one it was, but it couldn't last long. For one thing, she was so demanding a mistress that she came near to wearing me out, and if she was a novelty, she was one I didn't altogether enjoy. She was too imperious, and I prefer softer women who understand that it is my pleasure that counts. Not with Miss Rosanna, though; she *used* men. It was like being eaten alive, and God help you if you weren't ready to command. Everything had to be at her whim, and I got sick of it.

It was about a week after our first meeting that I finally lost my temper. We had had a tempestuous night, but when I wanted to go to sleep she had to chatter on—and even a husky Irish voice can get sickening when you've heard too much of it. And seeing me inattentive, she suddenly shouts, "On guard!" which was her war-cry before a tumble, and jumped on me again.

"In heaven's name!" says I. "Get off. I'm tired."

"Nobody gets tired of me," she flashed back, and started teasing me into action, but I was pegged out, and told her to let me alone. For a moment she persisted, and then she was sulky, and then in an instant she was in a raging fury, and before I knew it I had given her the back

24

of my hand and she was coming at me like a wildcat, screaming and clawing.

Now, I've dealt with raging women before, but I'd never met anything like her. She was dangerous—a beautiful, naked savage, flinging everything that came within reach, calling me the foulest names, and—I admit it freely—terrorising me to the point where I grabbed my clothes and ran for it. "Bastard and coward!" was the least of it, I remember, and a chamber pot smashing on the door-jamb as I blundered through. I roared threats at her from the corridor, at which she darted out, white with fury, flourishing a bottle, and I didn't stay for more. One way and another, I've probably had more practice in dressing running than most men, but this time I didn't bother until I'd got out of shot at the foot of the stairs.

I was badly shaken, I can tell you, and not my own man again till I was well away from her house and pondering, in my philosophic way, on means of getting my own back on the vicious, bad-tempered slut. It will seem to you to be the usual, sordid conclusion to so many Flashman amours, but I have dwelt on it at some length for good reason. It wasn't only that she was, in her way, as magnificent a creature as I've ever had the good fortune to mount, and comes back to my mind whenever I see a hair-brush. That alone would not be sufficient. No, my excuse is that this was my first encounter with one of the most remarkable women in my life—or in the life of anyone in the nineteenth century, for that matter. Who could have guessed then that Marie Elizabeth Rosanna James would turn a crowned head, rule a great kingdom, and leave a name to compare with Dubarry or Nell Gwynn? Well, she was Flashy's girl for a week, at least, which is something to boast of. But I was glad to be shot of her at the time, and not just because of the way she treated me: I discovered soon after that she hadn't been altogether truthful about herself. She hadn't mentioned, for example, that her soldier husband was in the process of divorcing her, which would have been enough to scare me away to less controversial beds if I'd known it sooner. Apart from the unpleasant social aspects of being cited, I couldn't have afforded it.

But she was important in my life in another way—she had been the means of my meeting the splendid Otto. You could say that it was through her that the mischief was born between him and me, and our enmity shaped his future, and the world's.

Nothing might have come of it, though, had I not run into him again, by pure chance, a month or so later. It was at Tom Perceval's place in Leicestershire, where I joined a party to see Nick Ward[7] fight some local pug, and to do a little hunting in Tom's coverts. Young Conyngham,[8] who was a fool of a gambler, was there, and old Jack Gully, who had once been Champion of England and was now a rich ironmaster and retired from the House of Commons as well; there were about a dozen others whom I've forgotten, and Speedicut, too—when I'd told him how *I'd* spent the night of his arrest, he just roared with laughter and cried "Flashy's luck! Well, only the brave deserve the fair!" And he insisted on telling everyone how it had happened, himself lying in a dirty cell full of drunkards while I was bumping a beauty.

Most of the company were at Tom's place when I arrived, and when he met me in the hall he told me:

"They're all old acquaintances but one, a foreigner that I can't get rid of, damn him. Friend of my uncle's, and wants to see something of our rustic ways while he's here. Trouble is, he's full of bounce, and some of the fellows are rather sick of it already."

It meant nothing until I went into the gunroom with him, where the boys were cheering up the cold night with punch and a roaring fire, and who should be there, very formal in long coat and trousers among all the buffs and boots, but Otto. He stiffened at the sight of me, and I brought up short.

The fellows gave a hurrah when I came in, and thrust punch and cheroots at me, while Tom did his duty by the stranger.

"Baron," says he—the brute has a title, thinks I—"permit me to present Captain Flashman. Flash, this is Baron Otto von . . . er, dammit . . . von Schornhausen, ain't it? Can't get my confounded tongue round it."

"Schonhausen," says Otto, bowing stiffly with his eyes on mine. "But that is, in fact, the name of my estate,

27

if you will pardon my correction. My family name is Bismarck."[9]

It's an old man's fancy, no doubt, but it seemed to me that he said it in a way that told you you would hear it again. It meant nothing to me, of course, at the time, but I was sure that it was going to. And again I felt that prickle of fear up my back; the cold grey eyes, the splendid build and features, the superb arrogance of the man, all combined to awe me. If you're morally as soft as butter, as I am, with a good streak of the toad-eater in you, there's no doing anything with people like Bismarck. You can have all the fame that I had then, and the good looks and the inches and the swagger—and I had those, too—but you know you're dirt to him. If you have to tangle with him, as the Americans say, you know you'll have to get drunk first; I was sober, so I toadied.

"Honoured to make your acquaintance, Baron," says I, giving him my hand. "Trust you're enjoying your visit."

"We are already acquainted, as I'm sure you remember," says he, shaking hands. He had a grip like a vice; I guessed he was stronger than I was, and I was damned strong, in body at least. "You recollect an evening in London? Mrs James was present."

"By God!" says I, all astounded. "So I do! Well, well! And here you are, eh? Damme, I never expected . . . well, Baron, I'm glad to see you. Aye, hum. I trust Mrs James is well?"

"Surely I should ask you?" says he, with a thin smile. "I have not seen the . . . lady, since that evening."

"No? Well, well. I haven't seen a great deal of her lately myself." *I* was prepared to be pleasant, and let bygones be bygones, if he was. He stood, smiling with his mouth, considering me.

"Do you know," says he at length, "I feel sure I have seen you before, but I cannot think where. That is unusual, for I have an excellent memory. No, not in England. Have you ever been in Germany, perhaps?"

I said I hadn't.

"Oh, well, it is of no interest," says he coolly, meaning that *I* was of no interest, and turned away from me.

I hadn't liked him before, but from that moment I hated Bismarck, and decided that if ever the chance came to do him a dirty turn, I wouldn't let it slip past me.

Tom had said he was full of bounce, and at supper that night we got a good dose of it. It was very free and easy company, as you can imagine, with no women present, and we ate and drank and shouted across the table to our heart's content, getting pretty drunk and nobody minding his manners much. Bismarck ate like a horse and drank tremendously, although it didn't seem to show on him; he didn't say much during the meal, but when the port went round he began to enter the conversation, and before long he was dominating it.

I'll say this for him, he wasn't an easy man to ignore. You would have thought that a foreigner would have kept mum and watched and listened, but not he. His style was to ask a question, get an answer, and then deliver judgement—for instance, he says to Tom, what was the hunting like, and Tom remarking that it was pretty fair, Bismarck said he looked forward to trying it, although he doubted if chasing a fox could hold a candle to the boar-hunting he had done in Germany. Since he was a guest, no one pulled his leg, although there were a few odd looks and laughs, but he sailed on, lecturing us about how splendid German hunting was, and how damned good at it he was, and what a treat we were missing, not having wild pigs in England.

When he had done, and there was one of those silences, Speed broke it by remarking that I had done some boar-hunting in Afghanistan; the fellows seemed to be looking to me to take the talk away from Bismarck, but before I had the chance he demanded:

"In Afghanistan? In what capacity were you there, Captain Flashman?"

Everyone roared with laughter at this, and Tom tried to save his guest embarrassment by explaining that I had been soldiering there, and had pretty well won the war single-handed. He needn't have minded, for Bismarck never turned a hair, but began to discourse on the Prussian Army, of all things, and his own lieutenant's commission, and how he regretted that there were so few chances of active service these days.

"Well," says I, "you can have any that come my way, and welcome." (This is the kind of remark that folk love to hear from a hero, of course.) The fellows roared, but Bismarck frowned.

"You would avoid dangerous service?" says he.

"I should just think I would," say I, winking at Speed. If only they had known how true that was. "Damned unpleasant, dangerous service. Bullets, swords, chaps killing each other—no peace and quiet at all."

When the laughter had died down, Tom explained that I was joking; that I was, in fact, an exceptionally brave man who would miss no chance of battle and glory. Bismarck listened, his cold eye never leaving me, and then, would you believe it, began to lecture us on a soldier's duty, and the nobility of serving one's country. He obviously believed it, too, he rolled it out so solemnly, and it was all some of the younger men could do to keep their faces straight. Poor old Tom was in an anguish in case we offended his guest, and at the same time obviously nearly out of patience with Bismarck.

"I wish to God my uncle had found some other poor devil to bear-lead him," says he later to Speedicut and me. "Was there ever a bigger bore and ass? How am I to deal with the fellow, eh?"

We couldn't help him; in fact I resolved to keep as far out of Bismarck's way as possible. He unsettled me; he was so damned superior. Tom was wrong in one thing: Bismarck wasn't an ass, whatever else he might be. In some ways he was like that outstanding idiot Cardigan, under whom I had served in the 11th Hussars, but only on the surface. He had the same splendid certainty in everything he said and did; he looked on the world as created for him alone; he was right, and that was that. But where Cardigan's arrogant eye had the shallow stare of the born fool, Bismarck's didn't. You could see the brain at work behind it, and those who listened only to his rather monotonous sermonisings and noticed only his lack of humour—of *our* kind of humour, anyway—and put him down as a pompous dullard were well wide of the mark.

I wanted nothing to do with him, anyway, but in that short visit at Tom's place Bismarck still contrived to touch me on the raw twice—and in the only two things that I am any good at, too. Coward and rascal that I've always been, I have had two talents, for foreign tongues and for horses. I can master almost any language in short time, and ride anything with a mane and tail. Looking back, I can almost believe that Bismarck smelled these two gifts and set out to hip me over them.

I don't remember how the conversation at one breakfast came to touch on foreign speech—usually it was women and drink and horses and pugs, with an occasional high flight on something like the scandalous rate of income tax at 7d in the pound.[10] But it did, and my gift was mentioned. Bismarck, lounging back in his chair, gave a sneering little laugh and said that it was a useful talent in head-waiters.[11]

I was furious, and tried to think of some cutting retort, but couldn't. Later it occurred to me that I might have fixed him with a look and said it was also a useful gift in German pimps, but it was too late then. And you could never be quite sure with his remarks whether he was jibing or simply stating what he thought was a fact, so I just had to ignore him.

The second set-down came on a day's hunting, when we had had poor sport and were riding home. Conyngham, drawing rein on top of a slight rise from which you could

31

see miles of rolling countryside in every direction, points to a church which was just visible in the distance through the late afternoon haze, and cries out:

"Who's for a steeplechase?"

"Oh, too much of a fag," says Tom. "Anyway, it's getting dark and the beasts may go wrong. I vote for home."

"Steeplechase?" says Bismarck. "What is that?"

It was explained to him that the object was to race straight across country for the steeple, and he nodded and said it was an excellent sport.

"Good for you!" cries Conyngham. "Come on, you fellows! You, Flashy, are you game?"

"Too far," says I, for like Tom I didn't fancy taking hedges on wettish country with the light starting to fail.

"Nonsense!" cries Bismarck. "What, gentlemen, are the English backward in their own game? Then you and I, Marquis, shall we have it out together?"

"With you! Tally-ho!" yells Conyngham, and of course the other asses took off after them. I couldn't hang back, so cursing Bismarck I clapped in my heels and gave chase.

Conyngham led the field over the first meadows, with Bismarck close behind, but a couple of hedges checked them, and the rest of us caught up. I hung back a little, for steeplechasing in the style of your old-fashioned bucks, when you just go hell-for-leather at everything, is as quick a road to a broken neck as I know. If you have an eye for ground, and watch how the leaders jump and land, you can reap the benefit of their discoveries without the risk of going first. So I rode a nice easy chase for the first mile or so, and then we came into light woodland, with trees well spaced out, and I touched my hunter and moved up.

There is a moment every jockey knows, when he feels his mount surge forward, and he lies with his head down being brushed by the mane, and sees the gap narrowing ahead of him, and knows he has the legs of the field. I felt it then as I thundered past the ruck, hearing the thud of the hooves and seeing the clods thrown up from the wet turf, feeling the wind in my face as the trees flew past; even now I see the scarlet coats in the fading light, and smell the rain-sodden country, and hear the yelps of the fellows as they cheered each other on and laughed and cursed. God, it was good to be young and English then!

We thundered through the woodland like a charge of dragoons and were out on a long, rising incline. Conyngham held the lead to the crest, but as we came over and down it was the turn of the heavier men; Bismarck went past him, and then I, too; we pounded down to the hedgerow, Bismarck went over like a bird—he could ride, I may say—and I launched my hunter at the same gap and came through on his heels. I stayed with him, over hedges, lanes, ditches, and fences, until I saw the steeple perhaps half a mile away, and now, thinks I, is the time to get my nose in front.

I had the speed in hand; his head came round as I drew level, and he hammered in his heels and plied his crop, but I knew I had the distance of him. He was leading by half a length as we took a rail fence; then we were on pasture with only one hedge between us and the common that ran up to the churchyard. I inched up level and then led by a head, scanning the distant hedge for a good jump. It was a nasty one, high hawthorn with trees at intervals throwing their shade over the hedgerow; there was one place that looked likely, where the hawthorn thinned and only a couple of rails covered the gap. I clapped in my heels and made for it; first over was a certain winner. As we closed in, with me half a length in front, I realised that even at the rails the jump was a good five feet; I didn't half fancy it, for as Hughes pointed out, Flashman was good only at those games which didn't entail any physical risk. But there was nothing for it; I had Bismarck headed and must keep my lead, so I steadied the hunter for the jump, and then out of nowhere came Bismarck's grey at my elbow, challenging for the jump.

"Give way!" I roared. "My jump, damn your eyes!"

By God, he paid not the slightest heed, but came boring in, neck and neck with me for the fence. We were almost knee to knee as we rushed down on it.

"Get out, blast you!" I yelled again, but he was just staring ahead, teeth clenched and whip going, and I knew in an instant that it was a case of pull up or have the most unholy smash as two horses tried to take a jump where there was only space for one.

As it was, I came within an ace of a hellish tumble; I reined back and at the same time tried to swerve from the gap; the hunter checked and swung away and we scraped along the face of the hedge with no more damage than a few scratches, while Master Bismarck cleared the rails with ease.

By the time I had trotted back, cursing most foully, the rest of the chase was thundering up; Bismarck was waiting at the lychgate looking cool and smug when we arrived.

"Don't you know to give way to the leader?" says I, boiling angry. "We might have broken our necks, thanks to you!"

"Come, come, Captain Flashman," says he, "it would have been thanks to *you* if we had, for you would have been foolishly challenging the stronger rider."

"What?" says I. "And who the devil says you are the stronger rider?"

"I won, did I not?" says he.

It was on the tip of my tongue to say that he had ridden foul, but the way the other chaps were hallooing, and telling him what a damned fine race he had ridden, I thought better of it. He had gone up in their estimation; he was a damned good-plucked 'un, they shouted, and they clapped him on the back. So I contented myself with suggesting that he learn the rules of horsemanship before he rode in England again, at which the others laughed and cried:

"That's right, Flash, damn his eyes for him!" and made

a joke out of bluff Flashy's bad temper. They hadn't been close enough to see exactly what had happened, and none of them would have imagined for a minute that neck-or-nothing Flashman would give way in the breach; but Bismarck knew, and it showed in his eyes and the cold smile he gave me.

But I had my own back on him before the week was out, and if my initial rudeness in London was the first spark in the mischief between us, what was now to come really started the fire.

It was on the last day, after we had been to see the fight between Nick Ward the Champion, and the local pug. It was a good afternoon's sport, with the pug getting his nose broken and half his teeth knocked out; Bismarck was greatly interested, and seemed to enjoy watching the loser being battered as much as I did myself.

At supper that night the talk was naturally of the fight, and old Jack Gully, who had refereed, held the floor. He wasn't normally an over-talkative man, despite the fact that he had been an M.P., but on his two loves—the prize ring and horseflesh—he was always worth listening to. Though it was more than thirty years since he had held the belt himself—and since retiring he had become most prosperous and was well received everywhere—he had known and seen all the greatest pugs, and was full of stories of such giants as Cribb and Belcher and the Game Chicken.[12]

Of course, the company would have listened all night—I don't suppose there was a man in England, Peel, Russell, or any of them, who could have commanded such universal attention as this quiet old boxing champion. He must have been close to sixty then, and white-haired, but you could see he was still fit as a flea, and when he talked of the ring he seemed to light up and come alive.

Bismarck, I noticed, didn't pay him much attention, but when Jack paused after a story, our German suddenly says:

"You make very much of this boxing, I see. Now,

it is an interesting enough spectacle, two of the lower orders thrashing each other with their fists, but does it not become boring after a while? Once, or even twice, perhaps, one might go to watch, but surely men of education and breeding must despise it."

There was a growl round the table, and Speed says:

"You don't understand it because you're a foreigner. It is our game in England. Why, in Germany, according to what you've said, fellows fight duels without any intent to kill each other, but just to get scars on their heads. Well, we wouldn't think much of that, let me tell you."

"The *schlager* endows a man with honourable scars," says Bismarck. "What honour is there in beating an opponent with your fists? Besides, our duelling is for gentlemen."

"Well, as to that, mynheer," says Gully, smiling, "gentlemen in this country ain't ashamed to use their fists. I know I wish I'd a guinea for every coroneted head I've touched with a straight left hand."

"Mine for one, any time you please, Jack," cries Conyngham.

"But in the use of the *schlager* there is soldierly skill," Bismarck insisted, and rapped his fist on the table. Oho, thinks I, what's this? Has our Prussian friend perhaps got a little more liquor on board than usual? He was a mighty drinker, as I've said, but it occurred to me that he might not be holding it so well tonight.

"If you think there's no skill in prize-fighting, my friend, you're well out of court," says one of the others, a heavy-faced Guardee named Spottswood. "Didn't you see Ward, this afternoon, take the starch out of a chap three stone heavier than himself?"

"Oh, your fellow Ward was swift and strong," says Bismarck. "But speed and strength are common enough. I saw no sign of skill in that butchery."

And he emptied his glass as though that settled the matter.

"Well, sir," says old Jack, smiling, "there was skill

a-plenty, and you can take my word for it. You wouldn't
see it, 'cos you don't know what to look for, just as I
wouldn't know what to look for in your schlag-what-
you-call-ems."

"No," says Bismarck, "likely you would not." And the
tone of his voice made Gully look sharp at him, although
he said nothing. Then Tom Perceval, sensing that there
might be trouble if the subject wasn't changed, started to
say something about hunting, but I had seen my chance to
set this arrogant Prussian down, and I interrupted him.

"Perhaps you think boxing is easy," says I to Bismarck.
"D'ye fancy you could hold your own in a mill?"

He stares at me across the table. "With one of those
brawlers?" says he at length. "A gentleman does not come
to physical contact with those people, surely?"

"We don't have serfs in England," says I. "There isn't
a man round this table wouldn't be glad to put 'em up
with Nick Ward—aye, and honoured, too. But in your
case—suppose there was a sporting German baron whose
touch wouldn't sully you? Would you be ready to try it
with him?"

"Hold on, Flash—" says Perceval, but I carried on.

"Or a gentleman from among ourselves, for example?
Would you be ready to go a round or two with one of us?"

Those cold eyes of his were damned uncomfortable
on me, but I held his gaze, for I knew I'd got him. He
considered a moment, and then said:

"Is this a challenge?"

"Good God, no," says I. "Only you think that our good
old game is just a brawl, and I'd like to show you different.
If I were asked, I'd be ready enough to try my hand at this
schlager business of yours. Well, what d'ye say?"

"I see you are smarting for revenge after our race the
other day," says he, smiling. "Very well, Captain, I shall
try a round with you."

I believe he had weighed me up for a coward who
wouldn't be much good, in which he was right, and that he

also thought—like many another ignoramus—that boxing was pure brute force and nothing more, in which he was wrong. Also, he had seen that a good part of it was body wrestling, of which no doubt he had some experience. And he knew he was pretty well as big and strong as I. But I had a surprise in store for him.

"Not with me," says I. "I'm no Nick Ward. Anyway, my idea is instruction, not revenge, and the best instructor in the whole wide world is sitting within ten feet of you." And I nodded at Gully.

All I intended was to make a fool of Bismarck, which I knew Gully could do with one hand behind his back, and so cut his comb for him. I hadn't any hope that Gully would hurt him, for unfortunately old Jack, like most champions, was a gentle, kindly sort of fool. Indeed, at my proposal, he burst out laughing.

"Lord, Flashy," says he. "D'ye know how much I used to be paid to come up to scratch? And you want to see it free, you dog!"

But Bismarck wasn't laughing. "That is a foolish proposal," says he. "Mr Gully is too old."

Gully's laugh was wiped off his face at once. "Now, wait a moment, mynheer," says he, but I was ahead of him again.

"Oh, is that it?" says I. "You wouldn't be chary about milling with a professional, would you?"

Everyone was talking at once, of course, but Bismarck's voice cut through them.

"I have no interest in whether he is a professional or not—"

"Or the fact that he was once in jail?" says I.

"—but only in the fact that he is very much older than I. As to his being in prison, what has that to do with anything?"

"You know best about that," says I, sneering.

"Now, dammit, hold on here," says Perceval. "What the devil is all this? Flashy—"

"Ah, I'm sick of his airs," says I, "and his sneers at Jack there. All right, he's your guest, Tom, but he goes a bit far. Let him put up or shut up. I only suggested he should try a round with a real boxer, to show him that his jibes were wide of the mark, and he turns up his nose as though Gully weren't good enough for him. It's the wrong side of enough, I say."

"Not good enough?" roars Jack. "What's this . . .?"

"No one said anything of the sort," cries Tom. "Flashy, I don't know what you're driving at, but—"

"Captain Flashman's intention is apparently to annoy me," says Bismarck. "He has not succeeded. My only objection to boxing with Mr Gully was on the score of his age."

"That'll do about my age, thank'ee!" says Jack, going red. "I'm not so old I can't deal with anyone who don't know his place!"

They calmed him down, and there was a lot of hubbub and noise and nonsense, and the upshot was that most of them, being slightly fuddled anyway, got the notion that I had suggested, friendly-like, to Bismarck, that he try a round with Gully, and that somehow he had insulted old Jack and looked down on him. It was Spottswood who calmed things over, and said there was no cause for shouting or hard feelings.

"The point is, does the Baron want to try his hand in a friendly spar? That's all. If so, Jack'll oblige, won't you, Jack?"

"No, no," says Jack, who was cooled again. "Why, I haven't stood in a ring for thirty years, man. Besides," he added, with a smile, "I didn't understand that our guest was eager to try me."

That brought him a lofty look from Bismarck, but Spottswood says:

"Tell ye what, Jack; if you'll spar a round or two with him, I'll sell you Running Ribbons."

He knew Jack's weak spot, you see; Running Ribbons

was own brother to Running Reins, and a prime goer.[13] Jack hummed and hawed a bit, saying no, no, his fighting days were long done, but the fellows, seeing him waver, and delighted at the thought of watching the famous Gully in action (and no doubt of lowering Bismarck a peg or two) urged him on, cheering him and slapping him on the shoulder.

"Well, well," says Jack at last, for his flash of ill-temper had quite gone now, and he was his placid self, "if you must have it, I'll tell you what I'll do. To convince the Baron here, that there's maybe more in the Noble Art than meets his eye, I'll engage to stand up in front of him, with my hands down, and let him try to plant me a few facers. What d'ye say to that, sir?" he asks Bismarck.

The German, who had been sitting very disdainful, looked interested despite himself.

"You mean you will let me strike you, without defending yourself?"

Jack grins at him. "I mean I'll let you *try*," says he.

"But I *must* strike you—unless you run away."

"I reckon you're not too clever in our lingo yet," says Jack, smiling, but looking keen. "What with 'too old' and 'running away', you know. But don't worry, mynheer— I'll stand my ground."

There was a great commotion while the table was thrust against one wall, and the carpet rolled up, and everyone piled furniture to the sides of the room to leave space for the exhibition. Perceval was the only one who wasn't delighted at the prospect; "'Tain't fair," says he, "not to a guest; I don't like it. Ye'll not hurt him, Jack, d'ye hear?"

"Not a hair of his head," says old Jack.

"But his vanity may be a bit bruised when he discovers it ain't so easy to hit a good milling cove as he imagines," says Speed, laughing.

"That's what I don't like either," says Perceval. "It looks as though we're making a fool of him."

"Not us," says I. "He'll be doing it himself."

"And serve the German windbag right," says Spottswood. "Who's he to tell us our faults, damn him?"

"I still don't like it," says Perceval. "Curse you, Flash, this is your doing." And he mooched away, looking glum.

At the other end of the room Conyngham and one of the other chaps were helping Bismarck off with his coat. You could see he was wondering how the devil he had got into this, but he put a good face on it, pretending to be amused and interested when they fastened the gloves on him and Jack, and explained what was expected of him. Spottswood led the two of them to the centre of the floor, where a line had been chalked on the boards, and holding one on either hand, called for silence.

"This ain't a regular mill," says he ("Shame!" cries someone). "No, no," says Spottswood, "This is a friendly exhibition in the interests of good sportsmanship and friendship between nations. ('Hurrah!' 'Rule Britannia!' from the fellows). Our old and honoured friend, Jack Gully, champion of champions—" at this there was a great hurrah, which set old Jack grinning and bobbing—"has generously engaged to let Herr Otto von Bismarck stand up to him and try, if he can, to hit him fair on the head and body. Mr Gully engages further not to hit back, but may, if he wishes, use his hands for guarding and blocking. I shall referee"—cries of "Shame!" "Watch out for him, Baron, he's a wrong 'un!"—"and at my word the contestants will begin and leave off. Agreed? Now, Baron, you may hit him anywhere above the waist. Are you ready?"

He stepped back, leaving the two facing each other. It was a strange picture: the big candelabra lit the room as clear as day, shining on the flushed faces of the spectators sitting or squatting on the furniture piled round the panelled walls; on the sporting prints and trophies hung above them; on the wide, empty polished floor; on the jumble of silver and bottles and piled plates on the table with its wine-stained cloths; on the two men toe to toe at

41

the chalk line. There was never a stranger pair of millers in the history of the game.

Bismarck, in his shirt and trousers and pumps, with the big padded mauleys on his fists, may have been awkward and uncertain, but he looked well. Tall, perfectly built and elegant as a rapier, with his fair cropped head glistening under the light, he reminded me again of a nasty Norse god. His lips were tight, his eyes narrow, and he was studying his man carefully before making a move.

Gully, on the other hand—oh, Gully! In my time I've seen Mace and Big Jack Heenan and little Sayers, and I watched Sullivan beat Ryan[14] and took $10 off Oscar Wilde over that fight, too, but I doubt if any of them could have lived with Gully at his best. Not that I ever saw that best, but I saw him face up to Bismarck, nearly sixty years old, and that is enough for me. Like most poltroons, I have a sneaking inward regard for truly fearless, strong men, fools though they may be, and I can have an academic admiration for real skill, so long as I don't suffer by it. Gully was fearless and strong and incredibly skilful.

He stood on the balls of his feet, head sunk between his massive shoulders, hands down, his leathery brown face smiling ever so slightly, his eyes fixed on Bismarck beneath beetling brows. He looked restful, confident, indestructible.

"Time!" cries Spottswood, and Bismarck swung his right fist. Jack swayed a little and it went past his face. Bismarck stumbled, someone laughed, and then he struck again, right and left. The right went past Jack's head, the left he stopped with his palm. Bismarck stepped back, looking at him, and then came boring in, driving at Jack's midriff, but he just turned his body sideways, lazily almost, and the German went blundering by, thumping the air.

Everyone cheered and roared with laughter, and Bismarck wheeled round, white-faced, biting his lip. Jack, who didn't seem to have moved more than a foot, regarded him with interest, and motioned him to come on again. Slowly, Bismarck recovered himself, raised his hands and then shot out his left hand as he must have seen the pugs do that afternoon. Jack rolled his head out of the way and then leaned forward a little to let Bismarck's other hand sail past his head.

"Well done, mynheer," he cried. "That was good. Left and right, that's the way. Try again."

Bismarck tried, and tried again, and for three minutes Jack swayed and ducked and now and then blocked a punch with his open hand. Bismarck flailed away, and never looked like hitting him, and everyone cheered and roared with laughter. Finally Spottswood called, "Time", and the German stood there, chest heaving and face crimson with his efforts, while Jack was as unruffled as when he started.

"Don't mind 'em, mynheer," says he. "There's none of 'em would ha' done better, and most not so well. You're fast, and could be faster, and you move well for a novice."

"Are you convinced now, Baron?" says Spottswood.

Bismarck, having got his breath back, shook his head.

"That there is skill, I admit," says he, at which everyone raised an ironical cheer. "But I should be obliged," he goes on to Jack, "if you would try me again, and this time try to hit me in return."

At this the idiots cheered, and said he was damned game and a sportsman, and Perceval said he wouldn't have it, and demanded that the bout should stop at once. But old Jack, smiling his crooked smile, says:

"No, no, Tom. This fellow's more of a boxing man than any of you know. I'd not care to mill with anyone who didn't hit back. I'll spar, gentle-like, and when he goes home he can say he's been in a fight."

So they went to it again, and Jack moved about now, smooth as a dancer for all his years, and tapped his glove on Bismarck's head and chin and body, while the other smashed away at him and hit nothing. I encouraged him by haw-hawing every time he missed, for I wanted him to realise what an ass he looked, and he bore in all the harder, flailing at Jack's head and shoulders while the old champion turned, feinted and slipped away, leaving him floundering.

"That's enough!" shouts someone. "Time out, you fellows, and let's drink to it!" and there were several voices which cried aye, aye, at which Jack dropped his hands and looked to Spottswood. But Bismarck rushed in, and Jack, in fending him off with a left, tapped him a little harder than he meant to, and bloodied his nose.

That stopped the German in his tracks, and Jack, all crestfallen, was stepping in to apologise, when to everyone's amazement Bismarck ran at him, seized him round the waist, swung him off his feet, and hurled him to the floor. He landed with a tremendous crash, his head striking the boards, and in a moment everyone was on his feet, shouting and cheering. Some cried "Foul!" while others applauded the German—they were the drunker ones—and then there was a sudden hush as Jack shook his head and slowly got to his feet.

He looked shaken, and furious, too, but he had himself in hand.

"All right, mynheer," says he. "I didn't know we was holding and throwing." I don't suppose anything like it had happened to him in his life before, and his pride was wounded far worse than his body. "My own fault, for not looking out," says he. "Well, well, let it go. You can say you've downed John Gully," and he looked round the room, slowly, as though trying to read what everyone was thinking.

"Best stop now, I think," says he at last.

"You do not wish to continue?" cries Bismarck. He looked fairly blown, but the arrogant note in his voice was there, as ever.

Gully stared at him a moment. "Best not," says he.

The room was uncomfortably quiet, until Bismarck laughed his short laugh and shrugged his shoulders.

"Oh, very well," says, he, "since you do not wish it."

Two red spots came into Jack's pale cheeks. "I think it's best to stop now," says he, in a hard voice. "If you're wise, mynheer, you'll make the most of that."

"As you please," says Bismarck, and to my delight he added: "It is you who are ending the bout, you know."

Jack's face was a study. Spottswood had a hand on his shoulder, and Perceval was at his side, while the rest were crowding round, chattering excitedly, and Bismarck was looking about him with all his old bounce and side. It was too much for Jack.

"Right," says he, shaking Spottswood off. "Put your hands up."

"No, no," cries Perceval, "this has gone far enough."

"I quit to nobody," says Jack, grim as a hangman. " 'End the bout', is it? I'll end it for him, sure enough."

"For God's sake, man," says Perceval. "Remember who you are, and who he is. He's a guest, a stranger—"

"A stranger who threw me foul," says old Jack.

"He don't know the rules."

"It was a mistake."

"It was a fair throw."

"No t'wasn't."

Old Jack stood breathing heavily. "Now, look'ee," says he. "I give it him he threw me not knowing it was an unfair advantage, when I was off guard on account of having tapped his claret. I give it him he was angry and didn't think, 'cos I'd been making a pudding of him. I'll shake hands wi' him on all of that—but I won't have him strutting off and saying I asked to end the fight. Nobody says that to me—no, not Tom Cribb himself, by God."

Everyone began to yammer at once, Perceval trying to push them away and calm Jack down, but most of us well content to see the mischief increase—it wasn't every day one could see Gully box in earnest, which he seemed ready to do. Tom appealed to Bismarck, but the German, smiling his superior smile, just says:

"I am prepared to continue."

After that, try as Tom might, he was over-ruled, and presently they were facing up to each other again. I was delighted, of course; this was more than I had hoped for, although I feared that Gully's good nature would make him let Bismarck off lightly. His pride was hurt, but he was a fair-minded fool, and I guessed he would just rap the German once or twice, smartly, to show him who was master and let it go at that. Perceval was hoping so, at all events. "Go easy, Jack, for God's sake," he cried, and then they set to.

I don't know what Bismarck hoped for. He wasn't a fool, and Gully had demonstrated already that the German was a child in his hands. I can only suppose that he thought he had a chance of throwing Gully again, and was too damned conceited to escape gratefully. At any rate, he went in swinging both arms, and Jack rapped him over the heart and then cracked him a neat left on the head when he was off balance, which knocked him down.

"Time!" cries Spottswood, but Bismarck didn't understand, and bounding up he rushed at Gully, and with a lucky swing, caught him on the ear. Jack staggered, righted himself, and as if by instinct smacked two blows into Bismarck's belly. He went down, gasping and wheezing, and Perceval ran forward, saying that this was the end, he would have no more of it.

But the German, when he had straightened up, got his breath back and wiped the trickle of blood from his nose, was determined to go on. Gully said no, and Bismarck sneered at him, and the upshot was that they squared away again, and Gully knocked him off his feet.

But still he got up, and now Gully was sickened, and refused to go on, and when he held out his hand Bismarck struck at him, at which Gully hammered him one in the face, which sent him headlong, and on the instant Gully was cursing himself for a bad-tempered fool, and calling for Spottswood to take off his gloves, and Tom was raising Bismarck off the floor, and a splendidly gory face he presented, too. And there was a tremendous hubbub, with drunk chaps crying "Shame!" and "Stop the fight!" and "Hit him again!" and Perceval almost crying with mortification, and Gully stamping off in a corner, swearing he hadn't meant to hurt the fellow, but what could he do? and Bismarck white-faced, being helped into one of the chairs, where they sponged his face and gave him brandy. There were apologies, and protestations, and Gully and Bismarck finally shook hands, and Jack said he was ashamed of himself, as an Englishman, and would Bismarck forgive him? Bismarck, with his mouth puffed and split where Jack's last blow had caught him, and his fine aristocratic nose crusted with his own blood—I'd have given twenty guineas to see it properly smashed—said it was nothing, and he was obliged to Mr Gully for the instruction. He then added that he was capable of continuing, and that the fight had not been stopped at *his* request, at which old Jack took a big breath but said nothing, and the others cheered and Conyngham cried:

"Good for the Prussian! A dam' game bird he is! Hurrah!"

This was the signal for the drinking to start again, in earnest, while two of the company, flown with pugilistic ardour, put on the mauleys and began to spar away drunkenly, and losing their tempers, finished up savaging each other on the floor. Perceval stayed by Bismarck, muttering apologies while the German waved them away and sipped brandy through his battered mouth. Gully simply went over to the sideboard and poured drink into himself until he was completely foxed; no one had ever seen him so shaken and unhappy before, or known him drink more than the most modest amount. But I knew why he was doing it; he was ashamed. It is a terrible thing to have ideals and a conscience, to say nothing of professional pride. He told me later he would have been better to suffer being thrown; beating Bismarck had been the most shameful thing he ever did, he said.

I'd have been delighted to do it, personally, if I'd had his skill; I'd have left that German upstart without a tooth in his head. As it was, when the boozing was at its height, and the uproar was deafening, I chanced by where Bismarck was still sitting, sipping delicately at his glass. He turned and caught my eye, frowned, and said:

"Still I cannot place you, Captain. It is most intriguing; but it will come back, no doubt. However, I trust you were not disappointed with your evening's entertainment."

"It might have been better," says I, grinning at him.

"Even so, you contrived very well. I have you to thank for these," and he touched his lips and reddened nose. "One day I shall hold you to your promise, and show you the *schlager* play. I look forward to that; we shall see how much credit you obtain from *my* country's sport."

"More than you've got from mine, I hope," says I, laughing.

"Let us hope so," says he. "But I doubt it."

"Go to the devil," says I.

He turned away, chuckling to himself. "After you, I think."

One of the difficulties of writing your memoirs is that they don't run smooth, like a novel or play, from one act to the next. I've described how I met Rosanna James and Otto, but beyond a paragraph in *The Times* announcing her divorce from Captain James towards the end of the year, I didn't hear of her again for months. As for Bismarck, it was a few years before I ran into him again, and then it was too soon.

So in the first place I must skip over a few months to my second meeting with Rosanna, which was brought about because I have a long memory and a great zeal in paying off old scores. She had put herself on the debit side of Flashy's ledger, and when the chance came to pay her out I seized on it.

It was the following summer, while I was still in London, officially waiting for Uncle Bindley at the Horse Guards to find me an appointment, and in fact just lounging about the town and leading the gay life. It wasn't quite so gay as it had been, for while I was still something of an idol in military circles, my gloss was beginning to wear a bit thin with the public. Yesterday's hero is soon forgotten, and while Elspeth and I had no lack of invitations during the season, it seemed to me that I wasn't quite so warmly fêted as I had been. I wasn't invariably the centre of attraction any longer; some chaps even seemed to get testy if I mentioned Afghanistan, and at one assembly I heard a fellow say that he personally knew every damned stone of Piper's Fort by now, and could have conducted sightseers over the ruins.

That's by the way, but it was one of the reasons that I began to find life boring me in the months that followed, and I was all the readier for mischief when the chance came.

I forget exactly what took me to one of the Haymarket theatres on an afternoon in May—there was an actress, or an acrobat she may have been, whom I was pushing about just then, so it may have been her. In any event, I was standing in the wings with some of the Gents and Mooners,[15] during a rehearsal, when I noticed a female practising dance-steps on the other side of the stage. It was her shape that caught my eye, for she was in the tight fleshings that ballet-dancers wear, and I was admiring her legs when she turned in profile and to my astonishment I recognised Rosanna.

She was wearing her hair in a new way, parted in the centre, and held behind her head in a kerchief, but there was no mistaking the face or the figure.

"Splendid piece, ain't she?" says one of the Mooners. "They say Lumley"—he was the manager—"pays her a fortune. 'Pon my soul, I would myself, what?"

Oho, I thought to myself, what's this? I asked the Mooner, offhand, who she might be.

"Why, she's his new danseuse, don't you know," says he. "It seems that opera hasn't been bringing in the tin lately, so Lumley imported her specially to dance between the acts. Thinks she'll make a great hit, and with those legs I'll be bound she will. See here." And he pushed a printed bill into my hand. It read:

HER MAJESTY'S THEATRE
Special Attraction

Mr Benjamin Lumley begs to announce that between the acts of the Opera, Donna Lola Montez, of the Teatro Real, Seville, will have the honour to make her first appearance in England in the Original Spanish dance, El Oleano.

"Ain't she a delight, though?" says the Mooner. "Gad, look at 'em bouncing when she struts!"

"That's Donna Lola Montez, is it?" says I. "When does she perform, d'ye know?"

"Opens next week," says he. "There'll be a crowd and a half, shouldn't wonder. Oh, Lovely Lola!"

Well, I'd never heard of Lola Montez, but I saw there was something here that needed going into. I made a few discreet inquiries, and it seemed that half the town was talking about her already, for Lumley was making a great to-do about his beautiful new attraction., The critics were slavering in advance about "the belle Andalusian", and predicting a tremendous success, but nobody had any notion that she wasn't a genuine Spanish artiste at all. But I was in no doubt about her; I'd been close enough to Rosanna James to be sure.

At first I was just amused, but then it occurred to me that here was a heaven-sent opportunity to have my own back on her. If she was exposed, denounced for what she really was, that would put paid to her making a hit. It would also teach her not to throw piss-pots at me. But how to do it best? I pondered, and in five minutes I had it pat.

I remembered, from the conversations we had had during our passionate week, her mention of Lord Ranelagh, who was one of the leading boys about town just then. She was forever chattering about her admirers, and he was one she had turned down; snubbed him dead, in fact. I knew him only to see, for he was a very top-flight Corinthian, and didn't take much heed even of heroes if they weren't out of the top drawer (and I wasn't). But all I'd heard suggested that he was a first-class swine, and just the man for me.

I hunted him out at his club, slid inside when the porter wasn't looking, and found him in the smoke-room. He was lying on a couch, puffing a cigar with his hat over his brows; I spoke right out.

"Lord Ranelagh," says I. "How are you? I'm Flashman."

He cocked an eye lazily under the brim of his hat, damned haughty.

"I'm certain I haven't had the honour," says he. "Good day to you."

"No, no, you remember me," says I. "Harry Flashman, you know."

He pushed his hat right back, and looked at me as if I was a toad.

"Oh," says he at length, with a sneer, "The Afghan warrior. Well, what is it?"

"I took the liberty of calling on your lordship," says I, "because I chanced to come across a mutual acquaintance."

"I cannot conceive that we have any," drawls he, "unless you happen to be related to one of my grooms."

I laughed merrily at this, although I felt like kicking his noble backside for him. But I needed him, you see, so I had to toad-eat him.

"Not bad, not bad," says I. "But this happens to be a lady. I'm sure she would be of interest to you."

"Are you a pimp, by any chance? If so—"

"No, my lord, I'm not," says I. "But I thought you might be diverted to hear of Mrs James—Mrs Elizabeth Rosanna James."

He frowned, and blew ash off his ridiculous beard, which covered half his shirt-front.

"What of her, and what the devil has she to do with you?"

"Why, nothing, my lord," says I. "But she happens to be taking the stage at Her Majesty's next week, masquerading as a famous Spanish dancer. Donna Lola Montez, she calls herself, and pretends to be from Seville. An impudent imposture."

He digested this, while I watched his nasty mind working.

"How d'ye know this?" says he.

"I've seen her at rehearsal," says I, "and there's no doubt about it—she's Rosanna James."

"And why should this be of interest to me?"

I shrugged at this, and he asked what *my* purpose was in telling him.

"Oh, I was sure you would wish to be at her first performance—to pay your respects to an old friend," says I. "And if so, I would solicit a place for myself in your party. I entertain the same affection for her that I'm sure your lordship does."

He considered me. "You're a singularly unpleasant creature," says he. "Why don't you expose her yourself, since that's obviously what you want?"

"Your lordship, I'm sure, has a style in these things. And you are well known, while I . . ." *I* didn't want to be the centre of any scandal, although I wanted to have a front seat to see the fun.

"I can do your dirty work, eh? Well, well."

"You'll go?"

"That is no concern of yours," says he. "Good day."

"May I come?"

"My dear sir, I cannot prevent you going where you choose. But I forbid you absolutely to address me in public."

And he turned over on his side, away from me. But I was satisfied; no doubt he would go, and denounce "Donna Lola". He had his own score to pay off, and was just the sort of mean hound who would do it, too.

Sure enough, when the fashionable crowd was arriving at Her Majesty's the following Monday, up rolls Lord Ranelagh with a party of bloods, in two coaches. I was on hand, and tailed on to them at the door; he noticed me, but didn't say anything, and I was allowed to follow into the omnibus-box which he had engaged directly beside the stage. One or two of his friends gave me haughty stares, and I took my seat very meek, at the back of the box, while his lordship showed off at the front, and his friends and he talked and laughed loudly, to show what first-rate bucks they were.

It was a splendid house—quite out of proportion to the opera, which was "The Barber of Seville". In fact, I was astonished at the gathering: there was the Queen Dowager in the Royal Box, with a couple of foreign princelings; old Wellington, wrinkled and lynx-eyed, with his Duchess; Brougham, the minister, the Baroness de Rothschild, Count Esterhazy, the Belgian ambassador, and many others. All the most eminent elderly lechers of the day, in fact, and I hadn't a doubt that it wasn't the music they had come for. Lola Montez was the attraction of the night, and the talk through the pit was of nothing else. Rumour had it that at certain select gatherings for the highest grandees in Spain, she had been known to dance nude; it was also being said that she had once been the leading light of a Turkish harem. Oh, they were in a fine state of excitement by the time the curtain went up.

My own idea of theatrical entertainment, I admit, is the music-hall; strapping wenches and low comedians are my line, and your fine drama and music bore me to death. So I found "The Barber of Seville" a complete fag: fat Italians screeching, and not a word to be understood. I read the programme for a bit, and found more entertainment in the advertisements than there was on the stage—"Mrs Rodd's anatomical ladies' stays, which ensure the wearer a figure of astonishing symmetry"; I remember thinking that the leading lady in "The Barber" could have profited by Mrs Rodd's acquaintance. Also highly spoken of were Jackson's patent enema machines, as patronised by the nobility when travelling. I wasn't alone, I noticed, in finding the opera tedious; there were yawns in the pit, and Wellington (who was near our box) began to snore until his Duchess dug him in the ribs. Then the first act ended, and when the applause died away everyone sat up, expectant; there was a flourish of Spanish music from the orchestra, and Lola (or Rosanna) shot dramatically on to the stage.

I'm no authority on the dance; the performer, not the performance, is what I pay to see. But it seemed to me that she was damned good. Her striking beauty brought the pit up with a gasp: she was in a black bodice, cut so low that her breasts seemed to be in continual danger of popping out, and her tiny pink skirt showed off her legs to tremendous advantage. The slim white neck and shoulders, the coal-black hair, the gleaming eyes, the scarlet lips curled almost in contempt—the whole effect was startling and exotic. You know these throbbing, Spanish rhythms; well, she swayed and shook and stamped her way through them in splendid passion, and the audience sat spellbound. She was at once inviting and challenging; I doubt if there was any gesture or movement in the whole dance that a magistrate could have taken exception to, and yet the whole effect of it was sensual. It seemed to say "Bed me—if you dare", and every man in the place was taking her clothes off as he watched. What the women thought I can't imagine, but I guess they admired her almost as much as they disliked her.[16]

When she finished abruptly, with a final smash of her foot and clash of cymbals from the orchestra, the theatre went wild. They cheered and stamped, and she stood for a moment still as a statue, staring proudly down at them, and then swept straight off the stage. The applause was deafening, but she didn't come back, and there were sighs and a few groans when the curtain went up again on the next act of the opera, and those damned Macaronis began yelping again.

Through all this Ranelagh had sat forward in his chair, staring at her, but never said a word. He didn't pay the least attention to the opera, but when Lola came on for her second dance, which was even more tempestuous than the first, he made a great show of examining her through his glasses. Everyone else was doing the same, of course, in the hope that her bodice would burst, which it seemed likely to do at any moment, but when the applause broke out, wilder than ever, he kept his glasses glued to his eyes, and when she had gone he was seen to be frowning in a very puzzled way. This was all leading up to the denouement, of course, and when she bounced on, snapping her fan, for the third time, I heard him mutter to his nearest neighbour:

"You chaps keep your eyes on me. I'll give the word, mind, and then we'll see some fun."

She swirled through the dance, showing splendid amounts of her thighs, and gliding about sinuously while peeping over her fan, and at the finish there was a perfect torrent of clapping and shouting, with bouquets plopping down on to the stage and chaps standing up and clapping wildly. She smiled now, for the first time, bowing and blowing kisses before the curtain, and then suddenly, from our box there was a great hissing in unison, at which the applause faltered and died away. She turned to stare furiously in our direction, and as the hissing rose louder than ever there were angry shouts and cries from the rest of the theatre. People craned to see what the row was about, and then Ranelagh climbs to his feet, an imposing figure with his black beard and elegant togs, and cries out, very distinctly:

"Why, this is a proper swindle, ladies and gentlemen! That woman isn't Lola Montez. She's an Irish girl, Betsy James!"

There was a second's silence, and then a tremendous hullabaloo. The hissing started again, with cries of "Fraud!" and "Impostor!", the applause began and sputtered out, and angry cat-calls and boos sounded from the gallery. In a moment the whole mood of the theatre had changed; taking their cue from Ranelagh and his toadies, they began to howl her down; a few coins clattered on the stage; the conductor, gaping at the audience with his mouth open, suddenly flung down his baton and stamped out; and then the whole place was in a frenzy, stamping and calling for their money back, and shouting to her angrily to get back to the bogs of Donegal.

She was standing blazing with fury, and when she moved towards our box some of the chaps scrambled back to get out of harm's way. She stood a moment, her bosom heaving, her eyes sweeping the box—oh, yes, she recognised *me* all right, and when she began to curse at us I think it was me as much as Ranelagh she was getting at. Unfortunately, she swore in English, and the mob caught it and yelled louder than ever. Then she dashed down the bouquet she was holding, stamped on it, kicked it into the orchestra, and with one last damnation in our direction, ran from the stage as the curtain fell.[17]

I must say I was delighted; I hadn't thought it could go off so well. As we crowded out of the place—"The Barber", of course, was entirely forgotten in the sensation—I came up to Ranelagh's elbow and congratulated him; I couldn't have paid her out so splendidly myself, and I told him so. He gave me a cold nod and sailed off, the snobbish bastard, but I wasn't in a mood to mind too much; that was me quits with Mistress Lola for her brickbats and insults, and I went home in high good humour.

She was finished on the London stage, of course. Lumley dismissed her, and although one or two attempts were made to present her at other theatres, the damage was done. All sorts of people now seemed to remember her as Mrs James, and although she wrote a letter of denial to the press, no one believed it. A few weeks later she had disappeared and that, thought I, was the end of Lola Montez so far as I was concerned, and good riddance. A brilliant bed-mate, I don't deny, in her way, and even now the picture of her kneeling naked among the bed-clothes can set me itching—but I'd never liked her particularly, and was glad to see her sent packing.

But it wasn't the end of her, by any means. Although it was some years before I saw her again—in circumstances that I couldn't have dreamed of—one heard of her from time to time through the papers. And always it was sensational news; she seemed to have a genius for thrusting herself into high places and creating scandal. First there was a report of her horse-whipping a policeman in Berlin; next she was dancing on the tables during a civic banquet in Bonn, to the outrage of Prince Albert and our Queen, who were on a State visit at the time. Then she was performing in Paris, and when the audience didn't take to her she stripped off her garters and drawers and flung them at the gallery; she started a riot in the streets of Warsaw, and when they tried to arrest her she held the peelers off with pistols. And of course there were scores of lovers, most of them highly-placed: the Viceroy of Poland, the Tsar of Russia (although I doubt if that's true), and Liszt the musician.[18] She took up with him two or three times, and once to get rid of her he locked her in a hotel room and sneaked out by the back door.

I met him, later on, by the way, and we discussed the lovely Lola and found ourselves much in agreement. Like me, he admired her as a tumble, but found her all too overpowering. "She is a consuming fire," he told me, shaking his white head ruefully, "and I've been scorched—oh, so often." I sympathised; she had urged me on in love-making with a hair-brush, but with him it had been a dog-whip, and he was a frail sort of fellow, you know.

At all events, these scraps of gossip reached me from time to time over the next few years. In that time I was out of England a good deal—as will be set down in another packet of my memoirs, if I'm spared to write them. My doings in the middle forties of the century don't fit in with my present tale, though, so I pass them over for the moment and come to the events to which my meeting with Lola and Otto Bismarck was the prelude.

I can see, now, that if I hadn't deserted Speedicut that night, hadn't been rude to Bismarck, hadn't set Jack Gully on to give him a beating, and finally, hadn't taken my spite out on Lola by peaching on her to Ranelagh—without all these "if's" I would have been spared one of the most frightening and incredible experiences of my life. Another glorious chapter in the heroic career of Harry Flashman would not have been written, and neither would a famous novel.

However, I've seen too much of life to fret over if's and but's. There's nothing you can do about them, and if you find yourself at the end of the day an octogenarian with money in the bank and drink in the house—well, you'd be a fool to wish that things had fallen out differently.

Anyway, I was home again in London in '47, with cash in my pocket for once—my own cash, too, dishonestly got, but no dirtier than the funds which old Morrison, my father-in-law, doled out as charity to keep us respectable "for my wee daughter's sake". His wee daughter, my Elspeth, was as pleased to see me as she ever was; we still suited very well between the sheets, however much she was playing loose with her admirers. I had ceased worrying about that, too.

However, when I arrived home, hoping for a few months' rest to recover from the effects of a pistol-ball which had been dug out of the small of my back, there was a nasty shock awaiting me. My dear parents-in-law, Mr and Mrs Morrison of Paisley, were now in permanent residence in London; I hadn't seen much of them, thank God, since I had married their beautiful, empty-headed trollop of a daughter several years before, when I was a young subaltern in Cardigan's Hussars. We had detested each other then, they and I, and time hadn't softened the emotion, on either side.

To make matters worse, my father was away from home. In the past year or two the old fellow had been hitting the bottle pretty hard—and pretty hard for him meant soaking up liquor in every waking moment. Once or twice they had to put him away in a place in the country where the booze was sweated out of him and the pink mice which nibbled at his fingers and toes were shoo'ed away—that was what *he* said, anyway—but it seemed that they kept coming back, and he was off getting another "cure".

"A fine thing," sniffed old Morrison—we were at dinner on my first evening home, and I had hoped to have it in bed with Elspeth, but of course we had to do "the polite" by her parents—"a fine thing, indeed. He'll drink himsel' intae the grave, I suppose."

"Probably," says I. "His father and grand-father did, so I don't see why he shouldn't."

Mrs Morrison, who in defiance of probability had grown with the years even more like a vulture, gave a gasp of disgust at this, and old Morrison said he didn't doubt that the son of the house would follow in his ancestors' besotted footsteps.

"Shouldn't wonder," says I, helping myself to claret. "I've got a better excuse than they had."

"And whit does that mean, sir?" bridled old Morrison. I didn't bother to tell him, so he started off on a great rant about ingratitude and perversity, and the dissolute habits of myself and my family, and finished up with his age-old lamentation about his daughter having married a wastrel and a ruffian, who hadn't even the decency to stay at home with his wife like a Christian, but must be forever wandering like Ishmael . . .

"Hold on," says I, for I was sick of this. "Since I married your daughter I have been twice abroad, on my country's service, and on the first occasion at least I came home with a good deal of credit. I'll wager you weren't slow to boast about your distinguished son-in-law when I came back from India in '42."

"And what have ye made of it?" sneers he. "What are ye? A captain still, and like to remain one."

"You're never tired of reminding Elspeth in your letters that you keep this family, this house, and the rest of it. Buy me a majority, if military rank means so much to you."

"Damn yer impudence!" says he. "Is it no' enough that I keep you and yer drunken father oot o' the poor's-hoose, where ye belong?"

"I'd have thought so," says I, "but if you want me to shoot up the military tree as well—why, it costs money, you know."

"Aye, weel, deil's the penny ye'll get from me," snaps he. "Enough is bein' spent on wanton folly as it is," and it seemed to me he darted a look at his vinegary spouse, who sniffed and coloured a bit. What's this, I wondered: surely she hasn't been asking him to buy *her* a pair of colours: Horse Guards wouldn't have taken her, anyway, not for a commission: farrier-sergeant, perhaps, but no higher.

No more was said at dinner, which ended in a merry atmosphere of poisonous ill-will, but I got the explanation from Elspeth when we had retired for the night. It seemed that her mother had been growing increasingly concerned at her inability to get Elspeth's two virgin sisters married off: the oldest girl, Mary, had been settled on some commercial creature in Glasgow, and was breeding at a rare rate, but Agnes and Grizel were still single. I said surely there were enough fortune-hunters in Scotland ready to take a shot at her father's money, but she said no, her mother had discouraged them. She was flying higher, reasoning that if Elspeth had been able to get me, who had titled relatives and was at least half-way into the great world of fashionable society, Agnes and Grizel could do even better.

"She's mad," says I. "If they had your looks it might be

61

a half-chance, but one sight of your dear parents is going to scare any eligible sprig a mile off. Sorry, m'dear, but they ain't acceptable, you know."

"My parents certainly lack the advantages," says Elspeth seriously. Marrying me had turned her into a most wonderful snob. "That I admit. But father is extremely rich, as you are aware—"

"To hear him, it's no fault of ours if he is."

"—and you know, Harry, that quite a few of our titled acquaintances are not too nice to look above a fine dowry. I think, with the right introductions, that Mama might find very suitable husbands for them. Agnes is plain, certainly, but little Grizel is really pretty, and their education has been quite as careful as my own."

It isn't easy for a beautiful woman with blue eyes, a milky complexion, and corn-gold hair to look pompous, especially when she is wearing only a French corset decorated with pink ribbons, but Elspeth managed it. At that moment I was overcome again with that yearning affection for her that I sometimes felt, in spite of her infidelities; I can't explain it, beyond saying that she must have had some magic quality, something to do with the child-like, thoughtful look she wore, and the pure, helpless stupidity in her eyes. It is very difficult not to like a lovely idiot.

"Since you're so well-educated," says I, pulling her down beside me, "let's see how much you remember." And I put her through a most searching test which, being Elspeth, she interrupted from time to time with her serious observations on Mrs Morrison's chances of marrying off the two chits.

"Well," says I, when we were exhausted, "so long as I ain't expected to help launch 'em in Society, I don't mind. Good luck to it, I say, and I hope they get a Duke apiece."

But of course, I had to be dragged into it: Elspeth was quite determined to use my celebrity for what it was still worth, on her sisters' behalf, and I knew that when she was insistent there was no way of resisting her. She controlled the purse-strings, you see, and the cash I had brought home wouldn't last long at my rate of spending, I knew. So it was a fairly bleak prospect I had come back to: the guv'nor away in the grip of the quacks and demon drink, old Morrison in the house carping and snuffling, Elspeth and Mrs Morrison planning their campaign to inflict her sisters on unsuspecting London, and myself likely to be roped in—which meant being exposed in public alongside my charming Scotch relations. I should have to take old Morrison to my club, and stand behind Mrs Morrison's chair at parties—no doubt listening to her teaching some refined mama the recipe for haggis—and have people saying: "Seen Flashy's in-laws? They eat peat, don't you know, and speak nothing but Gaelic. Well, it wasn't English, surely?"

Oh, I knew what to expect, and determined to keep out of it. I thought of going to see my Uncle Bindley at the Horse Guards, and beseeching him to arrange an appointment for me to some regiment out of town—I was off the active list just then, and was not relishing the idea of half-pay anyway. And while I was hesitating, in those first few days at home, the letter came that helped to solve my difficulties for me and incidentally changed the map of Europe.

It came like the answer to a pagan's prayer, along with a dun from some tailor or other, an anti-popish tract, a demand for my club subscription, and an invitation to buy railway shares—all the usual trash. Why I should remember the others, I don't know. I must have a perverse memory, for the contents of the big white envelope should have been enough to drive them out of my head.

It was a fine, imposing cover—best quality paper, with a coat-of-arms on the back, which I have before me now. There was a shield, quartered red, blue, blue, and white, and in the quarters were a sword, a crowned lion, what looked like a fat whale, and a pink rose. Plainly it was either from someone of tremendous rank or the manufacturers of a new brand of treacle.[19]

Inside there was a letter, and stamped at the top in flowery letters, surrounded by foliage full of pink-bottomed cupids, were the words, "Gräfin de Landsfeld". And who the deuce, I wondered, might she be, and what did she want with me.

The letter I reproduce exactly as it now lies in my hand, very worn and creased after sixty years, but still perfectly legible. It is, I think, quite the most remarkable communication I have ever received—even including the letter of thanks I got from Jefferson Davis and the reprieve I was given in Mexico. It said:

> Most Honoured Sir,
>   I write to you on instruction of Her Grace, the Countess de Landsfeld, of whom you had the honour to be acquainted in Londres some years ago. Her Grace commands me to inform you that she holds the warmest recollection of your friendship, and wishes to convey her strongest greetings on this occasion.

I made nothing of this. While I couldn't have recited the names of *all* the women I had known, I was pretty clear that there weren't any foreign countesses that had slipped my mind. It went on:

> Sir, while Her Grace doubts not that your duties are of the most important and exacting nature, she trusts that you will have opportunity to consider the matter which, on her command, I am now to lay before you. She is confident that the ties of your former friendship, no less than the chivalrous nature of which she has such pleasing memory, will prevail upon you to assist her in a matter of the most extreme delicate.

Now he's certainly mad, this fellow, thinks I, or else

he's got the wrong chap. I don't suppose there are three women in the world who ever thought me chivalrous, even on short acquaintance.

Her Grace therefore directs me to request that you will, with all speed after receiving this letter, make haste to present yourself to her in München, and there receive, from her own lips, particulars of the service which it is her dearest wish you will be obliged to render to her. She hastens to assure you that it will be of no least expense or hardship to you, but is of such particular nature that she feels that you, of all her many dear friends, are most suitable to its performing. She believes that such is the warmth of your heart that you will at once agree with her, and that the recollection of her friendship will bring you at once as an English gentleman is fitting.

Honoured Sir, in confidence that you will wish to assist Her Grace, I advise you that you should call on William Greig & Sons, attorneys, at their office in Wine Office Court, Londres, to receive instruction for your journey. They will pay £500 in gold for your travelling, etc. Further payments will be received as necessary.

Sir, Her Grace commands me to conclude with the assurance of her deepest friendship, and her anticipation of the satisfaction of seeing you once again.

Accept, dear Sir, etc.,
R. Lauengram,
Chamberlain.

My first thought was that it was a joke, perpetrated by someone not quite right in the head. It made no sense; I had no idea who the Gräfin de Landsfeld might be, or where "München" was. But going over it again several times, it occurred to me that if it had been a fake, whoever had written it would have made his English a good deal worse than it was, and taken care not to write several of the sentences without howlers.

But if it was genuine, what the devil did it mean? What was the service (without expense or hardship, mark you) for which some foreign titled female was willing to slap £500 into my palm—and that only a first instalment, by the looks of it?

I sat staring at the thing for a good twenty minutes, and the more I studied it the less I liked it. If I've learned one thing in this wicked life, it is that no one, however rich, lays out cash for nothing, and the more they spend the rummer the business is likely to be. Someone, I decided, wanted old Flashy pretty badly, but I couldn't for the life of me think why. I had no qualification that I knew of that suited me for a matter of the most "extreme delicate": all I was good at was foreign languages and riding. And it couldn't be some desperate risk in which my supposed heroism would be valuable—they'd as good as said so. No, it beat me altogether.

I have always kept by me as many books and pamphlets on foreign tongues as I can collect, this being my occasional hobby, and since I guessed that the writer of the letter was pretty obviously German I turned up an index and discovered that "München" was Munich, in Bavaria. I certainly knew no one there at all, let alone a Gräfin, or Countess; for that matter I hardly knew any Germans, had never been in Germany, and had no acquaintance with the language beyond a few idle hours with a grammar some years before.

However, there was an obvious way of solving the mystery, so I took myself off to Wine Office Court and looked up William Greig & Sons. I half expected they would send me about my business, but no; there was as much bowing and scraping and "Pray to step this way, sir" as if I had been a royal duke, which deepened my mystification. A young Mr Greig smoothed me into a chair in his office; he was an oily, rather sporty-looking bargee with a very smart blue cutaway and a large lick of black hair—not at all the City lawyer type. When I presented my letter and demanded to know what it was all about, he gave me a knowing grin.

"Why, all in order, my dear sir," says he. "A draft for £500 to be issued to you, on receipt, with proof of identity—well, we need not fret on that score, hey? Captain Flashman is well enough known, I think, ha-ha. We all remember your famous exploits in China—"

"Afghanistan," says I.

"To be sure it was. The draft negotiable with the Bank of England. Yes, all in perfect order, sir."

"But who the devil is she?"

"Who is who, my dear sir?"

"This Gräfin what's-her-name—Landsfeld."

His smile vanished in bewilderment.

"I don't follow," says he, scratching a black whisker. "You cannot mean that you don't have the lady's acquaintance? Why, her man writes to you here . . ."

"I've never heard of her," says I, "to my knowledge."

"Well," says he, giving me an odd look. "This is dam—most odd, you know. My dear sir, are you sure? Quite apart from this letter, which seems to suggest a most, ah . . . cordial regard, well, I had not thought there was a man in England who had not heard of the beauteous Countess of Landsfeld."

"Well, you're looking at one now," says I.

"I can't believe it," cries he. "What, never heard of the Queen of Hearts? La Belle Espagnole? The monarch, in all but name, of the Kingdom of Bavaria? My dear sir, all the world knows Donna Maria de—what is it again?" and he rummaged among some papers—"aye, here it is 'Donna Maria de Dolores de los Montez, Countess of Landsfeld'. Come, come, sir, surely now . . ."

At first the name meant nothing, and then it broke on me.

"De los Montez? You don't mean Lola Montez?"

"But who else, sir? The close friend—indeed, some

67

say more than friend—of King Ludwig. Why, the press is never without some fresh sensation about her, some new scandal . . ." and he went on, chattering and smirking, but I never heeded him. My head was in a spin. Lola Montez, my Rosanna—a Countess, a monarch in all but name, a royal mistress by the sound of it. And she was writing to me, offering me hard cash—plainly I needed more information.

"Forgive me, sir," says I, breaking in on his raptures. "The title misled me, for I'd never heard it before. When I knew Lola Montez she was plain Mrs James."

"Oh, dear me, my dear sir," says he, very whimsical. "Those days are far behind us now! Our firm, in fact, represented a *Mrs James* some years ago, but we never talk of her! Oh, no, I daresay not! But the Countess of Landsfeld is another matter—a lady of quite a different colour, ha-ha!"

"When did she come by the title?"

"Why, some months ago. How you should not . . ."

"I've been abroad," says I. "Until this week I hadn't seen an English newspaper in almost a year. I've heard of Lola Montez's doings, of course, any time over the past three years, but nothing of this."

"Oh, and such doings, hey?" says he, beaming lewdly. "Well, my dear sir, your friend at court—ha-ha—is a very great lady indeed. She has the kingdom under her thumb, makes and breaks ministers, dictates policies—and sets all Europe by the ears, upon my word! Some of the stories—why, there is an article in one of the sheets calling her 'The Modern Messalina' "—he dropped his voice and pushed his greasy face towards me—"and describing her picked bodyguard of splendid young men—what, sir, hey? She goes abroad with a guard of cuirassiers riding behind her coach, sets her dogs on whoever dares to cross her path—why, there was some unfortunate who didn't doff his cap, sir—flogged almost to death! True, sir. And none dare say her nay. The King dotes on her, his courtiers and ministers hate her but go in fear and trembling, the students worship her. For luxury and extravagance there has been nothing like her since La Pompadour, they say. Why, sir, she is the nine-day wonder!"

"Well, well," says I. "Little Mrs James."

"Pray, sir!" He pretended distress. "Not that name, I beg you. It is the Countess of Landsfeld who is your friend, if I may be so bold as to remind you."

"Aye, so it is," says I. "Will you tell me what she wants of me, then?"

"My dear sir," says he, smirking. "A matter of 'the most delicate', is it not? What that may be—surely you are in a better position than I to say, eh? Ha-ha. But you will be going to Bavaria, I take it, to hear the particulars 'from her own lips'?"

That was what I was asking myself. It was unbelievable, of course: Lola a queen, to all intents—that was wild enough. But Lola seeking my help—when our last encounter had been distinguished by the screaming of abuse and the crashing of chamberpots—to say nothing of the furore at the theatre when she had seen me among her betrayers . . . well, I know women are fickle, but I doubted if she remembered *me* with any affection. And yet the letter was practically fawning, and she must have dictated the sense of it, if not the words. It might be she had decided to let bygones be bygones—she was a generous creature in her way, as so many whores are. But why? What could she want me for—all she knew of me was my prowess in bed. Did the *maîtresse en titre* want to instal me as her lover? My mind, which is at its liveliest in amorous imagination, opened on a riotous vision of Flashy, Pride of the Hareem . . . but no. I have my share of conceit, but I could not believe that with the pick of all the young stallions of a palace guard, she was yearning for my bonny black whiskers.

And yet here was a lawyer, authorised on her behalf, ready to advance me £500 to go to Munich—ten times more than was necessary for the journey. It made no sort of sense—unless she *was* in love with me. But that was out of court; I'd been a good enough mount for a week or so, no doubt, but there had been nothing deeper than that, I was certain. What service, then, could I perform that was so obviously of importance?

I have a nose for risk; the uneasy feeling that had come over me on first reading her letter was returning. If I had any sense, I knew, I would bid the greasy Mr Greig good-day and tell him to tear his draft up. But even the biggest coward doesn't run until some hint of danger appears, and there was none here at all—just my uneasy instinct. Against which there was the prospect of getting away from my damned relations—oh, God, and the horrors of accompanying the Morrisons into Society—and the certainty of an immediate tidy sum, with more to follow, and sheer curiosity, too. If I did go to Bavaria, and the signs were less pleasant than appeared at present—well, I could cut stick if I wanted. And the thought of renewing acquaintance with Lola—a 'warm' and 'friendly' Lola—tickled my darker fancies: from Greig's reports, even if they were only half true, it sounded as though there was plenty of sport at the Court of Good King Ludwig. Palace orgies of Roman proportions suggested themselves, with old Flashy waited on like a Sultan, and Lola mooning over me while slaves plied me with pearls dissolved in wine, and black eunuchs stood by armed with enormous gold-mounted hair-brushes. And while cold reason told me there was a catch in it somewhere—well, I couldn't *see* the catch, yet. Time enough when I did.

"Mr Greig," says I, "where can I cash this draft?"

Getting away from London was no great bother. Elspeth pouted a little, but when I had given her a glimpse—a most fleeting one—of Lauengram's signature and of the letter's cover, and used expressions like "special military detachment to Bavaria" and "foreign court service", she was quite happily resigned. The idea that I would be moving in high places appealed to her vacant mind; she felt vaguely honoured by the association.

The Morrisons didn't half like it, of course, and the old curmudgeon flew off about godless gallivanting, and likened me to Cartaphilus, who it seemed had left a shirt and breeches in every town in the ancient world. I was haunted by a demon, he said, who would never let me rest, and it was an evil day that he had let his daughter mate with a footloose scoundrel who had no sense of a husband's responsibilities.

"Since that's the case," says I, "the farther away from her I am, the better you should be pleased."

He was aghast at such cynicism, but I think the notion cheered him up for all that. He speculated a little on the bad end that I would certainly come to, called me a generation of vipers, and left me to my packing.

Not that there was much of that. Campaigning teaches you to travel light, and a couple of valises did my turn. I took my old Cherrypicker uniform—the smartest turnout any soldier ever had anywhere—because I felt it would be useful to cut a dash, but for the rest I stuck to necessaries. Among these, after some deliberation, I included the duelling pistols that a gunsmith had presented to me after the Bernier affair. They were beautiful weapons, accurate enough for the most fastidious marksman, and in those days when revolving pistols were still crude experimental toys, the last word in hand guns.

But I pondered about taking them. The truth was, I didn't want to believe that I might need them. When you are young and raw and on the brink of adventure, you set great store by having your side-arms just right, because you are full of romantic notions of how you will use them. Even I felt a thrill when I first handled a sabre at practice with the 11th Light Dragoons, and imagined myself pinking and mowing down hordes of ferocious but obligingly futile enemies. But when you've seen a sabre cut to the bone, and limbs mangled by bullets, you come out of your daydream pretty sharp. I knew, as I hesitated with those pistols in my hands, that if I took them I should be admitting the possibility of my own sudden death or maiming in whatever lay ahead. This was, you see, another stage in my development as a poltroon. But I'd certainly feel happier with 'em, uncomfortable reminders though they were, so in they went. And while I was at it, I packed along a neat little seaman's knife. It isn't an Englishman's weapon, of course, but it's devilish handy sometimes, for all sorts of purposes. And experience has taught me that, as with all weapons, while you may not often need it, when you do you need it badly.

So, with a word to Uncle Bindley at Horse Guards—who said acidly that the British Army *might* survive my absence a while longer—and with half of my £500 in my money belt (the other half was safe in the bank), I was ready for the road. Only one thing remained to do. I spent a day searching out a German waiter in the town, and when I had found a likely fellow I offered him his fare home and a handsome bonus, just to travel along with me; I had no German at all, but with my gift for languages I knew that if I applied myself on the journey to Munich I should have at least a smattering by the time I arrived there. I've often said that the ideal way to learn a language is in bed with a wench, but failing that an alert, intelligent travelling

72

companion is as good a teacher as any. And learning a new tongue is no hardship to me; I enjoy it.

The fellow I picked on was a Bavarian, as luck had it, and jumped at the chance of getting home. His name, I think, was Helmuth, but at any rate he was a first-rate choice. Like all Germans, he had a passion for taking pains, and when he saw what I wanted he was all enthusiasm. Hour after hour, in boat, train, and coach, he talked away to me, repeating words and phrases, correcting my own pronunciation, explaining grammatical rules, but above all giving me that most important thing of all—the rhythm of the language. This is something which only a few people seem to have, and I am lucky to be one. Let me catch the rhythm, and I seem to know what a man is saying even if I haven't learned all the words he uses. I won't pretend that I learned German in a fortnight, but at the end of that time I could pass my own elementary test, which is to say to a native: "Tell me, speaking slowly and carefully, what were your father's views on strong drink," or religion, or horses, or whatever came to mind—and understand his reply fairly well. Helmuth was astonished at my progress.

We did not hurry on the journey, which was by way of Paris, a city I had often wanted to visit, having heard that debauchery there was a fine art. I was disappointed: whores are whores the world over, and the Parisian ones are no different from any other. And French men make me sick; always have done. I'm degenerate, but they are dirty with it. Not only in the physical sense, either; they have greasy minds. Other foreigners may have garlic on their breaths, but the Frogs have it on their thoughts as well.

The Germans are different altogether. If I wasn't an Englishman, I would want to be a German. They say what they think, which isn't much as a rule, and they are admirably well ordered. Everyone in Germany knows his place and stays in it, and grovels to those above him, which makes it an excellent country for gentlemen and bullies. In England, even in my young day, if you took liberties with

73

a working man you would be as likely as not to get a fist in your face, but the lower-class Germans were as docile as niggers with white skins. The whole country is splendidly disciplined and organised, and with all their docility the inhabitants are still among the finest soldiers and workers on earth—as my old friend Bismarck has shown. The basis of all this, of course, is stupidity, which you must have in people before you can make them fight or work successfully. Well, the Germans will trouble the world yet, but since they are closer to us than anyone else, we may live to profit by it.

However, all this I was yet to discover, although I had an inkling of it from studying Helmuth on our journey. I don't bore you with details of our travels, by the way; nothing happened out of the ordinary, and what I chiefly remember is a brief anxiety that I had caught the pox in Paris; fortunately, I hadn't, but the scare I got prejudiced me still further against the French, if that were possible.

Munich, when we reached it, I liked the look of very well. It was clean and orderly on the surface, prices were far below our own (beer a halfpenny a pint, and a servant could be hired at two shillings a week), the folk were either civil or servile, and the guide-book which I had bought in London described it as "a very dissolute capital". The very place for old Flash, thinks I, and looked forward to my stay. I should have known better; my eagerness to see Lola again, and my curiosity about what she wanted, had quite driven away those momentary doubts I had felt back in London. More fool I; if I had known what was waiting round the corner I would have run all the way home and felt myself lucky to be able to run.

We arrived in Munich on a Sunday, and having dismissed Helmuth and found a hotel in the Theresienstrasse, I sat down to consider my first move. It was easy enough to discover that Lola was installed in a personal palace which the besotted Ludwig had built specially for her in the Barerstrasse; presumably I might stroll round and announce my arrival. But it pays to scout whenever you can, so I decided to put in an hour or two mooning round the streets and restaurants to see what news I could pick up first. I might even gain some hint of a clue to why she wanted me.

I strolled about the pleasant streets for a while, seeing the Hofgarten and the fine Residenz Palace where King Ludwig lived, and drank the excellent German beer in one of their open-air beer-gardens while I watched the folk and tried out my ear on their conversation. It could hardly have been more peaceful and placid; even in late autumn it was sunny, and the stout contented burghers with their pleasant-faced wives were either sitting and drinking and puffing at their massive pipes, or sauntering ponderously on the pavements. No one hurried, except the waiters; here and there a group of young fellows in long cloaks and gaudy caps, whom I took to be students, stirred things a little with their laughter, but for the rest it was a drowsy, easy afternoon, as though Munich was blinking contentedly in the fine weather, and wasn't going to be bustled by anybody.

However, one way and another, by finding a French newspaper and getting into talk with people who spoke either French or English, I picked up some gossip. I soon found that one did not need to ask about Lola; the good Muncheners talked about her as Britons do about the weather, and with much the same feeling—in other words, they thought she was bad and would get worse, but that nothing could be done about her anyway.

She was, it seemed, the supreme power in Bavaria. Ludwig was right under her thumb, she had swept out the hostile Ultramontane cabinet and had it replaced largely with creatures of her own, and despite the fact that she was a staunch Protestant, the Catholic hierarchy were powerless against her. The professors, who count for much more there than do ours in England, were solidly against her, but the students were violently split.

75

Some detested her, and had rioted before her windows, but others, calling themselves the Allemania, constituted themselves her champions and even her bodyguard, and were forever clashing with her opponents. Some of these Allemania were pointed out to me, in their bright scarlet caps; they were a tough-looking crew, tight-mouthed and cold-eyed and given to strutting and barking, and people got out of their way pretty sharp.

However, with Ludwig infatuated by her, Lola was firmly in the saddle, and according to one outspoken French journalist whose story I read, her supremacy was causing alarm far outside Bavaria. There were rumours that she was an agent of Palmerston, set on to foment revolution in Germany; to the other powers, striving to hold down a growing popular discontent that was spreading throughout Europe, she appeared to be a dangerous threat to the old regime. At least one attempt had been made to assassinate her; Metternich, the arch-reactionary master of Austria, had tried to bribe her to leave Germany for good. The truth was that in those days the world was on the edge of general revolution; we were coming out of the old age and into the new, and anything that was a focus of disorder or instability was viewed with consternation by the authorities. So Lola was not popular; the papers fumed against her, clergymen damned her in their sermons as a Jezebel and a Sempronia, and the ordinary folk were taught to regard her as a fiend in human shape—all the worse because the shape was beautiful.

Here ends Professor Flashman's historical lecture, much of it cribbed from a history book, but some of it at least learned that first day in the Munich beer-gardens.

One thing I was pretty sure of, and it flies in the face of history: whatever may be said, Lola was secretly admired by the common people. They might shake their heads and look solemn whenever her cavalry escort drove a way for her through a crowd of protesting students; they might look shocked when they heard of the orgies in the

76

Barerstrasse palace; they might exclaim in horror when her Allemania horse-whipped an editor and smashed his presses—but the men inwardly loved her for the gorgeous hoyden she was, and the women hid their satisfaction that one of their own sex was setting Europe by the ears. Whenever the insolent, tempestuous Montez provoked some new scandal, there was no lack of those who thought, "Good for you," and quite a few who said it openly.

And what the devil did she want with me? Well, I had come to Munich to find out, so I scribbled a note that Sunday evening, addressed to the Chamberlain Lauengram, saying that I had arrived and was at his disposal. Then I wandered over to the Residenz Palace, and looked at Lola's portrait in the public gallery—that "Gallery of Beauties" in which Ludwig had assembled pictures of the loveliest women of his day. There were princesses, countesses, actresses, and the daughter of the Munich town-crier, among others, and Lola looking unusually nun-like in a black dress and wearing a come-to-Jesus expression.[20] Underneath it was inscribed a verse written by the king, who was given to poetry, which finished up:

> Oh, soft and beauteous as a deer
> Art thou, of Andalusian race!

Well, he was probably in a position to know about that. And to think that only a few years ago she had been a penniless dancer being hooted off a London stage.

I had hoped, considering the urgency of Lauengram's original letter to me, to be bidden to Lola's palace on the Monday, but that day and the next went by, and still no word. But I was patient, and kept to my hotel, and on the Wednesday morning I was rewarded. I was finishing breakfast in my room, still in my dressing-gown, when there was a great flurry in the passage, and a lackey came to announce the arrival of the Freiherr von Starnberg, whoever he might be. There was much clashing and stamping, two cuirassiers in full fig appeared behind the lackey and stationed themselves like statues on either side of my doorway, and then in between them strolled the man himself, a gay young spark who greeted me with a flashing smile and outstretched hand.

"Herr Rittmeister Flashman?" says he. "My privilege to welcome you to Bavaria. Starnberg, very much at your service." And he clicked his heels, bowing. "You'll forgive my French, but it's better than my English."

"Better than my German, at any rate," says I, taking stock of him. He was about twenty, of middle height and very slender, with a clean-cut, handsome face, brown curls, and the wisp of a moustache on his upper lip. A very cool, jaunty gentleman, clad in the tight tunic and breeches of what I took to be a hussar regiment, for he had a dolman over his shoulder and a light sabre trailing at his hip. He was sizing me up at the same time.

"Dragoon?" says he.

"No, hussar."

"English light cavalry mounts must be infernally strong, then," says he, coolly. "Well, no matter. Forgive my professional interest. Have I interrupted your breakfast?"

I assured him he had not.

"Splendid. Then if you'll oblige me by getting dressed, we'll lose no more time. Lola can't abide to be kept waiting." And he lit a cheroot and began to survey the room. "Damnable places, these hotels. Couldn't stay in one myself."

I pointed out that I had been kept kicking my heels in one for the past three days, and he laughed.

"Well, girls will be girls, you know," says he. "We can't expect 'em to hurry for mere men, however much they expect *us* to jump to it. Lola's no different from the rest—in that respect."

"You seem to know her very well," says I.

"Well enough," says he negligently, sitting himself on the edge of a table and swinging a polished boot.

78

"For a messenger, I mean," says I, to take some of the starch out of him. But he only grinned.

"Oh, anything to oblige a lady, you know. I fulfil other functions, when I'm so inclined." And he regarded me with an insolent blue eye. "I don't wish to hurry you, old fellow, but we are wasting time. Not that I mind, but she certainly will."

"And we mustn't have that."

"No, indeed. I imagine you have some experience of the lady's fine Latin temper. By God, I'd tame it out of her if she was mine. But she's not, thank heaven. I don't have to humour her tantrums."

"You don't, eh?"

"Not hers, nor anyone else's," says Master von Starnberg, and took a turn round the room whistling.

Cocksure men irritate me as a rule, but it was difficult to take offence at this affable young sprig, and I had a feeling that it wouldn't do me much good if I did, so while he lounged in my sitting-room I retired to the bed-chamber to dress. I decided to wear my Cherrypicker rig, with all the trimmings of gold-laced blue tunic and tight pants, and when I emerged Starnberg cocked an eye and whistled appreciatively.

"Saucy regimentals," says he. "Very pretty indeed. Lola may not mind too much having been kept waiting, after all."

"Tell me," I said, "since you seem to know so much: why do you suppose she sent for me?—I'm assuming you know that she did."

"Oh, aye," says he. "Well, now, knowing Lola, I suggest you look in your mirror. Doesn't that suggest an answer?"

"Come now," says I, "I know Lola, too, and I flatter as easily as the next man. But she would hardly bring me all the way from England, just to . . ."

"Why not?" says he. "She brought me all the way from Hungary. Shall we go?"

He led the way down to the street, the two cuirassiers marching at our heels, and showed me into a coach that was waiting at the door. As he swung himself in beside me, with his hand on the window-frame, his sleeve was slightly pulled back, and I saw the star-shaped white scar of a bullet-wound on his wrist. It occurred to me that this von Starnberg was a tougher handful than he looked at first sight; I had noticed the genuine cavalry swing, toes pointing, as he walked, and for all his boyishness there was a compact sureness about him that would have sat on a much older man. This is one to keep an eye on, thinks I.

Lola's house was in the best part of Munich, by the Karolinen Platz. I say "house", but it was in fact a little palace, designed by King Ludwig's own architect, regardless of expense. It was the sight of it, shining new, like a little fairy-tale castle from Italy, with its uniformed sentries at the gate, its grilled windows (a precaution against hostile crowds), its magnificent gardens, and the flag fluttering from its roof, that brought it home to me just how high this woman had flown. This magnificence didn't signify only money, but power—unlimited power. So why could she want me? She couldn't *need* me. Was she indulging some whim—perhaps going to repay me for being in Ranelagh's box the night she was hissed off the stage? She seemed to be capable of anything. In a moment, after clapping eyes on her palace, I was cursing myself for having come—fear springs eternal in the coward's breast, especially when he has a bad conscience. After all, if she was so all-powerful, and happened to be vindictive, it might be damned unpleasant . . .

"Here we are," says Starnberg, "Aladdin's cave."

It almost justified the description. There were flunkeys to hand us out, and more uniformed sentries in the hall, all steel and colour, and the splendour of the interior was enough to take your breath away. The marble floor shone like glass, costly tapestries hung on the walls, great mirrors reflected alcoves stuffed with white statuary and choice furniture, above the staircase hung a chandelier which appeared to be of solid silver, and all of it was in a state of perfection and brilliance that suggested an army of skivvies and footmen working full steam.

"Aye, it's a roof over her head, I suppose," says Starnberg, as we gave our busbies to a lackey. "Ah, Lauengram, here is Rittmeister Flashman; is the Gräfin receiving?"

Lauengram was a dapper little gentleman in court-dress, with a thin, impassive face and a bird-like eye. He greeted me in French—which I learned later was spoken a good deal out of deference to Lola's bad German—and led us upstairs past more lackeys and sentries to an anteroom full of pictures and people. I have a soldier's eye for such things, and I would say the loot value of that chamber would have kept a regiment for life, with a farm for the farrier-sergeant thrown in. The walls appeared to be made of striped silk, and there was enough gold on the frames to start a mint.

The folk, too, were a prosperous-looking crew, courtly civilians and military in all the colours of the rainbow; some damned handsome women among them. They stopped their chattering as we entered, and I took advantage of my extra three inches on Starnberg to make a chest, touch my moustache, and give them all the cool look-over.

He had barely started to introduce me to those nearest when a door at the far end of the room opened, and a little chap came out backwards, stumbling over his feet, and protesting violently.

"It is no use, madame!" cries he, to someone in the far room. "I have not the power! The Vicar-General will not permit! Ach, no, lieber Herr Gott!" He cowered back as some piece of crockery sailed past him and shattered on the marble floor, and then Lola herself appeared in the doorway, and my heart took a bound at the sight of her.

She was beautiful in her royal rage, just as I remembered, although now she had clothes on. And although her aim seemed as vague as ever, she appeared to have her wrath under better control these days. At all events, she didn't scream.

"You may tell Dr Windischmann," says she, her rich husky voice charged with contempt, "that if the king's best friend desires a private chapel and confessor, she shall have one, and he shall provide it if he values his office. Does he think he can defy me?"

"Oh, madame, please," cries the little chap. "Only be reasonable! There is not a priest in Germany could accept such a confession. After all, your highness is a Lutheran, and—"

"Lutheran, fiddlesticks! I'm a royal favourite, you mean! That's why your master has the impertinence to flout me. Let him be careful, and you, too, little man. Lutheran or not, favourite or not, if I choose to have a chapel of my own I shall have it. Do you hear? And the Vicar-General himself shall hear my confession, if I think fit."

"Please, madame, oh, please!" The little fellow was on the verge of tears. "Why do you abuse me so? It is not my fault. Dr Windischmann objects only to the suggestion of a private chapel and confessor. He says . . ."

"Well, what does he say?"

The little man hesitated. "He says," he gulped, "he says that there is a public confessional at Notre-Dame, and you can always go there when you want to accuse yourself of any of the innumerable sins you have committed." His voice went up to a squeal. "His words, madame! Not mine! Oh, God have mercy!"

As she took one furious step forward he turned and ran for his life past us, his hands over his ears, and we heard his feet clatter on the stairs. Lola stamped her foot, and shouted after him, "Damned papist hypocrite!", and at this the sycophantic crowd in the ante-chamber broke out in a chorus of sympathy and reproach.

"Jesuit impertinence!"
"Intolerable affront!"

82

"Scandalous insolence!"

"Silly old bastard." (This was Starnberg's contribution.)

"Impossible arrogance of these prelates," says a stout, florid man near me.

"I'm Church of England myself," says I.

This had the effect of turning attention on me. Lola saw me for the first time, and the anger died out of her eyes. She surveyed me a moment, and then slowly she smiled.

"Harry Flashman," says she, and held out a hand towards me—but as a monarch does, palm down and pointing to the ground between us. I took my cue, stepping forward and taking her fingers to kiss. If she wanted to play Good Queen Bess, who was I to object?

She held my hand for a moment afterwards, looking up at me with her glowing smile.

"I believe you're even handsomer than you were," says she.

"I would say the same to you, Rosanna," says I, cavalier as be-damned, "but handsome is too poor a word for it."

Mind you, it was true enough. I've said she was the most beautiful girl I ever met, and she was still all of that. If anything, her figure was more gorgeous than I remembered, and since she was clad in a loose gown of red silk, with apparently nothing beneath it, I could study the subject without difficulty. The effect of her at close quarters was dazzling: the magnificent blue eyes, the perfect mouth and teeth, the white throat and shoulders, and the lustrous black hair coiled up on her head—yes, she was worth her place in Ludwig's gallery. But if she had ripened wonderfully in the few years since I had last seen her, she had changed too. There was a composure, a stateliness that was new; you would always have caught your breath at her beauty, but now you would feel a little awe as well as lust.

I was leering fondly down at her when Starnberg chimes in.

" 'Rosanna'?" says he. "What's this, Lola? A pet name?"

83

"Don't be jealous, Rudi," says she. "Captain Flashman is an old, very dear friend. He knew me long before—all this," and she gestured about her. "He befriended me when I was a poor little nobody, in London." And she took my arm in both of hers, reached up, and kissed me, smiling with her old mischief. Well, if that was how she chose to remember our old acquaintance, so much the better.

"Listen, all of you," she called out, and you could have heard a pin drop. "The Rittmeister Flashman is not only the closest to my heart of all my English friends—and those, you remember, include the noblest in the land—but the bravest soldier in the British Army. You see his decorations"—she leaned across me to touch my medals, and the presence of two almost naked, beautifully rounded breasts just beneath my face was delightfully diverting. Lola was always vain of her bosom,[21] and wore it all but outside her gown; I wished I had had a pinch of snuff to offer her. "Who ever saw a young captain with five medals?" she continued, and there was a chorus of murmured admiration. "So you see, he is to be honoured for more reasons than that he is my guest. There is no soldier in Germany with a higher reputation as a Christian champion."

I had sense enough to look quizzical and indulgent at this, for I knew that the most popular heroes are those who take themselves lightly. I had heard this kind of rot time without count in the past few years, and knew how to receive it, but it amused me to see that the audience, as usual, took it perfectly seriously, the men looking noble and the women frankly admiring.

Having delivered her little lecture, Lola took me on a tour of introduction, presenting Baron this and Countess that, and everyone was all smirks and bows and polite as pie. I could sense that they were all scared stiff of her, for although she was her old gay self, laughing and chattering as she took me from group to group, she was still the grande dame under the happy surface, with a damned imperious eye. Oh, she had them disciplined all right.

Only when she had taken me apart, to a couch where a flunkey served us Tokay while the others stood at a respectful distance, did she let the mask drop a little, and the Irish began to creep back into her voice.

"Let me look at you comfortably now," says she, leaning back and surveying me over her glass. "I like the moustaches, Harry, they become you splendidly. And the careless curl; oh, it's the bonny boy still."

"And you are still the most beautiful girl in the world," says I, not to be outdone.

"So they say," says she, "but I like to hear it from you. After all, when you hear it from Germans it's no compliment—not when you consider the dumpy cows they're comparing you with."

"Some of 'em ain't too bad," says I carelessly.

"Ain't they, though? I can see I shall have to keep an eye on you, my lad. I saw Baroness Pechman wolfing you up a moment ago when she was presented."

"Which one was she?"

"Come, that's better. The last one you met—over there, with the yellow hair."

"She's fat. Overblown."

"Ye-es, poor soul, but some men like it, I'm told."

"Not I, Rosanna."

"Rosanna," she repeated, smiling. "I like that. You know that no one ever calls me by that name now. It reminds me of England—you've no notion how famous it is to hear English again. In conversation, I mean, like this."

"Was that why you sent for me—for my conversation?"

"That—and other things."

"What other things?" says I, seeing a chance to get down to business. "What's this very delicate matter that your chamberlain talked about?"

"Oh, that." She put on a coy look. "That can wait a little. You must know I have a new motto since I came to Bavaria: 'pleasure before business'." She gave me a sleepy look from beneath those glorious black lashes that made my heart skip a little. "You wouldn't be so ungallant as to hurry me, would you, Harry?"

"Not where business is concerned," says I, leering again. "Pleasure's another matter."

"Wicked," she says, smiling lazily, like a sleek black cat. "Wicked, wicked, wicked."

It is remarkable what fatuities you can exchange with a beautiful woman. I can think shame when I consider the way I sat babbling with Lola on that couch; I would ask you only to remember that she was as practised a seductress as ever wore out bed linen, and just to be beside her, even in a room full of people, was in itself intoxicating. She was overpowering, like some rich tropical flower, and she could draw a man like a magnet. The same Dr Windischmann, Vicar-General, whose name she had been taking in vain so recently, once said that there was not even a priest in his charge who could have been trusted with her. Liszt put it more bluntly and accurately when he observed to me: "As soon as you meet Lola, your mind leaps into bed."

Anyway, I mention this to explain how it was that after a few moments with her I had forgotten entirely my earlier misgivings about her possible recollection of our parting in London, and my fears that she might harbour a grudge against me for the Ranelagh affair. She had charmed me, and I use the word exactly. Laughing and talking with her over the Tokay, only one thought was in my mind: to get her bedded as swiftly as might be, and the devil with anything else.

While we were chatting so amiably and I, poor ass, was succumbing to her spell, more people were arriving in the ante-room, and presently she had them called up, with Lauengram playing the major-domo, and talked to them in turn. These levées of hers were quite famous in Munich, apparently, and it was her habit to hold court to all sorts of folk: not just distinguished visitors and such odds and ends as artists and poets, but even statesmen and ambassadors. I don't recall who was there that morning, for between Lola and the Tokay I was not paying much heed, but I know they scraped and fawned to her no end.

Presently she announced that we would all go to see her cuirassiers at exercise, and there was a delay while she went off to change; when she returned it was in full Hussar rig, which showed off her curves admirably and would have caused the police to be called in London. The sycophants "Ooh-ed" and "Aah-ed" and cried "Wunderschön!", and we all trooped after her to the stables and rode out to a nearby park where a couple of squadrons of cavalry were going through their paces.

Lola, who was riding a little white mare, took great pleasure in the spectacle, pointing with her whip and exclaiming authoritatively on the manoeuvres. Her courtiers echoed her applause faithfully, all except Rudi Starnberg, who I noticed was watching with a critical eye, like myself. I ought to know something about cavalry, and certainly Lola's cuirassiers were a smart lot on parade, and looked very well as they thundered past at the charge. Starnberg asked me what I thought of them; very fine, I said.

"Better than the British?" says he, with his cocky grin.

"I'll tell you that when I've seen 'em fight," says I, bluntly.

"You won't deny they're disciplined to perfection," cries he.

"On parade," says I. "No doubt they'd charge well in a body, too. But let's see 'em in a mêlée, every man for himself; that's where good cavalry prove themselves."

This is true; of course, no one would run faster from a mêlée than I, but Starnberg wasn't to know that. For the first time he looked at me almost with respect, nodding thoughtfully, and admitted I was probably right.

Lola got bored after half an hour or so, and we returned to her palace, but then we had to turn out again because she wanted to exercise her dogs in the garden. It seemed that whatever she did, everyone else was expected to tag after her, and by God, her amusements were trivial. After the dogs, there was music indoors, with a fat bastard of a tenor sobbing his soul out, and then Lola sang herself—she had a fine contralto, as it happens—and the mob raised the roof. Then there was a reading of poetry, which was damnable, but would probably have been even more painful if I had been able to understand it fully, and then more conversation in the ante-room. The centre of it was a long-jawed, tough-looking fellow whose name meant nothing to me at the time; he talked interminably, about music and liberal politics, and everyone lionised him sickeningly, even Lola. When we went into an adjoining room for a buffet—"erfrischung" as the Germans call it—she introduced him to me as Herr Wagner, but the only conversation we had was when I passed him the ginger and he said "danke". (I've dined out on that incident since, by the way, which shows how ridiculous people can be where celebrities are concerned. Of course, I usually expand the story, and let on that I told him that "Drink, puppy, drink" and "The British Grenadiers" were better music than any damned opera, but only because that is the sort of exaggeration that goes well at dinner parties, and suits my popular character.)[22]

But my memories of that afternoon are necessarily vague, in view of what the night was to bring forth. Briefly, I stayed at the palace all day, being unconscionably bored, and impatient to get Lola by herself, which looked like being damned difficult, there was such a crowd always in attendance on her. From time to time we had a word or two, but always with others present, and when we dined I was halfway down the table, with the fat Baroness Pechman on one side of me, and an American whose name I've forgotten on the other.[23] I was pretty piqued with Lola for this; quite apart from the fact that I thought I deserved a place near her at the table top, the Yankee was the damnedest bore you ever met, and the giggling blonde butterball on my other side was infuriating in her shrieks of amusement at my halting German. She also had a tendency to let her hand stray on to my thigh beneath the table—not that I minded the compliment, and she would have been pretty enough in a baby-faced way if she had weighed about six stones less, but my mind was on the lovely Lola, and she was a long way off.

Being bored, I was careless, and didn't keep too close an eye on my glass. It was a magnificent dinner, and the wines followed each other in brilliant succession. Everyone else punished them tremendously, as the Germans always do, and I simply followed suit. It was understandable, but foolish; I learned in later years that the only safe place to get drunk is among friends in your own home, but that evening I made a thorough pig of myself, and the long and short of it was that "Flashy got beastly drunk", to quote my old friend Tom Hughes.

Not that I was alone; the talk got steadily louder, faces got redder, jokes got coarser—the fact that half those present were women made no difference—and eventually they were roaring and singing around the table, or staggering out to be sick, no doubt, and what conversation there was consisted of shouting at full pitch. I remember there was an orchestra playing incessantly at one end of the hall, and at one point my American companion got up unsteadily on to his chair, amid the cheers of the multitude, and conducted them with a knife and fork. Presently he tumbled down, and rolled under the table. This is an orgy, thinks I, but not a proper orgy. I got it into my head—quite understandably—that such a bacchanalia should be concluded in bed, and naturally looked round for Lola. She had left the table, and was standing off in an alcove at one side, talking to some people; I got up and weaved my way through such of the guests as were standing about—those who were fit to stand, that is—until I fetched up in front of her.

I must have been heroically drunk, for I can remember

her face swimming in and out of focus; she had a diamond circlet in her dark hair, and the lights from the chandelier made it glitter dazzlingly. She said something, I don't recall what, and I mumbled:

"Let's go to bed, Lola. You an' me."

"You should lie down, Harry," says she. "You're very tired."

"Not too tired," says I. "But I'm damned hot. Come on, Lola, Rosanna, let's go to bed."

"Very well. Come along, then." I'm sure she said that, and then she turned away, and I followed her out of the din and stuffiness of the banqueting chamber into a corridor; I was weaving pretty recklessly, for I walked into the wall once, but she waited for me, and guided me to a doorway, which she opened.

"In here," she said.

I stumbled past her, and caught the musky sweetness of her perfume; I grabbed at her, and dragged her to me in the darkness. She was soft and thrilling against me, and for a moment her open mouth was under mine; then she slipped away, and I lost my balance and half-fell on to a couch. I called out to her to come back, and heard her say, "A moment; just in a moment," and then the door shut softly.

I half-lay on the couch, my head swimming with drink and my mind full of lustful thoughts, and I believe I must have passed into a brief stupor, for suddenly I was aware of dim light in the room, and a soft hand was stroking my cheek.

"Lola," says I, like a moon-calf, and then there were arms round my neck and a soft voice murmuring in my ear, but it was not Lola. I blinked at the face before me, and my hands came in contact with bare, plump flesh—any amount of it. My visitor was Baroness Pechman, and she was stark naked.

I tried to shove her off, but she was too heavy; she clung to me like a leech, murmuring endearments in German, and pushing me back on the couch.

"Go away, you fat slut," says I, heaving at her. "Gehen Sie weg, dammit. Don't want you; want Lola."

I might as well have tried to move St Paul's; she was all over me, trying to kiss me, and succeeding, her fat face against mine. I cursed and struggled, and she giggled idiotically and began clawing at my breeches.

"No, you don't," says I, seizing her wrist, but I was too tipsy to be able to defend myself properly, or else she was strong for all her blubber. She pinned me down, calling me her duckling, of all things, and her chicken, and then before I knew it she had suddenly hauled me upright and had my fine Cherrypicker pants round my knees, and was squirming her fat backside against me.

"Oh, eine hammelkeule!" she squeaked. "Kolossal!"

No woman does that to me twice; I'm too susceptible. I seized handfuls of her and began thrusting away. She was not Lola, perhaps, but she was there, and I was still too foxed and too randy to be choosy. I buried my face in the blonde curls at the nape of her neck, and she squealed and plunged in excitement. And I was just settling to work in earnest when there was a rattle at the door handle, the door opened, and suddenly there were men in the room.

There were three of them; Rudi Starnberg and two civilians in black. Rudi was grinning in delight at the sight of me, caught flagrante seducto, as we classical scholars say, but I knew this was no joke. Drunk as I was, I sensed that here was danger, dreadful danger when I had least expected it. It was in the grim faces of the two with him, hard, tight-lipped fellows who moved like fighters.

I shoved my fat baroness quickly away, and she went down sprawling flabbily on her stomach. I jumped back, trying to pull up my breeches, but cavalry pants fit like a skin, and the two were on me before I could adjust myself. Each grabbed an arm, and one of them growled in execrable French:

"Hold still, criminal! You are under arrest!"

"What the devil for?" I shouted. "Take your hands off me, damn you! What does this mean, Starnberg?"

"You're arrested," says he. "These are police officers."

"Police? But, my God, what am I supposed to have done?"

Starnberg, arms akimbo, glanced at the woman who had climbed to her feet, and was hastening to cover herself with a robe. To my amazement, she was giggling behind her hand; I wondered was she mad or drunk.

"I don't know what you call it in English," says he coolly, "but we have several impolite names for it here. Off you go, Gretchen," and he jerked a thumb towards the door.

"In God's name, that's not a crime!" I shouted, but seeing him silent and smiling grimly, I struggled for all I was worth. I was sober enough now, and horribly frightened.

"Let me go!" I yelled. "You must be mad! I demand to see the Gräfin Landsfeld! I demand to see the British Ambassador!"

"Not without your trousers, surely," says Rudi.

"Help!" I roared. "Help! Let me loose! You scoundrels, I'll make you pay for this!" And I tried in frenzy to break from the grip of the policemen.

"Ein starker mann," observed Rudi. "Quiet him."

One of my captors shifted quickly behind me, I tried to turn, and a splitting pain shot through the back of my head. The room swam round me, and I felt my knees strike the floor before my senses left me.

I wonder sometimes if any man on earth has come to in a cell more often than I have. It has been happening to me all my life; perhaps I could claim a record. But if I did some American would be sure to beat it at once.

This awakening was no different from most of the others: two damnable pains, one inside and one outside my skull, a stomachful of nausea, and a dread of what lay ahead. The last was quickly settled, at any rate; just as grey light was beginning to steal through the bars of my window—which I guessed was in a police station, for the cell was decent—a uniformed guard brought me a mug of coffee, and then conducted me along a corridor to a plain, panelled room containing a most official-looking desk, behind which sat a most official-looking man. He was about fifty, with iron grey hair and a curling moustache, and cold eyes flanking a beaky nose. With him, standing at a writing pulpit beside the desk, was a clerk. The guard ushered me in, bleary, unshaven, blood-stained, and in the fiend's own temper.

"I demand to be allowed to communicate with my ambassador this instant," I began, "to protest at the outrageous manner in which—"

"Be quiet," says the official. "Sit down." And he indicated a stool before the desk.

I wasn't having this. "Don't dare to order me about, you cabbage-eating bastard," says I. "I am a British officer, and unless you wish to have a most serious international incident to answer for, you will—"

"I will certainly have you whipped and returned to your cell if you do not curb your foul tongue," says he coldly. "Sit."

I was staring, flabbergasted at this, when a cheerful voice behind me said:

"Better sit down, old fellow; he can do it, you know," and I wheeled round to find Rudi Starnberg lolling against a table by the door, which had hidden him from me when I came in. He was fresh and jaunty, with his undress cap tilted forward rakishly over one eye, smoking a cheroot in a holder.

"You!" cried I, and got no further. He shushed me with a gesture and pointed to the stool; at the same time the official rapped smartly on his table, so I decided to sit. My head was aching so much I doubt if I could have stood much longer anyway.

"This is Doctor Karjuss," says Rudi. "He is a magistrate and legal authority; he has something to say to you."

"Then he can start by telling me the meaning of this dastardly ill-treatment," cries I. "I've been set upon, my skull cracked, thrown into a filthy cell, denied the right to see my ambassador, and God knows what else. Yes, by the lord, I've been threatened with flogging, too!"

"You were placed under arrest last night," says Karjuss, who spoke tolerable French. "You resisted the officers. They restrained you; that is all."

"Restrained me? They bloody well half-killed me! And what is this damned nonsense about arrest? What's the charge, hey?"

"As yet, none has been laid," says Karjuss. "I repeat, as yet. But I can indicate what they may be." He sat very prim and precise, his cold eyes regarding me with distaste. "First, obscene and indecent conduct; second, corruption of public morals; third, disorderly behaviour; fourth, resisting the police; fifth—"

"You're mad!" I shouted. "This is ridiculous! D'you imagine any court in the world would convict me of any of this, on the strength of what happened last night? Good God, there is such a thing as justice in Bavaria, I suppose—"

"There is indeed," snaps he. "And I can tell you, sir, that I do not merely imagine that a court could convict you—I *know* it could. And it will."

My head was reeling with all this. "Oh, to the devil! I'll not listen to this! I want to see my ambassador. I know my rights, and—"

"Your ambassador would be of no help to you. I have not yet mentioned the most serious complaint. It is possible that a charge of criminal assault on a female may be brought against you."

At this I staggered to my feet in horror. "That's a lie! A damned lie! My God, she practically raped *me*. Why, she—"

"That would not be the evidence she would give before a judge and jury." His voice was stone cold. "Baroness Pechman is known as a lady of irreproachable character. Her husband is a former Commissioner of Police for Munich. I can hardly imagine a more respectable witness."

"But . . . but . . ." I was at a loss for words, but a horrible thought was forming in my brain. "This is a plot! That's it! It's a deliberate attempt to discredit me!" I wheeled on Starnberg, who was negligently regarding his nails. "You're in this, you rascal! You've given false witness!"

"Don't be an ass," says he. "Listen to the magistrate, can't you?"

Stunned and terrified, I sank on to the stool. Karjuss leaned forward, a thin hand tapping the table before him. I had the impression he was enjoying himself.

"You begin to see the seriousness of your position, sir. I have indicated the charges which could be brought—and without doubt, proved—against you. I speak not as an examining magistrate, but as a legal adviser, if you like. These are certainties. No doubt you would persist in denial; against you there would be at least four witnesses of high character—the two police officers who apprehended you, Baroness Pechman, and the Freiherr von Starnberg here. Your word—the word of a known duellist over women, a man who was expelled for drunken behaviour from his school in England—"

"How the devil did you know that?"

"Our gathering of information is thorough. Is it not so? You can guess what your word would count for in the circumstances."

"I don't care!" I cried. "You can't hope to do this! I'm a friend of the Gräfin Landsfeld! She'll speak for me! By God, when she hears of this, the boot will be on the other foot . . ."

I went no further. Another horrid thought had struck me. Why hadn't the all-powerful Lola, whose lightest word was law in Bavaria, intervened by now? She must know all about it; why, the ghastly affair had happened in her own palace! She had been with me not five minutes before . . . And then, in spite of my aching, reeling head, the full truth of it was plain. Lola knew all about it, yes; hadn't she lured me to Munich in the first place? And here I was, within twenty-four hours of meeting her again, trapped in what was obviously a damnable, deliberate plot against me. God! Was this her way of punishing me for what had happened years before, when I had laughed at her humiliation in London? Could any woman be so fiendishly cruel, hating so long and bitterly that she would go to such lengths? I couldn't believe it.

And then Karjuss spoke to confirm my worst fears.

"You can hope for no assistance whatever from the Gräfin Landsfeld," says he. "She has already disclaimed you."

I took my aching head in my hands. This was a nightmare; I couldn't believe it was happening.

"But I've done nothing!" I burst out, almost sobbing. "Oh, I galloped that fat trot, yes, but where's the crime in that? Don't Germans do it, for Christ's sake? By God, I'll fight this! My ambassador—"

"A moment." Karjuss was impatient. "It seems I have talked to no purpose. Can I not convince you that, legally, you are without hope? And, on conviction, I assure you, you could be imprisoned for life. Even on the minor charges, it would be possible to ensure a maximum sentence of some years. Is that clear? This, inevitably, is what will happen if, by insisting on seeing your ambassador, and enlisting his interest, you cause the whole scandal to become public. At the moment, I would remind you, no charges have been formulated."

"And they needn't be," says Rudi from behind me. "Unless you insist, of course."

This was too much for me; it made no sense whatever.

"No one wants to be unpleasant," says Rudi, all silky.

"But we have to show you where you stand, don't you see? To let you see what *might* happen—if you were obstinate."

"You're blackmailing me, then!" I stared from the thin-lipped Karjuss to the debonair stripling. "In God's name, why? What have I done? What d'ye want me to do?"

"Ah!" says he. "That's better." He tapped me twice smartly on the shoulder with his riding-switch. "Much better. Do you know, Doctor," he went on, turning to Karjuss, "I believe there is no need to trouble you any longer. I'm sure the Rittmeister Flashman has at least realised the—er, gravity of his situation, and will be as eager as we all are to find a mutually satisfactory way out of it. I'm deeply obliged to you, Doctor."

Even in my scared and bewildered state, I noticed that Karjuss took his dismissal as a lackey does from a master. He stood up, bowed to Starnberg, and with his clerk at his heels, strode out of the room.

"That's better too," said young Rudi. "I can't endure these damned scriveners, can you? I wouldn't have troubled you with him, really, but there's no doubt he explains legal technicalities well. Cigar? No?"

"He's explained nothing, except that I'm the object of a damned conspiracy! God, why do you do this to me? Is it that damned bitch Lola? Is this how she takes her revenge on me?"

"Tut-tut," says Rudi. "Be calm." He seated himself on the edge of Karjuss's desk, swung his legs a moment, and looked at me thoughtfully. Then he gave a slow chuckle.

"It's too bad, really. I don't blame you for being annoyed. The truth is, we haven't been quite honest with you. You're sure you won't have a cigar? Oh, well, here's how it is."

He lit himself another weed, and held forth.

"I think Karjuss has convinced you that you're in a most devilish mess. *If* we choose, we can shut you up for ever, and your own ambassador, and your government,

97

would be the first to say 'Amen'. Considering the charges, I mean."

"Trumped-up lies!" I shouted. "False blasted witnesses!"

"But of course. As you yourself said, a dastardly plot. But the point is—you're caught in it, with no choice but to do as you're told. If you refuse—the charges are brought, you're convicted, and good-night."

And the insolent young hound grinned pleasantly at me and blew a smoke-ring.

"You devil!" cries I. "You—you dirty German dog!"

"Austrian, actually. Anyway, you appreciate your position?"

Oh, I appreciated it, no question of that. I didn't understand how, or why, they had done this to me, but I was in no doubt of what the consequences would be if I didn't play their infernal game for them—whatever it was. Blustering hadn't helped me, and a look at Rudi's mocking face told me that whining wouldn't either. Robbed of the two cards which I normally play in a crisis, I was momentarily lost.

"Will you tell me why you've done this—why to me? What can you want of me, in heaven's name?"

"There is a service—a very important service—which only you can perform," says he. "More than that I can't say, at the moment. But that is why you were brought to Munich—oh, it was all most carefully planned. Lola's letter—dictated by me, incidentally—was not altogether inaccurate. 'Most delicate' really sums it up."

"But what service could there possibly be that only I—"

"You'll have to wait and see, and for heaven's sake stop expostulating like the victim in a melodrama. Take my word for it, we didn't go to so much trouble for nothing. Now, you're a sensible man, I'm sure. Will you bow to the inevitable, like a good chap?"

"That bitch Lola!" I growled. "She's up to the neck in this—this villainy, I suppose."

"Up to a point, not up to the neck. She was the means

of getting you to Germany, but it wasn't her idea. We employed her assistance—"

" 'We'? Who the devil's 'we'?"

"My friends and I. But you shouldn't be too hard on her, you know. I doubt if she bears you any ill-will—in fact, I think she's rather sorry for you—but she knows which side her bread is buttered. And powerful as she is, there are those in Germany whom even she finds it wise to oblige. Now, no more silly questions: are you going to be a good boy or aren't you?"

"It seems I've no choice."

"Excellent. Now, we'll have that crack in your head seen to, get you a bath and some clean linen, and then—"

"What then?"

"You and I will make a little journey, my dear Flashman. Or, may I call you Harry? You must address me as Rudi, you know; 'dirty dog' and 'devil' and 'swine' and so on are all very well between comparative strangers, but I feel that you and I may be on the brink of a really fruitful and profitable friendship. You don't agree? Well, I'm sorry, but we'll see. Now, if you'll come along, I have a closed carriage waiting which will take us to a little place of mine where we'll have you repaired and made all klim-bim, as the Prussians say. Devilish places, these jails, aren't they; no proper facilities for a gentleman at all . . ."

Well, what could I do, but trot along at his heels with a mouthful of apprehension? Whatever "they" were up to, I was in for it, and in the meantime there was nothing to do but go with the tide. With my sure instinct, I knew that the "service" I was being blackmailed into was sure to be unpleasant, and quite likely damned dangerous, but my queasy guts didn't interfere with my logical process. I'm a realist, and it was already in my mind that in whatever lay ahead—a journey, initially, according to Rudi—some opportunity of escape must surely present itself. Unless you are actually locked up, escapes are not as difficult as many folk think; you simply bolt, seize the first available horse, and go like hell for safety—in this case probably the Austrian frontier. Or would Switzerland be better? It was farther, but Rudi and his sinister friends probably had influence in Austria. And they would not reckon on me trying a forced ride to the Swiss border . . .

"Oh, by the way," says Rudi, as we left the police office and he handed me into a carriage, "to a man of action like yourself it may seem that an opportunity will arise of giving me the slip. Don't try it. I would kill you before you'd gone five yards." And he smiled genially as he settled himself opposite me.

"You're mighty sure of yourself," growls I.

"With cause," says he. "Look here." He gave his right arm a shake, and there was a pocket pistol in his right hand. "I'm a dead shot, too."

"Naturally," says I, but I decided it was probably true. Anyone who keeps a pistol in his sleeve can usually use it.

"And, in all modesty, I'm probably your master with the sabre as well—or with a knife," says Master Rudi, putting his pistol away. "So you see, it wouldn't pay you to run for it."

I said nothing, but my spirits sank a few notches lower. He was going to be an efficient watch-dog, rot him, the more so since he believed me to be "a man of action". He knew enough of my reputation, no doubt, to put me down as a desperate, dangerous fellow who didn't give a damn for risks. If he'd known me for the poltroon I was he might have been less alert.

So in the meantime, I was at the mercy of Freiherr Rudolf von Starnberg, and if I'd known him then as I knew him later I'd have been even more nervous than I was. For this gay, devil-may-care youngster, with his curly head and winning smile, was one of the hardest cases I've ever encountered—a thoroughly bad, unscrupulous and fatally dangerous ruffian—and, as you can imagine, I have known a few. Not many of them, scoundrels that they were, delighted in wickedness for its own sake, but Rudi did.

He enjoyed killing, for example, and would kill laughing; he was without shame where women were concerned, and without pity, too. I dare say there may have been crimes he didn't commit, but it can only have been for want of opportunity. He was an evil, vicious, cruel rascal.

We got on very well, really, I suppose, all things considered. This was not just because I shared most of his vices, but because he believed erroneously that I shared his only virtue, which was courage. He was too young to know what fear was, and he imagined that I was as big a daredevil as he was himself—my Afghan reputation was pretty glorious, after all. But in addition I must admit that he could be a good companion when he chose—he had a great fund of amiable conversation and a filthy mind, and loved the good things of life—so it was not difficult to get along with him.

He was all consideration that first day. At the house he took me to there was a most competent French valet who dressed and bathed my head, provided me with a bath and a suit of my own clothes—for they had brought my baggage from my hotel—and later cooked us both a most splendid omelette before we set off for the station. Rudi was in haste to catch the train: we were bound for Berlin, he told me, but beyond that I could get nothing out of him.

"Wait and see," says he. "And while you're waiting, I'd be obliged if you would stop talking French and practise your German—you're going to need it."

With that mysterious instruction I had to be content—and I had to be obedient, too, for devil a word of French would he say or listen to from then on. However, with a bottle of hock inside me, the unknown future looked a little less bleak, and when we boarded the evening train I was at least momentarily resigned to my situation. Time enough to start fretting again when we reached Berlin.

The journey took us three days, although nowadays you would do it in a matter of hours. But those were the early years of railways, and the line between Munich and Berlin was not complete. I know we did part of the trip by coach, but I can't recall where; one night we spent in Leipzig, certainly, but I was paying no great heed to my surroundings. As the miles went by my apprehension was growing again—what the devil did "they" want me for? I tried several times to pump Rudi, but without success.

"You'll find out in good time," was all he would say, with a knowing grin. "I'll tell you this much—*I'd* do the job in a moment if I had the chance. I envy you, indeed. But you're the only man for it—and don't fret: it's well within your powers."

That should have cheered me up, but it didn't. After all, my powers, so far as he and the world knew them, were all concerned with war, slaughter, and heroism, and I wanted none of that if I could help it. But I had sense enough not to let him get a glimpse of my lily liver; no doubt, if my worst fears were realised, he'd see all he wanted of it, in time.

We spent much of our time in the train playing piquet and écarté, and recognised each other as fairish sharps, but neither of us was able to take much interest in the game. I was too inwardly nervous, and he was too busy keeping an eye on me—he was one of these extraordinary folk who can be on the hair trigger of action for days and nights on end, and not once in that journey was there a decent chance to take him unawares. Not that I'd have dared to try if there had been; I had got a healthy respect for young Rudi by now, and didn't doubt that he would shoot me without the slightest hesitation, and take his chance on the consequences.

So we came to Berlin, on a night of bitter snow and wind, and there was another coach at the station to whirl us away through the busy lamp-lit streets. Even with our fur-collared coats, and rugs and hot bricks, it was damnably chilly in that coach after the warmth of the train, and I wasn't cheered by the fact that our journey was obviously not going to be a short one—that much was clear from the fact that we had a couple of hampers of food with us and a basket of bottles as well.

It lasted another three days, what with snow-choked roads and the coach shedding a wheel, and damned uncomfortable it was. I guessed we were travelling west, at about twenty miles a day, but beyond that there was nothing to be learned from the dreary German landscape. The snow stuck to the windows, and the coach was like an ice-house; I cursed and grumbled a good deal, but Starnberg sat patiently in his corner, huddled in his great-coat, whistling softly through his teeth—his observations were either insolently cheerful or caustic, and I couldn't decide which I disliked more.

It was towards evening on the third day that I awoke from a doze to find Rudi with the window down, peering out into the dusk. The snow had stopped for the moment, but there was a keen wind whistling into the coach, and I was about to tell him brusquely to shut the window before we froze, when he pulled his head in and said:

"Journey's end, thank God. Now for some decent food at last and a proper bed."

I leaned forward to look out, and I've seen cheerier prospects. We were rolling slowly up a long avenue of trees towards a huge, bleak house, half mansion, half castle; in the fading light, with the wintry sky behind it, it looked in silhouette like the setting for some gothic novel, all towers and spires and rugged stonework. There were lights in some of the windows, and a great lantern shone yellow above the pointed archway of its main door, but they served only to exaggerate the ancient gloom of the place. Childe Flashy to the Dark Tower came, thinks I, and tried not to imagine what lay within.

It proved to be a match for the exterior. We were shown into an immense, stone-flagged hall, hung round with faded tapestries and a few old trophies of arms and the chase; there were archways without doors leading out of it, and in keeping with a general air of medieval ghastliness,

103

there were even torches burning in brackets on the walls. The place felt like a tomb, and the ancient butler who received us would have made an excellent gravedigger.

But what daunted me most of all was the presence in the hall of a strapping trio of fellows, all of military cut, who welcomed Rudi and weighed me up with cold, professional eyes. One was a massive, close-cropped, typical Prussian, whose fleshy face was wealed with a great sabre cut from brow to chin; the second was a tall, supple, sinister gentleman with sleek black hair and a vulpine smile; the third was stocky and stout, balding and ugly. All were in undress uniforms, and as tough-looking a set of customers as you could wish for; my spirits sank even farther as I realised that with this crew on hand my chances of escape had dwindled out of sight.

Rudi performed introductions. "My friends Kraftstein" —the big Prussian clicked his heels—"de Gautet"—a bow from the sinister Scaramouche—"and Bersonin"—the bald ugly one barely nodded. "Like you and me, they are military men, as you see. You'll find they are devoted to your welfare and er . . . safekeeping," says Master Rudi pleasantly, "and any one of them is almost as tough as I am, nicht wahr?"

"Ich glaube es," says the sleek de Gautet, showing his teeth. Another confident bastard, and decidedly unpleasant.

While he and Kraftstein stayed talking with Rudi, I was conveyed to a room on the second floor by Bersonin, and while he kept a bleak eye on me I was graciously permitted to change, wash, and eat a meal which the ancient butler brought. It was tolerable food, with an excellent Rhenish, and I invited the taciturn Bersonin to join me in a glass, but he shook his head. I tried my German on him, but getting nothing but grunts for my pains I turned my back on him and devoted myself to my meal. If he wanted to play the jailer, he could be treated like one.

Presently back comes Master Rudi, very debonair in a clean shirt, freshly-pressed breeches and polished boots, with the Brothers Grimm, Kraftstein and de Gautet, at his heels.

"All fed and watered?" says he. "Capital. I can see you two have been getting along famously. I trust our good Bersonin hasn't overwhelmed you with his inconsequential chatter. No?" He grinned impudently at Bersonin, who shrugged and scowled. "My, what a madcap he is," went on Rudi, who had evidently dined too, and was back at the top of his most amiable form. "Well, come along with me, and we'll see what other entertainment this charming establishment can offer."

"All the entertainment I want is to find out what the devil I'm doing here," says I.

"Oh, you haven't long to wait now," says he, and he conducted me down the corridor, up another stairway, and into a long gallery. Just as we set foot in it, there sounded from somewhere ahead of us the unmistakable crack of a pistol-shot; I jumped, but Rudi only grinned over his shoulder.

"Rats," says he. "The place is thick with 'em. We've tried poison and dogs, but our host believes in more direct methods. There he goes again," he added, as another shot sounded. "They must be out in force tonight."

He paused in front of a stout, metal-studded door. "Here we are," cries he, throwing it wide, and waving me in. "Your patience is rewarded."

It was a fine, spacious room, far better appointed than anything I had seen so far, with carpet on the flags, a bright fire in the huge grate, solid-looking leather furniture, several shelves of books round the panelled walls, and a long, narrow polished table running down the centre under a brilliant candelabra. At the far end of the table sat a man, his feet cocked up on the board, reloading a long pistol, and at the sight of him I stopped as though I had walked into a wall. It was Otto von Bismarck.

In a lifetime that has included far too many unpleasant surprises, I can think of few nastier shocks than that moment. Strange as it seems, from the very start of this German affair, Bismarck had never even crossed my mind—probably because I didn't want to remember him. Having done the dirty on him in England with John Gully, I'd had no wish ever to meet him again—especially at such a disadvantage as now. Well, when you've caused a man to be cut up by a prize pug, and made him look an idiot into the bargain, you bar renewing his acquaintance in a lonely castle with four of his hired thugs ushering you into his presence.

Equally alarming was the discovery that he was at the bottom of the plot that had snared me: if it had looked sticky before, it looked a lot worse now.

"Welcome to Schönhausen, Mr Flashman," says he, with the vaguest curl of a smile at the corner of his mouth. "Pray be seated."[24]

Bersonin set a chair for me at the table end opposite Bismarck, and then took station by the door. The other three stood by the fireplace, Rudi leaning against the overmantel. Bismarck studied me along the table's length: he looked as nasty as ever, with those pale blue eyes and his arrogant stare. His face had roughened up a bit, though, since I first knew him, and he was sporting a heavy moustache; booze and guzzling had added a good deal of flesh to him, especially about the neck.

My heart was thumping like a hammer, and as always when I am scared half out of my wits my face was going red. Bismarck misread the signs.

"You don't appear pleased to see me," says he, laying

aside his pistol. "But then, why should you? There is a score to settle on my side; I still miss a tooth, thanks to your pugilist friend." He paused, while I quaked. "However, don't imagine that I contrived your coming all the way here from England just to settle a personal difference. It happens, amazing though it may seem, that I need you. What do you think of that?"

"My God," says I, "if that's so, why the devil didn't you ask me, like a civilised human being, instead of going through that damned charade in Munich? Of all the ridiculous, dangerous—yes, and damned bad-mannered—"

"Don't be a fool. We will not pretend that if I had asked you, you would have come. It was necessary to use guile and force, in turn, to ensure your presence here. And to further ensure that you would be—pliable. For you have been left in no doubt what will happen to you if you do not do exactly what I require."

"I've been left in no doubt that I've been bloody well kidnapped! And assaulted and falsely accused! I've been left in no doubt that you're a damned villain. And—"

"Shall we leave these vapourings?" he broke in harshly. "You know something of what I am, and I know exactly what you are—a brutal, lecherous ruffian. Yes, but with certain abilities, which you will use as I direct."

"What the devil *is* it you want, curse you? What use can I possibly be to you?"

"That is better. Give him a brandy, Kraftstein, and a cigar. Now then, Mr Flashman, you will listen to me, and what I tell you will never be repeated—never, as you love your life."

As I think back on it now, it is still difficult to believe that it happened—that I really sat in that long room, with a glass and a cigar, while that cold, masterful man who was to be the greatest statesman of his age, outlined to me the amazing plan which was to be the first, small stepping-stone in his great career. It was mad, incredible nonsense, but it is true. Bismarck then was nothing—in the political sense, anyway. But he had dreamed his dreams (as Lola had told me years before) and now he was setting about in that cold, German certainty, to make them realities. Strange, isn't it, that without me he could not have begun as he did? He needed the lecherous, brutal ruffian (an incomplete description, but Bismarck always was a great one for half-truths).

"Let me begin by asking you a question," says he. "What do you know of Schleswig and Holstein?"

"Never even met 'em," says I. Rudi laughed aloud, and de Gautet gave his sidelong smile.

Bismarck didn't show any amusement. "They are states," he said, "not persons. I shall tell you about them."

And he began to explain what historians call "the Schleswig-Holstein question". I won't bore you with it here, because even diplomats agree that it is the most infernally complex affair that ever bedevilled European politics. Nobody has ever got to the bottom of it—indeed, Palmerston once said that only three people understood it: one was Pam himself, and he had forgotten it, another was a famous statesman, and he was dead, and the third was a German professor, and he had gone mad thinking about it. So there. But the nub was that the two states, which lay directly between Denmark and the German Confederacy, were nominally ruled by the King of Denmark, although most of the inhabitants were Germans. Both Germany and Denmark claimed Schleswig and Holstein, and the people living there were forever arguing about who they should belong to.

That, then, was the famous question[25]—and of course, Bismarck knew the answer.

"It is beyond dispute," says he, "that these two states are German by right. It has become of the first import that they should be German in fact."

I couldn't see what the devil this had to do with me, and said so.

"Be silent, and listen," he snarled. "You will see very

soon. Now, answer me: in the intervals between your drinking and whoring and hunting, do you take any interest in politics?"

"Well, I'm a Tory, I suppose. Haven't ever bothered to vote, mind you. Why?"

"Gerrechter Herr Gott," says he. "This, gentlemen"—he glanced at the others—"is a specimen of the ruling caste of the most powerful country on earth—for the present. Incredible, is it not?" His eyes scornful, he turned back to me. "You know, in effect, nothing of affairs of state—your own, or any others. Very good. But even you, Mr Flashman, must be aware that of late, all over Europe, there have been storm clouds gathering. There is a dangerous sentiment of liberalism, fostered by so-called progressive groups of intellectuals, which is infecting the populaces of states. Discontent and disaffection have been created; everywhere there are movements for reform"—he spat the word out—"reform, that slogan of the shiftless by which they mean destruction of stability in the hope that they will find some pickings among the ruins. Reform! Yes, your own country has given in to it, as probably even you have heard—"

"Should think I have. My guv'nor lost his seat in the House."

"—and with what result? Concession has bred anarchy, as it always does. Are your masses satisfied? Of course not: they never are."

"Not that he ever spent much time there, of course . . ."

"But as yet England has not reaped the full consequence of her statesmen's stupidity. It will come in time, just as it is coming all over Europe. We have been wasted and enfeebled by peace these thirty years past, until there is hardly a man in Europe—I except Metternich—with the vision to see beyond the borders of his own state, to look past the petty trivialities of his own domestic politics, at the dark picture of the continent. They blind themselves to what is happening all about them; they consider only how to safeguard their own miserable little countries, with no thought for the whole. They cannot see, it seems, that unless those who lead and rule Europe stand together for the preservation of order and government, they will be swept away piecemeal on a rising tide of revolution."

He had worked himself into a mild passion by this time; his eyes were bright and he was crouched forward in his chair, hurling his words down the table at me.

"Well," says I, "I grant you things are a bit slack, here and there, and my wife has remarked that good servants are getting damned hard to find. But if you think England's in for revolution, you're well off the mark. We leave that sort of thing to Frogs and niggers."

"I am not interested in your imbecile observations. I tell you what *is*, in Europe, and what its consequences must be unless measures are taken to prevent it. Here, in Germany, we have the cancer in a malignant form: the liberal movements are afoot throughout the confederacy. As a member of the Prussian Diet I see them at work openly in Berlin; as a rural landowner I am aware of them even in the countryside. I see them sapping the strength of the German people. If such insidious doctrines have their way, in a loose, undisciplined confederacy such as ours, the result will be chaotic. Germany, and especially German unity, for which far-sighted men have laboured for generations, will receive a mortal blow, from which it might take a century to recover. That she cannot afford. The world is on the move: the great nations are already jockeying for position in the race for power which is sure to move with incredible swiftness, now that science and industry are providing the impetus. If Germany is to take her place among the leaders, she must have unity, she must have strength, she must have discipline"—his great fist smacked the table with each phrase—"she must submit herself to the guidance and government of a supreme authority, who will do for her what Napoleon did for France, what Washington did for America. These were

110

not liberals, Mr Flashman; these were not progressive intellectuals. Germany must have her Napoleon, if she is to have her—"

"Waterloo?" I was sick of all his bombast. Mind you, the moment I'd said it, I wished I hadn't, for he stopped dead and stared at me in silence with those blazing blue eyes. Then he sat back in his chair, and spoke quietly.

"There will be no Waterloo. However, this is academic, and certainly wasted on a mind such as yours. I have said enough, I think, to explain to you the necessity for ensuring that the spread of liberal thought must be checked before it breeds revolution proper. For this, there must be measures, wherever possible, to buttress existing government, and to preserve order. Stability must be maintained wherever seditious influences are at work. And nowhere are they more in evidence than in Schleswig and Holstein."

"I wondered when we should get back to them," says I, and glanced at the others to see how they had taken Bismarck's tirade. Young Rudi was blowing smoke rings at the ceiling, but de Gautet was all ears, and as for Kraftstein, he was pointing like a damned retriever, as though ready to bark in admiration. It occurred to me that if he found Bismarck's claptrap absorbing, there was probably no lack of other idiots in Germany who would do so too.

"If you care to study the map of Europe above that bookcase," Bismarck continued, "you will see that at the eastern limit of Holstein, where it adjoins Mecklenburg, there is a small duchy called Strackenz. It, like Schleswig and Holstein, has ties both with Germany and Denmark; like them, also, it is riven internally by contending parties. Being a rural, backward province, it is of less apparent importance than its larger neighbours, but this is an illusion. In fact, it is the spark on the tinder; if the dissension between the contending parties in Strackenz were to erupt

111

into disorder, this would undoubtedly be used by revolutionary elements as an excuse to foment unrest in the neighbouring provinces; Denmark and Germany could become involved—believe me, great wars have begun over smaller matters than Strackenz.

"Is it plain to you that the peace must be kept in this little province? If it is, then given time, German diplomacy will ensure the incorporation of Schleswig and Holstein into the German confederacy, and the process of our national unification will have begun. But if in the immediate future anything should occur to plunge Strackenz into unrest, if the rival factions there should be given any crisis to exploit—then, my work will be ruined before it has been commenced."

I can't say I gave a tuppenny damn about his work, or the building of a united German state, and I couldn't for the life of me see what all this had to do with me. Still, I could only listen. Bismarck was leaning forward again, staring at me and tapping the table.

"Such a crisis is at hand. Here are the facts. Strackenz is ruled by a Duchess Irma, who has recently reached marriageable age. She is exceedingly popular with her subjects, being young and personable and therefore supremely fitted to rule, in the eyes of superstitious peasants. It has been arranged that she should marry a prince of the Danish royal family, a nephew, in fact, of King Christian himself, one Prince Carl Gustaf. This informs you of the importance that Denmark attaches to even such a tiny province as Strackenz. The point is that the marriage will be hailed by the Danish faction in Strackenz, who are an unusually troublesome group—possibly because they are so far away from Denmark itself. And if *they* are contented, Strackenz will continue in peace. Its German population will know how to wait," he added with confidence.

I confess I stifled a yawn, but he ignored it.

"Politically, then, the match is not only desirable, but

essential. Its stabilising influence apart, I am not without hopes of Carl Gustaf, with whom I am acquainted. He would make a popular consort and ruler in Strackenz."

He hesitated, his eyes unwinking on mine, and I stirred impatiently.

"Well, then," says I, "good luck to the happy couple, and God bless 'em all and Tiny Tim. Will you come to the point as far as I'm concerned—if I am at all, which I'm beginning to doubt."

"Oh, you are," says he, nodding grimly. "I said there was a crisis in Strackenz. It is this: as things stand, the wedding, which is to be solemnised in six weeks' time, cannot take place."

"Can't it, now? Why not?"

"Prince Carl Gustaf, who is in many ways an admirable young man, has nevertheless his share of young men's folly." Bismarck paused. "He has contracted a social disease, which makes it impossible that he marry, at least for the time being."

"A what?"

"A social disease."

"You mean he's got a dose of clap?" I let loose a guffaw. "Well, that's damned inconsiderate of him. Bad luck on Duchess what's-her-name, too. Still, boys will be boys, eh? But that makes things awkward, I agree. What are you going to do about it?"

Bismarck didn't reply for a moment. There was a dead silence in the room, an expectant silence that made me uneasy.

"Well," says I at length. "What next?"

Bismarck stood up abruptly, went over to a desk against the wall, and took a small object from it. He weighed it in his hand as he paced slowly back to the table.

"If the wedding does not take place, Strackenz will explode. The Danish party will see to it; liberal agitators will whip up anti-German feeling with tales of a plot. But it is obviously impossible for Prince Carl to marry for

113

several months, when his . . . condition has responded to treatment."

He seemed to expect a comment, so I suggested the wedding be postponed.

"On what pretext? If the real reason were known, the marriage could never take place at all, obviously. And the Strackenz pot would boil over. At the moment, no one knows of Carl Gustaf's malady except his own physician, and two highly-placed Danish ministers. The rest of Denmark, like Germany and Strackenz, suspects nothing amiss, and expects the wedding to go forward."

"You say only three people know that this Prince has Cupid's measles? Then how do you . . ."

"I have my own sources. The three I mentioned, the Prince, and ourselves are the only people who know, rest assured." He juggled the object in his hand. "The wedding must take place."

"Well, he'll just have to marry her, clap and all, won't he? What else . . ."

"Out of the question," says de Gautet, speaking for the first time. "Humanitarian reasons apart, it would surely be discovered afterwards, and the ensuing scandal would have as disastrous an effect as a postponement of the marriage."

"Well, then, talk sense," says I. "If the Prince *can't* marry her in six weeks, the wedding's off, ain't it? You'll have to think of something else."

"We have," says Bismarck. "And the wedding will take place."

"You're talking bloody nonsense," says I. "Anyway, what the hell do I care? What has all this to do with me?"

Bismarck tossed down on the table the thing he had been holding. It slithered along the length of the wood and stopped in front of me. I saw it was a gold case, oval and about four inches long.

"Open it," says Bismarck.

I touched the catch, and the thing sprang open. In

114

it was a miniature, in very fine colour, showing a man in uniform, youngish, but with a completely bald head which gave him an unnatural look. He wasn't bad-looking, though, and it seemed to me I knew him . . . and then the case dropped from my fingers, and the room seemed to swim about me. For I did know him; saving the bald head, the face in the miniature was my own. It was all too familiar from my own mirror: the likeness was uncanny, exact.

"Prince Carl Gustaf of Denmark," says Bismarck, and his voice seemed to be coming through a fog.

I'm not often at a loss for words, but at that moment I sat stricken dumb. The enormity of the idea—for it was as plain as a pikestaff in an instant—was beyond reasonable comment. I just sat and gaped from them to the miniature and back, and Rudi's jovial laugh rang out.

"Magnificent!" cries he. "I'd not have missed that moment for a dukedom! I wish you could have seen your face—your *own* face, I mean."

"You will remember," says Bismarck, "that when we first met in London I was puzzled to remember where I had seen you before. I had not, of course—but I *had* seen the young Prince Carl when he visited Berlin. I realised then that you were *doppelgängers*, identical bodies, and regarded it as an interesting fact; no more. Three months ago, when I first learned of the Prince's indisposition, and that his response to treatment was too slow to make it possible that he be married on the required date, I remembered the fact again. I perceived that here lay a way out. At first, as you may appreciate, I rejected the notion as absurd. Then I applied myself to study it minutely, and saw that it was possible. Incredible, perhaps, but still possible. I planned it step by step, and saw that with proper care and preparation it was more than that—it was virtually certain of success. My decision taken, I set in motion the events that have brought you here to Schönhausen."

At last I found my tongue. "You're mad!" I shouted.

"You're a raving lunatic! You'd substitute *me* . . . for *him* . . . to . . . to . . . pose . . . to attempt the maddest, most ridiculous . . ."

"Silence!" he shouted, and came round the table, his face working with passion. "Do you suppose I have entered on this matter lightly? That I have not examined it, time and time again, before I determined on it? Do you imagine I designed the plan that has brought you here, and spent the time and money I have used, without being certain that I could complete the whole business?" He bent down, his face close to mine, and spoke rapidly and quietly. "Consider, if you have the intelligence, the minute thoroughness of the stratagem that has brought you this far. Planned, my English numbskull, with a care and precision that your slow wits cannot conceive."

"Genius," says Kraftstein, jerking his head like a doll.

"Only one thing was a matter of chance—your presence in England. It was the prerequisite, and by good fortune it was there. The rest—organisation." Bismarck took a breath and straightened up. "And as we have begun, so we will proceed."

Well, I saw one thing: he *was* mad; they all were. And, by God, if they thought they were dragging me into their lunacy, they had got the wrong man.

"I won't touch it," says I, "and that's flat. D'you think I'm as big a fool as you are? Good God, man, the thing's impossible; I wouldn't last five minutes as . . . a substitute for this poxed-up Danish fellow. And what then, eh?"

Bismarck considered me a moment. Then: "Fill his glass, Kraftstein." He walked back to his seat, and stretched his legs.

"It is, perhaps, unreasonable to expect you to accept the scheme without being convinced of its soundness. Tell me, why do you suppose it might fail?"

There were about seven hundred answers to that, and I burst out with the first one that came to mind.

"I couldn't get away with it! How could I pretend to be a Danish prince?"

"Take my word for it that you could. The likeness, believe me, is astounding. No one would suspect the imposture for a moment."

"But I don't speak Danish, dammit!"

"But you have a gift for languages, remember? In the few weeks available, you can be given a smattering. No more than that will be necessary, for His Highness speaks German indifferently well, as you will before you take his place. You have a tolerable fluency as it is."

"But . . . but . . . well, how the devil do you propose that I *should* take his place? Go to Denmark, I suppose, and present suitable references! Balderdash!"

"You need not go to Denmark. I have been in constant communication with Prince Carl Gustaf. Naturally, he does not know of our plan, but he does have great faith in me. One of the ministers I mentioned is in my employ. Through him, all has been arranged. The Prince will set out from Denmark when the time comes with his retinue; he has been led to believe that I have found a way out of his difficulties. He is rather a simple fellow, although amiable, and supposes that I can arrange matters. In that belief he will come to Holstein, en route to Strackenz, and in Holstein the substitution will take place. The mechanics you may leave to me."

It was like listening to some grotesque fairy-tale. The cool, precise way in which he told it was staggering.

"But . . . but this retinue—his people, I mean . . ."

"The minister who is my agent will accompany the Prince. His name is Detchard. With him at your side, you need have no fears. *And no one will suspect you*: why should they?"

"Because I'll give myself away in a hundred things, man! My voice, my actions—God knows what!"

"That is not so," said Bismarck. "I tell you, I know the Prince, his voice, his mannerisms—all of it. And I tell you that if you shave your head and upper lip, your own mothers would not know you apart."

"It's true," says Rudi, from the fireplace. "You aren't just alike: you're the same man. If you learn a few of his habits—gestures, that sort of thing—it can't fail."

"But I'm not an actor! How can I—"

"You wandered in Afghanistan disguised as a native, did you not?" says Bismarck. "I know as much about you as you do yourself, you see. If you can do that, you can easily do this." He leaned forward again. "All this has been thought of. If you were not a man of action, of proved resource and courage, of *geist und geschicklichkeit*, wit and aptitude, I would not have entertained this scheme for a moment. It is because you *have* all these things, and have proved them, that you are here now."

Well, that was all *he* knew. God help him, he believed the newspapers, and my huge, overblown reputation—he thought I was the daredevil Flash Harry of popular report, the Hero of Jallalabad, and all that tommy-rot. And there was no hope that I could persuade him otherwise.

"But my God!" says I, appalled. "What you are proposing is that I should go to Strackenz and *marry* this damned woman! I mean—I'm married already!"

"You are a Protestant. This will be a Roman ceremony. It will be in no way binding on you, morally or in fact."

"Who cares about that? What I mean is—I'd have to *live* with her, as King of Strackenz, or whatever it is. How could I? What about the real Prince Carl?"

"He will be kept close under lock and key, in a convenient place in Mecklenburg. He will there recover from his illness. And in due course I will explain matters to him—the full truth. I will point out to him that he has no choice but to continue with the remainder of my plan."

"And what's that, in God's name?"

"When he has recovered—in perhaps a month or two after your marriage—you will go hunting from a certain lodge. You will become separated from your companions.

They will find you, eventually, or rather they will find the real Prince. He will have fallen from his horse, and taken a slight graze on the head. It will necessitate some days' rest and recovery. Thereafter he will return to Strackenz City and his bride. If she notices any difference in him, it will be attributed to the effect of his head wound. But it will hardly cause her to suspect that he is not the man she married. I expect that they will live and rule long and happily together."

"And what the hell happens to me?"

"You, my dear sir, will by then be far over the frontiers of Germany—with ten thousand pounds sterling in your pocket." Bismarck permitted himself a smile. "We do not ask you to work for nothing, you see. Your silence will be assured—for if you decided to tell your incredible tale, who would believe it? But why should you? You will have come out of the affair most profitably."

Aye, profitably for you, thinks I, with a bullet in the back of my head or a knife between my ribs. It was as clear as day that at the end of the affair I'd be a heap safer dead than alive, from their point of view. I looked from Bismarck to the cheerfully smiling Rudi, who had perched himself on the table edge; to Kraftstein, frowning at me from his massive height; to de Gautet, with his snake's eyes—I even glanced round at Bersonin, glowering in silence by the door. By gum, I've seen some pretty sets of villains in my time, but I believe that if I were ever asked to recruit a band of cut-throats for some nefarious enterprise, Bismarck's beauties would head my list.

"I see what is in your mind," says Bismarck. He rose, taking out his cigar case, and presented me with a weed, which he lit for me from a candle. "You do not trust me. You believe that afterwards I should have you destroyed, nicht wahr? That I would break my promise."

"Oh, well," says I, "the thought hadn't occurred, but now that you mention it . . ."

"My dear Mr Flashman," says he, "credit me with

some intelligence. I have only to put myself in your shoes—as I'm sure you have just been putting yourself in mine. I should be highly suspicious, if I were you. I should require to be convinced that all was—above board, is it not?"

I said nothing, and he took a turn round the table.

"Ask yourself," says he, "what I have to gain by playing you false. Security? Hardly so, since you will be in no case, living, to do harm to us. As I've said, no one would believe your story, which indeed would incriminate you if you were foolish enough to tell it. What else? Killing you would present . . . problems. You are not a child, and disposing of you might well cause some unforeseen complication in my plans."

"We're honest with you, you see," says Rudi, and Kraftstein nodded vigorously. De Gautet tried to smile reassuringly, like a contrite wolf.

"And ten thousand pounds, you may believe me, is neither here nor there," went on Bismarck. "It is a cheap price to pay for laying the foundation of the new Germany—and that is what is at stake here. You may think we are daydreaming, that we are foolish visionaries—you may even think us villains. I do not care. It does not matter. It is a great thing that we are going to do, and you are only a tiny pawn in it—but, like all tiny pawns, vital. I need you, and I am willing to pay for what I need." He drew himself up, virile, commanding, and full of mastery. "You seek guarantees of my good faith. I have tried to show you that it is in my interest, and Germany's, to keep faith. To this I add my word as a *junker*, a soldier, and a gentleman: I swear on my honour that what I have promised I shall fulfil, and that when you have concluded your part in this scheme you shall have safe-conduct out of Germany, with your reward, and that no harm shall come to you."

He swung about on his heel and went back to his chair; the others sat dead still. And then, after just the right interval had elapsed, he added:

"If you wish, I can swear it on the Bible. For my own part, I believe that a man who will tell a lie will swear one also. I do neither. But I am at your disposal."

It was very prettily said. For a moment he almost had me believing him. But I'd moved in just as seedy company as friend Bismarck, and was up to all the dodges.

"I don't care about Bible oaths," says I. "And, anyway, I'm not sure that I like your little plot. I'm no pauper, you know—" which was a damned lie, but there—"and I'm not sweatin' to earn your ten thousand. It's dishonest, it's deceitful, and it's downright dangerous. If there was a slip, it would cost me my head—"

"And ours, remember," says de Gautet. "You would be in a position to betray us, if you were taken."

"Thanks very much," says I. "That would be a great consolation. But, d'you know, I don't think I care for the whole thing. I'm all for a quiet life, and—"

"Even in a Bavarian prison," says young Rudi sweetly, "serving ten years as a ravisher?"

"That cock won't fight," says I. "Even suppose you took me back to Munich now, how would you explain my absence between the supposed crime and my arrest? It might not be so easy."

That made them think, and then Bismarck chimed in.

"This is to waste time. Whatever pressures were used on you initially, the point is that you are here, now, and I need hardly tell you what will happen if you refuse my offer. We are very lonely here. None saw you come; none would ever see you go. Am I plain? You have no choice, in fact, but to do as I require, and collect the fee which, I promise, will be paid."

So there we were; the good old naked threat. They could slit my throat as neat as ninepence if they chose, and none the wiser. I was in a most hellish fix, and my innards were churning horribly. But there was no way out—and they *might* be honest at the end of the day. By God, I could use ten thou. But I couldn't believe they would come up to

121

scratch (I wouldn't have, in Bismarck's place, once I'd got what I wanted). I didn't even dare think of the risks of their hare-brained impersonation scheme, but on the other hand I couldn't contemplate the alternative if I refused. On the one side, a lunatic adventure fraught with frightful danger, and possibly a handsome reward; on the other side—death, no doubt at the bare hands of Herr Kraftstein.

"Tell you what, Bismarck," says I. "Make it fifteen thousand."

He stared at me coldly. "That is too much. The reward is ten thousand, and cannot be increased."

I tried to look glum, but this had cheered me up. If he was intending to play me false in the end, he wouldn't have hesitated to raise the stakes; the fact that he didn't suggested he might be going to level after all.

"You're no pauper, you know," chuckled Rudi, damn him.

I sat like a man undecided, and then I cried:

"I'll do it, then."

"Good man!" cries Rudi, and clapped me on the back. "I swear you're one after my own heart!"

De Gautet shook my hand, and announced that they were damned lucky to have such a resolute, resourceful, cool hand in the business with them; Kraftstein brought me another glass of brandy and pledged me; even Bersonin deserted his post at the door and joined in the toast. Bismarck, however, said no more than "Very good. We will begin our further preparations tomorrow," and then took himself off, leaving me with the four jacks in the pack. They were all affability now; we were comrades in fortune, and jolly good fellows, and they did their best to get me gloriously fuddled. I didn't resist; I was shaking with the strain and in need of all the fortifying liquor I could get. But through all their noisy bonhomie and back-slapping one thought kept pounding in my brain; oh, Jesus, in the soup again; how in God's name shall I get out this time?

You can guess how much sleep I had that first night at Schönhausen. Well liquored as I was when Bersonin and Kraftstein helped me to bed and pulled my boots off, my mind was all too clear; I lay there, fully clothed, listening to the wind whining round the turrets, and watching the candle shadows flickering on the high ceiling, and my heart was pumping as though I had run a race. The room was dank as a tomb, but the sweat fairly ran off me. How the devil had it all happened? And what the devil was I to do? I actually wept as I damned the folly that had ever made me come to Germany. I could have been safe at home, pleasuring myself groggy with Elspeth and sponging off her skinflint father, facing nothing worse than the prospect of bear-leading her family in Society, and here I was imprisoned in a lonely castle with five dangerous lunatics bent on dragooning me into a hare-brained adventure that was certain to put my head in a noose. And if I resisted, or tried to escape, they would wipe me out of existence as readily as they would swat a fly.

However, as usual, once I had cursed and blubbered myself empty, my mind started searching for some ray of comfort—anything to cling to, for if you are coward enough your vainest hopes can be magnified beyond all reason. Six weeks, Bismarck had said, before this impossible wedding—say five weeks or a month at least before my substitution for Carl Gustaf had to take place. Surely much could happen in that time. Clever and wary as they were, Bismarck's gang couldn't watch me all the time—in four weeks there must be a moment when such a practised absconder as myself could cut and run for it. A horse, that was all I needed, and a look at the sun or the stars, and I was confident that my terror could outstrip Bismarck's vengeance. God knew how far away the frontier was, but I was willing to wager my neck that I could reach it faster than any rider living. My neck, of course, was exactly what I would be wagering.

With these jolly musings I passed the night, imagining a

score of madcap means of escape—and as many nightmares in which Bismarck caught me in the act. It was all a waste of time, of course; within me I knew that anyone who could plot as subtly as he had done wasn't going to give me the ghost of a hope of escaping. And I had a shrewd suspicion that if a chance did arise, I'd be too funky to take it. These fellows would stop at nothing.

They proved it, too, on my first morning at Schönhausen.

The great oaf Kraftstein summoned me at dawn, and I was pulling on my boots when Rudi strode in, very fresh and whistling cheerfully, rot him.

"And did your highness sleep well?" says he. "I trust your highness is sufficiently rested after your journey."

I told him sourly that I wasn't in a mood for his comedy.

"Oh, no comedy at all," says he. "High drama, and unless you want it to develop into tragedy you'll act as you've never acted before. From this moment you are His Highness Prince Carl Gustaf, blood royal and Lord's anointed. Do you follow me? You speak German, and nothing else—your Danish we'll take care of presently—and you will comport yourself as a member of the Danish ruling house."

"Talk sense," I growled. "I don't know how."

"No, but we're going to teach you—your highness," says he, and for once his eyes had no laughter in them. "So. The first thing is to make you look the part. All right, Kraftstein."

And then and there, despite my protests, Kraftstein sat me in a chair and set to work, first cropping my hair and whiskers, and then soaping and shaving my skull. It was a long and unpleasant process, and when it was done and I looked in the glass I could have burst into tears. The ghastly creature with his great, gleaming dome of a skull was a horrid parody of me—my face, surmounted by a naked convict head.

124

"Damn you!" I burst out. "Damn you! You've ruined me!"

I expected them to mock me, of course, but neither twitched so much as a muscle.

"Your highness will be under the necessity of shaving your head daily," murmured Rudi. "Kraftstein will instruct you. Now, may I suggest that your highness wears uniform today?"

They had that, too; rather a trim rig, I had to admit, in bottle green, which fitted me perfectly and would have given me a fine dashing air if it hadn't been for that bald monstrosity above the collar.

"Admirable," says Rudi, standing back from me. "May I compliment your highness on your appearance?"

"Drop that, blast you!" I snarled at him. "If I have to play your damned game, you'll spare me your infernal nonsense until it starts, at least. I'm your prisoner, ain't I? Isn't that enough for you?"

He waited a moment, and then says, in exactly the same tone:

"May I compliment your highness on your appearance?"

I stood glaring at him, on the point of swinging my fist into his impassive face, but he just stared me down, and I found myself saying:

"All right. If you must—all right."

"Very good, your highness," says he gravely. "May I respectfully suggest that we go down to breakfast. I find that Schönhausen gives one a rare appetite—the country air, of course. Will you lead on, Kraftstein?"

I wasn't hungry, but Rudi attacked his food in good spirits, and chattered away throughout the meal. He treated me with a nice blend of familiarity and respect, and you would never have guessed if you had seen us that it was all a sham. He was a splendid actor, and although it would have made me feel a complete fool if I hadn't been too miserable to mind, I began to realise even then that there was method

125

in what he was doing. Kraftstein just put his head down and gorged, but on the one occasion he addressed me, he too called me "highness".

Bismarck came in just as we were finishing, and he for one wasn't playing charades. He stopped dead on the threshold, though, at sight of me, and then came into the room slowly, studying my face, walking round me, and examining me carefully for a minute or more. Finally he says:

"The likeness is astounding. In effect, he is Carl Gustaf."

"So your friends have been trying to convince me," I muttered.

"Excellent. It is not quite perfect, though. Two small details remain."

"What's that?" says Rudi.

"The scars. One either side, the left immediately above the ear, the one on the right an inch lower and running slightly downward—so." And he drew his finger across my shaven skin; the touch sent mice scampering down my spine.

"By heaven, you're right," says Rudi. "I'd forgotten. How do we give him those?"

My innards turned to water as Bismarck surveyed me with his icy smile.

"Surgery? It is possible. I've no doubt Kraftstein here could employ his razor most artistically . . ."

"You're not cutting my bloody head, you bastard!" I shouted, and tried to struggle out of my chair, but Kraftstein seized me with his enormous hands and thrust me back. I yelled and struggled, and he clamped his paw across my jaws and squeezed until the pain made me subside, terrified.

"But there is a better way," says Bismarck. "They can be administered in the proper form—with the *schlager*. De Gautet can do it without difficulty." He added, with a nasty look at me: "And it will satisfy a small debt that I owe to our friend here."

126

"Aye," says Rudi doubtfully, "but can he do it exactly—they must be in precisely the right places, mustn't they? No use giving him a wound where Carl Gustaf doesn't have one."

"I have every confidence in de Gautet," says Bismarck. "With a sabre he can split a fly on the wing."

I was listening to them appalled; these two monsters calmly discussing the best means of giving me a slashed head. If there is one thing I can't endure, it is pain, and the thought of cold steel slicing into my skull nearly made me swoon. As soon as Kraftstein took his hand away I was yammering at them; Bismarck listened scornfully for a few seconds, and then says:

"Silence him, Kraftstein."

The giant seized the nape of my neck, and a fearful pain shot down my back and across my shoulders. He must have fixed on some nerve, and I screamed and writhed in his grasp.

"He can go on doing that until you die," says Bismarck. "Now get up, and stop behaving like an old woman. It won't kill you to have a couple of cuts from a *schlager*. Every German youth is proud to take them; a little drink from the 'soup-plate of honour' will do you good."

"For God's sake!" I burst out. "Look, I've agreed to do what you want, but this is abominable! I won't—"

"You will," says Bismarck. "Prince Carl Gustaf has two duelling scars, received while he was a student at Heidelberg. There is no question of your impersonating him without them. I am sure," he went on, smiling unpleasantly, "that de Gautet will administer them as painlessly as possible. And if they cause you some trifling smart, you may console yourself that they have been paid for in advance, by your amiable friend Mr Gully. You recall the occasion?"

I recalled it all right, and it was no consolation at all. So now the swine was going to get his own back, and if I resisted I'd have Kraftstein pulling pieces out of me with his bare hands for my pains. There was nothing for it but to submit, and so I allowed myself to be led down to a big bare room off the courtyard where there were fencing masks and foils hung on the walls, and chalk lines on the floor, like a fencing school.

"Our gymnasium," says Bismarck. "You will spend some time here during your preparation—you are heavier than Carl Gustaf by a pound or two, I should judge. Perhaps we can relieve you of some of it this morning."

Coming from a man with sausages of fat beginning to bulge over his collar, this was pretty cool, but I was too busy gulping down my fear to mind. Presently de Gautet arrived, looking even more snake-like than he had the previous night, and when Bismarck explained what was to do, you could see the rascal's mouth start to water.

"You must be exact to the inch," says Bismarck. "Look here." He stood in front of me, drawing from his pocket the little miniature he had shown me last night, glancing at it and then at me and frowning. "You see how they run—so and so. Now, the crayon." And to my horror he took a fat black pencil which Kraftstein held out, and with great care began to mark on the skin of my head the places where the cuts were to go.

It was the final obscene touch that brought the bile up into my mouth, so that I almost spewed at him. He stood there, his face close to mine, hissing gently through his teeth and sketching away on my crawling flesh as though it had been a blackboard. I shuddered away, and he growled at me to be still. I was paralysed—I don't think that of all the beastly things that man ever did, or all the terror he caused me, that there was anything as loathsome as that casual marking of my skin for de Gautet to cut at. There is only one word for it—it was German. And if you don't understand what I mean, thank God for it.

At last he was done, and Kraftstein could arm us for the *schlager* play. It seemed horrible to me at the time, but looking back from the safety of old age I can see that it is more childish than anything else. For all their pride in taking scars to impress everyone with how manly they are, the Germans are damned careful not to cause themselves any serious damage. Kraftstein fitted big metal caps onto the crowns of our heads; they were equipped with spectacles of iron in front to protect the eyes and nose, and there were heavy padded stocks to go round our necks. Then there was a quilted body armour to buckle round our middles, with flaps to cover the thighs, and a padded bandage to wrap round the right arm from wrist to shoulder. By the time we were fully equipped I felt like Pantaloon with dropsy; it was so ridiculous that I almost forgot to be afraid.

Even when the *schlager* was put into my hand it looked such a ludicrous weapon that I couldn't take it seriously. It was more than a yard long, with a triangular blade, and had a huge metal bowl at the hilt to protect the hand: it must have been about a foot across.[26]

"The soup-plate of honour," says Bismarck. "You have used a sabre, I suppose?"

"Ask your man about that when we've finished," says I, blustering with a confidence I didn't feel: de Gautet was swishing his *schlager* in a frighteningly professional way.

"Very good," says Bismarck. "You will observe that your opponent's head is covered, as is yours, at all points except for the cheeks and lower temples. These are your targets—and his. I may tell you that, with de Gautet, you are as likely to hit those targets as I was to strike Mr Gully. You may cut, but not thrust. Do you understand? I shall call you to begin and to desist."

He stepped back, and I found myself facing de Gautet across the chalked floor; Rudi and Kraftstein had taken their places along the walls, but Bismarck stayed within a couple of yards of us, armed with a *schlager* to strike up our blades if need be.

De Gautet advanced, saluting with a flourish; in his padding he looked like some kind of sausage-doll, but his eyes were bright and nasty through the spectacles. I didn't salute, but came on guard sabre-fashion, right hand up above my head and blade slanting down before my face.

"Salute!" snaps Bismarck.

"Pish to you!" says I, guessing that it would offend his fine Teutonic spirit to ignore the formalities. I was getting cocky, you see, because all this paraphernalia had convinced me that the business wasn't really serious at all. I'm not a sabre expert—a strong swordsman, rather than a good one, was how the master-at-arms in the 11th Hussars had described me—and if I have to use one I'd rather it wasn't in single combat, but in a mêlée, where you can hang about on the outskirts, roaring your heart out and waiting for an opponent with his back turned. However, it seemed to me now that I ought to be able to guard the unprotected areas that de Gautet would be cutting at.

He came on guard, the blades grated between us, and then he twitched his wrist, quick as light, right and left, aiming deft little cuts at the sides of my head. But Flashy's nobody's fool; I turned my wrist with his, and caught the cuts on my own blade. He cut again, and the blade rang on my cap, but I broke ground and let go a regular round-house slash at him, like a dragoon full of drink. With the *schlager*, I learned later, you are supposed to employ only wrist cuts, but I was just an ignorant foreigner. My sweep, if it had landed, would have loosed Mr de Gautet's guts all over the floor, but he was quick and turned it with the forte of his blade.

He came in again, on guard, his narrow eyes on mine, and the blades rasped together. He feinted and cut hard, but I was there again, and as we strained against each other I sneered at him over the crossed blades and exerted all my strength to bear down his guard. I felt his blade giving before mine, and then it whirled like lightning and it was as though a red-hot iron had been laid against my right temple. The pain and shock of it sent me staggering

130

back, I dropped my *schlager* and grabbed at my face, and as Bismarck jumped between us I saw the most unpleasant sight I know, which is my own blood; it coursed down my cheek and on to my hand, and I howled and dabbed at the wound to try to staunch it.

"Halt!" cries Bismarck, and strode over to inspect my wound—not because he gave a tuppenny damn about me, but to see if it was in the right place. He seized my head and peered. "To an inch!" he exclaimed, and tipped his hand triumphantly to de Gautet, who smirked and bowed.

"Fahren sie fort!" cries Bismarck, stepping back, and signing to me to pick up my *schlager*. Shaking with pain and rage, and with the blood feeling as though it were streaming out of me, I told him what he could do with it; I wasn't going to stand up to be cut to bits for his amusement.

He went red with fury. "Pick it up," he rasped, "or I'll have Kraftstein hold you down and we'll set the other scar on you with a rusty saw!"

"It's not fair!" I shouted. "I think my skull's fractured!"

He damned me for a coward, snatched up the *schlager*, and thrust it into my hand. And in case worse should happen, I squared up to de Gautet again, resolving to take the other cut as quickly as possible, and then to settle the account in my own way, if I could.

He shuffled in, full of bounce, cutting smartly right and left. I parried them, tried a quick cut of my own, and then flicked up my point to leave my left side unguarded. Instinctively he slashed at the gap, and I took it with my eyes shut and teeth gritted against the pain. My God, but it hurt, and I couldn't repress a shriek; I reeled, but kept a tight grip on my *schlager*, and as de Gautet stepped back, satisfied with his butchery, and glanced towards Bismarck, I forced myself into a sudden lunge that sent my point through his lousy body.

The next thing I knew I had been hurled to the floor, and as I lay there, blinded with my own blood, all hell broke loose. Someone fetched me a tremendous kick in the ribs, I heard Rudi shouting and de Gautet groaning—delightful sound—and then I must have fainted, for when I opened my eyes I was sprawled on one of the benches, with Kraftstein sponging the blood from my face.

My first thought was: they'll settle my hash now, for certain, and then I realised that Bismarck and de Gautet had vanished, and only young Rudi was left, grinning down at me.

"I couldn't have done better myself," says he. "Not much, anyhow. Our friend de Gautet won't be quite so cock-a-hoop another time. Not that you've damaged him much—you barely nicked his side—but he'll ache for a day or two. So will you, of course. Let's have a look at your honourable scars."

My head was aching abominably, but when he and Kraftstein had examined it, they pronounced it satisfactory—from their point of view. De Gautet had laid his cuts exactly, and provided the wounds were left open they would quickly heal into excellent scars, Kraftstein assured me.

"Give you a most distinguished appearance," says Rudi. "All the little Prussian girls will be fluttering for you."

I was too sick and shocked even to curse at him. The pain seemed to be searing into my brain, and I was half-swooning as Kraftstein bandaged my skull and the pair of them supported me upstairs and laid me down on my bed. The last thing I heard before I slipped into unconsciousness was Rudi saying that it would be best if my highness rested for a while, and I remember thinking it odd that he had slipped out of his play-actor's role for a while and then back into it.

That was my only experience of *schlager*-play, and it was one too many. But it taught me something, and that was a fearful respect for Otto Bismarck and his ruffians. If they were capable of that kind of cold-blooded mutilation then there was nothing they wouldn't do; from that moment I put all thought of trying to escape from Schönhausen out of my mind. I hadn't the game for it.

As to the scars, they healed quickly under Kraftstein's care. I'll carry them to my grave, one close to my right ear, the other slightly higher, but just visible now that my hair is thinner. Neither is disfiguring, fortunately; indeed, as Rudi observed, there is something quite dashing-romantic about them. They've been worth a couple of campaigns, I often think, in giving people the wrong impression of my character.

They hurt most damnably for a couple of days, though, during which I kept to my room. That was all the convalescence they would allow me, for they were in a great sweat to begin what Rudi was pleased to call my "princely education".

This consisted of some of the hardest brain work I've ever had in my life. For a solid month, every waking hour, I lived, talked, walked, ate and drank Prince Carl Gustaf until I could have screamed at the thought of him—and sometimes did. At its worst it amounted to gruelling mental torture, but in recalling it now I have to admit that it was brilliantly done. I wouldn't have believed it possible, but the three of them—Rudi, Kraftstein, and Bersonin—came as close as one humanly could to turning me into another person.

They did it, subtly and persistently, by pretending from the first that I *was* Carl Gustaf, and spending hour after hour reminding me about myself. I suppose to approach the thing in any other way would have been useless, for it would have been constant admission of the imposture, and what an idiot, hare-brained scheme it was. They took me through that Danish bastard's life a hundred times, from the cradle upwards, until I swear I must have known more about him than he did himself. His childhood ailments, his relatives, his ancestors, his tutors, his homes, his playmates, his education, his likes, his dislikes, his habits—there wasn't a call of nature that he had

133

answered in twenty years that I wasn't letter-perfect in by the time they had done. Hour after hour, day after day, they had me sitting at that long table while they poured fact after fact into me—what food he liked, what pets he had had, what he read, what colour his sister's eyes were, what nursery name his governess had called him (Tutti, of all things), how long he had lived at Heidelberg, what his musical tastes were ("Fra Diavolo", by one Auber, had apparently impressed him, and he was forever whistling an air from it; it says something for their teaching that I've whistled it off and on for fifty years now). Where they had got all their information, God only knows, but they had two huge folders of papers and drawings which seemed to contain everything that he had ever done and all that was known about him. I couldn't tell you my own grandmother's Christian name, but God help me I know that Carl Gustaf's great-uncle's mastiff was called Ragnar, and he lived to be twenty-three.

"And what was your highness's favourite game when you were little?" Rudi would ask.

"Playing at sailors," I would reply.

"What was the English ship you boasted to your mother you had captured at Copenhagen?"

"The *Agamemnon*."

"How did you come to capture it?"

"How the blazes do I know? I was only three, wasn't I? I can't remember."

"You have been told. It was stuck in a mudbank. In your infant re-enactment you covered yourself in mud in a garden pond, don't you remember?"

That was the kind of thing I had to know, and when I protested that no one was ever likely to ask me what games I had played when I was little, they wouldn't argue, but would pass patiently on—to remind me of the fever I had had when I was fourteen, or the time I broke my arm falling from an apple tree.

All our talk was conducted in German, at which I made

capital progress—indeed, Rudi's one fear was that I might be too proficient, for Carl Gustaf apparently didn't speak it too well, for all his Heidelberg education. Bersonin, who despite his taciturnity was a patient teacher, instructed me in Danish, but possibly because he himself only spoke it at second hand, I didn't take to it easily. I never learned to think in it, which is unusual for me, and I found it ugly and dull, with its long vowels that make you sound as though you had wind.

But the real curse of my days was being instructed in the actual impersonation. We had the tremendous advantage, as I was to see for myself later, that Carl Gustaf and I were real *doppelgängers*, as like as two tits. Even our voices were the same, but he had mannerisms and tricks of speech that I had to learn, and the only way was for me to try attitudes and phrases over and over, in different styles, until Rudi would snap his fingers and exclaim: "Er ist es selbst! Now say it again, and yet again."

For example, it seemed that if you asked Carl Gustaf a question to which the normal answer would have been "yes" or "of course", he, instead of contenting himself with "ja", would often say "sicher", which means "positively, certainly", and he would say it with a jaunty air, and a little stab of his right fore-finger. Again, in listening to people, he would look past them, giving tiny occasional nods of his head and making almost inaudible grunts of agreement. Lots of people do this, but I don't happen to be one of them, so I had to practise until I found myself doing it almost without thinking.

And he had a quick, brisk laugh, showing his teeth—I worked at that until my throat smarted and my jaws ached. But this was easy compared with the contortions I went through in trying to mimic his trick of raising one eyebrow by itself; I came near to setting up a permanent twitch in one cheek, and eventually they decided to let it be, and hope that no one noticed that my eyebrows perversely worked together.

Fortunately, Carl Gustaf was a cheerful, easy-going chap, much as I am myself, but I had to work hard to try to correct the sulky look I get when I'm out of sorts, and my habit of glowering and sticking out my lower lip. This ray of Danish sunshine didn't glower, apparently; when he was in the dumps he showed it with an angry frown, so of course I had to knit my brows until they ached.

How well I learned my lessons you may judge when I tell you that to this day I have his trick of rubbing one hand across the back of the other (when thinking deeply), and that I entirely lost my own habit of scratching my backside (when puzzled). Royalty—I have Bersonin's solemn word for it—never claw at their arses to assist thought.

Now the result of all this, day after day, and of the unbroken pretence that my captors kept up, was remarkable and sometimes even frightening. I suppose I'm a good actor, to begin with—after all, when you've been shamming all your life, as I have, it must come pretty natural—but there were times when I forgot that I was acting at all, and began to half-believe that I was Carl Gustaf. I might be practising before the long cheval glass, with Rudi and Bersonin watching and criticising, and I would see this bald-headed young fellow in the green hussar rig flashing his smile and stabbing his forefinger, and think to myself, "Aye, that's me"—and then my mind would try to recapture the picture of the dark, damn-you-me-lad-looking fellow with the curly hair and whiskers—and I would discover that I couldn't do it. That was when I found it frightening—when I had forgotten what my old self looked like.

Mind you, my character didn't change; these flashes were only momentary. But I certainly began to believe that we would carry off the imposture, and the terror that I had originally felt about it subsided to a mere craven apprehension of what the end of it all might be—when payday came and the real Carl Gustaf had come back into his own.

However, that was in the future, and in the meantime

I was floating with the tide, as is my habit, and letting my puppet-handlers think that butter wouldn't melt in my mouth. For their part, they seemed delighted with my progress, and one day, about three weeks after I had come to Schönhausen, on an evening when Bismarck joined the rest of us at supper, I did something which convinced Rudi and Bersonin that the first round was won at least.

We were sitting down to table, myself at the head, as usual, and Bismarck plumped down in his chair before I did. Now I was so used by this time to being seated first that I simply stared at him, more in curiosity, I imagine, than anything else; and he, catching my glance, actually began to get to his feet. Rudi, who missed nothing, couldn't repress a chuckle and a delighted slap of his thigh.

"Right royal, Otto," says he to Bismarck. "He had you feeling like a bad-mannered little schoolboy there, I'll swear. Bravo, your highness, you'll do."

This was rather more familiarity with me than Rudi had allowed himself since my duel with de Gautet. It didn't matter to me, of course, but Bersonin was shocked, and muttered that Rudi was forgetting himself. It occurred to me then that I was not the only one who was beginning to believe in my own royalty. Anyway, I played up by remarking to Bersonin casually that the Freiherr was still at an age when impudence took precedence before dignity, and was this hock that we were to drink again to night?

Bismarck observed all this impassively, but I felt sure he was secretly impressed by the naturalness of my princely behaviour, and even more by his own momentary reaction to it.

I should say in passing that Bismarck's appearance that night was a rare one. For days at a time I never saw him, but from casual conversation among the others I gathered that he was frequently in Berlin—he was a member of their Parliament, apparently, when he wasn't kidnapping useful Englishmen and plotting lèse majesté. I also learned that he

had a wife in the capital, which surprised me; somehow
I had come to think of him as brooding malevolently in
his lonely castle, wishing he was Emperor of Germany. I
remembered that Lola had thought he was a cold fish where
women were concerned, but it seemed that this was only a
pose; before his marriage, apparently, he had been saddling
up with all the wenches on his estate and breeding bastards
like a buck rabbit. They called him the Schönhausen Ogre
in those days, but of late he had been devoting himself
to politics and his new wife, Bersonin said, and taking a
serious interest in his farm property. A likely tale, thinks
I; *his* only interest in politics was to get personal power,
no matter how, and to gorge himself with food, drink,
and women along the way. Nasty brute.

However, as I say, we didn't see much of him, or
of anyone else for that matter. They kept me pretty well
confined to one wing of the house, and although there
must have been servants I never saw one except the old
butler. There wasn't a woman in the place, which was a
dead bore, and when I suggested to Rudi that he might
whistle up a wench or two to pass the evenings he just
shook his head and said it was out of the question.

"Your highness must contain yourself in patience," says
he. "May I respectfully remind you that your wedding is
not far off?"

"Thanks very much," says I. "And may I respectfully
remind you that I'm feeling randified now, and in no mood
to hold myself in until my wedding to some young German cow who probably looks like a boatswain's mate."

"Your highness need have no fears on that score," says
he, and he showed me a portrait of Duchess Irma of
Strackenz which I must say cheered me up considerably.
She looked very young, and she had one of those cold, narrow disdainful faces that you find on girls who have always
had their own way, but she was a beauty, no question. Her
hair was long and blonde, and her features very fine and
regular; she made me think of a story I remembered from

138

my childhood about a snow princess who had a heart of ice. Well, I could warm this one up, always assuming our enterprise got that far.

"In the meantime," says I, "what say to some nice, hearty country girl? She could teach me some more German, you know, and I could teach her anatomy."

But he wouldn't hear of it.

So the weeks ran by, and I suppose that gradually the nightmare impossibility of my position must have begun to seem less incredible than it looks now, half a century after; whatever happens to you, however far-fetched, you get used to eventually, I've found, and when the time came to leave Schönhausen I was ready for it. I was in a fair funk, of course, but so heartily thankful to be getting out of that draughty mausoleum that even the ordeal ahead seemed endurable.

It must have been a week or so after the meeting with Bismarck that I've just described that I was summoned late one evening to his library. They were all there, Rudi, Bismarck, and the Three Wise Men, and I knew at once that something was up. Bismarck was still in his greatcoat, with the last snowflakes melting on its shoulders, and a little pool of water forming round each boot as he stood before the fire. He looked me over bleakly, hands behind his back, and then says:

"The scars are still too livid. Any fool can see they are recent."

This seemed an excellent reason to me for calling off the whole thing, but Kraftstein said in his ponderous way that he could attend to them; he had a salve which could disguise their pinkness and make them look like old wounds. This seemed to satisfy Bismarck, for he grunted and turned to Rudi.

"Otherwise he is ready? He can play the part? Your head depends on this, remember."

"His highness is ready to resume his duties," says Rudi.

Bismarck snorted. "His highness! He is an actor, hired to play a part. Better he should remember that, and the consequences of missing a cue—he'll be less liable to bungle it. Oh, yes Bersonin, I know all about your theories; I prefer realities. And the reality of this, Mr Flashman, is that tomorrow you leave for Strackenz. You know what is to do, the reward of success—and the price of failure." His cold eyes played over me. "Are you dismayed?"

"Oh, no," says I. "when it's all over I intend to go back to England and take the place of Prince Albert, don't you know."

Rudi laughed, but I saw Kraftstein shake his head—no doubt he was thinking that I didn't look enough like Prince Albert to get away with it.

"Sit down," says Bismarck. "Give him a brandy, de Gautet." He came to stand at the table head, looking down at me. "Listen to me carefully. When you leave here tomorrow you will be accompanied by Freiherr von Starnberg and de Gautet. They will take you by coach to the rendezvous we have appointed—you need to know nothing more than that it is a country mansion owned by a nobleman who is to play host to Prince Carl Gustaf for one night during his journey to Strackenz. The journey to the house will take two days, but we are allowing three, for safety.

"On the appointed day Carl Gustaf and his retinue will arrive at the mansion in the afternoon. It stands in wooded country, but is easily accessible; you will be waiting for evening, and when it comes von Starnberg and de Gautet will take you into the grounds under cover of darkness. You will be admitted by a man who is one of the only three in the world, outside this room, who is in our plot. His name is Detchard, a Danish minister entirely faithful to me. He will conduct you secretly to the Prince's apartment; in the meantime von Starnberg will be effecting the . . . removal of the real Prince. Have I made myself clear so far?"

140

By God he had, and as I listened all my old fears came galloping back with a vengeance. The thing was obvious lunacy, and this outrageous creature, standing so straight and immaculate in his greatcoat, was a dangerous maniac.

"But . . . but, look here," I began, "suppose something goes wrong—I mean, suppose somebody comes . . ."

He banged his fist on the table and glared at me. "Nothing will go wrong! No one will come! Righteous Lord God! Do you suppose I know nothing? Do you imagine I have not planned every detail? De Gautet! Tell him—what is the name of the serving-maid whose duty it will be to change the Prince's bed linen while he is at the house?"

"Heidi Gelber," says de Gautet.

"Starnberg—how do you reach the Prince's dressing-room from the door where Detchard will admit you?"

"Twelve paces along a passage, up the stairway to the right, left at the first landing, then ten paces along to a passage on the right. The Prince's dressing-room is the first door on the left."

"From door to door—fifty seconds," says Bismarck. "If you wish, I can tell you the precise nature of the furnishings in the Prince's chamber, and their positions in the room. For example, there is a statuette of a kneeling cupid on the overmantel. Now—are you convinced that my organisation is sound, and my information complete?"

"How do you know that some drunk footman won't come blundering along in the middle of everything?" I cried.

I thought he would hit me, but he restrained himself.

"It will *not* happen," he said. "Everything will fall out exactly as I have said."

There was no point in arguing, of course; I sat in despair while he went on.

"Once inside that room, you will be Prince Carl Gustaf. That is the fact of paramount importance. From that moment Flashman no longer exists—you understand? With you will be Detchard and the Prince's physician,

Orsted, who is also privy to our plans. If at any moment you are in doubt, they will guide you. And when you set out next morning on your royal progress across the border into Strackenz, you will find that among the dignitaries who will greet you will be both de Gautet and Starnberg—it has been arranged that they will join your train as gentlemen of honour. So you will not lack for friends," he added grimly. "Now drink your brandy."

I gulped it down; I needed it. At the back of my mind I suppose there had still been some futile hope that I would be able to slip out of this at the last moment, but Bismarck had squashed it flat. I was going to have to go through with it, with Rudi and de Gautet hovering alongside ready, at the first false move, to put a bullet into me, I didn't doubt. Why the hell, I asked myself for the thousandth time, had I ever come to this bloody country?

"The wedding will take place on the day after your arrival in the city of Strackenz," Bismarck went on, for all the world as though he had been telling me the time of day. "You have already received some instruction in the details of the ceremony, of course. And then—all plain sailing, as your people say."

He sat down, and poured himself a glass of brandy from the decanter. He sipped at it, while I sat mute, staring at my glass. "Well, Mr Flashman; what have you to say?"

"What the hell does it matter what I say?" I burst out. "I've no choice, damn you!"

To my amazement, he actually chuckled. He stretched his legs and twirled the stem of his glass between his fingers.

"None at all," says he, grinning. "Flashman, you should be glad. You will be making history—aye, great history. Do you realise, I wonder, the magnitude of what we are doing? We are nailing a little hinge to a door, a great door which will open to reveal the destiny of a greater Germany! And *you*—a half-pay officer of no account, a pawn even in your own country's affairs—*you* are going to make it possible! Can you imagine what it means?" The man was positively beaming now, with a kind of fierce joy in his eyes. "For we are going to *win*! We six here, we are staking ourselves, our lives, everything—and we are going to succeed! I look at you, and I know we cannot fail. God has sent you to Germany, and I send you now to Strackenz." There was a nice little comparison there, all right. "And in Strackenz you will play such a game as has never been played before in the history of the world. And you will not fail—I know it! What a destiny! To be one of the architects of the new Fatherland!" He lifted his glass. "I salute you, and drink to our enterprise!"

Believe it or not, he actually raised my spirits a little with that. Of course, it was all humbug, designed to put some backbone into me—that was all *he* knew—but the man was so supremely confident it was infectious: if he really believed we could bring it off—well, perhaps we could. The others cheered and we all drank, and Bismarck sighed and refilled his glass. I'd never seen him anything like this before; for the moment he was almost jovial, showing an entirely new side of his nature—all carefully calculated for my benefit, I imagine.

"How will we look back on this?" he mused. "When we are old, and in our country places, and the bold lads of a new day are elbowing for power in the chancelleries? I wonder." He shook his head. "I think I will wear leather breeches and allow myself to be laughed at in Stettin wool market, and sell two thalers cheaper to anyone who calls me 'baron'.[27] And you, Flashman—you will sit in your club in St James, and grow fat on port and your memories. But we will have lived, by God! We will have fought! We will have won! Is it not something to have moved great affairs, and shaped the course of time?"

No doubt I should have shared his enthusiasm, like Kraftstein, who was hanging on every word, and looking like a ruptured bullock. But all I could think to myself

143

was, God, I wish John Gully had really set to work on you. What I said aloud was:

"Herr Bismarck, I am much moved. And now, with your permission, I intend to get as drunk as possible. Afterwards, tomorrow, I shall be at your service, since I can't do anything else. But if I'm to shape the destiny of Europe, I'll need a good skinful of liquor inside me to set me off. So will you kindly oblige me with the bottle, and a cigar, and as many dirty drinking songs as you and your friends can remember? And if this seems to you a coarse and pagan spirit in which to approach our glorious adventure for the Fatherland, well—you've made your preparations; let me now make mine."

As a result of the night's excesses, which Bismarck didn't discourage, I had a raging headache and a heaving stomach on the morning of my departure from Schönhausen. So I remember very little of it, which is no loss. For that matter my recollections of the journey north to Strackenz are hazy, too; I've travelled too far in my time to be anything but bored by it, and there was nothing to see that I recall except flat snowy fields, the occasional village, and bleak woodlands of bare black trees.

Rudi was full of spirits as usual, and de Gautet was his smooth, civil self, but I knew he wouldn't forget or forgive that *schlager*-thrust in the guts. I hadn't forgotten the two cuts I owed him, either, so we were even there. He never referred to our encounter, but now and then in the coach I would catch his dark eyes on me, and then they would slide away, looking anywhere but at me. He was one who wouldn't be sorry of the excuse to draw a bead on my back if I tried to run for it.

Following Bismarck's lead, both of them had dropped the pretence of calling me "highness"—Bersonin's "theory", as Bismarck had called it, being well enough in my training period, I suppose, but now considered unnecessary. But they lost no chance of lecturing me on such subjects as the geography of Strackenz, the ceremonial forms of its court, and the details of the wedding ceremony. I suppose I took it all in, for there was nothing else to do, but it has all gone now.

We were three days on the road, and the last afternoon of the journey took us deep into forest-country, all ghostly and silent under the snow. It was very beautiful and solemn, with never a soul to be seen along the rough track winding among the trees, until about four in the afternoon we stopped in a little clearing where a small hut stood, with thin smoke wreathing up from its chimney into the steely sky.

There were two or three brisk-looking fellows in peasant clothes to rub down the horses and usher us into the cottage—not that I took them for peasants, for I heard two of them in talk with Rudi. They were gentlemen, by German standards, but tough, active customers for all that—the kind who'll cut your throat and send back the wine at dinner afterwards.

We had a meal, Rudi and I, while de Gautet paced up and down and peered out at the darkening sky and consulted his watch and fidgeted generally until Rudi told him to leave off, and made him sit down and have a glass of wine with us. I was getting fairly twitchy myself as the hours passed, and Rudi gave me a stiff brandy to steady me.

"Three hours from now," says he, "and you'll be tucked up in a silk night-gown with C.G. embroidered on it. God! I wish I was in your shoes. How many commoners have the chance to be royalty!"

"I'll show you one who's ready to resign his crown any time," says I. The shivers were beginning to run up my spine.

"Nonsense. Give you two days, and you'll be behaving as though you'd been born to the purple. Issuing royal decrees against virginity, probably. What time is it, de Gautet?"

"We should be moving." I heard the strain in his voice.

"Heigh-ho," says Rudi, stretching; he was as cool as though he was off for an evening stroll. "Come along, then."

There was a slight altercation just before setting out when de Gautet, officiously helping me into my cloak, discovered my pistols in the pockets. I'd had them concealed in a pair of boots in my baggage at Schönhausen,

146

and was determined that they were going with me. Rudi shook his head.

"Royalty don't carry side-arms, except for ceremony."

"I do," says I. "Either they go with me, or I don't go at all."

"What good d'you suppose they'll be, man?"

"None, I hope. But if the worst happens they'll perhaps buy me a little elbow-room."

De Gautet was in a sweat to be off, so in the end Rudi cursed and grinned and let me keep them. He knew I wouldn't be fool enough to make a bolt for it now.

With de Gautet leading, Rudi and I behind, and two of the others in the rear, we struck out through the trees, plodding ankle-deep through the snow. It was still as death all round, and hellish dark, but de Gautet led on unerringly for perhaps quarter of an hour, when we came to a high stone wall running across our front. There was a wicket, and then we were skirting past a thicket of high bushes which, by their regular spacing, must be in the garden of some great estate. Even in the darkness I could make out the level sweep of lawn under the snow, and then ahead of us were the blazing lights of a huge mansion, surrounded by terraces, and hedged about by avenues of clipped bushes.

De Gautet strode noiselessly up one of these, with us hard on his heels. There were stone steps rising to a wing of the house that seemed to be in darkness, and then we were clustered round a small doorway under a great stone lintel, and Rudi was softly whistling (of all things) "Marlbroug s'en va-t'en guerre". For a few seconds we waited, breathing hoarsely like schoolboys who have robbed an orchard, and then the door opened.

"Detchard?"

De Gautet went in, and we followed. There was a man in a frock-coat in the dimly-lit passage; he closed the door quickly behind us—the other two were still outside somewhere—and motioned us to silence. He was a tall, distinguished old file with a beaky nose and heavy lower lip; he had grey hair and a beard like a muffler round his jaw-line. He glanced keenly at me, muttered "Donner!", and turned to Rudi.

"A complication. His highness has retired early. He is already in his apartments."

Aha, thinks I, clever little Bismarck's bandobast[28] didn't allow for this; oh, Jesus, we're done for . . .

"No matter," says Rudi easily. "He has three rooms; he can't be in all of them at once."

This was gibberish to me, but it seemed to reassure Detchard. Without another word he led us along the passage, up a stair, into a well-lighted and carpeted corridor, and round a corner to a large double-door. He paused, listening, cautiously turned the handle, and peered in. A moment later we were all inside.

Detchard stood for a moment, and I could hear my heart thumping like a paddle-wheel. The sound of voices came softly through an adjoining door from the next room.

"His highness is in his bed-chamber," whispers Detchard.

Rudi nodded. "Strip," says he to me, and de Gautet bundled up my gear as I tore it off. He knotted it all in my cloak—I had just sense enough to remember my pistols, and thrust them hurriedly under a cushion—and then I was standing there, mother-naked, while Detchard listened with his ear to the panels of the communicating door.

"Lucky little Duchess Irma," murmurs Rudi, and I saw him grinning at me. "Let's hope the real prince is as royally endowed." He tipped me a mock salute, very debonair. "Bonne chance, your highness. Ready, de Gautet?"

Together they went to the communicating door, Rudi nodded, and in a moment they had opened it and slipped through, with Detchard behind them. There was a second in which the murmur of voices sounded louder, and then the door closed, and I was left, stark in a royal dressing-room in a German mansion, all alone and palpitating.

For a moment there wasn't a sound, and then something tumbled next door. Minutes passed, a door was shut somewhere, there was a muttering of voices in the corridor that sent me scampering behind the curtains, and then silence. Several minutes passed, and my teeth began to chatter with cold and apprehension. At last I peeped out, to see if there wasn't a gown or something to wrap up in: there was plenty of furniture in the room, the main article being an enormous decorated commode—it struck me as my usual luck that whereas most royal successions lead to a throne, mine had got me nothing so far but a thunderbox—but devil a rag of clothing beyond a couple of towels. So I wrapped up in the curtain as well as I could, and waited fearfully.

Then the door opened, and Detchard's voice said softly: "Wo sind sie?"

I poked my head out. He was carrying a big silk dressing-gown, thank God, and I grabbed at it, shuddering.

"His highness has left the house," says he. "Everything is in train. Is all well with you?"

"Oh, splendid—except that I'm almost frozen to death. Isn't there a fire, in God's name?"

"There is a stove in the bedroom," says he, and ushered me through to a splendid apartment, thickly-carpeted, with a huge four-poster bed richly-curtained, and a fine stove with its doors thrown wide to warm the room. While I thawed out Detchard stood with his grey head cocked, considering me and toying with his seals.

"It is truly amazing," says he, at last. "I did not believe it—but you are the same man. Wonderful!"

"Well, I hope the other one's warmer than I am. Haven't you any brandy?"

He poured me a glass, very carefully, and watched me gulp it down.

"You are nervous," says he. "Naturally. However, you will have the night to accustom yourself to the—ah, novelty of your situation. His highness retired early, with a

149

slight headache no doubt brought on by the fatigue of his journey, so you will be undisturbed. Your host, Count von Tarlenheim, has given particular instructions. You will meet him briefly tomorrow, by the way, before we set out for the border. An amiable dotard. His highness—or I should say, your highness—has been quite formal with him so far, so there will be no questions asked if you are no more forthcoming tomorrow than politeness demands."

"Thank God for that," says I. I wanted time to play myself in, so to speak, and the thought of chattering to a breakfast table was out of court altogether.

"The only people who have been close to you on the journey, apart from myself, are Dr Ostred, your physician, and young Josef, your valet. He has been in your service only a day, your old valet, Einar, having become indisposed shortly after we set out."

"Convenient," says I. "Will he live?"

"Of course. You are much concerned about him." He turned, and I leaped violently as the door opened, and a little anxious-looking chap came in.

"Ah, Ostred," says Detchard, and the little chap blinked, looked at me, at Detchard, and back at me again.

"I thought . . ." he stammered. "That is—your pardon, highness. I supposed . . . you had retired . . . that you would be in bed." He looked helplessly to Detchard, and I thought, by heaven, he thinks I'm the real man. He couldn't make out what had gone wrong. So here was a first-rate chance to put the thing to the test; if I could fool my own doctor I could fool anyone.

"I have a headache," says I, quite gently. "That doesn't mean that I have to take to my bed."

"No, no . . . of course not, highness." He licked his lips.

"Perhaps you might take his highness's pulse, doctor," says Detchard, and the little fellow came over and took my wrist as though it was made of porcelain. There were beads of sweat on his brow.

"A little swift," he muttered, and glanced at my face.

He was scared and puzzled, and then he literally leaped back as though he had seen a ghost.

"He . . . he . . ." he exclaimed, pointing.

"No, Ostred," says Detchard. "He is not the prince."

"But—" the little doctor gargled speechlessly, and I couldn't help laughing. "But he is—identical! Dear Jesus! I could not believe it! I was sure, when I saw him, that something had gone amiss—that it was still the prince. My God!"

"What gave him away?" asks Detchard.

"The scars. They are new, and pink."

Detchard snapped his teeth in annoyance. "The scars, of course. I had forgotten. That might have cost us dear. However, we have the means to put it right." And he took out a flask, which I suppose Rudi had given him, and daubed at my wounds until he and the doctor were satisfied.

"There," says Detchard. "When did you last shave your head?"

"Last night."

"It will do for the moment. Ostred will attend to it again tomorrow." He pulled out his watch. "Now, it may be best if you and I, doctor, return to our hosts." For my benefit he rattled off a few more details about Tarlenheim and the arrangements for the morning. "Your valet will look in shortly, to see you to bed," he concluded. "You may sleep easily, believe me. Now that I have seen you, my doubts are at rest. I seriously question if your own father would detect the imposture. Ha! You see—I said 'your' own father." He smiled grimly. "I half believe in you myself. And so, your highness, I have the honour to bid you good-night."

They withdrew, bowing, and left me trembling—but for once it wasn't funk. I was elated—I had fooled Ostred. By God, it was going to work. I took a turn round the room, grinning to myself, drank another glass of brandy, and another, and stood beaming at myself in the mirror.

Well, Prince Harry, thinks I, if only Elspeth could see you now. And old moneybags Morrison. And Lord God-almighty Cardigan. He'd be glad enough to have royalty back in his flea-bitten 11th Hussars. For I *was* royal, for the moment—a full-blown prince of the blood, no less, until—aye, until Bismarck's little game was played out. And then—oh, the blazes with him. I had another glass of brandy and took stock of my royal surroundings.

Sumptuous wasn't the word for them—silk sheets, lace pillow, solid silver cup and plate by the bed—with breast of chicken under a napkin, bigod, in case I felt peckish. I resisted a temptation to slip the plate into a pocket—plenty of time for lifting the lumber later. This was only a staging-post on the journey, after all; the pick of the loot would be in the palace of Strackenz. But I felt I could rough it here for the night—excellent liquor, a warm fire, cigars in a tooled leather box, even the pot under the bed was of the best china, with little fat-arsed cherubs running round it. I plumped back on the bed—it was like floating on a cloud. Well, thinks I, they may talk about cares of state, and uneasy lies the head and all that tommy-rot, but this is the life for old Flashy. You may take my word for it, next time you hear about the burdens of monarchy, that royalty do themselves damned proud. I've been one; I know.

My eye fell on an ornament on the mantel; a carved kneeling figure. A little prickle ran through me as I realised that this was the cupid Bismarck had mentioned—by jove, he knew his business, that one. Down to the last detail. I rolled off the bed and looked at it, and felt a slight glow of pleasure as I realised it wasn't a cupid after all—it was a nymph. The great Otto wasn't infallible then, after all. It was most obviously a nymph, and contemplating it I realised there was one thing missing from my princely paradise. Bronze nymphs don't compare to real ones: I hadn't had a woman since the blubbery Baroness Pechman had been so rudely plucked from my embrace—and I hadn't really been able to get to proper grips with her before Rudi had interrupted us. Fat and all as she was, the thought of her was making me feverish, and at that moment there was a soft tap at the door and a slim, very sober-looking fellow slipped in. This was obviously Josef, my valet.

I was on guard again in a moment.

"Is there anything your highness requires?" says he.

"I don't think so, Josef," says I, and gave a yawn. "Just going to bed." And then a splendid idea occurred to me. "You may send up a chambermaid to turn down the covers."

He looked surprised. "I can do that, sir."

Now, Flashy would have growled: "Damn your eyes, do as you're bloody well told." But Prince Carl Gustaf merely said, "No, send the chambermaid."

He hesitated a second, his face expressionless. Then: "Very good, your highness." He bowed and went to the door. "Goodnight, highness."

Of course, it was a dam-fool thing to do, but what with the brandy and my randy thoughts, I didn't care. Anyway, wasn't I a prince? And the real Carl Gustaf was no monk, by all accounts—and damned careless about it, too. So I waited in lustful anticipation, until there was another knock, and a girl peeped in when I called out to enter.

She was a pretty, plump little thing, curly-haired and as broad as she was long, but just the thing for me with my thoughts running on Baroness Pechman. She had a bright eye, and it occurred to me that Josef was perhaps no fool. She curtsied and tripped across to the bed, and when I sauntered over—slipping the door-bolt on the way—and stood beside her, she giggled and made a great show of smoothing out my pillow.

"All work and no play isn't good for little girls," says I, and sitting on the bed I pulled her on to my knee. She hardly resisted, only trying to blush and look demure, and when I pulled down her bodice and kissed her breasts she

153

cooed and wriggled her body against mine. In no time we were thrashing about in first-rate style, and I was making up for weeks of enforced abstinence. She was an eager little bundle, all right, and by the time she had slipped away, leaving me to seek a well-earned rest, I was most happily played out.

I've sometimes wondered what the result of that encounter was, and if there is some sturdy peasant somewhere in Holstein called Carl who puts on airs in the belief that he can claim royal descent. If there is, he can truly be called an ignorant bastard.

There are ways of being drunk that have nothing to do with alcohol. For the next few days, apart from occasional moments of panic-stricken clarity, I was thoroughly intoxicated. To be a king—well, a prince—is magnificent; to be fawned at, and deferred to, and cheered, and adulated; to have every wish granted—no, not granted, but attended to immediately by people who obviously wish they had anticipated it; to be the centre of attention, with everyone bending their backs and craning their necks and loving you to ecstasy—it is the most wonderful thing. Perhaps I'd had less of it than even ordinary folk, especially when I was younger, and so appreciated it more; anyway, while it lasted I fairly wallowed in it.

Of course, I'd had plenty of admiration when I came home from Afghanistan, but that was very different. Then they'd said: "There's the heroic Flashman, the bluff young lionheart who slaughters niggers and upholds old England's honour. Gad, look at those whiskers!" Which was splendid, but didn't suggest that I was more than human. But when you're royalty they treat you as though you're God; you begin to feel that you're of entirely different stuff from the rest of mankind; you don't walk, you float, above it all, with the mob beneath, toadying like fury.

I had my first taste of it the morning I left Tarlenheim, when I breakfasted with the Count and about forty of his crowd—goggling gentry and gushing females—before setting out. I was in excellent shape after bumping the chambermaid and having a good night's rest, and was fairly gracious to one and all—even to old Tarlenheim, who could have bored with the best of them in the St James clubs. He remarked that I looked much healthier this morning—the solicitous inquiries after my headache would have put a Royal Commission on the plague to shame—and encouraged, I suppose, by my geniality, began to tell me about what a hell of a bad harvest they'd had that year. German potatoes were in a damnable condition, it seemed.[29] However, I put up with him, and presently, after much hand-kissing and bowing, and clanking of guardsmen about the driveway, I took my royal leave of them, and we bowled off by coach for the Strackenz border.

It was a fine, bright day, with snow and frost all over the place, but warm enough for all that. My coach was a splendid machine upholstered in grey silk, excellently sprung, and with the Danish Royal arms on the panels. (I remembered that the coach Wellington had once taken me in looked like a public cab, and rattled like a wheelbarrow.) There were cuirassiers bumping along in escort—smart enough—and a great train of other coaches bringing up the rear. I lounged and had a cheroot, while Detchard assured me how well things had gone, and would continue to go—he needn't have bothered, for I was in an exalted state of confidence—and then presently we rolled through our first village, and the cheering began.

All along the road, even at isolated houses, there were smiling faces and fluttering handkerchiefs; squires and peasants, farm-girls and ploughmen, infants waving the red and white Danish colours and the curious thistle-like emblem which is the badge of Holstein,[30] labourers in their smocks staring, mounted officials saluting—the whole countryside seemed to have converged on the Strackenz road to see my royal highness pass by. I beamed and

155

waved as we rushed past, and they hallooed and waved back all the harder. It was a glorious dream, and I was enjoying it to the full, and then Detchard reminded me drily that these were only Holsteiners, and I might save some of my royal energy for the Strackenzians.

It was at the border, of course, that the real circus began. There was a great crowd waiting, the toffs to the fore and the mob craning and hurrahing at a more respect-ful distance. I stepped out of the coach, at Detchard's instruction, and the cheers broke out louder than ever—the crashing three-fold bark that is the German notion of hip-hip-hip-hooray. An elderly cove with snow-white hair, thin and hobbling stiffly, came forward bowing and hand-kissing, to bid me welcome in a creaking voice.

"Marshal von Saldern, Constable of Strackenz," whis-pered Detchard, and I grasped the old buffer's hand while he gushed over me and insisted that this was the greatest day in Strackenz's history, and welcome, thrice welcome, highness.

In turn I assured him that no visitor to Strackenz had ever arrived more joyfully than I, and that if their welcome was any foretaste of what was to come then I was a hell of a fortunate fellow, or words to that effect. They roared and clapped at this, and then there were presentations, and I inspected a guard of honour of the Strackenz Grenadiers, and off we went again, with von Saldern in my coach, to point out to me objects of interest, like fields and trees and things—the old fellow was as jumpy as a cricket, I realised, and babbled like anything, which I accepted with royal amiability. And then he had to leave off so that I could devote myself to waving to the people who were now lining the road all the way, and in the distance there was the sound of a great throng and a tremendous bustle; far away guns began to boom in salute, and we were rolling through the suburbs of the city of Strackenz itself.

The crowds were everywhere now, massed on the pave-ments, waving from the windows, crouching precariously on railings, and all yelling to beat the band. There were flags and bunting and the thumping of martial music, and then a great archway loomed ahead, and the coach rolled slowly to a halt.

The hubbub died away a little, and I saw a small procession of worthies in robes and flat caps approaching the coach. Ahead was a stalwart lad carrying a cushion with something on it.

"The keys to the city," quavered von Saldern. "For your highness's gracious acceptance."

Without a thought, I opened the door and jumped down, which I gather was unexpected, but was a happy act, as it turned out. The crowds roared at the sight of me, the band began booming away, and the little burgomaster took the keys—huge heavy things on an enormous collar—and begged me to accept them as an earnest of the loyalty and love of the city.

"Your city, highness," he squeaked. "And your home!"

I knew enough to say that I was deeply sensible of the great honour done me, and to give him the keys back again. And being somewhat exalted, I felt it appropriate to slip my sword-belt over my head, present the weapon to him, and say that it would be ever-ready in the defence of Strackenzian honour and independence, or some such stuff.

I didn't know it, but that brief speech had an enormous political implication, the Danish-Strackenzians being in a great sweat about the German threat to their liberty, and the German-Strackenzians bursting to get away from Danish sovereignty. Anyway, the yell of applause that greeted it was startling, the little burgomaster went red with emotion, and taking the sword he pressed it back on me, tears in his eyes, and calling me the champion of Strackenzian freedom. I don't know which side *he* was on, but it didn't seem to matter; I believe if I'd shouted "Chairs to mend!" they'd have cheered just as loud.

I was then invited to enter the city, and it seemed a good notion to me to ride in on horseback rather than go in the coach. There was delight and confusion at this; orders were shouted, officers scampered to and fro, and then a cavalryman led forward a lovely black gelding, speed written in every line of him, and I mounted amid scenes of enthusiasm. I must have looked pretty fine, if I say it myself; they had dressed me that morning all in pale blue, with the blue sash of the Order of the Elephant over my shoulder (I've worn it in the last few years, by the way, at London functions, to the surprise and scandal of the Danish Embassy, who wondered where the deuce I'd got it. I referred them to former Chancellor Bismarck). The uniform set off my excellent stature famously, and since my disgusting bald head was covered by a plumed helmet, à la Tin-bellies, I've no doubt I looked sufficiently dashing.[31]

The band played, the cheering re-echoed, and I rode through the gateway into the city of Strackenz. Flowers were showered from the balconies, girls blew kisses, the troops lining the street struggled to hold back the press, and I waved and inclined my princely head, left and right, and smiled on my loyal subjects-to-be.

"Well, he can ride," someone called out, and a wit in the crowd shouted back "Aye, Duchess Irma will find out all about that," at which there was some commotion. I was aware that for all the adulation and hurrahing, there were those in the crowd who stood silent, and even some who looked positively hostile. These would be the Germans, no doubt, who didn't want to see the state bound any closer to Denmark. However, they were a small minority, in the city at all events, and for the most part it was flowers and laughter all the way, with Prince Charming flashing his smile to the prettiest girls and feeling no end of a fellow.

Probably because I was enjoying myself so much, it was no time at all to the town hall. I should say that Strackenz isn't much of a city, being no greater than one of our market towns, although it has a cathedral and a ducal palace of some pretension. For that matter the whole duchy isn't more than a dozen miles across by about thirty in length, having been whittled down over the centuries from a fair-sized province. But it was a perfect hotbed of nationalist emotions, German and Danish, and fiercely proud of its traditions, including its ducal house. The Danish faction were overjoyed at the impending marriage, hence their tumultuous welcome of me.

At the town hall there were more dignitaries, and bowing and scraping, and I was presented with an ornamental casket bearing the city's arms, and invited to sign an order for a jail clearance—it being the custom here, as elsewhere, to celebrate joyous occasions by letting all the hooligans and harlots out of the local clink. How this is supposed to add to the general jollity I've never understood—furthermore, although I've been in half the lock-ups between Libby Prison[32] and Botany Bay myself, no one has ever held a clearance that benefited me. I'm against 'em, on principle, but I saw nothing for it here but to sign, until the moment I actually took the pen in my hand and realised, with a fearful qualm, that one thing my instructors hadn't taught me was how to forge Carl Gustaf's signature. I didn't even know what his writing looked like. Probably I could have signed my own fist and no one would ever have spotted a difference, but at the time I didn't dare to risk it.

For what seemed a year I hesitated, at the great burgomaster's table, with the long roll of parchment stretched out in front of me, and my pen poised, while the crowd goggled expectantly and the little burgomaster stood waiting to pounce on my signature with the sand-caster. And then my mother-wit came back to me, and I laid down the pen and said, very quietly and seriously, that before signing such a delivery—which I reminded them was a grave matter indeed—I would wish to hear a report from the justices assuring me that no malefactor who might prove a danger to the commonweal would be enlarged by the amnesty. It could wait, I said firmly, for a day or two, and added that

159

I would find other and better ways of marking this happy occasion of my arrival.

That pious old hypocrite, Arnold, my headmaster, would have loved every word of it, but there was a general air of disappointment round the table, although one or two of the toadies muttered about a prudent prince and wagged their heads approvingly. The little burgomaster looked ready to cry, but agreed that my wishes would be met to the letter.

They all cheered up, though, at the next act of the comedy, when a small child was led in to present me with a peach that they had been preparing for me in the hothouse of the local orphanage. I say led in, because the child was so lame he had to go on little crutches, and there were sighings and affected cooings from the females present. I'm no hand with children at all, and have found them usually to be detestable, noisy, greedy little brats, but it seemed best to be monstrously pleasant to this one. So instead of just accepting the gift I racked my brains quickly for a touching gesture, and was inspired to pick him up—he was no size at all—and sit him on the table, and talk to him, and insisted that we eat the peach between us, then and there. He laughed and cried together, and when I patted his head according to form, he fastened on to my hand, and kissed it. The females were all snivelling foully by this time, and the men were looking pitying and noble. I felt ashamed, and still do. It is the only time in my life I have felt ashamed, which is why I put it on record here, and I still don't know why.

Anyway, I left the town hall in a thoroughly ill temper, and when they told me that next on the programme was a visit to the local academy, I as near as not told them I'd had enough of their damned infants for one day. But I didn't, of course, and presently I was being conducted through the school by the professor, who made an oration in my honour in Greek and then put up his best boys to construe for my entertainment. The things these honest asses imagine will delight royalty!

Of course the selected pupils were the usual mealy wretches who are put up in all schools everywhere on such occasions. Pious, manly little villains of the type I used to oppress myself in happier days—Tom Brown could have made a football side out of 'em, I don't doubt, and had them crying "Play up!" and telling the truth fit to sicken you. So I decided on a bit of mischief, and looked to the back of the school for the local Flashman—aye, there he was, a big, surly lout biting his nails and sneering to himself.

"There's a likely lad, professor," says I. "Let's hear him construe."

So, willy-nilly, they had to put the brute up, and he was paper-colour at the shock of it. Of course he floundered and grunted and glared round for inspiration, and the goody-goodies giggled and nudged each other, and the professor's frown grew blacker every minute.

"Stand down, sir," says he grimly, and to me: "He shall be corrected, highness, I assure you."

"That's your sort, professor," says I. "Lay on with a will." And I left in excellent humour. There would be a raw backside in that school by night, or I was mistaken—mind you, I'd sooner it had happened to the clever little sneaks, but no doubt my counterpart would pass his smarts on to them in turn.

The crowds still filled the streets for my final progress to the palace, which was a fine imposing pile on the outskirts of town, with pillars and balconies, and the running lion flag of Strackenz floating from its roof with the Danish colours alongside. The people were jammed up to the railings, and the sweep of the drive beyond was lined with the yellow-jacketed infantry of the Duchess's guard, all in glittering back-and-breasts, with drawn swords. Trumpeters blew a fanfare, the crowd surged and shouted, and I cantered up the gravel to the broad palace steps. There I turned and waved, for the last time, and wondered why people will make such a fuss over royalty. It's the same with us; we have our tubby little Teddy, whom everyone pretends is the first gentleman of Europe, with all the virtues, when they know quite well he's just a vicious old rake—rather like me, but lacking my talent for being agreeable to order. Anyway, I was aboard Lily Langtry long before he was.

That by the way; all such lofty philosophical thoughts were driven from my mind when I entered the palace, for there I met the Duchess I was to marry next day in the old Cathedral of Strackenz, and it is a tribute to her that while I have only the haziest memories of the brilliant throng that crowded the marble staircase and great ballroom, my first glimpse of her remains fresh in my mind to this day. I can still see her, standing slim and straight on the dais at the far end of the room, with the ducal throne framed in crimson behind her, watching me as I approached, with the spectators suddenly hushed, and only the sound of my marching feet echoing through the silence.

This was one of the moments when it struck me: this is all a fraud, it isn't real. Here was I, not Prince Carl Gustaf of the ancient royal house of Oldenbourg, but rascally old Flashy of the vulgar and lately-arrived house of Flashman, striding ahead to claim my noble bride. God, I remember thinking, the things people get me into, and that thought probably prevented me from wearing the devil-may-care leer that I normally assume in the presence of beautiful women.

She *was* beautiful, too—far more so than her portrait had made her out. She couldn't have been more than twenty, but already she had the hard, cold loveliness that you find only among Northern women, with their fine, long features looking as though they had been carved from marble. Her figure, in an ivory dress with a train that spread out behind her, was perhaps a trifle on the slim side, with a hint of boyishness about it, but everything

162

was there and in good parade order. She was crowned with a little silver diadem sparking with stones, and her shining fair hair was pulled back and rolled into some kind of jewelled net behind her head. The effect of it all—so pale and pure and perfect—was rather awe-inspiring; I felt almost afraid of her.

The way she looked at me didn't help matters—the grey eyes were cold and proud, and I thought: this is a spoiled, arrogant madame if ever I saw one. Whatever her feelings might be about a duty marriage, she didn't seem to care for me at first glance; I knew she was looking at my glistening bald head, and I thought angrily what a damned shame it was I hadn't my natural adornments of curly mane and whiskers. The hand she held out for me to kiss was as pale and chilly as mist in a cemetery, and just about as welcoming. I took it, murmuring about pleasure and honour and deeply heartfelt felicitous gratification, and felt it quiver ever so slightly before it was withdrawn.

So there we stood together on the dais, with me wondering what to say next, and then someone in the watching multitude began to clap, and in a moment they were crowding forward to get a closer look, I suppose, at the pair of us, and everyone was pleased and happy and clapping away like mad. I found myself grinning and nodding at them, but her grace stood there quite serene, with never a smile, as though this was her due, and rather a bore.

Well, thinks I, this is going to be a chilly wooing, and then an old cove in a frock coat with orders on his breast came bowing up beside us, and turned to the throng with his hand raised for silence. This turned out to be the Chief Minister, one Schwerin; he made a neat little speech in which he managed to wrap up a nice complimentary welcome for me, a note of homage for the duchess (who couldn't get too much of it, as I discovered), a patriotic boost for Strackenz, coupled with the state of Denmark, and a hint to the mob to keep their distance and stay out

163

of the buffet next door until her grace and I saw fit to lead the way.

That was about the size of it, and the good folk—who were a very well-trained court—chattered respectfully among themselves while Schwerin brought forward the more distinguished to be presented to me. These included the various emissaries to Strackenz, the British one among them, and I found myself thanking God that I'd never moved in diplomatic circles at home, or he might have remembered me. As it was, he and the others made their bows, and when they had withdrawn the Duchess indicated to me that we should sit down. We did so, both rather stiff, and while the noble assembly pretended not to notice, we began to get acquainted. It was formality carried to nonsense, of course, and if I didn't have a clear memory of our opening exchanges I wouldn't believe them.

Duchess Irma: I trust your highness's journey has not been tedious.

Flashy: Indeed, no, although I confess I have counted every moment in my impatience to be here.

Duchess: Your highness is very gracious. We of Strackenz can only hope that you are not too disappointed in us—we are very small and provincial here.

Flashy (very gallant): No one could be disappointed who was welcomed by so beautiful and noble a hostess.

Duchess: Oh. (Pause). Was the weather cold on your journey?

Flashy: At times. Occasionally it was quite warm. Nowhere so warm, however, as I find it here. (This with a flashing smile.)

Duchess: You are too hot? I shall order the windows opened.

Flashy: Christ, no. That is . . . I mean, the warmth of your welcome . . . and the people in the streets, cheering . . .

Duchess: Ah, the people. They are rather noisy.

Well, I don't give up easy, but I confess I was fairly stumped here. Usually, with young women, I get along all too well. Formal chit-chat isn't my style—a little gallantry, a few jocularities to see if she will or she won't, a pinch on the buttocks, and off we go. Either that, or off I go. But I couldn't make anything of the Duchess Irma; she kept her head tilted high and looked past me, so composed and regal that I began to wonder, was she perhaps terrified out of her wits? But before I could take soundings on that, she rose, and I found myself escorting her into the antechamber, where great tables were laid out with silver plate and crystal, and a most scrumptious spread was served by flunkies while a little orchestra struck up in the gallery overhead. I was sharp-set, and while one of the Duchess's ladies looked after her, I laid into the ham and cold fowls, and chatted affably to the nobs and their ladies, who were making the most of the grub themselves, as the Germans always do.

This kind of function normally bores me out of mind, and beyond the fact that the food was unusually excellent, and that the Duchess seemed intent on not being left alone with me for more than a moment at a time, I haven't any sharp recollection of it. I remember turning once, in that gay company with its buzz of well-bred conversation, and catching her eyes fixed on me; she looked quickly away, and I thought, my God, I'm *marrying* that woman tomorrow. My heart took a skip at the thought; she was unutterably lovely. And then it took a lurch as I remembered the appalling risk that I ran every moment I was in Strackenz, and wondered what the penalty might be for marrying the heir to the throne under false pretences. Death, certainly. I tried to smile politely at the eager, sycophantic faces around me, and to listen to their incredible inanities of small-talk, while my mind raced away looking for a way out, even although I knew it didn't exist.

I probably drank a little more than I should have done—although I was pretty careful—but at any rate the desperate

165

feeling passed. The good will of the Strackenzians towards me was so evident, and so fulsomely expressed, that I suppose it overcame me and banished my fears. I found I could even talk to the Duchess without embarrassment, although it was obvious to me, if not to anyone else, that she didn't like me; she remained haughty and distant—but then, she seemed to be the same to everyone, and they swallowed it and sucked up to her.

Afterwards old Schwerin and a couple of his ministerial colleagues—I forget their names—took me aside and discussed the next day's ceremony. They were fairly vague, as I remember, and gassed a good deal about the political advantage of the match, and the popular satisfaction, and how it would have a good and stabilising effect.

"Her grace is very young, of course," says old Schwerin. "Very young." He gave me rather a sad smile. "Your highness is not so very much older, but your education, at a great court, and your upbringing have perhaps prepared you better for what lies before you both." (You little know, old son, thinks I.) "It is a great responsibility for you, but you will bear it honourably."

I murmured noble nothings, and he went on:

"It is much to ask of two young folk—I often feel that such marriages of state would be the better of—ah—longer preparation. Perhaps I am a sentimentalist," says he, with a senile smirk, "but it has always seemed to me that a courtship would not be out of place, even between royal personages. Love, after all, does not come in a day."

It depends what you mean by love, thinks I, and one of the others says to Schwerin:

"You have a great heart, Adolf."

"I hope I have. I hope so. And your highness, I know, has a great heart also. It will know how to understand our—our little Irma. She is very much like a daughter to us, you see"—he was going pink about the eyes by this time—"and although she seems so serene and proud beyond her years, she is still very much a child."

Well, I could agree with him that she was an unusually arrogant little bitch for her age, but I kept a princely silence. He looked almost pleading.

"Your highness," he said at last, "will be kind to our treasure."

Strange, my own father-in-law had struck something of the same note before I married Elspeth; it's a polite way of suggesting that you don't make too much of a beast of yourself on the honeymoon. I assumed a look of manly understanding.

"Sirs," says I. "What can I say, except that I trust I shall always bear myself to your duchess as I would to the daughter of my oldest and dearest friend."

That cheered them up no end, and presently the reception began to draw to a close, and the noble guests imperceptibly melted away; Schwerin beamed paternally on the Duchess and myself, and hinted that as the next day was going to be an exhausting one, we should take all the rest we could beforehand. It was still only early afternoon, but I was dog-tired with the novelty and excitement of the morning, and so we said our formal goodbyes to each other. I made mine as pleasant as I could, and the Duchess Irma received it with an inclination of her head and gave me her hand to kiss. It was like talking to a walking statue.

Then Detchard, who had been hovering off my port quarter for several hours, closed in and with attendant flunkies escorted me to the suite reserved for me in the west wing of the palace. They would have made a great fuss of me, but he shooed them away, and what I thought rather odd, he also dismissed Josef, who was waiting to unbutton me and remove my boots. However, I realised he wished us to be private, and when we passed through into my main salon I understood why, for Rudi Starnberg and de Gautet were waiting for us.

The sight of them damped my spirits; it was a reminder of what I was here for, with my custodians dogging me all

167

the time. From being the prince I was become play-actor
Flashy again.

Rudi sauntered across and without so much as by-
your-leave took hold of my wrist and felt my pulse.

"You're a cool hand," says he. "I watched you down
below, and on my oath, you looked a most condescending
tyrant. How does it feel to play the prince?"

I hadn't been used to this kind of talk in the past
few hours, and found myself resenting it. I damned his
impudence and asked where the blazes he had been all
day—for he and de Gautet had been supposed to meet
me with the others at the frontier.

He cocked an eyebrow at me. "Regal airs, eh? Well,
highness, we've been busy about affairs of state if you
please. Your affairs, your state. You might show a little
appreciation to your loyal servants." He grinned insolently. "But of course, the gratitude of princes is proverbial."

"Then don't presume on it—even with temporary royalty," I growled. "You can both go to the devil. I want
to rest."

De Gautet considered me. "A little drunk perhaps?"

"Damn you, get out!"

"I do believe the infection has really taken," chuckled
Rudi. "He'll be calling the guard in a moment. Now,
seriously, friend Flashman"—and here he tapped me on
the chest—"you can put away your ill-temper, for it won't
answer. It ain't our fault if the Duchess hasn't languished
at you. No, you needn't damn my eyes, but listen. Certain
things have happened which may—I say may only—affect
our plans."

My stomach seemed to turn to ice. "What d'ye mean?"

"By ill chance, one of the Danish Embassy at Berlin—a fellow Hansen, a senior official—arrived today in
Strackenz. He was on his way home, and broke his journey
here to attend the wedding. There was no convenient way
to get rid of him, so he will be there tomorrow."

"Well, what about it?" says I. "There will be plenty

of Danes in the Cathedral, won't there? What's one more or less?"

Detchard spoke from behind me. "Hansen has been a friend of Carl Gustaf's from childhood. Indeed, the most intimate of all his companions."

"Your resemblance to Carl Gustaf is uncanny," put in de Gautet. "But will it deceive his oldest playmate?"

"Jesus!" I sat stricken. "No, no, by God, it won't! It can't! He'll know me!" I jumped up. "I knew it! I knew it! We're done for! He'll denounce me! You . . . you bloody idiots, see what you've done, with your lunatic schemes! We're dead men, and . . ."

"Lower your voice," says Rudi, "and take a grip on your nerves." He pushed me firmly back into my chair. "Your mind's disordered—which is not surprising. Bersonin warned us that even a strong man may show signs of hysteria in the kind of position you're in . . ."

"He's no fool, that one, is he?" cried I. "What the hell can I do? He'll give me away, this Hansen, and . . ."

"He will not," says Rudi firmly. "Take my word for it. I can see this thing clearly, which you can't, being the principal actor, and I tell you there is not the slightest risk—provided you keep your head. He'll meet you for a moment at the reception after the wedding, shake your hand, wish you well, and whist!—that is all. He's not looking for an impostor, remember. Why should he?"

"We would not have told you," said Detchard, "if it could have been avoided. But if we had not you might unwittingly have made some fatal blunder."

"That's it exactly," says Rudi. "You had to be ready for him. Now, we have decided what you shall say when he approaches you in the reception line. Detchard here will be at your elbow, and will whisper 'Hansen' when he reaches you. At the sight of him you'll start, look as delighted as you know how, seize his right hand in both of yours, shake it hard, and exclaim: 'Erik, old friend, where did you spring from?' Then, whatever he says in reply, you'll give

169

your merriest laugh and say: 'This is the happiest surprise of this happy day. God bless you for coming to wish me joy.' And that will be all. I'll see to it that he doesn't get near you before you leave for the lodge at Strelhow, where your honeymoon is being spent."

"And suppose he sees through me, what then?" This news had left me sick with fright. "Suppose he isn't to be put off with this nonsense about happy surprises, and I have to talk to him longer?" I had a dreadful vision. "Suppose he shouts, 'That's not the prince?' What'll you do then?"

"I'll have done it long before he shouts anything," says Rudi quietly. "You may rely on that."

I wasn't so easily reassured. My cowardly instincts were in full cry, and it took all Rudi's and Detchard's arts of persuasion to convince me that the risk wasn't so terrible—indeed, that if I played my part properly, it was barely a risk at all.

"Conduct yourself as you were doing an hour ago," says Rudi, "and the thing's as safe as sleep. Courage, man. The worst's past. You've pulled the wool over all the eyes in Strackenz this day, and right royally, too." I thought there was even a hint of envy in his voice. "All that's to do now is stand up in church with the delightful Duchess, say your vows, and then off for a blissful idyll in your forest love-nest. Aye, let your mind run on the pleasures of putting that dainty little pullet to bed." He nudged me and winked lewdly. "I'll wager the next Duke of Strackenz has fine curly whiskers, for all that his father won't have a hair on his face to bless himself with."

Of course, as so often turns out, there wasn't time to be frightened. Ostred gave me a sleeping draught that night, and in the morning it was all mad bustle and hurry, with never fewer than a dozen folk round me from the moment I rose, dressing me, pushing me, instructing me, reminding me—I felt like a prize beast in the ring as I was conducted down the great marble staircase to the waiting coach that was to carry me to the Cathedral. As we paused on the steps, the sound thundered up from the waiting thousands beyond the palace railings, the cannon boomed in the park, and a great cheer rolled across the steep roofs of Strackenz City.

"God save Prince Carl!"

"Wherever he may be," muttered Rudi. "Forward, your highness!"

It should have been a day to remember, I suppose, but how much of detail does one recall of one's own wedding?—and it was my second, as you know. It seems now like a strange dream, driving through the packed streets in the sunshine, with the roar of the people buffeting my ears, the blare of the trumpets, the clatter of hooves, and the coloured bunting fluttering bravely in the morning breeze—but what sticks in my mind is the red birthmark on the back of the coachman's head, which under his hat was as bald as my own.

And then there was the sudden dimness and hush of the great Cathedral, the pungent smell of the church, the soaring stained glass and the carpeted stone flags underfoot. There was the rustle as hundreds of people rose to their feet, the solemn booming of a great organ, and the hollow thud of my own footsteps on the stones. And there was the shrill sweetness of the choristers, and people softly moving to and fro about me, and the splendid figure of the Bishop of Strackenz, bearded to the eyes, and for all the world like Willie Grace, the great cricket champion nowadays.

I remember standing very lonely and afraid, wondering if perhaps there was such a place as Hell after all—a question which had occupied me a good deal as a small boy, especially when Arnold had been terrifying us with sermons about Kibroth-Hattaavah,[33] where I gathered all kinds of fornication and fun took place. Well, what I was doing in that Cathedral would have ensured me a single ticket to damnation, no doubt of that, but I consoled

171

myself with the thought that the hereafter was the last thing to worry about just then.

And I remember, too, the Duchess suddenly at my side, pale and wondrously lovely in her white gown, with her golden hair crowned with a fillet of brilliant stones. And her tiny hand slipping into mine, her clear voice answering the Bishop, and then my own, husky and nervous. They pressed a ring into my hand, and I fumbled it on to her tiny finger, my palms sweating, and kissed her on the cheek when the old Bishop gave the word. She stood like a wax dummy, and I thought, poor old Carl Gustaf, having to live with this cold fish all his life, and the choir let go a great blast of sound as they placed the ducal coronets on our heads, and the Duchess took the gold staff of her sovereignty and the Sword of State was buckled round my waist.

Then the whole congregation rose and sang a hymn of rejoicing, and various minor clergy decked us out in the remaining Crown Jewels. I must say that for a small state Strackenz was remarkably well off in this respect; apart from the coronets and staff, there were rings for my fingers and a magnificent solid gold chain set with emeralds which they hung round my unworthy neck; it had a star of diamonds pendent from it that must have weighed half a pound.

The Duchess did rather better, she being the reigning prince while poor old Flash was just her consort. (It struck me then, and it strikes me now, that the Salic Law was a damned sound idea.) She had a collar of solid gems, and her rings would have knocked mine all to pieces. Soldierly instinct dies hard, and as the hymn drew to a close I was mentally computing the worth of all this jewelled splendour, and how it could best be stowed: emerald chain in one side pocket, collar in t'other, rings and similar trifles in the fobs—the coronets would be bulky, but they could probably be bent flat for convenience. And the staff was slender enough to stick down your boot.

Of course, I'd probably never have the chance to lay my itchy fingers on this magnificent collection of loot again, but it does no harm to take stock in advance: you never know what opportunities may arise. The Crown Jewels of the Duchy of Strackenz would have kept me and a dozen like me in tremendous style for life, and they looked eminently portable. I decided to keep them in mind.

There was a final hallelujah and amen, and then we were out in the sunlight again with the crowd deafening us and the great bells of the Cathedral pealing overhead. There was an open State coach in which we rode side by side, with the Duchess's bridesmaids facing us, and I played up to the mob and waved and beamed, while my bride stirred a languid hand in their direction. She did manage a smile or two, though, and even condescended to exchange a few civilities with me, which was a great advance. Never mind, thinks I, it'll soon be ho for the hunting lodge and beddy-byes, and then we'll bring the roses back to those pearly cheeks.

We drove slowly, so that the populace could get a good look at us, and their enthusiasm was so tremendous that the infantry lining the road had to link arms to hold them back. There were children waving flags and screaming, girls fluttering their handkerchiefs, fellows throwing their hats in the air, and old women sobbing and mopping at themselves. At one point the troops gave way, and the crowd clamoured right up to the coach, stretching over to touch us as though we were holy relics: if only they'd known they'd have scampered off far enough in case they caught Flashy's Evil. The Duchess wasn't too pleased at being adored so closely, and looked ahead pretty stiff, but I shook hands like a good 'un and they cheered me hoarse.

At this point there was an odd incident. Above the cheering I was aware of a voice shouting from the back of the crowd—no, not shouting, but declaiming. It was a strong, harsh trumpet of a voice, although its words were lost in the tumult, and its owner was a most odd-looking fellow who had scrambled up onto some kind of hand-cart and was haranguing the mob full blast. There were soldiers struggling through the press to get at him, and a knot of sturdy, sober-looking chaps round the cart as though to shield the orator, so I gathered he must be denouncing us, or threatening a breach of the peace.

He wasn't a big chap, in height, but he was built like a bull across the shoulders, with a huge, shaggy head and a beard like a sweep's broom. Even at that distance I could see the flashing eyes as he thundered out his message, thumping the air with his fist and laying it off like a Mississippi camp-meeting preacher full of virtue and forty-rod whisky. The people nearest him and his group were shouting threats at him, but he kept bawling away, and it looked to me as though an excellent brawl was in prospect; unfortunately, just as the soldiers reached him and were trying to haul him down, the coach moved out of vision, so I didn't see how it came out.[34]

The Duchess had seen it, too, and we were no sooner at the palace than she summoned Schwerin to the ante-room where we were resting and pitched straight into him.

"Who was that agitator? How dared he raise his voice against me, and whose neglect allowed it to happen?" Her voice was perfectly level, but she was obviously in a furious bait, and the old minister fairly cowered before the slip of a girl. "Have he and his rabble been arrested?"

Schwerin wrung his hands. "Highness, that this should have happened! It is deplorable. I do not know who the man was, but I will ascertain. I believe he was one of the socialist orators—"

"Orator?" says the Duchess, in a tone that would have frozen brandy. "Revolutionary upstart! And on my wedding day!" She turned to me. "It is my shame, and my country's, that this affront should have taken place in your highness's presence, on this sacred occasion."

Well, I didn't mind. I was more interested in her cold rage at what she conceived an affront to her noble dignity;

she had a fine, spoiled conceit of herself to be sure. I suggested that the man was probably drunk, and that he had done no harm anyway.

"Denmark must be fortunate in its security against such dangerous criminals," says she. "In Strackenz we find it prudent to take sterner measures against these . . . these orators! Schwerin, I hold you responsible; let me hear presently that they have been arrested and punished."

It would have sounded pompous from a bench of bishops; from a nineteen-year-old girl it was ridiculous, but I kept a straight face. I was learning fast about my little Irma; an imperious young piece. I found myself hoping that she would be thwarted of her vengeance on my big-headed revolutionary; whoever he was, he had looked the kind of likely lad who would sooner spar with the peelers than eat his dinner, and keep things lively all round.

When she had sent Schwerin packing, and her ladies had adjusted invisible flaws in her appearance, we proceeded with tremendous ceremony to the great ballroom, where the brilliant throng had already assembled for the reception. This is a bigger "do" than old Morrison gave for Elspeth and me in Paisley, thinks I, but I'll wager they can't drink more than those Scotch rascals did. The place was a blaze of splendid uniforms and gowns; orders, medals, and jewellery twinkled everywhere; aristocratic backs bent and a hundred skirts rustled in curtsies as we took our place on the dais for the guests to file by with their respectful congratulations. You never saw such a pack of noble toadies in your life, smirking their way past. They all fawned over the Duchess, of course, the square-heads clicking their heels and bowing stiffly, the dagoes bending double—for we had a fine selection from half the countries in Europe. After all, Duchess Irma was the cousin of our own Britannic Majesty—which made me a sort-of-cousin-in-law to her and Albert, I suppose—and everyone wanted to have a grovel to us. I was delighted to see, though, that the British Ambassador confined himself to a jerky little bow and a "Felicitations, ma'am, and much happiness to both your highnesses." That's the style, thinks I; good old England and damn all foreigners.

I just stood there, nodding my head up and down until my neck creaked, smiling and murmuring my thanks to each passing face—fat, thin, sweating, straining, smiling, adoring, they came in all sizes and expressions. And then Detchard's voice behind me whispered "Hansen," and I glanced sharply to see a fair-haired, long-jawed young fellow just straightening up from his bow to the Duchess. He turned to me, smiling expectantly, and in my sudden nervousness I took a step forward, grinning like a death's head, I shouldn't wonder, grabbed him by the hand, and cried:

"Erik, old friend, this is the most springing surprise of my happy day!" or something equally garbled; I know that I bungled the words hopelessly, but he just laughed and pumped my hand.

"Dear Carl—highness—I had to come to wish you joy." He had that manly, sentimental look, misty-eyed yet smiling, which I personally can only manage in drink. "God bless you both!"

"God bless you, too, old friend," says I, wringing hard at him, and then his smile faded, a puzzled look came into his eyes, and he stepped back.

God knows I've had my bad moments, but seldom such a qualm of sickening dread as I experienced then. I kept my aching grin, because I was so paralysed with panic that I couldn't move a muscle, waiting for the denunciation which I was certain was on his lips.

For a second he stared, and then he made a sudden, nervous gesture of apology and smiled again.

"Pardon," he said. "Your pardon, highness . . . Carl." He moved quickly aside to let in the next guest, bowed again, and then moved off towards the buffets, where the other guests were assembling. There I saw him turn, staring back at me, and presently he rubbed his brow with his fingers, gave his head a quick shake as a man will who is putting some trifle out of his mind, and gave his attention to a waiter who was proffering champagne.

I knew I was crimson with the shock, and one knee was trembling violently, but I forced myself to smile steadily as the guest before me bobbed in a deep curtsey, and her escort swept me a bow. I saw the concern in their faces—when I turn red I'm a daunting sight—so I forced a laugh.

"Forgive me," I told them. "I'm out of breath with saying 'thank you' to several hundred people." They were delighted at being so familiarly addressed by royalty, and then the crisis was past and I had time to steady myself.

But it had been a horrible moment, and I must have gone through the rest of that reception like a man in a dream, for I can remember nothing more until I was back in my own room, alone with Detchard, Rudi and de Gautet, drinking brandy from a glass that rattled against my teeth.

"It was a bad moment," was Rudi's verdict. "For a second I thought we were gone. I had him covered from my pocket, and I swear if he had taken an instant longer to smile I'd have shot him down and claimed he was preparing to assassinate you. And God knows what might have come of that. Phew!"

"But he saw I wasn't the Prince!" I beat on the arm of my chair. "He saw through me! Didn't he? You saw him, de Gautet—didn't he?"

"I doubt it," says he. "For a moment he *thought* there was something strange about you—and then he told himself it was his own imagination. You saw him shake his head—he had tried to puzzle it out, but couldn't—and now he no more doubts you than he doubts himself."

"By God, I hope so." I attacked the brandy again. "Suppose he thinks better of it, though—becomes suspicious?"

"He's being watched every moment he is in Strackenz," says Rudi. "We have other reasons for keeping a sharp eye on Master Hansen."

177

"What's that?"

"Oh, his journey here wasn't only to dance at your wedding. We know that for months now he and other members of the Danish government have been in correspondence with the more militant Danish faction in Strackenz—people like the Eider Danes[35] over the border, only rather more dangerous. They watch everything German like hawks, hold secret meetings, that sort of thing. There's talk of a clandestine organisation, the 'Sons of the Volsungs', dedicated to fly to arms in the event of any threat from Berlin to Strackenzian independence." Rudi grinned pleasantly. "We'll settle with those gentlemen when the time comes. For the present, neither they nor friend Hansen need trouble you. The game's all but won, my boy"— and he slapped me on the shoulder. "With the wedding behind us there's nothing to do but sit out the weeks until Otto gives the word that our good Carl Gustaf is ready to resume the rôle in which you are proving such a distinguished understudy. Then back to merry England for you—and let's hope the delectable Irma isn't too disappointed in the change, shall we?"

This was all very well, but I was by no means sure that the worst was past. I'd had some nasty turns in my brief life as Prince Carl Gustaf, and it seemed odds on there being a few more before they'd sweated the clap out of him and he could succeed me on the consort's throne. And even then, would Bismarck keep faith? I didn't want to think about that just yet, but it was always at the back of my mind. Sufficient unto the day is the evil thereof, but you have to watch your step at night, too.

I was still shaking with the Hansen business, and for that matter I was probably suffering from the strain of two days' imposture—at any rate, I punished a half bottle of brandy there and then without noticeable effect, which is always a sign that the funks have got me good and proper. Rudi, although he watched me closely, whistling through his teeth, didn't say me nay; there was no further official

178

business that day, only the drive to the hunting lodge at Strelhow, ten miles from the city, and I didn't have to be stone-cold sober for that.

We were to set out in mid-afternoon, and presently Josef and various minions were admitted to begin my preparations for the road. There was a great bustle as trunks and boxes were taken below stairs, and I was divested of my ceremonial uniform and kitted out in cutaway and topper, as befitted a gentleman bent on his honeymoon. I was sufficiently recovered from my nervous condition—or else the booze was beginning to work—to be able to discuss with Rudi the merits of checked or striped trousers, which had been the great debate among the London nobs that year.[36] I was a check-er myself, having the height and leg for it, but Rudi thought they looked bumpkinish, which only shows what damned queer taste they had in Austria in those days. Of course, if you'll put up with Metternich you'll put up with anything.

While we were talking, an officer of the palace guard put in an appearance, with an escort carrying drawn sabres, to collect the crown jewellery which Josef had removed with my uniform. They had taken my coronet and State sword on our return from the cathedral, but my chain and rings remained, and these were now carefully stowed in velvet-lined cases and given to the guard to carry away.

"Pretty things," says Rudi, cocking his cheroot thoughtfully between his teeth. "Where are you taking them, Fahnrich?"

"To the clock-room, herr baron," says the young officer, clicking his heels.

"Aye, that's a strange place, surely. Wouldn't a dungeon be safer?"

"If you please, herr baron, the clock-room is in the top of the main tower of the palace. The tower has one stair, which is under constant guard." The youth hesitated. "I believe they are kept there because in the old Duke's time it was his grace's delight to visit the clock-room every day and examine the state treasure."

I was taking this in, for what it was worth, and noting that Rudi von Starnberg was showing an uncommon interest in it, too. Dishonest young pup; I knew what he was thinking.

We left the palace on the stroke of three, to be cheered out of town by the loyal Strackenzians, who had been making the most of the free buffets and unlimited wine being dispensed in all the public buildings. The whole population seemed to be half-shot, and the applause as we drove through the streets was abandoned and hilarious. I sat with the Duchess in an open landau, accompanied by Rudi and a strikingly pretty red-haired lady-in-waiting whose foot he kept stroking with his boot during the journey. Otherwise he was on his best behaviour, which meant that his conduct stopped just short of open insolence.

However, Irma was in no frame of mind to notice; she was in something of a pet, chiefly, I gathered, because Schwerin had not been able to report the apprehension of the agitator who had been abusing us on our drive from the cathedral. And there had been difficulties with her trousseau, the people who were waving us goodbye were over-familiar in their expressions, the open carriage was not suitable for such a cold day—and so on, every damned thing seemed to be wrong, for no obvious reason. To me it seemed that, whatever the rest of her trousseau was like, her blue travelling gown and fur hat, à la hussar, became her admirably. I said so, and she condescended to acknowledge the compliment, but very formally. We were still as distant as dowagers in church, and it struck me again that for all her prim composure, she was probably quaking underneath. I found this gratifying, and resolved to let her stew in it for a while; I wasn't over-solicitous, and for most of the journey we rode in silence.

It was a sunny afternoon, and warm in spite of Irma's complaint. The road from Strackenz runs through some splendid forest country, which encloses an unusual feature for that part of the world in a short range of little crags and cliffs called the Jotun Gipfel. They are very pretty, very wild, as our late Queen would say, and rather like the English lake hills in miniature. Apart from a few shepherds' huts they are fairly empty, most of the inhabitants of Strackenz province living down in the flat lands near the city, but they contain one or two beautiful mountain tarns, in one of which stands the old castle of Jotunberg, which was the stronghold of the Dukes of Strackenz in the bad old days. It was kept now by the Bülow family, a Strackenzian branch of the great German house of that name.

The hunting lodge of Strelhow stands some miles from the Jotun Gipfel, tucked away in the woods a little distance off the main road. It has been the country seat of the ruling house for generations, and is an excellent little box, all rough timber and fur rugs, with fine open fires, leaded windows, comfortable appointments, and plenty of room—altogether a bang-up place. We were travelling fairly informally; there were two Strackenzian aides for me, apart from de Gautet and Rudi, and the Duchess had three ladies and about five maids—God knows why she needed all those. Detchard had come, too, but elected to stay in the village, and of course I had Josef with me. There were other servants, and various grooms and attendants, and it looked like being quite a lively country party. And it was—lively and deathly.

We arrived at the lodge just before dusk. My bride was nervous and irritable, and had the servants who came out to greet us scurrying in all directions. There was a meal prepared in the panelled dining-room, with a cheery blaze in the grate, and all looking mighty snug and inviting, but she excused herself and went off above-stairs with her lady-in-waiting and a cloud of lackeys hovering in her wake. However, we men-folk were sharp-set and fell on supper with a will, and after that the port and brandy, and before long we were making a good roaring evening

181

of it. What with sensing that her haughty highness was out of sorts, and the food and wine, I was in excellent trim, and although de Gautet was his usual saturnine self—I was growing to loathe that sleek, silent smile—Rudi and the two Strackenzians took their cue from me and caroused like cricketers.

For all their other faults, I must own that Germans are excellent fellows at a gorging-and-drinking party. Rudi was in fine fettle, with his tunic undone and his curly hair a-tumble, leading the singing in a capital baritone (but his eyes were still bright and clear; I doubt if he was ever the worse for drink in his life, that one). I was ladling the liquor down at a fair rate, and had just reached that state where I begin to search for mischief, when a footman brought down word that her grace the duchess was about to retire, and requested that the disturbance of the evening should cease.

At this the others fell silent. Rudi sat back in his chair and smiled into his glass; the Strackenzians glanced uneasily at each other. I got to my feet, staggering a little and upsetting my chair, and said that if her grace was retiring, so was I. I bade them goodnight, and walked—rather unsteadily, I imagine—to the door.

One of the Strackenzian aides jumps up, and asked, could he help my highness?

"No, thank'ee, my son," says I. "I'm of age, you know."

At which he fell back, blushing, and as I strode out I heard Rudi laughing and calling out:

"Gentlemen, a toast! The Prince Carl Gustaf, coupled, if you follow me, with her grace the Duchess of Strackenz."

I blundered upstairs, shed my clothes in my dressing-room, thrust Josef out, threw on a gown, and strode through into the bedroom. I was full of booze and lewdness, and the sight of Irma, caught unawares, standing there in a white nightgown, did nothing to sober me. Her cold, proud beauty brought out the worst in me, I threw off the gown, and she shrieked and covered her eyes.

"Cheer up, little wife," says I, "there won't be any more singing downstairs," and I stooped and whipped the nightdress clean off, over her head. She gave a little cry, and since I maintain that the best way to deal with nervous females is to treat 'em hearty, I lifted her up bodily, popped her on, and stumped round the room singing:

"This is the way the ladies ride, trit-trot, trit-trot, trit-trot."

As near as I can remember I sang it in English, but I doubt if she noticed. At all events I know we finished the business on the bed, with me laughing weakly and babbling about "hobble-dee, hobble-dee, and down in a ditch" and assuring her that she was a damned fine duchess and a credit to her country.[37]

I suppose I dozed off, but I woke up and had at her again, and being slightly more sober by this time I was aware that she lay as still as a corpse, and didn't enter into the fun of the thing at all. If it had been any other woman I'd have smartened her up with a few cuts across the rump, but with a duchess one ought to practise patience, I felt.

And I was right, you see, because after that I went to sleep, leaving her lying there, with her eyes closed, like a beautiful ghost in the candlelight, and what should awaken me—I don't know how many hours later—but a tiny hand creeping across my thigh, and long hair snuggling up to my face, and I thought, well, damme, royal or not, they're all alike under the skin. I was beat, I can tell you, but one must act like a gentleman, so I went to work again, and this time she clung like a leech. Just like Elspeth, I remember thinking—all chaste purity to look at, maidenly beauty personified, and randy as a monkey.

I've known too many women, far too many, to claim to understand 'em. Their minds work in ways too mysterious for me to fathom; anyway, my studies have generally been confined to their bodies, which perhaps accounts for it. But I know that Duchess Irma of Strackenz was a different woman after that night—to me, at any rate. She had

183

been a proud, autocratic, thoroughly spoiled little brat the day before; nervous as a mouse and as cold as a whale's backside. And I'd not have been surprised if after the way I'd handled her, she'd been put off men for good. But next morning she was positively meek, in a thoughtful but apparently contented way, and very attentive to me; she seemed to be in a state of wonder, almost, and yet she was ready to talk to me, and what was even more remarkable, listen to me, too—not that I'm a great hand at conversation in the mornings.

I don't mention this in a boastful way, or to suggest that with a chap like me it's just a matter of catch 'em young, treat 'em rough, roger 'em hard, and they eat out of my hand. Far from it; I've used women that way, and had them try to repay me with cold steel, or run a mile next time I looked at them. But with Irma, for some reason, it had quite the opposite effect; I can say that from that night on, as long as I knew her, she treated me with something near to worship. Which shows you how stupid a love-struck young woman can be.

All this, of course, made for a most happy sojourn at Strelhow. There was plenty to do during the day, what with picnic parties—for although some snow still lay, it was pleasantly warm for the season—and shooting in the woods, and riding (on horses) in the afternoon, and in the evening we had musical entertainment from the ladies, or played billiards, and the food and drink were of the best. I began to feel like royalty again, with people waiting on me hand and foot, and jumping to my slightest wish, and it is mighty pleasant to have a beautiful young duchess hanging on your arm, adoring you, even if she does keep you from getting much sleep at nights. It was the life, all right—lazing, feasting, shooting, tickling the pills in the billiard room and sweating it out in bed with Irma—all the trivial amusements that are simply nuts to chaps like me.

Rudi and de Gautet were the only flies in the ointment, for their very presence was a constant jog to my memory of the business in hand. But strangely enough, I became a little closer to de Gautet, for I discovered that he shared one of my chief interests, which is horseflesh. He was an authority, of the true kind who never pretends more than he knows, and in the saddle he was nearly as good as I was myself, which is to say he would have been top-notch among any horsemen in the world—even the Cheyennes of the American plains, who are the best I know. We rode together a good deal, but I made sure we always had one of the Strackenzians or a couple of grooms along—I'm nervous about going into the woods alone with fellows whom I've cut open with a *schlager*, and who I'm pretty sure haven't forgotten it.

De Gautet, at any rate, was a silent, unassertive fellow, which was more than could be said of the bold Rudi. Now that he was confident I could play my role in perfect safety, he was treating me exactly as he would have used the real Prince Carl, which is to say with his customary impertinence. Of course, he cared for no one, and even let his bright eye play over Irma, while he would address her with that half-mocking deference which he seemed to reserve for his social superiors. She was woman enough to be taken by his good looks and easy charm, but she sensed, I think, that here was a real wrong 'un, and confessed to me on one occasion that she was sure he was not a gentleman. I promised to replace him with a new aide when we returned to the city—and took some malicious pleasure in telling him about it later, so that he should realise that one woman, at least, had read him correctly. But he was only amused.

"I knew the chit had no taste," says he. "Why, she's taken to you. But don't imagine you can get rid of me so easily, your highness—I'm your loyal, obedient, and ever-present servant until the time comes to end our little comedy." He blew a smoke-ring and eyed me, tongue in cheek. "I think you'll be sorry when it's over, won't you? Princely life suits you, or I'm mistaken."

In fact, he *was* mistaken. Oh, it was very idyllic there in Strelhow, and I was idler than even royalty usually are, but already I had a notion that the future that faced Carl Gustaf wasn't going to be all roses and wine. It may seem rare to be a crowned head, and no doubt if you're an absolute monarch with unlimited power, it's right enough—but a prince consort, which is more or less what I was, isn't quite the same thing. He can't trim the heads off those he don't like, or order up any good-looking skirt who takes his fancy. He's always one step behind his adoring spouse, and even if she dotes on him—and who knows how long that will last?—he still has to get his own way, if he wants it, *through* her good leave. Even in those blissful early days with Irma, I could see how it would be, and I didn't much like it. God knows how our late lamented Albert stuck it out, poor devil. If I'd been him, six months would have seen me on the boat back to Saxe-Coburg or wherever it was. But perhaps he didn't mind playing second fiddle—he wasn't English.

However, I consoled myself that I was having the best of both worlds—my luxurious enslavement was both enjoyable and temporary. Now and then I fretted a little over what the outcome of the comedy would be, but there was nothing to be done about it. Either Bismarck would keep his bargain or he wouldn't—and I forced myself to put the latter possibility out of my mind. This is the real coward's way, of course—I wanted to believe he would play fair, and so I did, even though common sense should have warned me that he wouldn't. And as so often happens, I almost fell a prey to my own comfortable, lily-livered hopes.

We had been about ten days at Strelhow, I suppose, when one evening we were in the billiard room, and the talk turned to horses. Someone—Rudi, I think—mentioned the fine stable kept by a gentleman over beyond the Jotun Gipfel; I expressed interest, and it was suggested that next day we should ride over and call on him. It was all very easy and casual, like any of the other expeditions and picnics we had enjoyed, and I gave it no thought at all.

So next morning de Gautet and one of the Strackenzian aides and I set off. The quickest way was through the Jotun Gipfel on horseback, and Irma came with us by carriage as far as the road allowed. Thereafter we turned off towards the crags, she fluttering her handkerchief lovingly after her departing lord, and presently we were climbing into the hills by one of the bridle-paths that are the only tracks through that wild and picturesque little region.

It was a splendid day for such a jaunt, clear and sunny, and the scenery was pleasant—any of our Victorian artists would have sketched it in a moment, with its nice little crags and trees and occasional waterfalls, and would have thrown in a couple of romantic shepherds with whiskers and fat calves for good measure. But we saw no one as we moved up towards the summit, and I was enjoying the ride and musing on last night's sporting with Irma, when the Strackenzian aide's horse went lame.

I've often wondered how they arranged that, for the horse *was* certainly lame, and I doubt if the aide—his name was Steubel, just a boy—had anything to do with it. I cursed a bit, and de Gautet suggested we turn and go back. The boy wouldn't hear of it; he would walk his horse slowly down to Strelhow, he said, and we should go on. De Gautet looked doubtful—he was a clever actor, that one—but I was fool enough to agree. I can't think, now, how I was so green, but there it was. I never thought of foul play—I, who normally throw myself behind cover if someone breaks wind unexpectedly, was completely off guard. I had my pistols, to be sure, and even my knife, for I'd got into the wise habit of going armed whenever I left the lodge; but de Gautet's manner must have disarmed me completely.

We went on together, and about twenty minutes after parting from Steubel we had reached the summit, a pleasant little tree-fringed plateau, split by a deep gorge through

187

which a river rushed, throwing up clouds of mist against the rocky sides. The whole table-top was hemmed in by trees, but there was a clear patch of turf near the edge of the gorge, and here we dismounted to have a look down into the bottom, a hundred feet below. I don't care for heights, but the scene was so pleasant and peaceful that I never felt a moment's unease, until de Gautet spoke.

"The Jotunschlucht," says he, meaning the gorge, and something in his voice sounded the alarm in my brain. It may have been the flatness of his tone, or the fact that he was closer behind me than I felt he should have been, but with the instinct of pure panic I threw myself sideways on the turf, turning as I fell to try to face him.

If his pistol hadn't misfired he would have got me; I heard the click even as I moved, and realised that he had been aiming point-blank at my back. As I tried to scramble up he dropped it with an oath, drew its mate from beneath his tunic, and levelled it at me. I screamed, "No! No!" as he thumbed back the lock, and he hesitated a split second, to see if I should leap again, and to make sure of his aim.

In a novel, of course, or a play, murders are not committed so; the villain leers and gloats, and the victim pleads. In my practical experience, however, killing gentlemen like de Gautet are far too practised for such nonsense; they shoot suddenly and cleanly, and the job's done. I knew I had perhaps a heart-beat between me and damnation, and in sheer terror I snatched the seaman's knife from the top of my boot and hurled it at him with all my force, sprawling down again as I did so.

If I've had more than my share of bad luck in my life, I've had some good to make up for it. I had some now; the knife only hit him butt first, on the leg, but it caused him to take a quick step back, his heel caught on a stone or tuft, he overbalanced, the pistol cracked, the ball went somewhere above my head, and then I was on top of him, smashing blindly with my fists, knees, and anything else, trying to beat him into the ground.

He was tall and active, but nothing like my weight, and Flashy in the grip of mortal fear, with nowhere to run to and no choice but to fight, is probably a dreadful opponent. I was roaring at the top of my voice and clawing at him for dear life; he managed to shove me off once, but he made the error of lunging for the fallen knife, and I was able to get one solid, full-blown boot against the side of his head. He groaned and fell back, his eyes rolling up in his head, and collapsed limply on the turf.

For a moment I thought I'd killed him, but I didn't wait about to see. The training of years asserted itself, and I turned and bolted headlong down the path, with no thought but to put as much distance as I could between me and the scene of possible danger. Before I'd gone far I had to stop to be sick—no doubt from the shock of my narrow escape—and during the pause I had time to consider what I was doing. Where could I run to? Not back to Strelhow, for certain; the Bismarck gang had shown their hand now, and my life wouldn't be worth a china orange if I went anywhere they could come at me. And why had they tried to kill me now? What purpose was there in having me dead·before the real Carl Gustaf was ready to take my place? Maybe he was ready—although if he'd been rotten with pox they had tidied him up mighty quick. Or had Bismarck's whole tale been pure moonshine? Maybe Carl Gustaf was dead, maybe—oh, maybe a thousand things. I had no way of knowing.

As I think I've said before, while fear usually takes control of my limbs, particularly my running equipment, it seldom prevents me from thinking clearly. Even as I stood there spewing I knew what had to be done. It was essential that I make tracks out of Strackenz at once. But reason told me that to do that in safety I must have a clear notion of what my enemies were up to, and the only man who could tell me that was de Gautet, if he was still alive. The longer I hesitated, the longer he had to revive; my pistols were in my saddle holsters at the summit, so back

189

up the track I went at full speed, pausing only near the top to have a stealthy skulk and see how the land lay.

The horses had gone, scared no doubt by the pistol shot, but de Gautet was still where I had left him. Was he shamming? It would have been like the foxy bastard, so I lay low and watched him. He didn't stir, so I tossed a stone at him. It hit him, but he didn't move. Reassured, I broke cover, snatched up the knife, and crouched panting beside him. He was dead to the world, but breathing, with a fine red lump on his skull; in a moment I had his belt off and trussed his elbows with it; then I pulled off his boots, secured his ankles with my own belt, and felt comfortably safer. Several excellent ideas were already forming in my mind about how to deal with Master de Gautet when he came to, and I waited with a pleasant sense of anticipation. He had a hole in one sock, I noticed; there would be holes in more than that before I'd finished with the murderous swine.

Presently he groaned and opened his eyes, and I had the pleasure of watching his expression show bewilderment, rage, and fear all in turn.

"Well, de Gautet," says I. "What have you got to say, you back-shooting rat, you?"

He stayed mum, glaring at me, so I tickled him up with the knife and he gasped and cursed.

"That's it," says I, "get some practice. And see here: I'm not going to waste time with you. I'm going to ask questions, and you'll answer 'em, smartly, d'you see? Because if you don't—well, I'll show you the advantages of an English public school education, that's all. Now, first, why did you try to kill me? What are you and our good friend Otto Bismarck up to?"

He struggled, but saw it was no go and lay still.

"You will learn nothing from me," says he.

"Your error," says I. "See here."

By good luck I had a piece of string with me, which I looped over two of his toes, placing a nice sharp pebble in between them. I put a stick through the loop and twisted it a little. It always used to liven the Rugby fags up, although of course one couldn't go too far with them, and de Gautet's response was gratifying. He squealed and writhed, but I held his legs down easily.

"You see, my boy," says I, "You'd better open your potato trap or it'll be the worse for you."

"You villain!" cries he, sweating with fear. "Is this how you treat a gentleman?"

"No," says I, enjoying myself. "It's how I treat a dirty, cowardly, murdering ruffian." And I twisted the stick, hard. He screamed, but I kept on twisting, and his yells were such that I had to stuff my glove in his mouth to quiet him. I'd no real fear of interruption, for he had been at such pains to get me alone that I doubted if any of his precious friends were in the district, but it seemed best to keep him as mum as possible.

"Nod your head when you've had enough, de Gautet," says I cheerfully. "When I've broken all your toes I'll show you how the Afghan ladies treat their husbands' prisoners."

And I went back to work on him. I confess that I thoroughly enjoyed it, as only a true coward can, for only your coward and bully really understand how terrible pain can be. De Gautet wasn't much braver than I am; a few more twists and he was jerking his head up and down like Punch, and for some reason this put me into a great fury. I gave him a few more twists for luck, until the string broke. Then I pulled the gag out.

He was groaning and calling me filthy names, so I taught him manners with the point of the knife in his leg.

"Now, you bastard, why did you try to kill me?"

"It was the Baron's order. Ah, dear God!"

"Never mind God. What for? What about my ten thousand pounds, damn you?"

"It . . . it was never intended that you would be paid."

191

"You mean I was to be murdered from the start, is that it?"

He rolled over, moaning and licking his lips, looking at me with terror in his eyes.

"If I tell you . . . all . . . oh, my feet! If I tell you . . . do you swear, on your honour as a gentleman, to let me go?"

"Why should I? You'll tell me anyway. Oh, all right then, on my honour as a gentleman. Now, then."

But he insisted that I swear on my mother's memory, too—what he thought all that swearing was worth I can't imagine, but he wasn't feeling himself, I dare say, and foreigners tend to take an Englishman's word when he gives it. That's all they know.

So I swore his oaths, and it all came tumbling out. The Prince Carl Gustaf hadn't had pox at all; he was clean as an old bone. But Bismarck had plotted with Detchard to spirit him away and put me in his place—as they had indeed done. The pox story had simply been an excuse for my benefit, and if it seems ludicrously thin now I can only assert that it seemed damned convincing coming from Bismarck in his lonely stronghold with Kraftstein waiting to fillet me if I didn't believe it. Anyway, their little plan was that after a few days, when Strackenz was convinced it had got a genuine consort for its Duchess, I was to be murdered, in the Jotun Gipfel, and de Gautet was to vanish over the German border. There would be a hue and cry, and my body would be found and carried back to Strackenz amid general consternation.

And then, wonder of wonders, papers would be found in my clothing to suggest that I wasn't Prince Carl at all, but a daring English impostor called Flashman, an agent of Lord Palmerston, if you please, and up to God-knows-what mischief against the security and well-being of the Duchy of Strackenz. There would be chaos and confusion, and a diplomatic upheaval of unprecedented proportions.

I couldn't take it in at first. "You bloody liar! D'ye

expect me to believe this cock-and-bull? For that matter, who in the world would credit it?"

"Everyone." His face was working with pain. "You are *not* the Prince—you would be identified for what you really are—even if it took time, witnesses who knew you could be brought. Who would doubt it?—it is true."

My brain was reeling. "But, in God's name, what for? What could Bismarck gain from all this?"

"The discredit of England—your Lord Palmerston. Utter bewilderment and rage, in Strackenz. Dane and German are on a knife-edge here—there would be blood-shed and disorder. That is what the Baron wants—ah, Herr Gott, my feet are on fire!"

"Damn your feet! Why the hell does he want bloodshed and disorder?"

"As a—pretext. You know that Strackenz and Schleswig and Holstein are bitterly divided between Dane and German. Disorder in one would spread to the others—the old rivalry between Berlin and Copenhagen would be fanned into flame—for the sake of German interest, Berlin would march into Strackenz, then into the other two. Who could stop her? It is only the—excuse—that is lacking."

"And how would my murder be explained, in God's name?"

"It would not need—explaining. That you were an English agent—that would be enough."

Well, that seemed the silliest bit of all, to me, and I said so—who was going to buy me as an agent?

"Feel the lining of your tunic—on the right side." For all his pain, he couldn't keep a grin of triumph off his face. "It is there—feel."

By God, it was. I ripped out the lining with my knife, and there was a paper, covered in tiny cryptograms—God knows what they meant, but knowing Bismarck I'll wager it was good, sound, incriminating stuff. I sat gazing at it, trying to understand what de Gautet had been telling me.

"It has all been exactly planned," says he. "It could not fail. Confusion and riot must follow on your death—and Germany would seize the opportunity to march."

I was trying vainly to make sense of the whole, incredible scheme—and to find a flaw in it.

"Aha, hold on," says I. "This is all very fine—but just because Bismarck has fine ideas about marching into Strackenz don't mean a thing. There's a government in Berlin, I believe—suppose they don't share his martial ardour—what then?"

"But it is planned, I tell you," cries he. "He has friends —men of power—in high places. It is concerted—and when the chance comes in Strackenz, they will act as he says. He can force the thing—he has the vision—*das genie*."

Aye, perhaps he had the genius. Now, of course, I know that he could have done it—I doubt if there was any diplomatic coup that that brilliant, warped intelligence couldn't have brought off; for all that he was the most dreadful bastard who ever sat in a chancellery, he was the greatest statesman of our time. Yes, he could have done it—he did, didn't he, in the end, and where is Strackenz now? Like Schleswig and Holstein, it is buried in the German empire that Otto Bismarck built.

It was just my bad luck that I had been cast—through the sheer chance of an uncanny resemblance—to be the first foundation-stone of his great dream. This was to be his initial step to power, the opening move in his great game to unify Germany and make it first of the world's states. Squatting there, on the damp turf of the Jotun Gipfel, I saw that the crazy scheme in which he had involved me had a flawless logic of its own—all he needed was something to strike a spark in Strackenz, and I was the tinder. Thereafter, with him gently guiding from the wings, the tragic farce could run its course.

De Gautet groaned, and brought me back to earth. He was lying there, this foul brute who would have put a bullet in my back—aye, and had already planted his sabre cuts in my skull. In a rage I kicked him—this was the pass that he and his damned friends had brought me to, I shouted, stranded in the middle of their blasted country, incriminated, helpless, certain to be either murdered by Bismarck's crew or hanged by the authorities. He roared and pleaded with me to stop.

"Aye, you can howl now," says I. "You were ready enough an hour ago to show me no mercy, curse you!" A thought struck me. "I don't suppose you showed any to that poor Danish sod, either. Where's Carl Gustaf, then? Lying somewhere with his throat cut and a letter in his pocket saying: 'A present from Flashy and Lord Palmerston'?"

"No, no—he is alive—I swear it! He is being kept—safe."

"What for? What use is he to bloody Bismarck?"

"He was not to be—nothing was to befall him—until—until . . ."

"Until I'd had my weasand slit? That's it, isn't it? You dirty dogs, you! Where is he then, if he's still alive?"

At first he wouldn't say, but when I flourished the knife at him he changed his mind.

"In Jotunberg—the old castle of the Duke. Yonder, over the crags—in the Jotunsee. I swear it is true. He is under guard there—he knows nothing. The Baron leaves nothing to chance—if aught had gone wrong, he might have been needed—alive."

"You callous hound! And otherwise—he would have got a bullet, too, eh?"

I had to give him some more toe-leather before he would answer, but when he did it was in some detail. To ensure that no mischance should lead to his being rescued, Carl Gustaf was in a dungeon in the castle, with a handy shaft in its floor that came out somewhere under the Jotunsee. His body would never be found once they popped him down there—which they would certainly do once they heard that my corpse had been delivered back to

195

Strackenz, and the uproar over my identity was going nicely. Well, it looked bad for Carl Gustaf in any event—not that it was any concern of mine, but it helped to fan my righteous indignation, which was powerful enough on my own behalf, I can tell you.

"De Gautet," says I. "You're a foul creature—you don't deserve to live another minute—"

"You swore!" He babbled, struggling in his bonds. "You gave me your solemn promise!"

"So I did," says I. "To let you go, wasn't it? Well, I will. Come along, let's have you up."

I dragged him to his feet, and took my belt from round his ankles. He could hardly stand with the pain of his toes, and I had to support him.

"Now, de Gautet," says I. "I'm going to let you go—but where, eh? That's the point, ain't it?"

"What do you mean?" His eyes were staring with fear. "You promised!"

"So did Bismarck—so did you. You're a dirty creature, de Gautet; I think you need a wash." I propelled him to the edge of the precipice, and held him for a second. "I'll let you go, all right, you murderous cur—down there."

He let out a shriek you could have heard in Munich, and tried to wrench free, but I held him fast and let him look, just to let him know he was really going to die. Then I said: "Gehen sie weg, de Gautet," and gave him a push.

For an instant he tottered on the brink, trying to keep his balance, and screaming hoarsely; then he fell out and down, and I watched him turn slowly over in the air, crash onto the jutting rocks half-way down the cliff, and spin outwards, like a rag-doll with his legs waving, before he vanished into the spray at the precipice foot.

It was an interesting sight. I'd killed before, of course, although never in what you might call cold blood, but I've never felt anything but satisfaction over the end of de Gautet. He deserved to die, if anyone ever did. He was a heartless, cruel rascal, and I'd have been lucky to come off as easily if things had been the other way round. I'm not justifying myself, either for torturing him or killing him, for I don't need to. Both had to be done—but I'm honest enough to admit I enjoyed doing them. He was a good horseman, though.

However, his death, though first-rate in its way, solved nothing so far as my immediate comfort and safety were concerned. I was still in the very devil of a pickle, I realised, as I gazed round the empty clearing and tried to decide what to do next. It was certain that de Gautet had arranged some means of getting word quickly to Rudi and Co. to say that Flashy was a goner and all was well. How long would it be before they realised something had gone wrong? An hour or two? A day? I must assume it would be sooner rather than later—and then the hunt would be up with a vengeance, with me as the poor little fox. I had to get out of Strackenz at once—but where to?

These thoughts put me into a blue funk, of course, and I paced up and down that summit muttering "Where? where? Oh, Jesus, how can I get out of this?" Then I steadied up, telling myself that when you've been hounded by Afghans and come safe home, you need hardly take the vapours over a pack of Germans. Which is just rubbish, of course, as I assured myself a second later; one's as beastly dangerous as the other. Still, this was a comparatively civilised country, I spoke the language tolerably, and I'd had enough experience of skulking, surely, to get me out of it. I hadn't a horse, and only a knife for protection—de Gautet's empty pistols were useless—but the first thing was to get down from the Jotun Gipfel, and plot my course as I went.

Before starting out, I burned the incriminating papers they had sewn in my tunic. Then I took to the woods at right angles from the path we had been following, scrambling down over mossy rocks and through thick brushwood; it wasn't easy going, but I was too busy with my thoughts to notice much. One point stuck clear in my mind, and it was the advice given by the late lamented Sergeant Hudson when he and I were on the run from the Afridis on the Jallalabad road: "When the bastards are after you, go in the direction where they'll never think o' looking for you—even if it's right back in their faces."

Well, I wasn't going to Strelhow, that was flat. But if I was Bismarck or Rudi, where would I expect Flashy to run? North, for certain, towards the coast, less than a hundred miles away. So that was out of court. Of the other directions, which was the *least* likely for a fugitive? All were hazardous, since they would take me long journeys through Germany, but south seemed the most dangerous of all. By God, the last place they would expect me to make for was Munich, at the far end of the country, where all the bother had begun.

My legs trembled at the thought, but the more I considered it the better it seemed. They'd never believe I'd risk it, so they wouldn't look thereaway. It was horribly chancy, but I was certain that if Hudson had been with me that was the way he'd have pointed. Let me get a horse—no matter how—and I could be over the Strackenz border by nightfall and galloping south. I'd have to beg, hire, borrow, or steal, changes on the way—well, it wouldn't be the first time. I might even use the railway, if it seemed safe to do so. At any rate I was free, for the moment, and if they could catch old Flashy with the wind up him—well, they were smarter fellows than I thought they were.

I hurried on down the hillside, and found myself after half an hour or so on more level land, where the trees thinned out. There was a wisp of smoke coming from behind a copse, and I stole forward cautiously to have a look-see. There was a little farm-building with great trees behind it, but no one about except a few cows in the field to one side and an old dog drowsing in the yard. It didn't look like the kind of place where the new ducal consort of Strackenz would be known, which suited me—the fewer folk who got a glimpse of me, the less chance Bismarck's bullies had of getting on my track.

I was wondering whether to go forward boldly, or scout round for a horse to pinch, when the farm door opened and an old man in gaiters and a sugar-loaf hat came out. He was a peasant, with a face like a walnut, and when he saw me he brought up short and stood glowering at me, the way country folk do at everyone who hasn't got dung on his boots. I gave him a civil good day, and told him my horse had thrown me while I was riding in the Jotun Gipfel; could he oblige me with a remount, for which I would pay generously? And I showed him a handful of crowns.

He mumbled a bit, watching me with the wary, hostile eyes of the old, and then said that his daughter was in the house. She turned out to be a big, strapping creature, plain enough in the face, but just about my weight, so I gave her my best bow and repeated my request with a charming smile. The long and short of it was that they sat me down in the kitchen with some excellent beer and bread and cheese while the old man went off round the house, and presently came back to say that Franz had gone to find Willi, who would be able to borrow Wolf's horse, no doubt, and if the gentleman would be pleased to rest and eat, it would be along in a little while.

I was happy enough with this, for neither of them seemed to have any notion of who I was—or rather, who I was supposed to be—and it gave me the chance to get something under my belt. They were both a little in awe, though, at having such a fine gentleman in their humble home, and seemed too tongue-tied to say much. If the dotard hadn't been there I dare say I could have had the buxom piece dancing the mattress quadrille within the hour, but as it was I had to confine my refreshment to the victuals and beer.

After an hour had passed, though, I began to get restless. I'd no wish to linger here, with Rudi possibly combing the Jotun Gipfel for me already, and when a second hour passed, and then a third, I became feverish. The old clod kept assuring me, in answer to my impatient demands, that Wolf or Franz or Willi would soon be along, with the horse. An excellent horse, he added. And there seemed to be nothing to do but wait, chewing my nails, while the old man sat silent, and the woman went very soft-footed about her work.

It was four hours before they came, and they didn't have a horse. What they did have, though, was weapons. There were four of them, hefty lads in peasant clothes, but with a purposeful look about them that suggested they didn't give all their time to ploughing. Two had muskets, another had a pistol in his belt, and the leader, who was a blond giant at least a head taller than I, had a broadsword, no less, hanging at his side. I was on my feet, quaking, at the sight of them, but the big fellow held up a hand and made me a jerky bow.

"Highness," says he, and the others bobbed their heads behind him. My bald head was evidently better known than I'd realised. Uneasily, I tried to put on a bold front.

"Well, my lads," says I cheerfully, "have you a horse for me?"

"No highness," says the big one. "But if you will please to come with us, my master will attend to all your needs."

I didn't like the sound of this, somehow.

"Who is your master, then?"

"If you please, highness, I am to ask you only to come with us. Please, highness."

He was civil enough, but I didn't like it.

"I want a horse, my good fellow, not to see your master. You know who I am, it seems. Well, bring me a horse directly."

"Please, highness," he repeated stolidly. "You will come with us. My master commands."

At this I became very princely and peremptory, but it didn't do a straw's worth of good. He just stood there insisting, and my bowels went more chilly every moment. I hectored and stormed and threatened, but in the end there was nothing for it. I went with them, leaving the farm couple round-eyed behind us.

To my consternation they led me straight back towards the Jotun Gipfel, but although I protested they held their course, the big fellow turning every now and then to mutter apologies, while his pals kept their muskets handy and their eyes carefully on me. I was beside myself with fright and anger; who the devil were they, I demanded, and where was I being taken? But not a word of sense was to be had from them, and the only consolation I could take was a vague feeling that whoever they were, they weren't Rudi's creatures, and didn't seem to mean me any harm—as yet.

How far we tramped I don't know, but it must have taken fully two hours. I wouldn't have believed the Jotun Gipfel was so extensive, or so dense, but we seemed to be moving into deeper forest all the time, along the foot of the crags. The sun was westering, so far as I could judge, when I saw people ahead, and then we were in a little clearing with perhaps a dozen fellows waiting for us; stalwart peasants like my four guards, and all of them armed.

There was a little cabin half-hidden among the bushes at the foot of a small cliff that ran up into the overhanging forest, and before the cabin stood two men. One was a tall, slender, serious-looking chap dressed like a quality lawyer, and grotesquely out of place here; the other was burly and short, in a corduroy suit and leggings, the picture of a country squire or retired military man. He had grizzled, close-cropped hair, a bulldog face, and a black patch over one eye. He was smoking a pipe.

They stood staring at me, and then the tall one turned and said urgently to his companion: "He is wrong. I am sure he is wrong."

The other knocked out his pipe on his hand. "Perhaps," says he. "Perhaps not." He took a step towards me. "May I ask you, sir, what is your name?"

There was only one answer to that. I took a deep breath, looked down my nose, and said:

"I think you know it very well. I am Prince Carl Gustaf. And I think I may be entitled to ask, gentlemen, who you may be, and what is the explanation of this outrage?"

For a man with his heart in his mouth, I think I played it well. At any rate, the tall one said excitedly:

"You see! It could not be otherwise. Highness, may I . . ."

"Save your apologies, doctor," says the short one. "They may be in order, or they may not." To me he went on: "Sir, we find ourselves in a quandary. I hear you say who you are; well, my name is Sapten, and this is Dr Per Grundvig, of Strackenz. Now, may I ask what brings you to Jotun Gipfel, with your coat muddied and your breeches torn?"

"You ask a good deal, sir!" says I hotly. "Must I remind you who I am, and that your questions are an impertinence? I shall . . ."

"Aye, it sounds like the real thing," says Sapten, smiling a grim little smile. "Well, we'll see." He turned his head. "Hansen! Step this way, if you please!"

And out of the hut, before my horrified gaze, stepped the young man who had greeted me at the wedding reception—Erik Hansen, Carl Gustaf's boyhood friend. I felt my senses start to swim with sick terror; he had sensed something wrong then—he couldn't fail to unmask me now. I watched him through a haze as he walked steadily up to me and gazed intently at my face.

"Prince Carl?" he said at last. "Carl? Is it you? Is it really you?"

I forced myself to try to smile. "Erik!" God, what a croak it was. "Why, Erik, what brings you here?"

He stepped back, his face white, his hands trembling. He looked from Sapten to the doctor, shaking his head. "Gentlemen, I don't know . . . it's he . . . and yet . . . I don't know . . ."

202

"Try him in Danish," says Sapten, his single grey eye fixed on me.

I knew then I was done for. Bersonin's efforts had been insufficient to give me more than the crudest grasp of one of the hardest tongues in Europe. It must have shown in my face as Erik turned back to me, for the damned old villain Sapten added:

"Ask him something difficult."

Erik thought a moment, and then, with an almost pleading look in his eyes, spoke in the soft, slipshod mutter that had baffled my ear at Schönhausen. I caught the words "Hvor boede" and hardly anything else. Christ, he wanted to know where somebody lived, God knows who. Desperately I said:

"Jeg forstar ikke" to show that I didn't understand, and it sounded so hellish flat I could have burst into tears. Slowly an ugly look came over his fair young face.

"Ny," he said slowly. "De forstar my ikke." He turned to them, and said in a voice that shook: "He may be the devil himself. It is the Prince's face and body. But it is not Carl Gustaf—my life on it!"

There wasn't a sound in the clearing, except for my own croaking breaths. Then Sapten put his pipe in his pocket.

"So," says he. "Right, my lad, into that hut with you, and if you make a wrong move, you're with your Maker. Jacob," he shouted. "Sling a noose over the branch yonder."

Cowards, as Shakespeare has wisely observed, die many times before their deaths, but not many of them can have expired in spirit more often than I. And I've seldom had better reason than when Sapten threw that order to his followers; there was an air of grim purpose about the man that told you he would do exactly what he promised, and that offhand instruction was more terrible than any mere threat could have been. I stumbled into the hut and collapsed on a bench, and the three followed me and closed the door.

"Now," says Sapten, folding his arms, "who are you?"

There was no question of brazening it out, any more than there was hope of making a run for it. My only chance lay in talking my way out of the noose—not that the three grim faces offered any encouragement. But anyway, here goes, thought I, reminding myself that there's no lie ever invented that's as convincing as half-truth.

"Gentlemen," I began, "believe me, I can explain this whole fearful business. You're quite right; I am not Prince Carl Gustaf. But I most solemnly assure you that these past few days I have had no choice but to pretend that I was that man. No choice—and I believe when you have heard me out you will agree that the true victim of this abominable hoax is my unhappy self."

"Like enough," says Sapten, "since you'll certainly hang for it."

"No, no!" I protested. "You must hear me out. I can prove what I say. I was forced to it—dreadfully forced, but you must believe me innocent."

"Where is the Prince?" burst out Hansen. "Tell us that, you liar!"

I ignored this, for a good reason. "My name is Arnold—

Captain Thomas Arnold. I'm a British Army officer"—and my idiot tongue nearly added "of no fixed abode"—"and I have been kidnapped and tricked into this by enemies of Strackenz."

That threw them into a talking; both Grundvig and Hansen started volleying questions at me, but Sapten cut them off.

"British Army, eh?" says he. "How many regiments of foot guards have you?—quick, now."

"Why, three."

"Humph," says he. "Go on."

"Well," says I. "It's an incredible tale . . . you won't believe it . . ."

"Probably not," says Sapten, whom I was liking less and less. "Get to the point."

So I told it them, from the beginning, sticking as close as I could to the truth. My brain was working desperately as I talked, for the tale wouldn't do entirely as it stood. I left Lola Montez out of it, and invented a wife and child for myself who had accompanied me to Germany—I was going to need them. I described my abduction in Munich, without reference to Baroness Pechman, and related the Schönhausen episode exactly as it had happened.

"Otto Bismarck, eh?" says Sapten. "I've heard of him. And young Starnberg—aye, we know of that one."

"This is unbelievable," exclaims Grundvig. "The man is plainly lying in everything he says. Why, who could . . ."

"Easy, doctor," says Sapten. "Unbelievable—yes." He pointed at me. "*He's* unbelievable, too—but he's sitting here in front of us." He nodded to me. "Continue."

Thank God there was at least one cool head among them. I went on, relating how I came to Strackenz, how I had gone through the farce in the Cathedral, how de Gautet had tried to murder me, and how I had killed him in fair fight at the top of the Jotun Gipfel that morning. Sapten's icy eye

205

never left my face, but Grundvig kept giving exclamations of incredulity and horror, and finally Hansen could contain himself no longer.

"*Why* did you do it? My God, you villain, *why*? Have you no shame, no honour? How could you live, and commit such a monstrous crime?"

I looked him full in the face, like a man struggling with tremendous emotion. (I was, and it was funk, but I tried to look as though I was bursting with wrought-up indignation and distress.)

"Why, sir?" says I. "You ask 'why'. Do you suppose I would have consented to this infamy—have played this awful masquerade—unless they had compelled me with a weapon that no man, however honourable, could resist?" I gave a mighty gulp. "They held my wife and child, sir. Do you realise what that means?" I shouted the question at him, and decided that this was the time to break down. "My God, my God!" I exclaimed. "My precious jewels! My little golden-headed Amelia! Shall I ever see thee again?"

It would have had them thumping on the seat-backs in any theatre in London, I'll swear, but when I raised my head from my hands there was no sign of frantic applause from this audience. Hansen looked bewildered and Grundvig's long face was working with rage; Sapten was filling his pipe.

"And Prince Carl Gustaf—where's he?" he asked.

I had thought, at the beginning, that eventually I might bargain with them—my life for the information—but now instinct told me that it wouldn't answer. Sapten would have hanged me on the spot, I'm sure—anyway, it wouldn't have suited the character I was trying desperately to establish. In that, I saw, lay my only hope—to make them believe that I had been a helpless victim of a dastardly plot. And God help me, wasn't it true?

So I told them about Jotunberg, and the plans for disposing of Carl Gustaf. Grundvig clasped his temples,

Hansen exclaimed in horror, Sapten lit his pipe and puffed in silence.

"Aye," says he, "and then what? This fellow tried to murder you—you killed him, you say. What did you propose to do next?"

"Why—why—I hardly knew. I was distraught—my wife and child—the fate of the prince—I was half-mad with anxiety."

"To be sure," says he, and puffed some more. "And this was all played out, you tell us, so that this Otto Bismarck could start to build a German Empire? Well, well."

"You've heard what I've told you, sir," says I. "I warned you it was incredible, but it's true—every word of it."

Grundvig, who had been pacing up and down, spun on his heel.

"I for one cannot believe it! It is impossible! Major, Erik! Would anyone but a madman credit such a story? It is not to be imagined!" He glared at me. "This man—this scoundrel—can you believe anyone as infamous as he has confessed himself to be?"

"Not I, for one," says Hansen.

Sapten scratched his grizzled head. "Just so," says he, and my heart sank. "But I suggest, doctor, and you too, Erik, that there's a question to be asked. Can either of you—" and his bright eye went from one to the other—"looking at this fellow here, a man who we know has successfully imposed himself for two weeks on a whole nation—can either of you, in the face of the fact, suggest a better story than he's told us?"

They stared at him. He nodded at me.

"There he is. Account for him." He knocked out his pipe. "If he has lied—then what's the true explanation?"

They babbled a good deal at this, but of course there was no answering him. My story was enough to defy imagination, Sapten agreed—but any alternative must be equally incredible.

"If we can accept that a *doppelgänger* of the Prince's

can take his place for two weeks—and we know that has happened—then I for one can accept anything," says he.

"You mean you believe him?" cries Grundvig.

"For want of evidence to disprove his story—yes." My heart fluttered up like a maiden's prayer, "You see," says Sapten grimly, "it fits. Haven't we been starting at every German shadow this twenty years back? You know that, Grundvig. Isn't fear for the security of our duchy the reason we're here? What are we Sons of the Volsungs for?" He shook his head. "Show me a hole in this fellow's tale, for I can't see one."

At this they went into a frantic discussion, which of course got them nowhere. Baffled, they turned back on me.

"What are we to do with him?" says Grundvig.

"Hang him," snaps Hansen. "The swine deserves it."

"For the crime he has committed against our duchess," says Grundvig, glowering at me, "he deserves no less."

They were all looking like Scotch elders in a brothel, but I saw that here was my cue again. I looked bewildered, and then let outraged indignation take its place.

"What do you mean by that?" I cried.

"You were married to her for more than a week," says Sapten significantly.

I made hoarse noises of fury. "You infamous old man!" I shouted. "D'you dare to suggest? . . . My God, sir, have you forgotten that I am a British officer? Have you the effrontery to imply that I would . . ."

I choked as with great rage, but I doubt if Sapten was much impressed. The other two looked doubtful, though.

"I am not so dead to honour," says I, trying to look noble and angry together, "that I would stoop to carry my imposture as far as that. There are some things that no gentleman . . ." And I broke off as though it was too much for me.

"It must have been thought strange," mutters Grundvig. Palpitating, I maintained a stiff silence.

They were quiet for a moment, contemplating their duchess's virginity, I suppose. Then Grundvig said:

"Do you swear . . . that . . . that . . ."

"My word of honour," says I, "as a British officer."

"Oh, well, that settles it," says Sapten, and I'll swear his mouth twitched under his moustache. "And at the risk of seeming disloyal, gentlemen, I'd suggest that the fate of Prince Carl Gustaf is perhaps as important as what may or mayn't have happened to . . . well, let it be." He swung round on me. "You'll stay here. If you move outside this hut you're a dead man—which you may be, anyway, before we're done. I suggest we continue our deliberations elsewhere, doctor. If what we have learned today is true, we haven't much time to prevent our duchess becoming a widow before she's been a bride. To say nothing of saving her duchy for her. Come."

The door slammed behind them, and I was left alone with my thoughts. Not pleasant ones, but they could have been worse. They seemed to have accepted my story, and I was pretty sure that the fictitious parts of it would defy their efforts to pick holes—they weren't important lies, anyway, but merely colour to enhance my character of innocent-in-the-grip-of-cruel-fate. Best of all, I was reasonably sure they weren't going to hang me. Sapten was the strong mind among them, and while I read him as one who wouldn't think twice about taking human life if he had to, there didn't seem any good reason why they should do away with me. He was a realist, and not swayed by emotion like Grundvig and Hansen. But Grundvig, too, I believed would stop short of murder—he seemed a decent, sensitive sort of fool. Hansen was the one I offended most, probably because he was the Prince's close friend. He would have slaughtered me for old time's sake, so to speak, but I fancied he would be out-voted.

So there I was, with nothing to do but wait and think. At least I was safe from Bismarck's bravos, which was something. If these were the Sons of the Volsungs—the clandestine Danish sympathisers whom Rudi had spoken of with contempt—I couldn't be in better hands, from that point of view. Rudi, it seemed to me, had under-estimated them; I had no idea what they could do about rescuing their precious prince from Jotunberg, and didn't care either, but they looked a lively and workmanlike lot. It was pleasant to think that they might put a spoke in bloody Otto's little wheel, after all—Sapten was just the man for that, if I knew anything. He was steady, and saw quickly to the heart of things, and seemed to be full of all the best virtues, like resolution and courage and what-not, without being over-hampered by scruple. Given him on the retreat from Kabul our army would have got home safe enough, and probably brought all the loot of the Bala Hissar into the bargain.

Anyway, I wasn't too displeased with my own situation, and passed the time wondering when they would let me go. God knows why I was so optimistic—reaction, possibly, after having escaped unpleasant death twice in one day—but I ought to have known better. If I had been thinking clearly I'd have realised that from their point of view, the safest place for me was six feet under, where I couldn't cause any scandal. As it was, what they got me into was very nearly as bad, and caused me to die several more of Shakespeare's deaths.

I was left alone for several hours, during which time the only soul I saw was the big peasant, who brought me some food and beer (still addressing me as "highness", but in a rather puzzled way). It was night before my three inquisitors returned, and I noticed that both Sapten and Hansen were splashed with mud about the legs, as though they'd ridden hard. Sapten set down a lamp on the table, threw aside his cloak, and eyed me grimly.

"Captain Arnold," says he, "if that is your name, you puzzle me. I don't like being puzzled. As these gentlemen here have pointed out, no sane man would believe your story for a moment. Well, maybe I'm not sane, but I've decided to believe it—most of it anyway. I don't know whether you're the biggest knave or the unluckiest wretch who ever drew breath—I incline to the first view, personally, having a nice nose for knavery—no, don't bother to protest, we've heard all that. But I can't be sure, you see, and it suits me to assume that you're honest—up to a point. So there."

I kept quiet, fearful and hopeful together. He produced his pipe and began to rub tobacco.

"Fortunately, we can test you and serve our own ends at the same time," he went on. "Now then,"—he fixed me with that cold eye—"here's the point. Victim or scoundrel, whichever you may be, you've committed a monstrous wrong. Are you prepared to help to set it right?"

With those three grim faces on me in the lamplight, I was in no doubt about the right answer here—no doubt at all.

"Gentlemen," says I, "God bless you. Whatever I can do"—and I couldn't think, thank God, that there was much—"that I shall do, with all the power at my command. I have been thinking, as I sat here, of the terrible—"

"Aye, we know," Sapten cut in. "You needn't tell us." He lit his pipe, pup-pup-pup, and blew smoke. "All we want is yes or no, and I take it the answer's yes."

"With all my heart," I cried earnestly.

"I doubt it," says Sapten, "but never mind. You're a soldier, you say. Tell me—have you seen much service?"

Well, I could answer truthfully to that—I had seen plenty, and I didn't see any need to tell him that I'd been sweating with panic all through it. Like a fool, I implied that I'd been in some pretty sharp stuff, and come out with (in all manly modesty) some distinction. The words were out before I realised that I might be talking myself into more trouble.

"So," says he, "well enough—you've the look of a man of your hands. We may have cause to be glad of that. Now then, here's the position. You tell us that Prince Carl Gustaf is in Jotunberg under guard of Bismarck's men, and that they can do away with him—and leave no evidence—at the first sign of alarm. They'll weight his body, shove it down this hell-hole of theirs—and good-bye." I noticed Grundvig shudder. "So if we were to storm the place—and it wouldn't be easy—all that we would find would be a party of gentlemen who no doubt would have an innocent tale of being the guests of Adolf Bülow, the owner—he's tactfully out of the country, by the way. And we'd have lost Prince Carl. The Jotunsee is deep, and we'd never even find his body."

Hansen gave a little gasp, and I saw there were absolute tears on his cheek.

"So that won't do," says Sapten, puffing away. "Now—suppose we leave Jotunberg alone. Suppose we return you to Strelhow, and wait and see what our German friends in the castle do then. It would gain us time."

By God, I didn't like this. De Gautet might have failed with me, but some one else would surely succeed—the last place I wanted to be was anywhere on public view in Strackenz.

"They would hardly murder the prince," says Grundvig, "while you were on the consort's throne. At least, they have not done it yet."

"It offers us time," repeated Sapten slowly, "but what could we do with it, eh?"

I tried to think of something—anything.

"Perhaps if I were to abdicate," I suggested hurriedly. "I mean . . . if it would help . . ."

"Waiting increases the risks, though," went on Sapten, as though I hadn't spoken. "Of your discovery; of the Prince's murder."

"We cannot leave him there, with those villains!" burst out Hansen.

"No, so we've rejected that," says Sapten. "And we come back to the only course—a desperate and dangerous one, for it may cost his life in the end. But nothing else remains."

He paused, and I felt my spine dissolve. Oh, Jesus, here it was again—whenever I hear the words "desperate and dangerous" I know that I'm for it. I could only wait to hear the worst.

"To storm Jotunberg is impossible," says Sapten. "It stands in the lake of the Jotunsee, and only at one point is it accessible from the shore, where a causeway runs out towards it. There were two guards on the causeway tonight, at the outer end, where the gap between causeway and castle is spanned by a drawbridge. That bridge is raised, which is a sign that those within know that their plans have gone astray. Doubtless when the man you killed this morning failed to return to his friends, they took alarm. Two of them, at any rate, rode into the castle tonight—Hansen and I saw them; a youngster, a gay spark, for all he looked little more than a boy, and a big ruffian along with him—"

"Starnberg and Kraftstein," says I. "Major Sapten, they are a devilish pair—they'll stop at nothing!"

"Well, how many more were already in the castle, we don't know. Probably no more than a handful. But we could never hope to surprise them. So we must find another way, and quickly." He sat back. "Erik, it is your scheme. Let him hear it."

One look at Hansen's face—his eyes were glittering like a fanatic's—prepared me for the worst.

"Where a storming party must fail, we may prevail by stealth. Two brave men could cross the Jotunsee at night from the opposite bank, by boat as close as they dared, and then by swimming. Part of the fortress is in ruin; they could land in the darkness, enter the castle silently, and discover where the prince is hidden. Then, while one guarded him, the other would hasten to the drawbridge and lower it so that our people, hidden on the shore, could storm across the causeway. They could

213

easily overpower its garrison—but somehow the prince's life would have to be preserved while the fighting lasted. Whether this could be done—" he shrugged. "At least the two who had entered first could die trying."

And the very fact that they were telling me this informed me who one of those two was going to be. Of all the lunatic, no-hope schemes I ever heard, this seemed to be the primest yet. If they thought they were going to get me swimming into that place in the dark, with the likes of Rudi and Kraftstein waiting for me, they didn't know their man. The mere thought was enough to set my guts rumbling with fright. I'd see them damned first. I'd sooner be—swinging at the end of Sapten's rope? That was what would happen, of course, if I refused.

While I was gulping down these happy thoughts, Grundvig—whom I'd known from the first was a clever chap—sensibly suggested that where two men could swim, so could a dozen, but Hansen shook his fat head with determination.

"No. Two may pass unobserved, but not more. It is out of the question." He turned to look at me, his face set, his eyes expressionless. "I shall be one of the two—Carl Gustaf is my friend, and if he is to die I shall count myself happy to die with him. You do not know him—yet without you, he would not be where he is. Of all people, you at least owe him a life. Will you come with me?"

Whatever I may be, I'm not slow-witted. If ever there was a situation made for frantic pleading in the name of common sense, I was in it now—I could have suggested that they try to bargain with Rudi, or send a messenger to Bismarck (wherever he was) and tell him that they were on to his games; I could have gone into a faint, or told them that I couldn't swim, or that I got hay fever if I went out after dark—I could simply have roared for mercy. But I knew it wouldn't do; they were deadly serious, frightened men—frightened for that Danish idiot, instead of for themselves, as any sane man would have

214

been—and if I hesitated, or argued, or did anything but accept at once they would rule me out immediately for a coward and a hypocrite and a backslider. And then it would be the Newgate hornpipe for Flashy, with the whole damned crew of Sons of the Volsungs hauling on the rope. I knew all this in the few seconds that I sat there with my bowels melting, and I heard a voice say in a deadly croak:

"Yes, I'll come."

Hansen nodded slowly. "I do not pretend that I take you from choice; I would sooner take the meanest peasant in our band. But you are a soldier, you are skilled in arms and in this kind of work." (Dear lad, I thought, how little you know.) "You are a man of resource, or you could never have done the infamous thing that has brought you here. Perhaps there is a queer fate at work in that. At all events, you are the man for this."

I could have discussed that with some eloquence, but I knew better. I said nothing, and Hansen said: "It will be for tomorrow night, then," and he and Grundvig got up and went without another word.

Sapten lingered, putting on his cloak, watching me. At last he spoke.

"It is one of the lessons a man learns as he grows old," says he, "to put away desires and emotions—aye, and even honour—and to do what must be done with the tools to hand, whatever they may be. So I let you go with Hansen tomorrow. Succeed in what is to do, for as God's my witness, if you don't I'll kill you without pity." He turned to the door. "Perhaps I misjudge you; I don't know. In case I am guilty of that, I promise that whatever befalls, I shall not rest until I have ensured the safety of that wife and daughter who so concerned you earlier today, but whom you seem to have forgotten tonight. Take comfort from the knowledge that little golden-haired Amelia is in my thoughts." He opened the door. "Goodnight, Englishman."

And he went out, no doubt very pleased with himself.

I spent the next hour frantically trying to dig under the wall of the cabin with my bare hands, but it was no go. The earth was too hard, and full of roots and stones; I made a pitifully small scrape, and then hurriedly filled it in again and stamped it down in case they saw what I'd been up to. Anyway, even if I had succeeded in breaking out, they'd have run me to earth in the forest; they were trained woodsmen and I'd no idea where I was.

Once my initial panic had passed, I could only sit in miserable contemplation. There was a slim chance that before tomorrow evening something might happen to change Hansen's lunatic plan—or I might receive a heaven-sent opportunity to escape, although I doubted that. Failing these things, I should certainly be launched—literally, too—into the most dangerous adventure of my life, and with precious little prospect of coming through it. So I would end here, in a god-forsaken miserable German ruin, trying to rescue a man I'd never met—I, who wouldn't stir a finger to rescue my own grandmother. It was all too much, and I had a good self-pitying blubber to myself, and then I cursed and prayed a bit, invoking the God in whom I believe only in moments of real despair to intervene on my behalf.

I tried to console myself that I'd come out of desperate straits before—aye, but wasn't my luck about due to run out, then? No, no, Jesus would see the repentant sinner right, and I would never swear or fornicate or steal or lie again—I strove to remember the seven deadly sins, to make sure I missed none of them, and then cudgelled my brains for the Ten Commandments, so that I could promise never to break them again—although, mind you, I'd never set up a graven image in my life.

I should have felt purified and at peace after all this, but I found I was just as terrified as ever, so I ended by damning the whole system. I knew it would make no difference, anyway.

That next day was interminable; my heart was in my

mouth every time footsteps approached the cabin door, and it was almost a relief when Sapten and his two companions came for me in the evening. They brought a good deal of gear with them, explaining that we should make all our preparations here before setting out, and just the activity of getting ready took my mind momentarily off the horrors ahead.

First Hansen and I stripped right down, so that we could be rubbed all over with grease as a protection against the cold when we took to the water. Sapten whistled softly when he saw my scars—the place where a pistol ball had burrowed from my side towards my spine, the whip-marks left by the swine Gul Shah, and the white weal on my thigh where my leg was broken at Piper's Fort. It was an impressive collection—and even if most of them were in the rear, they weren't the kind of decorations you normally see on a coward.

"You've been lucky," says he. "So far."

When we had been thoroughly greased, we put on rough woollen underclothes—a most disgusting process—and then heavy woollen shirts and smocks, tucked into our breeches. We wore stockings and light shoes, and Sapten bound bandages round our wrists and ankles to keep our clothing gathered in place.

"Now, then," says he, "to arms," and produced a couple of heavy broadswords and an assortment of hunting knives. "If you want fire-arms you'll have to persuade our friends in Jotunberg to give you some," he added. "Useless to try to take them with you."

Hansen took a sword and a long dagger, but I shook my head.

"Haven't you a sabre?"

Sapten looked doubtful, but a search among his band of brigands outside produced the required article—it was old but a good piece of steel, and I shuddered inwardly at the sight of it. But I took it—if I have to fight, God forbid, I'll do it with a weapon I understand, and if I was no Angelo[38] with a sabre, at least I'd been trained in its use. For the rest, they gave me back my seaman's knife, and each of us was provided with a flask of spirits.

We carried the swords on our backs, looped securely at shoulder and waist, and Hansen bound a length of cord round his middle. There was some debate as to whether we should take flint and steel, but there seemed no point to it. Finally, we each had an oilskin packet containing some meat and bread and cheese, in case, as Sapten cheerfully remarked, we had time to stop for a snack.

"You may feel the need of something when you get out of the water," he added. "Eat and drink if chance serves. Now, then, Mr Thomas Arnold, attend to me. From here we ride to the Jotunsee, which will take us the best part of three hours. There the boat is waiting, with two stout men at the oars; they will take you as close to the castle as seems advisable—there is a moon, but we can't help that. The clouds are thick, so you should get close in unobserved. Then you swim for it—and remember, they will be watching and listening in yonder."

He let me digest this, his head cocked and his hands thrust deep in his pockets—strange how these pictures stay with one—and then went on:

"Once inside the castle, Hansen is in command, you understand? He will decide how to proceed—who is to guard the prince, who to lower the bridge. So far as we know, it is wound up and down by a windlass. Knock out the pin and the bridge will fall. That will be our signal to storm the causeway—fifty men, led by myself and Grundvig here." He paused, pulling out his pouch. "It is not our intention to leave any survivors of the garrison."

"They must all die," says Grundvig solemnly.

"To the last man," says Hansen.

It seemed to call for something from me, so I said: "Hear, hear."

"Serve us well in this," added Sapten, "and the past will

be forgotten. Try to play us false—" He left it unspoken. "Now, is all clear?"

It was clear, right enough, all too clear; I did my best not to think of it. I didn't want to know any more dreadful details—indeed, the only question in my mind was a completely unimportant one, and had nothing to do with what lay ahead. But I was curious, so I asked it.

"Tell me," I said to Hansen. "Back in Strackenz City— what made you think I wasn't Carl Gustaf?"

He stared at me in surprise. "You ask now? Very well—I was not sure. The likeness is amazing, and yet . . . there was something wrong. Then I knew, in an instant, what it was. Your scars are in the wrong places—the left one is too low. But there was more than that, too. I don't know—you just were *not* Carl Gustaf."

"Thank'ee," says I. Poor old Bismarck—wrong again.

"How did you come by these scars?" asked Sapten.

"They cut them in my head with a *schlager*," says I, offhand, and Grundvig drew in his breath. "Oh, yes," I added to Hansen, "this is no *kindergarten* you are venturing into, my lad. These are very practical men, as you may discover." I was eager to take some of the bounce out of him.

"That'll do," growls Sapten. "All ready, then? Lassen sie uns gehen."

There were horses outside, and men moving about us in the gloom; we rode in silent cavalcade through the woods, along a path that wound upwards into the Jotun Gipfel, and then down through dense thickets of bush and bracken. There was no chance of escape, even if I had dared; two men rode at my stirrups all the way. We halted frequently—while scouts went ahead, I suppose—and I took the opportunity to sample the contents of my flask. It held brandy, about half a pint, and it was empty by the time the journey was half done. Not that it made much odds, except to warm me; I could have drunk a gallon without showing it just then.

At last we halted and dismounted; shadowy hands took my bridle, and I was pushed forward through the bushes until I found myself on the banks of a tiny creek, with water lapping at my feet. Hansen was beside me, and there was much whispering in the dark; I could see the vague outline of a boat and its rowers, and then the moon came out from behind the clouds, and through the tangled branches at the creek's mouth I saw the choppy grey water of the lake, and rising out of it, not three furlongs off, the stark outline of Jotunberg.

It was a sight to freeze your blood and make you think of monsters and vampires and bats squeaking in gloomy vaults—a gothic horror of dark battlements and towers with cloud-wrack behind it, silent and menacing in the moonlight. My imagination peopled it with phantom shapes waiting at its windows—and they wouldn't have been any worse than Rudi and Kraftstein. Given another moment I believe I would have sunk down helpless on the shore, but before I knew it I was in the boat, with Hansen beside me.

"Wait for the moon to die." Sapten's hoarse whisper came out of the dark behind, and presently the light was blotted out, and Jotunberg was only a more solid shadow in the dark. But it was still there, and all the more horrid in my mind's eye. I had to grip my chin to stop my teeth chattering.

Sapten muttered again in the gloom, the boat stirred as the dim forms of the rowers moved, and we were sliding out of the creek onto the face of the Jotunsee. The breeze nipped as we broke cover, and then the bank had vanished behind us.

It was as black as the earl of hell's weskit, and deadly silent except for the chuckle of water under our bow and the soft rustle as the oarsmen heaved. The boat rocked gently, but we were moving quite quickly, with the dim shape of the castle growing bigger and uglier every moment. It seemed to me that we were rowing dangerously close to it; I could see the faint glare of a light at one of the lower windows, and then Hansen softly said "Halt", and the oarsmen stopped rowing.

Hansen touched my shoulder. "Ready?" I was trying to suppress the bile of panic that was welling up into my throat, so I didn't answer. "Folgen sie mir ganz nahe," says he, and then he had slipped over the side like an otter, with hardly a sound.

For the life of me I couldn't bring myself to follow; my limbs were like jelly; I couldn't move. But petrified though I was, I knew I daren't stay either; let me refuse now, and Sapten would make cold meat of me very shortly afterwards. I leaned over the side of the boat, clumsily trying to copy Hansen, and then I had overbalanced, and with an awful, ponderous roll I came off the gunwale and plunged into the Jotunsee.

The cold was hideous, cutting into my body like a knife, and I came up spluttering with the sheer pain of it. As I gasped for breath Hansen's face came out of the darkness, hissing at me to be quiet, his hand searching for me underwater.

"Geben sie acht, idiot! Stop splashing!"

"This is bloody madness!" I croaked at him. "Christ, it's mid-winter, man! We'll freeze to death!"

He grabbed my shoulder while we trod water, snarling at me to be quiet. Then, turning from the boat, he began to strike out slowly for the castle, expecting me to follow. For a second I considered the possibility, even at this late hour, of making for the shore and taking my chance in the woods, but I realised I could never swim the distance—not at this temperature, and with the sabre strapped to my back and my sodden clothes dragging at me. I had to stay with Hansen, so I struck out after him, as quietly as I could, sobbing with fear and frustration.

God, I remember thinking, this is too bad. What the hell had I done to deserve this? Left alone I'm a harmless enough fellow, asking nothing but meat and drink and

221

a whore or two, and not offending anyone much—why must I be punished in this hellish fashion? The cold seemed to be numbing my very guts; I knew I couldn't go much longer, and then a blinding pain shot through my left leg, and I was under water, my mouth filling as I tried to yell. Flailing with my good leg I came up, bleating for Hansen.

"Cramp!" I whimpered. "Christ, I'll drown!" Even then, I had sense enough to keep my voice down, but it was loud enough to reach him, for next time I went under he hauled me up again, swearing fiercely at me to be quiet, and to stop thrashing about.

"My leg! my leg!" I moaned. "Jesus, I'm done for. Save me, you selfish bastard! Oh, God, the cold!" My leg was one blinding pain, but with Hansen gripping me and holding my face above water I was able to rest until gradually it subsided to a dull ache; I stretched it cautiously, and it seemed to be working again.

When he was sure I could swim on, he whispered that we must hurry, or the cold would get us for certain. I was almost past caring, and told him so; he and his bloody prince and Sapten and the rest of them could rot in hell for me, I said, and he struck me across the face and threatened to drown me if I didn't keep quiet.

"It's your life, too, fool!" he hissed. "Now be silent, or we're lost."

I called him the filthiest names I knew (in a whisper), and then he swam on, with me behind him, striking out feebly enough, but it wasn't far now; another couple of freezing minutes and we were under the lee of the castle wall, where it seemed to rise sheer out of the water, and there wasn't a sight or sound to suggest we had been heard.

Hansen trod water in front of me, and when I came up with him he pointed ahead, and I saw what seemed to be a shadowy opening at the foot of the wall.

"There," says he. "Silence."

"I can't take much more of this," I whispered feebly. "I'll freeze, I tell you—I'm dying—I know I am. God damn you, you scabby-headed Danish swine, you . . . wait for me!"

He was swimming slowly into the gap in the wall; and at that moment the moon chose to come out again, striking its cold light on the rearing battlement above us, and showing that the gap was in fact a tiny harbour, cut out of the rock of the Jotunberg itself. To the left and ahead it was enclosed by the castle wall; to the right the wall seemed to be ruined, and there were dark areas of shadow where the moonlight didn't penetrate.

I felt a chill that was not from the water as I paddled slowly towards it; exhausted and shocked as I was, I could smell danger from the place. When you burgle a house, you don't go in by the open front door. But Hansen was already out of sight in the shadow; I swam after him round an angle of the rock, and saw him treading water with his hand up on the stone ledge that bordered the harbour. When he saw me he turned face on to the stone, put up his other hand, and heaved himself out of the water.

For a second he hung there, poised, straining to pull his body onto the ledge; the moonlight was full on him, and suddenly something glittered flying above the water and smacked between his shoulder blades; his head shot up and his body heaved convulsively; for a second he hung, motionless, and then with a dreadful, bubbling sigh he flopped face down on the stone and slid slowly back into the water. As he slipped under I could distinctly see the knife-hilt standing out of his back; then he was floating, half-submerged, and I was scrabbling frantically away from him choking back the shriek of terror in my throat.

There was a low, cheerful laugh out of the shadows above me, and then someone whistled a line or two of "Marlbroug s'en va t-en guerre".

"Swim this way, Flashman, Prince of Denmark," said Rudi's voice. "I have you beaded, and you won't float long if I put lead ballast into you. Come along, there's a good chap; you don't want to catch cold, do you?"

He watched me as I clambered miserably out, shaking with fright and cold, and stood hand on hip, smiling easily at me.

"This is a not entirely unexpected pleasure," says he. "I had a feeling you would turn up, somehow. Eccentric way you have of arriving, though." He nodded towards the water. "Who's our dead friend?"

I told him.

"Hansen, eh? Well, serve him right for a meddling fool. I did him rather proud, I think—twenty-five feet, an uncertain light, and a rather clumsy hunting-knife—but I put it right between his shoulders. Rather pretty work, wouldn't you say? But you're trembling, man!"

"I'm cold," I chattered.

"Not as cold as he is," chuckled this hellish ruffian. "Well, come along. Ah, but first, the formalities." He snapped his fingers, and two men came out of the shadows behind him. "Michael, take the gentleman's sabre, and that most un-English knife in his belt. Excellent. This way."

They took me through a ruined archway, across a paved yard, through a postern-like door in what seemed to be the main keep, and into a vast vaulted hall with a great stone stairway winding round its wall. To my left was a lofty arch through which I could see dimly the outline of massive chains and a great wheel: I supposed this would be the drawbridge mechanism—not that it mattered now.

Rudi, humming merrily, led the way upstairs and into a chamber off the first landing. By contrast with the gloomy medieval stonework through which we had come, it was pleasantly furnished in an untidy bachelor way, with clothes, papers, dog-whips, bottles, and so on scattered everywhere; there was a fire going and I made straight for it.

"Here," says he, pushing a glass of spirits into my hand. "Michael will get you some dry clothes." And while

224

I choked over the drink, and then stripped off my soaking weeds, he lounged in an armchair.

"So," says he, once I had pulled on the rough clothes they brought, and we were alone, "de Gautet bungled it, eh? I told them they should have let me do the business—if *I'd* been there you would never even have twitched. Tell me what happened."

Possibly I was light-headed with the brandy and the shock of what I had been through, or my fear had reached that stage of desperation where nothing seems to matter; anyway, I told him how I had disposed of his colleague, and he chuckled appreciatively.

"You know, I begin to like you better and better; I knew from the first that we'd get along splendidly. And then what? Our Dansker friends got hold of you, didn't they?" Seeing me hesitate, he leaned forward in his chair. "Come along, now; I know much more than you may think, and can probably guess the rest. And if you hold back, or lie to me—well, Mr Play-actor, you'll find yourself going for a swim with friend Hansen, I promise you. Who sent you here? It was the Danish faction, wasn't it—Sapten's precious bandits?"

"The Sons of the Volsungs," I admitted. I daren't try to deceive him—and what would have been the point?

"Sons of the Volsungs! Sons of the Nibelungs would be more appropriate. And you and Hansen were to try to rescue Carl Gustaf? I wonder," he mused, "how they found out about him. No matter. What did you expect to accomplish, in heaven's name? Two of you couldn't hope . . . ah, but wait a moment! You were the mine under the walls, weren't you? To open the way for the good Major Sapten's patriotic horde." He gave a ringing laugh. "Don't look so surprised, man! D'ye think we're blind in here? We've been watching them scuttle about the shore all day. Why, with a night-glass in the tower we watched your boat set out an hour ago! Of all the bungling, ill-judged, badly-managed affairs! But what would one expect from

225

that pack of yokels?" He roared with laughter again. "And how did they coerce you into this folly? A knife at your back, no doubt. Well, well, I wonder what they'll think of next?"

Now, I was beginning to get some of my senses back, what with the warmth and the rest of sitting down. I was out of the frying-pan into the fire, no question, but I couldn't for the life of me see why he had killed Hansen and taken me prisoner—unless it was for information. And when he had got all that he wanted, what was he going to do with me? I could guess.

"Yes, what *will* they think of next?" He sauntered in front of the fireplace, slim and elegant in his tight-fitting black tunic and breeches, and turned to flash his teeth at me. "Suppose you tell me?"

"I don't know," says I. "It was . . . as you've guessed. We were to try to release him and let down the bridge."

"And if that failed?"

"They didn't say."

"Mm. Do they know our garrison?"

"They think . . . only a few."

"Well guessed—or well spied out. Not that it'll help them. If they try to storm the place their dear Prince will be feeding the fishes in the Jotunsee before they're over the causeway—do they know that, I wonder?"

I nodded. "They know all about it."

He grinned happily. "Well, then, we needn't fret about them, need we? It gives us time to consider. How many men have they over yonder, by the way? And be very, very careful how you answer."

"I heard them say fifty."

"Wise Flashman. I knew, you see." Suddenly he clapped me on the shoulder. "Would you like to meet your royal twin? I've been longing to bring the pair of you face to face, you know—and you can see, at the same time, the excellent arrangements we have for his . . . shall we say, security?—in the event of burglars. Come along." He flung

226

open the door. "Oh, and Flashman," he added, carelessly smiling. "You will bear in mind that I'm *not* de Gautet, won't you? You'll do nothing foolish, I mean? You see, it would be a great waste, because I think . . . I think we may be able to try out a little scheme of mine together, you and I. We'll see." He bowed and waved me through. "After you, your highness."

We went down to the great hall, and there Rudi turned into a side-passage, and down a steep flight of stone steps which spiralled into the depths of the castle. There were oil lamps at intervals, glistening on the nitre which crusted the bare stone, and in places the steps were slippery with moss. We came out into a flagged cloister, with mighty, squat columns supporting the low ceiling; the place was in shadow, but ahead of us light shone from an archway, and passing through we were in a broad stone chamber where two men sat over cards at a rough table. They looked up at our approach, one with his hand on a pistol; they were burly, tall fellows in what looked like cavalry overalls, and their sabres hung at their elbows, but I wasn't concerned with them. Beyond them was a great iron grille, stretching from floor to ceiling, and before it stood Kraftstein, his huge hands on his hips, like an ogre in the flickering lamplight.

"Here he is, Kraftstein," says Rudi lightly. "Our old drinking-companion from Schönhausen. Aren't you pleased, now, that I didn't let you shoot him in the water? Kraftstein's got no manners, you know," he added over his shoulder to me. "And how is our royal guest this evening?"

Kraftstein said nothing, but having glowered at me he turned and drew a bolt in the grille. Rudi waved me through the gate as it groaned back on its hinges, and with the hair prickling on my neck, but spurred by curiosity, I passed through.

The grille, I saw, cut off the end of the vault, and we were in an enclosure perhaps forty feet deep and half as wide. At the end, opposite me, a man lay on a low couch set against the wall; there was a table with a lamp beside him, and at the sound of the creaking hinge he sat up, shading his eyes and peering towards us.

For some reason I felt a nervousness that had nothing to do with the danger of my situation; I felt I was about to see something uncanny—and this although I knew what it was going to be.

"Guten abend, highness," says Rudi, as we went forward. "Here's a visitor for you."

The man took his hand from his face, and I couldn't help letting out an exclamation. For there I sat, looking at me—my own face, puzzled, wary, and then in an instant, blank with amazement, the mouth open and eyes staring. He shrank back, and then suddenly he was on his feet.

"What is this?" his voice was strained and hoarse. "Who is this man?"

As he moved, there was a heavy, clanking noise, and with a thrill of horror I saw that there was a heavy chain on his left ankle, fettering him to a great stone weight beside the bed.

"May I have the honour to present an old acquaintance, highness?" says Rudi. "I'm sure you remember him, from your mirror?"

It was a weird experience, looking at that face, and hearing that voice when he spoke again—perhaps a trifle deeper than my own, I fancied, and now that I looked at him, he was a shade slimmer than I, and less tall by a fraction. But it was an amazing resemblance, none the less.

"What does it mean?" he demanded. "In God's name, who are you?"

"Until recently, he was Prince Carl Gustaf of Denmark," says Rudi, obviously enjoying himself. "But you'd regard him as a most presumptive heir to the title, I'm sure. In fact, he's an Englishman, your highness, who has been kind enough to deputise for you during your holiday here."

He took it well, I'll say that for him. After all, I'd known for weeks that my spitten image was walking about somewhere, but it was all new to him. He stared at me for a long moment, and I stared back, tongue-tied, and then he said slowly:

"You're trying to drive me mad. Why, I don't know. It is some filthy plot. In God's name, tell me, if you have any spark of pity or decency, what it means. If it is money you want, or ransom, I have told you—say so! If it is my life—well, damn you! take it!" He tried to stride forward, but the chain wrenched at his ankle and almost upset him. "Damn you!" he roared again, shaking his fist at us. "You vile, cowardly villains! Let me loose, I say, and I'll send that creature with my face straight to hell—and you, too, you grinning mountebank!" He was a fearsome sight, wrestling at his chain, and cursing like a Smithfield porter.

Rudi clicked his tongue. "Royal rage," says he. "Gently, your highness, gently. Don't promise what you couldn't perform."

For a moment I thought Carl Gustaf would burst himself with rage; his face was purple. And then his temper subsided, he strove to compose himself, and he jerked back his lips in that gesture that I had spent so many weary hours trying to copy.

"I forget myself, I think," he said, breathing hard. "To what end? Who you are, fellow, I don't know—or what this means. I'll not entertain you by inquiring any further. When you choose to tell me—if you choose to tell me—well! But understand," and he dropped his voice in a way which I knew so well, because I do it myself, "that you had better kill me and have done, because if you do not, by God's help I'll take such a revenge on you all . . ."

He left it there, nodding at us, and I had to admit that whatever our resemblance in looks, he was as different from me in spirit as day from night. You wouldn't

229

have got me talking as big as that, chained up in a dungeon—well, I've been in that very situation, and I blubbered for mercy till I was hoarse. I know what's fitting. But he didn't, and much good his defiance was doing him.

"Oh, never fear, highness," says Rudi. "We'll certainly kill you when the time is ripe. Remember the royal progress we have prepared for you."

And he pointed off to the side of the great cell; I looked, and my heart gave a lurch at what I saw.

To that side the flags sloped down in a depression, perhaps a dozen feet across and about four feet deep. The sloping stones looked smooth and slippery, and at the bottom of the shallow funnel which they formed there was a gaping hole, circular and more than a yard wide. Carl Gustaf's face went pale as he, too, looked, and his mouth twitched, but he said nothing. My skin crawled at the thought of what lay beyond the mouth of that shaft.

"Merry lads, the old lords of Jotunberg," says Rudi. "When they tired of you, down you went, suitably weighted—as our royal guest is here—and hey, splash! It's not a trip I'd care to take myself—but your highness may not mind so much when I tell you that one of your friends is waiting for you in the Jotunsee. Hansen, his name was."

"Hansen? Erik Hansen?" The prince's hand shook. "What have you done to him, you devil?"

"He went swimming at the wrong time of year," says Rudi cheerily. "So rash—but there. Young blood. Now, your highness, with your gracious permission, we'll withdraw." He made a mocking bow, and waved me ahead of him towards the grille.

As we reached it, Carl Gustaf suddenly shouted:

"You—you with my face! Haven't you a tongue in your head? Why don't you speak, damn you?"

I blundered out; that hellish place was too much for me; I could imagine all too clearly slithering down into that shaft—ugh! And these murdering monsters would do it to me as soon as to him, if it suited them.

Young Rudi's laughter rang after me as I stumbled through the vault; he strode up beside me, clapping his hand round my shoulders and asking eagerly what I had thought of meeting my double face to face—had it made me wonder who I was? Had I noticed the amazement of Carl Gustaf, and what did I suppose *he* was making of it all?

"I'll swear I hadn't realised how alike you were till I saw you together," says he, as we reached his room again. "It's supernatural. Do you know . . . it makes me wonder if Otto Bismarck didn't miss the true possibility of his scheme. By God!" he stopped dead, rubbing his chin. Then:

"You remember a few moments ago I spoke of a plan that you and I might try together? I'll be frank; it occurred to me the moment I saw you swimming in the lake, and realised that I had both the court cards in my hand, with no one but the worthy Kraftstein to interfere—and he doesn't count. The two court cards," he repeated, grinning, "and one of them a knave. Have a drink, play-actor. And listen."

You'll have noticed that since my arrival in Jotunberg I had said very little—and, of course, the situation was really beyond comment. Events in the past forty-eight hours had brought me to the point where intelligent thought, let alone speech, was well-nigh impossible. The only conscious desire I felt was to get out of this nightmare as fast as possible, by any means. And yet, the hectoring way in which this cocksure young upstart shoved me into a chair and commanded me to listen, stirred a resentment beneath my miserable fear. I was heartily sick of having people tell me to listen, and ordering me about, and manipulating me like a damned puppet. Much good it had done me to take it all meekly—it had been one horror after another, and only by the luck of the devil was I still in one piece. And here, unless I mistook the look in Starnberg's eye, was going to be another brilliant proposal to put me through the mill. Open defiance wasn't to be thought of, naturally, but

231

in that moment I felt that if I did manage to muster my craven spirits to do *something* on my own behalf, it probably couldn't be any worse than whatever he had in mind for me.

"Look here," says he, "how many of these damned Danes know that you are really an impostor?"

I could think of Grundvig and Sapten for certain; their peasant followers I wasn't sure of, but Rudi brushed them aside as unimportant.

"Two who matter," says he. "And on my side—Bismarck, Bersonin and Kraftstein—we can forget Detchard and that squirt of a doctor. Now—suppose our captive Prince goes down that excellent pipe tonight, and we let down the bridge to encourage your friends to attack? It would be possible to arrange a warm reception for them—warm enough to ensure that Grundvig and Sapten never got off that causeway alive, anyhow. Kraftstein could easily meet with a fatal accident during the fight— somehow I'm sure he would—and by the time the Sons of the Volsungs had fought their way in and cut up the survivors, you and I could be on our way to the shore, by boat. Then, back to Strackenz and the acclaim of everyone who has been wondering where their beloved prince has been. Oh, we could invent some tale—and who would there be to give you away? Detchard and the doctor daren't. Your Danish friends couldn't, being dead. And by this time Bismarck and Bersonin are far too busy, I'll be bound, to worry about Strackenz."

Seeing my bewildered look, he explained.

"You haven't heard the news, of course. Berlin is alive with alarms, it seems. The revolution's coming, my boy; the student rabble and the rest will have the King of Prussia off his throne in a week or two. So dear Otto has other fish to fry for the moment. Oh, it's not only in Germany, either; I hear that France is up in arms, and Louis-Phillipe's deposed, they say. It's spreading like wildfire."[39] He laughed joyously. "Don't you see, man?

232

It's a heaven-sent chance. We could count on weeks—nay, months—before anyone gave a thought to this cosy little duchy—or to the identity of the duchess's consort."

"And what use would that be to us?"

"God, you're brainless! To hold the reins of power—real power—in a European state, even a little one like Strackenz? If we couldn't squeeze some profit out of that—enough to set us up for life—before we took leave of 'em, then we aren't the men I think we are. D'you know what the revenues of a duchy amount to?"

"You're mad," I said. "Raving mad. D'you think I'd put my neck into that again?"

"Why not? Who's to stop you?"

"We wouldn't last a week—why, half the bloody peasants in Strackenz probably know that there are two Carl Gustafs loose about the place! They'll talk, won't they?"

"Bah, where's your spirit, play-actor?" he jeered. "Who would listen to them? And it's only for a few weeks—you've done it once already, man! And think of the fun it would be!"

They are rare, but they do exist, and you can only call them adventurers. Rudi was one; it was the excitement, the mischief, that he lived for, more than the reward; the game, not the prize. Mad as hatters, mark you, and dangerous as sharks—they are not to be judged by the standards of yellow-bellies like me. Flashy don't want anything to do with 'em, but he knows how their minds work. Because of this, I was wondering furiously how to deal with him.

"You can go back to your pretty duchess, too," says he.

"Don't want her," says I. "I've had her, anyway."

"But there's a fortune in it, man!"

"I'd rather be alive and poor, thank'ee."

He stood considering. "You don't trust me, is that it?"

"Well," says I, "now that you mention it . . ."

"But that's the point!" He clapped his hands. "We are the ideal partners—neither of us trusts the other an inch, but we need each other. It's the only guarantee in any business. You're as big a rascal as I am; we would sell each other tomorrow, but there isn't the need."

Our financiers know all this, of course, but I've often thought that our diplomatists and politicians could have gone to school to Professor Starnberg. I can see him still, arms akimbo, flashing eyes, curly head, brilliant smile, and ready to set fire to an orphan asylum to light his cheroot. I'm a dirty scoundrel, but it has come to me naturally; Rudi made a profession out of it.

"Come on, man, what d'you say?"

I caught the note of impatience in his voice; careful, now, I thought, or he'll turn vicious. His scheme was unthinkable, but I daren't tell him so. What was the way out, then? I must pretend to go along with him for the moment; would a chance of escape offer? It was growing on me that the only safe way out—or the least risky—was to find some way of doing what Sapten had wanted. How could I get the drawbridge down; would I survive the assault that would follow? Aye, but for the moment, pretend.

"Could we make certain of Sapten and Grundvig?" I asked doubtfully.

"Be sure of that," says he. "There are two little cannon below stairs—ornamental things, but they'll work. Load 'em with chain, and we'll sweep that causeway from end to end when the rescuers come charging home."

"There are fifty of them, remember; have you enough here to man the guns and hold the place until we can get away?"

"Two of us, the three you saw in the cellar, and another three in the tower," says he. "Then there are two on the causeway, but they'll go in the first rush. They needn't concern us." Oh, he was a born leader, all right. But now I knew how many men he had, and where they were. The vital fact was that there was no one, apparently, guarding the drawbridge mechanism on the inside.

"So," he cried, "you're with me?"

234

"Well," says I, doubtfully, "if we can be sure of holding those damned Volsungs on the bridge long enough . . ."

"We'll concentrate all our force by the guns at the drawbridge arch," says he. "Why, we can have all ready in half an hour. Then, down with the bridge, and let the flies come streaming towards our parlour." His eyes were shining with excitement, and he put out his hand. "And then, my friend, we embark on our profitable partnership."

Suddenly it struck me that it was now or never; he would move fast, and somehow I had to forestall him while his small forces were still scattered about the castle and all unsuspecting. I fought down my rising fear of what was to do, steeling myself for a desperate effort. My hand was sweating in his grasp.

"Let's drink to it!" cries he exultantly, and turned to the table, where the bottles stood.

Oh, Jesus, good luck to me, I thought. I moved up to his side, and as he splashed brandy into the glasses I made a swift examination of the other bottles standing by. A sturdy flask caught my eye, and I made a careless show of examining it, turning it by the neck to see the label. He was so confident in his youth and strength and arrogance that he never thought of being caught off-guard—why should he worry, in a castle held by his men, with only the feeble-spirited Flashman to be watched?

"Here," says he, turning with a glass, and I breathed a silent prayer, shifted my hand on the bottle neck, and swung it with all my force at his head. He saw the movement, but had no time to duck; the flask shattered on his temple with an explosion like a pistol-shot, and he staggered back, wine drenching his hair and tunic, and hurtled full length to the floor.

I was beside him in a flash, but he was dead to the world, with a great ugly gash welling blood among his curls. For a few seconds I waited, listening, but there was no sound from without. I rose, my heart pounding, and

235

strode quickly across the room, pausing only to take up a sabre from a rack in the corner. I'd done it now, and was in a state of active funk, but there was nothing for it but to hurry ahead and hope.

The door creaked abominably as I pulled it gently open and peeped out. All was still; the stair-lamps shone dimly on the great empty hall. There was no sound of footsteps. I closed the door softly and tiptoed to the top of the stairs, keeping close to the wall. Through the great arch across the hall I could see the wheel and chains of the drawbridge; they looked gigantic, and I wondered uneasily could I lower the bridge single-handed, and would I have the time to do it before someone came into the hall?

I cursed myself for not finishing Starnberg off while I had the chance; suppose he came to? Should I go back and settle him? But I baulked at that, and every second I lingered now increased the chance of discovery. Gulping down my fear I sped down the steps and across the hall, taking cover in the shadows of the archway, holding my breath and trying to listen above the thumping of my heart. Still no sound, and the lighted entrance to the passage leading to the dungeons, which I could see from my hiding-place, remained empty. I stole across to the great wheel, gently laid my sabre on the flags, and tried to make out how the mechanism worked.

There was a big handle on the wheel, with room for at least two men; that was how they wound it up. But there must be a brake on the wheel to hold it; I fumbled in the dark, chittering with fright, and could find nothing that seemed to answer the case. The chains were taut with strain, and when I went farther into the arch I found that its outer end was closed by the raised wooden bridge itself; it was at least ten feet broad and might be three times that in length, for its upper end was lost in the dark above my head; faint streaks of moonlight came through at either side.

Well, at least there were no doors or portcullis to worry

236

about; once the bridge was down the way was open—if I could get it down, and if it survived the fall. The bloody thing looked as though it weighed a ton; when it crashed down across the gap to the causeway there would be no need of any further signal to Sapten and his boarding-party—they would hear the row in Strackenz City. Aye, that would wake the castle, all right, and young Flash would have to light out full tilt for cover before the shooting started.

But I had to get the damned thing down first, by God; how long was it since I had left Rudi? Suppose he was stirring? In a panic I scurried back to the wheel, kicked my sabre in the dark, and sent it clattering across the flags, making a most hellish din. I grabbed at it, whispering curses, and at that moment came the blood-chilling sound of footsteps from the passage-way across the hall. I actually clapped my hand across my own mouth, and dived for the shelter of the wheel, burrowing in close at its foot and trying not to breathe while the steps tramped out into the hall.

There were two of them, Kraftstein and another. They stopped in the middle of the hall, and Kraftstein glanced upwards towards the room where I had left Rudi. Oh my God, I thought, please don't let them go up; let the lousy bastards go away.

"Was machen sie?" said the second one, and Kraftstein grunted something in reply which I didn't catch. The other one shrugged and said he was fed up with sitting in the cellar with Carl Gustaf for company, and Kraftstein remarked that at least he was better off than the guards out on the causeway. They laughed at that, and both looked towards the arch where I was hiding; I lay still as a corpse, my nerves almost snapping, watching them through the spokes of the wheel. And then I saw something that brought the icy sweat starting out of me: the hall light, casting its shaft into the mouth of my archway, was glittering on the point of the sabre that lay where I had knocked it, half in and half out of the shadow.

Oh Christ, they couldn't help but see it—it was shining like a blasted lighthouse. They were standing there, staring straight in my direction, not a dozen paces away; another few seconds and I believe I'd have come bolting out like a rabbit, and then the second one yawned enormously and said:

"Gott, Ich bin müde; wie viel uhr glauben sie dass es sei?"

Kraftstein shook his head. " 'Ist spät. Gehen sie zu bette."

I was willing them feebly both to go to bed, and at last the other one mooched off on his own; Kraftstein took a turn round the hall while my pulse increased to a sickening gallop, and then he went back into the passage leading below.

I waited, trembling, until his footsteps had died away, and then stole out and retrieved my sabre. To my disordered imagination it seemed incredible that there was still no sound from Rudi's room—though in fact it probably wasn't five minutes since I had left him. I came back to the wheel, forcing myself to inspect it calmly; it must be held at some point. I felt it all over, both sides, feeling sicker every moment—and then I saw it. Where its rims almost touched the ground there was a bolt thrust through one of the spokes into the housing of the windlass; if it was withdrawn, I guessed, the wheel would be released, but it wasn't going to be a simple business of pulling it out. It was going to have to be driven out with force.

Well, in God's name, there had to be something handy to knock it clear; I fumbled about in the shadows, ears pricked and whimpering nonsensical instructions to myself, but the best thing I could find was a heavy billet of wood among some rubbish in the corner. I could only hope that it would do; I was desperate by now, anyway, and I fairly sped round the other side of the windlass, praying audibly as I went, and bashed at the protruding end of the bolt with all my strength.

The thumping was fit to wake the dead; oh, Jesus, it wasn't moving! I belaboured the bolt frantically, swearing at it, and it moved in a fraction. I hammered away, and suddenly it shot out of sight, there was an ear-splitting clang, the wheel whirred round like some huge animal springing to life, and the handle shot by within an inch of braining me.

I flung myself out of the way, my ears filled with the shrieking and clanking of the chains as they rasped over their rollers; it sounded like a thousand iron demons banging on anvils in hell. But the bridge was falling; I saw it yawn away from the outer arch, and moonlight flooded in, and then with an appalling crash the great mass of wood fell outwards, smashing against the stonework of the causeway, leaping as if it were alive, and settling—oh, thank God!—across the gap.

The clap of the explosion was in my ears as I grabbed my sabre and took cover at the side of the archway. My first thought was to rush out across the bridge—anywhere out of that damned castle—but an outcry from the causeway stopped me. The guards! I couldn't see them, but they were there, all right, and then I saw a pin-point of light from the far end of the causeway, and the crack of a shot hard behind it. Sapten's merry men must be getting into action; there was a ragged volley from the shore and a scream, and I hesitated no longer. Anything emerging across that bridge was going to be a prime target; this was no place for Harry Flashman, and I fled back into the hall, looking for a safe corner to hide in until the forthcoming passage of arms was over. By God, I had done my share, and no mistake; not for me to try to steal all the glory which the Sons of the Volsungs so richly deserved.

Someone was running and yelling in the passage from the dungeons; another voice was bellowing from up aloft. The hall was going to be fairly busy in a moment or two,

239

so I scampered towards a doorway hitherto unnoticed, midway between the main gate and the dungeon passage. It was locked; I battered on it for a futile moment, and then swung round to look for another bolthole. But it was too late; Kraftstein was leaping across the hall, sword drawn, bawling to everyone to come and lend a hand; two more were emerging from beyond the stairs. I shrank back in the doorway—fortunately it was fairly deep, and they hadn't seen me, being intent on their yawning front door.

"Pistols!" roared Kraftstein. "Quickly, they're coming across! Heinrich! Back this way, man! Come on!" He vanished into the archway, with the other two close behind him; I heard them start shooting, and congratulated myself on having left them a clear field in that direction. Sapten wasn't going to have things all his own way, by the sound of things, and presently two more of the garrison came racing out of the dungeon arch, and another from the stairs; unless I had miscounted, the whole of the Jotunberg friendly society was now gathered in the main entrance—all except Rudi, who was presumably still stretched out above stairs, and bleeding to death, with any luck.

I wondered if the last man up from below had cut Carl Gustaf's throat and sent him down the pipe; not that I cared much, but the besiegers would probably feel better disposed towards me if they found him alive. However, he could take his chance; in the meantime, it seemed reasonable that I should seek out another refuge elsewhere; if I made a quick bolt for it there seemed little chance that the defenders would notice me—they were warmly engaged by the sound of yelling and banging from the direction of the drawbridge.

I peeped cautiously out; the dungeon passage seemed a good place, for I recollected openings off it where I ought to be able to lurk in comparative safety. The hall was empty; I made sure there was no one in sight at the main arch, and was flitting stealthily out when a voice from the stairway stopped me dead in my tracks, yelping as I did so.

"Hold on, play-actor! The comedy's not finished yet!"

Rudi was standing on the bottom step, leaning against the stone balustrade. He was grinning, but his face was ghastly pale, except down the right side, where the blood had dried in a dark streak. He had a sabre in his free hand, and he lifted the point in my direction.

"Bad form to sneak away without saying goodbye to your host," says he. "Damned bad form. Didn't they teach you manners at that English school of yours?"

I made a dart towards the dungeon passage, but with a speed that astonished me, considering the wound on his head, he bounded off the step and was there before me, slashing at me so close that I had to leap back out of harm's way. He laughed savagely and feinted to lunge, tossing the curls out of his eyes.

"Not quick enough, were we? It isn't de Gautet this time, you know."

I circled away from him, and he followed me with his eyes, smiling grimly and making his point play about in front of me. I heard a movement behind me, towards the arch, but before I could turn, he sang out:

"No, no, don't shoot! You attend to the rats outside! I'll settle the one in here!"

He advanced slowly, his eyes flashing as the light caught them.

"It isn't played out yet, you know," says he. "Perhaps your friends will find Jotunberg a tougher nut to crack than they imagined. And if they do—well, they'll find twin corpses to cheer 'em up!" He flicked out his point, and I parried it and sprang away. He laughed at that. "Don't like cold steel, do we? We'll like it even less in a minute. Come on guard, curse you!"

I couldn't fly; he'd have had his point through my back in a twinkling. So I had to fight. Not many foemen have seen old Flashy's face in battle, but Rudi was destined to be one of them, and I couldn't have had a more deadly opponent. I knew he would be as practised with a sword as he was with a knife or a pistol, which put him well above my touch, but there was nothing for it but to grip my hilt with a sweating hand and defend myself as long as I could. I could see only one faint hope; if he was so greedy for my blood that he wasn't going to let his pals intervene, there was just a chance that I might hold him off long enough for Sapten to overcome the defenders—if I wasn't a swordsman of his brilliance, I was at least as good as the master-at-arms of the 11th Hussars could make me, and I was strong enough, while Rudi must be weakened by the smash on the head I had given him.

Perhaps the thought showed in my face, for he laughed again and took a cut at me.

"You can have your choice of how you die," jeers he. "A nice thrust? Or a good backhand cut—it can take a head off very pretty, as I'm sure you know!"

And with that he came in, foot and hand, and had me fighting for my life as I fell back across the hall. His blade was everywhere, now darting at my face, now at my chest; now slashing at my left flank, now at my head—how I parried those thrusts and sweeps is beyond me, for he was faster than any man I'd ever met, and his wrist was like a steel spring. He drove me back to the foot of the stairs and then dropped his point, laughing, while he glanced towards the main gate, where the pistols were cracking away, and the smoke was drifting back like mist into the hall.

"Stand to 'em, Kraftstein!" he shouted. "What, they're only a pack of ploughmen! Fire away, boys! Sweep 'em into the lake!"

He waved his sabre in encouragement, and I seized the chance to take a wild slash at his head. By God, I nearly had him, too, but his point was up in the nick of time, and then he was driving in at me again, snarling and thrusting with such speed that I had to duck under his blade and run for it.

"Stand and fight, damn you!" cries he, coming after me. "Are you all white-livered, you damned British? Stand and fight!"

"What for?" I shouted. "So that you can show off your sabre-work, you foreign mountebank? Come and get me if you're so bloody clever! Come on!"

It was the last thing I'd have thought of saying to anybody, normally, but I knew what I was doing. I'd noticed, as he turned to follow me, that he had staggered a little, and as he stood now, poised to lunge, he was swaying unsteadily from side to side. He was groggy from his wound, and tiring, too; for all his speed and skill he wasn't as strong a man as I. If I could lure him away from the hall, away from the chance to call in his men, I might be able to exhaust him sufficiently to disable or kill him; at least I might hold him in play until Sapten and his damned dilatory Danes came on the scene. So I fell back towards the dungeon doorway, calling him an Austrian pimp, a bedroom bravo, a Heidelberg whoremaster, and anything else that came to mind.

Possibly he didn't need this kind of encouragement; it only seemed to amuse him, but he came after me hard enough, stamp-stamp-stamp, with arm and sabre straight as a lance when he lunged. I retreated along the passage nimbly, keeping him at full stretch, and got my footing on the steps. After that it was easier, for whoever had built the steps had known his business; they spiralled down to the right, so that I could fight with the wall to cover my open flank, while his was exposed.

"You can't run forever," cries he, cutting back-handed.

"So they told Wellington," says I, taking it on my hilt. "Why didn't you learn to fence properly, you opera-house buffoon?"

"Sticks and stones," laughs he. "We'll have room enough in a moment, and see how well *you* can fence without a wall to burrow under."

He came down the stairs at a run, thrusting close to the

wall, and I had to jump away and scramble downwards for dear life. He was at my back on the instant, but I won clear with a couple of swinging cuts and went headlong down the steps, stumbling at the bottom and only regaining my balance just in time as he followed me into the open.

"Close thing that time, play-actor," says he, pausing to brush the hair out of his eyes. He was breathing heavy, but so was I; if he didn't tire soon I was done for. He came at me slowly, circling his point warily, and then sprang, clash-clash, and I fell back before him. We were in the low cloister now, with plenty of pillars for me to dodge round, but try as I might I found him forcing me back towards the lighted arch leading to the guardroom and Carl Gustaf's cell. He was fighting at full pitch, his point leaping at me like quicksilver, and it was all I could do to keep my skin intact as he drove me through into the lighted area.

"Not much farther to run now," says he. "D'ye know any prayers, you English coward?"

I was labouring too hard to answer him with a taunt of my own; the sweat was coming off me like water, and my right wrist was aching damnably. But he was almost spent, too; as he cut at me and missed he staggered, and in desperation I tried the old Flashman triple pass—a sudden thrust at the face, a tremendous kick at his essentials, and a full-blooded downward cut. But where I had been to school, Rudi had graduated with honours; he side-stepped thrust and kick, and if I hadn't postponed my intended cut in favour of an original parry—a blind sideways sweep accompanied by a squeal of alarm—he would have had me. As it was his point raked my left forearm before I could get out of range. He paused, panting, to jeer at me.

"So that's the way gentlemen fight in England, is it?" says he. "No wonder you win your wars."

"You should talk, you back-stabbing guttersnipe." I was scared sick at the narrowness of my escape, and glad of the respite. "When did you last fight fair?"

"Let's see, now," says he, falling on guard again and

trying another thrust. "It would be '45, I think, or '46—I was young then. But I was never as crude as you—see now."

And making a play at my head he suddenly spat straight at me, and as I hesitated in astonishment he tried to run me through, but his tiredness betrayed him, and his point went wide.

"Now who's a gentleman?" I shouted, but his only answer was a laugh and a sudden rush that drove me back almost to the grille of Carl Gustaf's cell. One backward glance I had to take—God, the grille door was open, and I went through it like a jack rabbit, slamming it as he came rushing after. He got a foot in, and we heaved and cursed at each other. My weight must have told, but suddenly there was a shout behind me, and something crashed against the bars close to my head. It was a pewter pot—that damned Carl Gustaf was not only still alive but hurling his furniture at me. I must have relaxed instinctively, for Rudi forced the door back, and I went reeling into the middle of the chamber just as the royal idiot behind me let fly with a stool, which fortunately missed.

"I'm on your side, you crazy bastard!" I shouted. "Throw them at him!"

But he had nothing left now but his lamp, and he didn't apparently fancy leaving us in the dark; he stood staring while Rudi rushed me, slashing for all he was worth. I hewed desperately back; the sabres clanged hilt to hilt, and we grappled, kicking and tearing at each other until he broke free. I caught him a cut on the left shoulder, and he swore foully and sprang into the attack again.

"You'll go together, then!" he shouted, and drove me back across the cell. His face and shoulder were bleeding, he was all in, but he laughed in my face as he closed in for the kill.

"This way! This way!" bawls Carl Gustaf. "To me, man!"

I couldn't have done it, not for a kingdom; I could

245

feel my arm failing before Starnberg's cuts. One I stopped a bare inch from my face, and lurched back; his arm straightened for the thrust—and then in a moment he stopped dead, his head turning towards the grille, as a shot sounded from the stairs.

"Help!" yelled Carl Gustaf. "Quickly! This way!"

Rudi swore and sprang back to the grille door; there was the sound of shouting and feet clattering on the steps. He waited only an instant, and glanced back at me.

"Another time, damn you," he cried. "Au revoir, your highnesses!", and he swung his sabre once and let it fly at me, whirling end over end. It sailed over my head, ringing on the stones, but I had started back instinctively, my feet slipped out from under me, and I came crashing down on the flags. Christ! they weren't level! I was sliding backwards, and in a moment of paralysing horror I remembered the funnel and that ghastly pit at its base. I heard Carl Gustaf's cry of warning too late and Rudi's exultant yell of laughter; they seemed to slide upwards out of my sight as I clawed frantically at the slippery stone. I couldn't stop myself; my foot caught for an instant and I slewed round sprawling, helpless as a cod on a fishmonger's slab. Now I was sliding head first; I had an instant's glimpse of that hellish black hole as I slithered towards it, then my head was over the void, my arms were flailing empty air, and I shot over the lip, screaming, into the depths. Jesus, down the drain, went through my mind as I hurtled headlong towards certain death.

The pipe ran at an angle; my shoulders, hips and knees crashed against its sides as I rushed into the inky blackness. For sheer horror I have known nothing to come near it, for this without doubt was the end—the frightful, unspeakable finish; I was being shot into the bowels of hell beyond all hope, into eternal dark. Down I went, the ghastly wail of my own screams in my ears, and ever down, down, and then with shattering force I was plunged into icy water, plummeting through it like a

246

stone until it gradually drew me to a halt, and I felt myself rising.

For a moment I thought I must have shot out into the Jotunsee, a moment of frantic hope, but before I had risen a foot my back bumped against the pipe. Christ! I was trapped like a rat, for the shaft was too narrow to turn; I was head down with nothing to do but drown!

That I didn't go mad in that moment is still a wonder to me. I honestly believe that a brave man would have lost his reason, for he would have known he was beyond hope; only one of my senseless, unreasoning cowardice would have struggled still, stretching down with frantic fingers and clawing at the pipe beneath me. I had had no time to take breath before hitting the water; my mouth and nose were filling as my hands clawed at the pipe and found a ledge. I hauled with the strength of despair, and slid a little farther down the pipe; my fingers found another ledge and hauled again, but then my strength went and I found myself turning on my back. I was gulping water; the stifling agony in my throat was spreading to my chest; I beat feebly at the roof of the pipe, thinking Christ, Christ, don't let me die, don't let me die, but I am dying, I am—and as I felt my senses going I was dimly aware that my face was not against the pipe, but only my chest and body.

I can't remember thinking clearly what this meant, but I know that my hands came up beside my face, which had in fact come out of the pipe's end, and pushed punily at the stone that was imprisoning me. I must have thrust outwards, for I felt my body rasp slowly along the pipe as I tilted upwards. There was a dreadful roaring in my ears, and nothing but crimson before my eyes, but I could feel myself rising, rising, and I know a vague thought of floating up to heaven went through what remained of my consciousness. And then there was air on my face—cold, biting air—only for a second before the water enveloped me again. But half-dead as I was, my limbs must have

247

answered to the knowledge, for my head came into the air again, and this time I thrashed feebly and kept it above the surface. My sight cleared, and there was a starry sky above me, with a huge, white cold moon, and I was spewing and retching on the surface of the Jotunsee.

Somehow I kept afloat while the agony in my chest subsided and my senses came back enough for me to realise that the water was freezing cold, and threatening to suck me down once more. Sobbing and belching water, I paddled feebly with my hands, and looked about me; to my right the lake stretched away forever, but there on my left, looming upwards, was the great rock of Jotunberg with its beautiful, welcoming, splendid castle. It was a bare twenty yards away; I struggled with all my strength, kicking out against the water, and by the grace of God the rock when I reached it was shelving. I got my head and shoulders on to it and clawed my way out, and then I lay, helpless as a baby, with my face on that blessed cold wet stone, and went into a dead faint.

I think I must have lain there only a few minutes; perhaps the mental shock of the ghastly experience I had endured was greater than the physical one, for the next thing I remember is stumbling slowly over the rocks by the waterside, without knowing where or who I was. I sat down, and gradually it all came back, like a terrible nightmare; it took some moments before I could assure myself that I was alive again.

Looking back, of course, I realise that from the moment I slipped into the funnel in the dungeon until I clambered ashore again on the Jotunberg, can hardly have been more than two minutes. My initial plunge must have taken me to within a foot or two of the pipe's outlet; I had scrambled out by sheer panicky good luck, and floated to the surface. It was a miracle, no doubt, but a truly horrifying one. If I'm a coward, haven't I cause to be? Only those who know what it is to die can really fear death, I think, and by God I knew. It haunts me still; any time I have a bellyful of cheese or lobster I try to stay awake all night, for if I drop off, sure as fate, there I am again in that hellish sewer beneath Jotunberg, drowning upside down.

However, at the time, when I realised that I wasn't dead yet, but that I would be if I sat there much longer, of cold and exhaustion, I took stock of the situation. At the point where I had left the scene of the action so abruptly, it had sounded as though help had arrived. Presumably Kraftstein and his cronies had been overcome, and with any luck Rudi had met a well-deserved end into the bargain. Happy thought! maybe they had slung him down the pipe after me. I couldn't think of anyone I would rather have had it happen to. Anyway, they were probably getting Carl Gustaf out of his fetters by now, and all would be jollity. How would they respond to my reappearance? It would be a bit of a blow to them, after I had appeared to die so conveniently—would they be tempted to do the job properly this time? No, surely not—not after all I'd done for them, much against my will though it had been.

Anyway, it was settled for me. If I stayed there any longer I would certainly freeze to death. I must just go into the castle and take my chance.

From where I stood I could see the causeway, about a hundred yards ahead, and as I stumbled round the base of the island the drawbridge came into view. There were figures in the castle gateway, and they looked like Volsungs; sure enough, as I came closer, I saw that they were, so I hallooed and scrambled up the little rocky path that ended at the bridge's foot.

Three gaping, sturdy peasants, they helped me up and led me through the debris-strewn archway into the hall. God, what a mess it was. Kraftstein lay beside the wheel, with his skull split and his great hands crooked like talons; I remembered their grip and shuddered. Nearby were half a dozen other bodies—Sapten had kept his word, then; there would be no survivors of the Jotunberg garrison. There

249

was a pool of blood in the very centre of the hall, and lying in it was the fellow who had complained to Kraftstein of boredom; well, ennui wouldn't trouble him any longer. The smell of powder was harsh in my nostrils, and a faint cloud of it still hung in the shadows overhead.

The peasants pushed me down on to a bench, and while one helped me strip my sodden clothes—the second time that night—another washed the stinging gash in my arm and bandaged it round. The third, practical fellow, realising that I had to be clad in something, was pulling the garments off one of the corpses—he chose one who had been neatly shot in the head, and had been considerate enough not to bleed much—and I can't say that I felt any revulsion at all about wearing dead men's weeds. In fact, they fitted uncommon well.

Then they presented me with a flask of schnapps, and I sent half of it down my throat at once, and felt the fiery warmth running back along my limbs. I poured a little into my palm and rubbed it on my face and neck—a trick Mackenzie taught me in Afghanistan; nothing like it for the cold, if you can spare the liquor.

I sipped the rest slowly, looking round. There were several Volsungs in the hall, staring curiously about them, and I could hear the voices of others in the upper rooms; they seemed to have everything in hand. Of Sapten and Grundvig there was no sign.

Well, this was fine, so far as it went. I was beginning to feel excellent, now that the shock—no, the series of hellish frights—of the evening were wearing off, and I was savouring the blissful knowledge that here I was, hale and whole, with drink in me, warm clothes, and nothing more to fear. With every moment, as I realised what I had endured and escaped, my spirits rose; I could contemplate the future, for the first time in months, without feeling my bowels drooping down into my legs.

"Where's Major Sapten, then?" says I, and they told me he was down in the dungeon still; on no account, they said, was anyone to intrude. Well, I knew the prohibition wouldn't include me, so I brushed aside their protests with a show of princely authority—remarkable how habits stick, once learned—and marched across to the passage. I checked at the archway, though, and asked if they were sure all the defenders were dead, and they beamed and chorused "Jah, jah." I took a sabre along anyway—not for protection, but because I knew it would look well, and went down the staircase and into the cloister. Through the far archway I heard the murmur of voices, and as I came closer Sapten was saying:

"—Hansen's body in the moat. I wish we had laid Starnberg by the heels, though; that's one overdue in hell."

That was bad news; I took a hurried look round, and then cursed my nervousness. Wherever Rudi was, it wouldn't be here.

"It all passes belief," said another voice, and I recognised it as Carl Gustaf's. "Can it be true? A man who could take my place . . . an English impostor . . . and yet he came here, alone with Hansen, to try to save me."

"He didn't have much choice," growls Sapten. "It was that or a rope." Well, damn him; there was gratitude.

"Nay, nay, you wrong him." It was Grundvig now, excellent chap. "He tried to make amends, Sapten; no man could have done more. Without him . . ."

"Do I not know it?" says Carl Gustaf. "I saw him fight; he saved me from that scoundrel. My God! what a death!"

There was a pause, and then Sapten says:

"Aye, well, give him the benefit of the doubt. But, I have to say it, in dying he performed you a service, highness, for alive he might have been a confounded embarrassment."

Well, I wasn't standing for this—besides, I know a cue when I hear one. I stepped softly through the archway.

"Sorry to be inconvenient, major," says I, "but embarrassment or not, I am still here to serve his highness."

It produced a most satisfactory effect; Sapten spun round on his heel, his pipe clattering on the floor; Grundvig sprang up, staring in amazement; the Prince, who had been seated at the table, swore in astonishment; there were two others there, behind the Prince's chair, and doubtless they were suitably stricken, too.

Well, there was a fine babble and cries of wonder and inquiry, I can tell you; they were certainly surprised to see me, even if they weren't exactly overjoyed. Of course, it was a difficult situation for them; heroes are so much less of a nuisance when they're dead. There was even a hint of resentment, I thought, in the questions they poured at me—how had I escaped, where had I come from; I'll swear Sapten was on the brink of demanding what the devil I meant by it.

I answered fairly offhand, describing the plumbing system of Jotunberg briefly, and how I had escaped from the lake. Grundvig and the Prince agreed it was a marvel; Sapten recovered his pipe and stuffed it with tobacco.

"And so," says I, in conclusion, "I came back to offer my further services—if they are needed." And I laid my sabre gently on the table and stood back. This chap Irving has nothing on me.

There was an awkward, very long silence. Sapten puffed —*he* wasn't going to break it; Grundvig fidgeted, and then the Prince, who had been frowning at the table, looked up. God, he was like me.

"Sir," says he slowly, "these gentlemen have been telling me . . . what has happened in Strackenz of late. It—it defies understanding . . . mine at least. It seems you have been party to the most dastardly deception, the strangest plot, I ever heard of. Yet it seems it was against your will—is this not so?" He looked at the others, and Grundvig nodded and looked bewildered. "Perhaps I am not clear in my mind," the Prince went on, "after all this—" and he gestured about him, like a man in a fog, "—but at least I have the evidence of my eyes. Whoever you are, whatever the reasons for

252

what you did . . ." he broke off, at a loss, and then pulled himself together. "You saved my life tonight, sir. That much I know. If there has been wrong on your side—well, that is for your soul. But it has been cancelled out, for me at least." He looked at the others, Grundvig still nodding, Sapten puffing grimly and staring at his boots. Then Carl Gustaf stood up, and held out his hand.

I took it, very manly, and we shook and looked each other in the eye. It was not canny, that resemblance, and I know he felt the same eeriness as I did, for his hand fell away.

"Indeed, I think I am in your debt," says he, a little shaky. "If there is anything I can do . . . I don't know."

Well, to tell the truth, I hadn't been thinking of rewards, but he seemed to be hinting at something. However, I knew the best policy was to shut up, so I simply waited, and another uncomfortable silence fell. But this time it was Sapten who broke it.

"There's no question of debt," says he, deliberately. "Mr Arnold may be said to have made amends. He's lucky to go off with his life."

But at this Grundvig and the Prince cried out.

"At least we owe him civility," says the Prince. "Mr Arnold, you have had my thanks; understand it is the thanks of Strackenz and Denmark also."

"Aye, very fine," sneers Sapten. "But with your highness's leave, a clear passage to our frontier is the most, I think, that Mr Arnold will expect." He was pretty angry, all right; I began to understand that if Carl Gustaf hadn't survived it would have been waltzing matilda for Flashy if Sapten had had his way. I didn't think it politic to mention his promise on behalf of little golden-headed Amelia; the less said about her the better.

"At least he must be allowed to rest first," says the Prince, "and then conveyed in safety to the border. We owe him that."

"He can't stay here," croaked Sapten. "In God's name,

look at his face! We'll have difficulty preventing a scandal as it is. If there are two men with the prince's figurehead in the state, we'll never keep it quiet."

The Prince bit his lip, and I saw it was time for a diplomatic intervention.

"If your highness pleases," says I, "Major Sapten is right. Every moment I continue in Strackenz is dangerous, for both of us, but especially for you. I must go, and quickly. Believe me, it is for the best. And as the major has remarked, there is no debt."

Wasn't there, though! I kept my face smooth, but underneath I was beginning to smart with hurt and anger. I hadn't asked to be embroiled in the politics of their tin-pot little duchy, but I had been bloody near killed more times than I could count, cut and wounded and half-drowned, scared out of my wits—and all I was getting at the end of it was the sneers of Sapten and the handshake of his blasted highness. Ten minutes before I had been thankful to come out with a whole skin, but suddenly now I felt full of spite and anger towards them.

There was a bit of mumbling and grumbling, but it was all hypocrisy; indeed, I don't doubt that if Carl Gustaf had been given an hour or two longer to recover from the scare he had had, and his consequent gratitude to me, he would have been ready to listen to a suggestion from Sapten that I should be slipped back down the pipe for a second time—with my hands tied this time. After all, his face was like mine, so his character might be, too.

For the moment, though, he had the grace to look troubled; he probably thought he owed it to his princely dignity to do something for me. But he managed to fight it down—they usually do—and the upshot of it was that they agreed that I should ride out as quickly as possible. They would stay where they were for the night, so that his highness could rest and take counsel, and there was a broad hint that I had better be over the frontier by morning. Grundvig seemed the only one who was unhappy about my sudden dismissal; he was an odd one, that, and I gathered from what he said that he alone had come round to the view that I was more sinned against than sinning. He actually seemed rather sorry for me, and he was the one who eventually escorted me up from that dungeon, and ordered a horse to be found, and stood with me in the castle gateway while they went to the mainland for it.

"I am a father, too, you see," says he, pacing up and down. "I understand what it must mean to a man, when his loved ones are torn from him, and used as hostages against him. Who knows? I, too, might have acted as you did. I trust I should have behaved as bravely when the time came."

Silly bastard, I thought, that's all you know. I asked him what had happened to Rudi, and he said he didn't know. They had seen him vanish through a side door in the outer cell, and had given chase, but had lost him in the castle. Presumably he knew its bolt-holes, and had got away. I didn't care for the sound of this, but it was long odds I wouldn't run into him again, anyway. I wasn't planning on lingering—just long enough for the notion that was beginning to form in my mind.

Then one of the peasants returned with a horse, and a cloak for me. I asked a few directions of Grundvig, accepted a flask and a pouch of bread and cheese, and swung into the saddle. Just the feel of the horse moving under me was heartening; I could hardly wait to be away from that beastly place and everything in it.

Grundvig didn't shake hands, but he waved solemnly, and then I turned the horse's head, touched her with my heel, and clattered away across the bridge, out of the lives of Carl Gustaf, the Sons of the Volsungs, Old Uncle Tom Cobley, and all. I took the Strackenz City road, and never looked back at the cold pile of Jotunberg. I hope they all caught pneumonia.

You would think, no doubt, that after what I had gone through, I would have no thought but to get out of Strackenz and Germany as fast as a clean pair of heels could take me. Looking back, I wonder that I had any other notion, but the truth is that I did. It's a queer thing; while I'm the sorriest coward in moments of danger, there is no doubt that escape produces an exhilaration in me. Perhaps it is simple reaction; perhaps I become light-headed; perhaps it is that in my many aftermaths I have usually had the opportunity of some strong drink—as I had now—and that all three combine to produce a spirit of folly. God knows it isn't courage, but I wish I had a guinea for every time I've come through some hellish crisis, babbling thankfully to be still alive—and then committed some idiocy which I wouldn't dare to contemplate in a rational moment.

And in this case I was angry, too. To be harried and bullied and exposed to awful danger—and then just cut adrift with hardly a thank-you-damn-your-eyes from a man who, but for me, would have been feeding the fishes— God, I found myself hating that shilly-shally Carl Gustaf, and that sour-faced old turd Sapten—aye, and that mealy Grundvig, with his pious maundering. I'd pay them out, by gum, would I. And it would be poetic justice, too, in a way—Bismarck had promised me a grand reward; well, I'd come out of Strackenz with something for my pains.

And, of course, it was really safe enough. There was hardly any risk at all, for I had a certain start of several hours, and I'd know how to cover my tracks. By God, I'd show them; they'd learn that a little gratitude would have been starvation cheap. I could do their dirty work for them, and then I could just piss off, could I? They'd learn to think a little more of Harry Flashman than that, the mean bastards.

So I reasoned, in my logical way. But the main thing was, I was sure there was no danger in what I intended. And what is there, I ask you, that a man will not dare, so long as he has a fast horse and a clear road out of town?

The night sky was just beginning to lighten when I came to Strackenz city, with the dawn wind rustling the trees along the landstrasse. The suburbs were quiet as I cantered through, my hooves ringing on the cobbles; I skirted the old city to come to the ducal palace, where two sleepy sentries stared open-mouthed at me through the railings.

"Oeffnen!" says I, and while one tried to present arms and dropped his musket, the other made haste to swing open the gates. I clattered through, leaving them to marvel at the sight of their new prince, whose absence must have been the talk of the duchy, arriving unkempt and unshaven at this hour of the day.

There were more guards at the door, to whom I gave sharp orders to have a strong horse saddled and ready for me within ten minutes. I issued further instructions that no one was on any account to be allowed to leave the palace, nor was anyone to be admitted without reference to me. They saluted and stamped and fell over themselves in their hurry to obey; one flung open the doors for me, and I strode masterfully into the hall—this was going to be easy, thinks I.

A sleepy major-domo or night porter came starting out of the chair where he had been dozing; he cried out at the sight of me, and would have roused the place, but I hushed him with a word.

"Send someone to the kitchen," says I. "Get them to put together such cold foods as will go into a saddle-bag, and bring it here. Also some wine and a flask of spirits. Oh, and some money—bring a purse. Now, go."

"Your highness is riding out again?" quavers he.

"Yes," I snapped. "Beeilen sie sich."

"But, highness . . . I have instructions . . . her highness the duchess must be informed."

"The duchess? She's here? Not at Strelhow?"

"No, indeed, sir. She returned last night, after . . . after you were not to be found." His eyes were round with fright. "There has been terrible concern, highness. Orders have been issued that if word came about you, her highness was to know at once."

I hadn't counted on this; she ought to have been at Strelhow still, damn her. It complicated matters— or did it? I stood thinking quickly, while the major-domo hopped from one foot to the other, and made up my mind.

"Well, I'll tell her myself," says I. "Now, my good fellow, do exactly as I have told you—and the less said about my return the better—understand?"

I left him chattering obedience, and went up the great staircase four at a time, and strode along to the duchess's apartments. There were the usual yellow-jacketed sentries at her door, stiffening to attention at the sight of me, and rolling their eyes in astonishment—wouldn't have done for the 11th Hussars, I'll tell you. I thumped on the panels, and after a moment a feminine voice called out sleepily: "Wer klopft?"

"Carl Gustaf," says I, and to the sentries: "Let no one pass."

There was a feminine squeaking from within, and the door opened on the pert little red-haired lady-in-waiting whom Rudi had fancied; she was staring in astonishment with one eye and rubbing the sleep out of the other—a very pretty picture of disarray, with one tit peeping out of her night-dress. It's as well I'm leaving Strackenz, thinks I, for I wouldn't have been a faithful husband for long.

"Where's your mistress?" says I, and at that moment the inner door opened, and Irma appeared, a gown pulled hastily round her shoulders.

"What is it, Helga? Who was knock—", and then at the

258

sight of me she gave a little scream, swayed for a moment, and then flung herself forward into my arms. "Carl! Oh, Carl! Carl!"

Oh, well, I might have been faithful for a while, anyway; the feel of that warm young body against mine was like an electric shock, and it was no pretence when I hugged her to me and returned the kisses that she rained on my lips and cheeks.

"Oh, Carl!" She stared up at me, tears on her lovely face. "Oh, my dear, what has happened to your head?"

For a moment I didn't understand; then I remembered. My fine bald poll hadn't had the razor over it for two or three days now, and I was sporting a fine black bristle, like an old brush. Trust a woman to hit on the least important thing!

"Nothing, my dear darling," says I, and smothered her lovingly. "All's well, now that I have you again."

"But what has happened? Where have you been? I was mad with anxiety—" She gave a little scream. "You are wounded! Your arm—"

"There, there, sweeting," says I, giving her another squeeze for luck. "Set your fears at rest. It's a scratch, nothing more." I turned her round, murmuring endearments, and led her into her own bedchamber, away from the delighted and curious gaze of young Helga. I shut the door, and at once her questions broke out afresh. I hushed her and sat down on the edge of the bed—it would have been splendid to curl up with her, but there wasn't time.

"There has been a rebellion—a plot, rather, against the duchy. Your throne, our lives, were threatened." I cut short her cry of dismay. "It is all over—nearly over, at any rate. There is a little still to do, but thanks to the loyalty of certain of your subjects—our subjects—the worst is passed, and there is no more to fear."

"But . . . but I don't understand," she began, and then that beautiful face hardened. "Who was it? Those agitators—those creatures of the gutter! I knew it!"

"Now, now," says I soothingly, "calm yourself. It is all past; Strackenz is safe—and most of all, you are safe, my sweet." And I wrapped her up again, most enjoyably.

She began to tremble, and then to sob. "Oh, Carl, oh, thank God! You have really come back! Oh, my dear, I have been ready to die! I thought . . . I thought you were . . ."

"Ah, well, you see, I wasn't. There, there. Now dry your eyes, my darling, and listen." She blinked at me, dabbing at her eyelashes—God, she was a beauty, in her flimsy night-rail—they seemed to be wearing them very low in Strackenz that winter, and I was beginning to come all over of a heat, what with her nearness and the scent of her hair, and the troubled adoration in her lovely eyes.

"It is quite crushed, this—this plot," says I. "No, hear me out—I shall explain everything in time, but for the moment you must trust me, and do precisely as I say. It is done—finished—safe, all but for a few details, which require my attention . . ."

"Details? What details?"

"There's no time now. I must be away again." She cried out at this. "It is only for a moment, darling—a few hours, and I shall be with you, and we'll never be parted again—never."

She started to weep again, clinging to me, refusing to let me go, protesting that I would be going into danger, and all the rest of it. I tried to comfort her, and then the baggage opened her mouth on mine, and pushed her hand between my thighs, murmuring to me to stay.

By gum, it agitated me; I wondered if I had time? No, by God, I daren't—I had lost precious minutes already. She was stroking away, and my head was swimming with her, but I just put lust second to common sense for once, and forced her gently away.

"You must stay here," says I firmly. "With a strong guard on the palace and on your room itself. Oh, darling, believe me, it is vital! I would not go, but I must—and you must remember that you are a duchess, and the protector of your people—and, and all that. Now will you trust me, and believe me that I do this for the safety of Strackenz and my own darling?"

These royal wenches are made of stern stuff, of course; tell 'em it's for their country's sake and they become all proudly dutiful and think they're Joan of Arc. I gave her some more patriotism mixed with loving slush, and at last she agreed to do what she was told. I swore I'd be back in an hour or two, and hinted that we would stay in bed for a week, and at this she flung herself on me again.

"Oh, my darling!" says she, wriggling against me. "How can I let you go?"

"Just for a bit," says I. "And then—ah, but I can't stop now." She was getting me into a fever. "No, I promise I shall take care. I won't get hurt—and if I do, there'll be another chap along shortly—that is, no . . . I mean . . . I shall return, my darling." I gave her one last tremendous hug, and left her stretching out her arms to me. It was quite touching, really—she loved me, you know, and if I hadn't been in such a damned hurry I'd have been quite sorry to leave her.

Next door Mistress Helga had restored herself to decency, but from the flush on her cheeks I suspected she'd been listening at the door. I instructed her sternly to look after her mistress and to see that she kept to her room; then I stepped out into the passage. The sentries were stiff as ramrods; I repeated my orders that no one was to pass, either way, and set off for the clock tower.

It wasn't difficult to find; up another flight of the main stairs—there were two more sentries at the top, whom I sent to join Irma's guard—and then up a spiral stairway and along a short passage to a wrought-iron gateway. Just before the gate there was a little guard-room, where I found an ensign and two sentries; the men were playing cards and the ensign was lounging in a chair, but at sight

261

of me they were on their feet in an instant, goggling and fumbling with buttons. I lost no time.

"Fahnrich," says I, "there has been an attempt at a coup d'état. The duchess's life has been threatened."

They stared at me aghast.

"No time to tell you more," I went on briskly. "The situation is in hand, but I have to leave the palace at once in order to take charge at the scene of the outbreak. You understand? Now, then, what's your name?"

"W-w-wessel, please your highness," he stammered.

"Very good, Fahnrich Wessel. Now, attend to me. For the safety of the duchess, I have already mounted a guard on her apartments. You, with your men here, will proceed there at once, and you will take command. You will permit no one—no one, you understand—to pass into her highness's apartment until I return. Is that clear?"

"Why—why, yes, your highness. But our post here—the crown jewels . . ."

"There is a jewel, infinitely more precious to us all, to be guarded," says I portentously. "Now, take your men and go quickly."

"Of course, highness . . . on the instant." He hesitated. "But, pardon, highness—it is the first order of the palace guard that never shall the jewels be left unwatched. These are explicit instructions . . ."

"Fahnrich Wessel," says I, "do you wish to be a lieutenant some day? Or would you prefer to be a private? I know the sacred value of the regalia as well as you, but there are times when even jewels are unimportant." (I couldn't think of one, offhand, but it sounded well.) "So, off with you. I take full responsibility. Indeed, I'll do better. Give me the keys, and I shall carry them myself."

That settled it. He clicked his heels, squeaked at his men, and sent them off at the double. He took the keys from his own belt, and passed them to me as though they were red-hot; then he gathered up his sabre and cap and was off, but I called him back.

"Wessel," says I, in a softer voice. "You are not married?"

"No, highness."

"But you are perhaps a lover?"

He went pink. "Highness, I . . ."

"You understand, I think." I frowned and forced a smile together—one of those grimaces of the strong man moved—and laid a hand on his shoulder. "Take care of her for me, won't you?"

He was one of those very young, intense creatures of the kind you see addressing heaven in the background of pictures showing Napoleon crossing the Alps in dancing pumps; he went red with emotion.[40]

"With my life, highness," says he, gulping, and he snatched my hand, kissed it, and sped away.

Well, that was Ensign Wessel taken care of. He'd cut the whole bloody German army to bits before he let anyone near Irma. Likewise, and more important, he didn't doubt his prince for a minute. Ah, the ideals of youth, I thought, as I sorted out the keys.

There were three of them; one to the ironwork gate, a second to the door beyond it, and a third to the little cage, shrouded in velvet, which stood on a table in the centre of the small jewel-room. It was so easy I could have cheered. There was a valise in the guard-room, and I laid it open beside the table and went to work.

God, what a haul it was! There were the rings, the staff of sovereignty, the diamond-and-emerald gold chain, the duchess's collar, and the two crowns—they didn't have to be bent, after all. The Sword of State I left behind, as too unwieldy, but there were a couple of necklaces I hadn't seen before and a jewelled casket, so in they went.

I was sweating, not with exertion but excitement, as I shut the valise and strapped it up; it weighed about a ton, and suddenly I was asking myself: where was I going to fence this collection? Oh, well, time to worry about that when I was safe over the border, and back in England or

France. Thank God the only name Sapten and Co. knew me by was Thomas Arnold—they were welcome to call at *his* tombstone if they felt like it, and ask for their money back. They had no way of tracing me, even if they dared—for if they ever did ferret me out, what could they do that wouldn't cause an unholy international scandal? But they'd never even know where to look in England—I was safe as houses.

Aye—once I'd got away: time was flying. It was full dawn outside by now. I locked the cage, arranged its velvet cover, locked the door and the gate, and set off down the stairs, lugging my bag with me. I emerged cautiously at the head of the grand staircase—thanks to my sending the sentries away there wasn't a soul in sight. I stole down, and was tip-toeing towards the head of the last flight when I heard footsteps along the passage. Quickly I thrust the valise behind the base of a statue; I was just in time. Old Schwerin, the Chief Minister, still with his nightcap on and a robe-de-chambre flapping round his ankles, was hobbling along towards me, with a little knot of attendants fussing in his wake.

He was in a tremendous taking, of course; I thought the old ass would have a seizure. Forcing myself not to panic at the delay, I stilled his questions with the same recital of tommy-rot that I'd served up to Irma and the ensign—well, I say I stilled them, but he babbled on, demanding details and explanations, and eventually I only shut him up by taking a strong line, insisting on the need for haste on my part—I had to get back to the scene of the action at once, I told him.

"Oh, God!" groans he, and sank down on a sofa. "Oh, the unhappy country! What shall we do?"

"Nonsense, sir," says I, stifling a sudden desire to run for it, "I have told you the alarm is over—all but over, anyway. What remains to do is to see that no disorders follow—to quiet our contending factions, Danish and German, in the city itself. This shall be your first concern."

And for some reason I asked: "Which side are you on, by the way?"

He stopped moaning and gazed up at me like a dying retriever. "I am for Strackenz, highness," says he. He was no fool, this one, for all he was an old woman.

"Excellent!" I cried. "Then summon the ministers at once—you'd better get dressed first—and send these people"—I indicated his followers—"to wait upon the duchess."

It was going to be like a galloping field day at her apartments, but the more of them were out of the way the better.

"Above all," says I, "try to communicate as little disquiet as possible. Now set about it, if you please."

He gathered himself up, and shooed away the crowd.

"And yourself, highness?" he quavered. "You are going into danger? But you will take a strong escort with you?"

"No," says I, "the fewer who see me go, the better." That was God's truth, too. "Not another word, sir. For the duchess's sake, do as I have bidden you."

"You will have a care, highness?" he pleaded. "I beg of you. For her sake—and for our country's. Oh, but must you go?"

I was almost bursting with anxiety, but I had to humour the senile bastard.

"Sir," says, I, "have no fear. Briefly as I have been in Strackenz, I owe a debt to this duchy already, and I intend to pay it in full."

He drew himself upright and straightened his night-cap. "God bless you, highness," says he, all moist and trembling. "You are in the true mould of the Oldenbourgs."

Well, from what I've seen of European royalty, he may well have been right. I gave him my manliest smile, pressed his hand, and watched him totter away to guard the destiny of the duchy, God help it. He was going to have his work cut out.

As soon as he was round the corner I heaved out my

valise, adjusted it over my shoulder by a strap, and pulled my riding-cloak over that side. The swag had a tendency to clank as I walked, so I paced slowly down the broad staircase and across the hall; the little major-domo was waiting, hopping in anxiety. There was a horse at the door, he pointed out, and its saddle-bags were packed. I thanked him and walked out into the morning.

There were guardsmen there, of course, and a couple of officers all agog at the rumours that must have been flying about. I instructed them to post their men at the palace railings, and to let no one pass without my orders—with any luck they might blow Sapten's grizzled head off when he arrived. Then I mounted, very carefully, which is damned difficult to do when you have a stone or two of loot swinging under your cloak, took the reins in my free hand, and addressed the officers again:

"I ride to Jotunberg!"

I cantered off down the great carriage-sweep, and they opened the gates at my approach. I stopped at the sentry and quietly inquired which was the western road to Lauenburg, and he told me—that would reach Sapten's ears, for certain, and should set him on the wrong track. Five minutes later I was clattering out of Strackenz City, making south-east towards Brandenburg.

I've noticed that in novels, when the hero has to move any distance at all, he leaps on to a mettlesome steed which carries him at breakneck speed over incredible distances—without ever casting a shoe, or going lame, or simply running out of wind and strength. On my flight from Strackenz, admittedly, my beast bore up remarkably well, despite the fact that I rode him hard until we were over the border and into Prussia. After that I went easier, for I'd no wish to have him founder under me before I'd put some distance between myself and possible pursuit. But thirty miles, with my weight to carry, is asking a lot of any animal, and by afternoon I was looking for a place to lie up until he was fit for the road again.

We found one, in an old barn miles from anywhere, and I rubbed him down and got him some fodder, before using up some of my store of cold food for myself. I took a tack to the south next day, for it seemed to me on reflection that the wider I could pass from Berlin, the better. I know my luck—I was going to have to go closer to Schönhausen than was comfortable, and it would have been just like it if I'd run into dear Otto on the way. (As it happened, I needn't have worried; there was plenty to occupy him in Berlin just then.) But I had planned out my line of march: acting on the assumption that the safest route was through the heart of Germany to Munich, where I could choose whether to go on to Switzerland, Italy, or even France, I had decided to make first of all for Magdeburg, where I could take to the railway. After that it should be plain sailing to Munich, but in the meantime I would ride by easy stages, keeping to the country and out of sight so far as possible—my baggage wouldn't stand examination, if I ran across any of the great tribe of officials who are always swarming in Germany, looking for other folk's business to meddle in.

In fact, I was being more cautious than was necessary. There was no telegraph in those days to overtake the fugitive,[41] and even if there had been, and the Strackenzians had been silly enough to use it, no one in Germany would have had much time for me. While I was sneaking from one Prussian hedge to another with my bag of loot, Europe was beginning to erupt in the greatest convulsion she had known since Napoleon died. The great revolts, of which I had heard a murmur from Rudi, were about to burst on an astonished world: they had begun in Italy, where the excitable spaghettis were in a ferment; soon Metternich would be scuttling from Vienna; the French had proclaimed yet another republic; Berlin would see the barricades up within a month, and Lola's old leaping-partner, Ludwig, would shortly be bound for the knacker's yard. I knew nothing of all these things, of course, and I take some pride in the fact that while thrones were toppling and governments melting away overnight, I was heading for home with a set of crown jewels. There's a moral there, I think, if I could only work out what it was.

Possibly it doesn't apply only to me, either. You will recall that while the continent was falling apart, old England went her way without revolutions or disturbances beyond a few workers' agitations. We like to think we are above that sort of thing, of course; the Englishman, however miserably off he is, supposes that he's a free man, poor fool, and pities the unhappy foreigners raging against their rulers. And *his* rulers, of course, trade on that feeling, and keep him underfoot while assuring him that Britons never shall be slaves. Mark you, our populace may be wiser than it knows, for so far as I can see revolutions never benefited the ordinary folk one bit; they have to work just as hard and starve just as thin as ever. All the good they may get from rebellion is perhaps a bit of loot and rape at the time—and our English peasantry doesn't seem to go in for that sort of thing at home, possibly because they're mostly married men with responsibilities.

Anyway, the point I'm making is that I've no doubt the revolts of '48 did England a bit of good—by keeping out of them and making money. And that, as you've gathered, was the intention of H. Flashman, Esq., also.

However, things never go as you intend, even in European revolutions. My third night on the road I came down with a raging fever—fiery throat, belly pumping, and my head throbbing like a steam engine. I suppose it was sure to happen, after being immersed in icy water twice in one night, taking a wound, and being three parts drowned—to say nothing of the nervous damage I had suffered into the bargain. I had just enough strength to stumble out of the copse where I'd been lying up, and by sheer good luck came on a hut not far away. I pounded on the door, and the old folk let me in, and all I remember is their scared faces and myself staggering to a truckle bed, kicking my precious valise underneath, and then collapsing. I was there for the best part of a week, so near as I know, and if they were brave enough to peep into my bag while I was unconscious—which I doubt—they were too frightened to do anything about it.

They were simple, decent peasants, and as I discovered when I was well enough to sit up, went in some awe of me. Of course they could guess from my cut that I wasn't any common hobbledehoy; they hovered round me, and I suppose the old woman did a fair job of nursing me, and all told I counted myself lucky to have come upon them. They fed me as well as they could, which was damned badly, but the old chap managed to look after my horse, so that eventually I was able to take the road again in some sort of order, though still a trifle shaky.

I gave them a nicely-calculated payment for their trouble—too little or too much might have had them gossiping—and set out southward again. I was within

269

ride of Magdeburg, but having lost so much time by my sickness I was in a nervous sweat in case a hue and cry should have run ahead of me. However, no one paid me any heed on the road, and I came to Magdeburg safely, abandoned my horse (if I knew anything it would soon find an owner, but I didn't dare try to sell it), and took a train southward.

There was a shock for me at the station, though. Magdeburg had been one of the earliest cities in Germany to have the railway, but even so the sum of thalers they took for my fare left me barely enough to keep myself in food during the journey. I cursed myself for not trying to realise something on my horse, but it was too late now, so I was carried south with a fortune in jewels in my valise and hardly the price of a shave in my pocket.

Needless to say, this shortage of blunt worried me a good deal. I could get to Munich, but how the devil was I to travel on from there? Every moment I was in Germany increased the chances of my coming adrift somehow. I wasn't worried about being in Bavaria, for I was persuaded that Rudi's threats of criminal charges in Munich had been all trumped-up stuff to frighten me, and there was no danger on that score. And I was a long way from Strackenz, in the last place that Sapten—or Bismarck—would have looked for me. But that damned valise full of booty was an infernal anxiety; if anyone got a whiff of its contents I was scuppered.

So I gnawed my nails the whole way—God knows I was hungry enough—and finally reached Munich in a rare state of jumps, my belly as hollow as a coffin, and my problem still unsolved.

As soon as I stepped from the station, clutching my bag and huddling in my cloak, I felt the hairs rising on my neck. There was something in the air, and I've sensed it too often to be mistaken. I had felt it in Kabul, the night before the Residency fell; I was to know it again at Lucknow, and half a dozen other places—the hushed quiet that hangs over

270

a place that is waiting for a blow to fall. You sense it in a siege, or before the approach of a conquering army; folk hurry by with soft footsteps, and talk in low voices, and there is an emptiness about the streets. The life and bustle die, and the whole world seems to be listening, but no one knows what for. Munich was expectant and fearful, waiting for the whirlwind that was to rise within itself.

It was a dim, chilly evening, with only a little wind, but shops and houses were shuttered as against an impending storm. I found a little beer shop, and spent the last of my coppers on a stein and a piece of sausage. As I munched and drank I glanced over a newspaper that someone had left on the table; there had been student rioting, apparently over the closure of the university, and troops had been called out. There had been some sharp clashes, several people had been wounded, property had been destroyed, and the houses of prominent people had been virtually besieged.

The paper, as I recall, didn't think much of all this, but it seemed to be on the students' side, which was odd. There were a few hints of criticism of King Ludwig, which was odder still, journalists being what they are, and knowing which side their bread is buttered—at all events, they didn't see a quick end to the general discontent, unless the authorities "heeded the voice of popular alarm and purged the state of those poisons which had for all too long eaten into the very heart of the nation"—whatever that meant.

All in all, it looked as though Munich was going to be a warm town, and no place for me, and I was just finishing my sausage and speculating on how the devil to get away, when a tremendous commotion broke out down the street, there was a crash of breaking glass, and the voice of popular alarm was raised with a vengeance. Everyone in the shop jumped to his feet, and the little landlord began roaring for his assistants to get the shutters up and bar the door; there was a rising chorus of cheering out in the dark, the thunder of a rushing crowd, the shop window was shattered, and almost before I had time to get under

271

the table with my bag there was a battle royal in progress in the street.

Amidst the din of shouts and cheers and cracking timber, to say nothing of the babble in the shop itself, I grabbed my bag and was making for the back entrance, but a stout old chap with grey whiskers seized hold of me, bellowing to make himself heard.

"Don't go out!" he roared. "Here we are safe! They will cut you to pieces out there!"

Well, he knew what he was talking about, as I realised when the sound of the struggle had passed by, and we took a cautious peep out. The street looked as though a storm had swept through it; there wasn't a whole window or shutter left, half a dozen bodies, dead or unconscious, were lying on the road, and the pavement was a litter of brickbats, clubs, and broken glass. A hundred yards down the street a handcart was being thrown on to an improvised bonfire; there were perhaps a score of fellows dancing round it, and then suddenly there were cries of alarm and they broke and ran. Round the corner behind came a solid mob of youths, rushing in pursuit with their vanguard carrying a banner and howling their heads off; some carried torches and I had a glimpse of red caps as they bore down, chanting "Allemania! Allemania!"

More than that I didn't see, for we all ducked back inside again, and then they had stormed past like a charge of heavy cavalry, the sound of their chanting dying into the distance, and the occasional smashing of glass and crash of missiles grew fainter and fainter.

The old chap with whiskers was swearing fearfully beside me.

"Allemania! Scum! Young hounds of hell! Why don't the soldiers sabre them down? Why are they not crushed without mercy?"

I remarked that crushing them was probably easier said than done, from what I'd seen, and asked who they were. He turned pop-eyes on me.

"Where have you been, sir? The Allemania? I thought everyone knew they were the hired mob of that she-devil Montez, who is sent to trouble the world, and Munich in particular!" And he called her several unpleasant names.

"Ah, she won't trouble it much longer, though," says another one, a thin cove in a stove-pipe hat and mittens. "Her time is almost run."

"God be thanked for it!" cries the old chap. "The air of Munich will be sweeter without her and her filthy bordello perfumes." And he and the thin cove fell to miscalling her with a will.

Now, as you can guess, I pricked up my ears at this, for it sounded like excellent news. If the good Muncheners were kicking Lola out at last, they would get three cheers and a tiger from me. She had been in my mind, of course, ever since I'd decided to make for Munich, although I'd determined to keep well clear of her and the Barerstrasse. But if she had fallen from favour I was agog to hear all about it; I couldn't think of anything I'd rather listen to. I pressed the stout old fellow for details, and he supplied them.

"The king has given way at last," says he. "He has thrown her out—the one good thing to come out of all this civil unrest that is sweeping the country. Herr Gott! the times we live in!" He looked me up and down. "But you, then, are a stranger to Munich, sir?"

I said I was, and he advised me to continue to be one. "This is no place for honest folk these days," says he. "Continue your journey, I say, and thank God that wherever you come from has not been ruined by the rule of a dotard and his slut."

"Unless," says the thin chap, grinning, "you care to linger for an hour or two and watch Munich exorcising its demon. They stoned her house last night, and the night before; I hear the crowds are in the Barerstrasse this evening again; perhaps they'll sack the place."

Well, this was splendid altogether. Lola, who had dragged me into the horror of Schönhausen and Jotunberg at

Bismarck's prompting, was being hounded out of Munich by the mob, while I, the poor dupe and puppet, would be strolling out with my pockets lined with tin. She was losing everything—and I was gaining a fortune. It isn't often justice is so poetic.

True, I still had to solve my immediate problem of getting out of Munich without funds. I daren't try to pop any of my swag, and short of waylaying someone in an alley—and I hadn't the game for that—I could see no immediate way of raising the wind. But it was a great consolation to know that Lola's troubles were infinitely more pressing—by the sound of it she'd be lucky to get through the night alive. Would they sack her palace? The thought of being on hand to gloat from a safe distance was a famous one—if it *was* safe, of course.

"What about her Allemania?" I asked. "Won't they defend her?"

"Not they," says the thin man, sneering. "You'll find few of them near the Barerstrasse tonight—they riot down here, where they conceive themselves safe, but they'll risk no encounter with the folk who are crying 'Pereat Lola' at her gates. No," says he, rubbing his mittens, "our Queen of Harlots will find she has few friends left when the mob flush her out."

Well, that settled it; I wasn't going to miss the chance of seeing the deceitful trollop ridden out of town on a rail—supposing the Germans had picked up that fine old Yankee custom. I could spare an hour or two for that, so off we set, the thin chap and I, for the Barerstrasse.

A mob is a frightening thing, even when it is a fairly orderly German one, and you happen to be part of it. As we came to the Barerstrasse, across the Karolinen Platz, we found ourselves part of a general movement; in ones and twos, and in bigger groups, folk were moving towards the street where Lola's bijou palace stood; long before we reached it we heard the rising murmur of thousands of voices, swelling into a sullen roar as we came close to the fringes of the mob itself. The Barerstrasse was packed by an enormous crowd, the front ranks pressing up against the railings. I lost the thin chap somewhere in the press, but being tall, and finding a step on the opposite side to stand on, I could look out across the sea of heads to the line of cuirassiers drawn up inside the palace railings—she still had her guard, apparently—and see the lighted windows towards which the crowd were directing a steady stream of catcalls and their favourite chant of "Pereat Lola! Pereat Lola!" Splendid stuff; I wondered if she was quite such a proud and haughty madame now, with this pack baying for her blood.

There wasn't much sign that they would do anything but chant, however; I didn't know, then, that they were mostly there in the expectation of seeing her go, for apparently the word had gone round that she was leaving Munich that night. I was to be privileged to see that remarkable sight—and to share in it; I would have been better crawling out of Munich on my hands and knees, and all the way to the frontier, but I wasn't to know that, either.

I had been there about half an hour, I suppose, and was getting weary of it, and starting to worry again about my valise, which I was gripping tightly under my coat. It didn't look as though they were going to break in and drag her out, anyway, which was what I'd have liked, and I was wondering where to go next, when a great roar went up, and everyone began craning to see what was happening. A carriage had come from the back of the palace, and was drawn up at the front door; you could feel the excitement rising up from the mob like steam as they jostled for a better look.

I could see over their heads beyond the line of guardsmen to the front door; there were figures moving round the coach, and then a tremendous yell went up as the door opened. A few figures emerged, and then one alone; even at that distance it was obviously a woman, and the crowd began to hoot and roar all the louder.

"Pereat Lola! Pereat Lola!"

It was her, all right; as she came forward into the light that shone from the big lanterns on either side of the doorway I could recognise her quite easily. She was dressed as for travelling, with a fur beaver perched on her head, and her hands in a muff before her. She stood looking out, and the jeers and abuse swelled up to a continuous tumult; the line of guardsmen gave back ever so slightly as the folk in front shook their fists and menaced her through the railings.

There was a moment's pause, and some consultation among the group round her on the steps; then there were cries of surprise from the street as the coach whipped up and wheeled down towards the gates, for Lola was still standing in the doorway.

"She's not going!" someone sang out, and there was consternation as the gates opened and the coach rolled slowly forward. The crowd gave back before it, and it was able to move through the lane they made; the coachee was looking pretty scared, and keeping his whip to himself, but the mob weren't interested in him. He drove a little way, and then stopped not twenty yards from where I was; the crowd, murmuring in bewilderment, couldn't make out what it was all about. There was a man in the coach, but no one seemed to know who he was.

Lola was still standing on the steps of the house, but now she came down them and began to walk towards the gate, and in that moment the roar of the mob died away. There was a mutter of astonishment, and then that died, too, and in an almost eery silence she was walking steadily past the line of cuirassiers, towards the crowd waiting in the street.

For a minute I wondered if she was mad; she was making straight for the crowd who had been roaring threats and curses at her only a moment before. They'll kill her, I thought, and felt the hairs prickling on the nape of my neck; there was something awful in the sight of that small, graceful figure, the hat perched jauntily on her black hair, the muff swinging in one hand, walking quite alone down to the open gates.

There she stopped, and looked slowly along the ranks of the mob, from side to side. They were still silent; there was a cough, a stifled laugh, an isolated voice here and there, but the mass of them made never a sound, watching her and wondering. She stood there a full half-minute, and then walked straight into the front rank.

They opened up before her, people jostling and treading on each other and cursing to move out of her way. She never faltered, but made straight ahead, and the lane to her coach opened up again, the people falling back on both sides to let her through. As she drew closer I could see her lovely face under the fur hat; she was smiling a little, but not looking to either side, as unconcerned as though she had been the hostess at a vicarage garden party moving among her guests. And for all their hostile eyes and grim faces, not one man-jack made a move against her, or breathed a word, as she went by.

Years later I heard a man who had been in that crowd—an embassy chap, I think he was—describing the scene to some others in a London club.

"It was the bravest thing, by gad, I ever saw in my life. There she was, this slip of a girl, walking like a queen—my stars, what a beauty she was, too! Straight into that mob she went, that had been howling for her life and would have torn her limb from limb if one of them had given the lead. She hardly noticed them, dammit; just smiled serenely, with her head high. She was quite unguarded, too, but on she walked, quite the thing, while those cabbage-eating swabs growled and glared—and did nothing. Oh, she had the measure of those fellows, all right. But to see her, so small and defenceless and brave! I tell you, I never was so proud to be an Englishman as in that moment; I wanted to rush forward to her side, to show her there was a countryman to walk with her through that damned, muttering pack of foreigners. Yes, by gad, I would have been happy—proud and happy—to come to her assistance, to be at her side."

"Why didn't you, then?" I asked him.

"Why not, sir? Because the crowd was too thick, damme. How could I have done?"

No doubt he was damned glad of the excuse, too; *I* wouldn't have been at her side for twice the contents of my valise. The risk she ran was appalling, for it would probably have taken only one spark to set them rushing in on her—the way they had been baying for her only a few minutes before would have frozen any ordinary person's blood. But not Lola; there was no cowing her; she was showing them, deliberately putting herself at their mercy, daring them to attack her—and she knew them better than they knew themselves, and they let her pass without a murmur.

It was pure idiot pride on her part, of course; typically Montez—and of a piece with what she had done, I heard, in the previous night's disturbance, when they were throwing brickbats at her windows, and the crazy bitch came out on her balcony, dressed in her finest ball gown and littered with gems, and toasted them in champagne. The plain truth about her was that she didn't care a damn—and they went in awe of her for it.[42]

She reached the coach and the chap inside hopped out and handed her in, but the coachee couldn't whip up until the crowd began to disperse. They went quietly, almost hang-dog; it was the queerest thing you ever saw. And then the coach began to go forward, at a walk, and the coachee still didn't whip up, even when the way was quite clear.

I tagged along a little way in the rear, marvelling at all this and not a little piqued to see her get off scot-free. Why, the brutes hadn't even given her a rotten egg to remember them by, but that is like the Germans. Let anyone stand up to 'em and they shuffle and look at each other and touch their forelocks to him. An English crowd, now—they'd either have murdered her or carried her shoulder-high, cheering, but these square-heads didn't have the bottom to do either.

The coach went slowly across the Karolinen Platz, where there was hardly any crowd at all, and into the street at the far side. I was still following on, to see if something was going to happen, but nothing did; no one seemed to be paying any attention to it now, as it rolled slowly up the street—and in that moment I was suddenly struck by a wonderful idea.

I had to get out of Munich—suppose I caught up with the coach and begged her to take me with her? She couldn't still be holding a grudge against me, surely—not after what I'd suffered through her contrivance? She'd paid off any score she owed me over Lord Ranelagh, a dozen times over—if she didn't know that, I could damned soon tell her. And she was no longer in any position to have me arrested, or locked up; dammit, anyway, we had been lovers, once; surely she wouldn't cast me adrift?

If I'd had a moment to think, I dare say I wouldn't have done it, but it was a decision taken on the edge of an instant. Here was a chance to get out of Munich, and Germany too, probably, before the traps got after me—and in a moment I was running after the coach, gripping my valise, and calling out to it to stop. Possibly it was just my natural instinct: when in danger, get behind a woman's skirts.

The coachee heard me, and of course at once whipped up, thinking, I suppose, that some particularly bloodthirsty hooligan in the mob had changed his mind, and was bent on mischief. The coach rumbled forward, and I ran roaring in its wake, cursing at the driver to rein in, and trying to make him understand.

"Halt, dammit!" I shouted. "Lola! It's me—Harry Flashman! Hold on, can't you?"

But he just went faster than ever, and I had to run like billy-o, splashing through the puddles and bellowing. Luckily he couldn't go too fast over the cobbles, and I hove alongside, just about blown, and swung myself onto the side step.

"Lola!" I roared, "Look—it's me!" and she called out to the coachee to pull up. I opened the door and tumbled in.

The chap with her, her little servant, was ready to leap at me, but I pushed him off. She was staring at me as though I were a ghost.

"In heaven's name!" she exclaimed. "You!—what are you doing here? And what the devil have you done to your head?"

"Oh, my God, Lola!" says I, "I've had the very deuce of a time! Lola, you must help me! I've no money, d'you see, and that damned Otto Bismarck is after me! Look—you ask about my head? He and his ruffians tried to murder me! They did—several times! Look here." And I showed her the bandage sticking out of my left cuff.

"Where have you been?" she demanded, and I looked in vain for that womanly concern in her splendid eyes. "Where have you come from?"

"Up in the north," says I. "Strackenz—my God, I've had a terrible time. I'm desperate, Lola—no money, not a damned farthing, and I must get out of Germany, you see? It's life or death for me. I've been at my wit's end, and I was coming to you because I knew you'd help—"

"You were, were you?" says she.

"—and I saw you back there, with those villains menacing you—my God! you were magnificent, my darling! I've never seen such splendid spirit, and I've been in some tight spots, as you know. Lola—please, dear Lola, I've been through hell—and it was partly because of you. You won't fail me now, will you? Oh, my darling, say you won't."

I must say it was pretty good, on the spur of the moment; the distraught, pleading line seemed the best to follow, and I must have looked pretty wild—and yet harmless. She looked at me, stony-faced, and my spirits sank.

"Get out of my coach," says she, very cold. "Why should I help you?"

"Why—after what I've suffered? Look, they slashed me with sabres, those damned friends of yours—Bismarck and that swine Rudi! I've escaped by a miracle, and they're still after me—they'll kill me if they find me, don't you understand?"

"You're raving," says she, sitting there cold and beautiful. "I don't know what you're talking about; it has nothing to do with me."

"You can't be so heartless," says I. "Please, Lola, all I ask is to be allowed to leave Munich with you—or if you'll lend me some money, I'll go alone. But you can't refuse me now—I'm punished for whatever you had against me, aren't I? Good God, I wouldn't cast you adrift—you know that! We're both English, my darling, after all . . ."

I have an idea that I went down on my knees—it's all the harder to tip a grovelling creature out of a coach, after all, and she bit her lip and swore and looked both ways in distraction. Her little servant settled it for the time being.

"Let him stay, madame; it is not wise to linger here. We should hurry on to Herr Laibinger's house without delay."

She still hesitated, but he was insistent, and I raised the roof with my entreaties, so eventually she snapped to the coachee to drive on. I was loud in my gratitude, and would have described the events leading up to my present situation at some length, but she shut me up pretty sharp.

"I have some concerns of my own to occupy me," says she. "Where you have been or what devilment you've been doing you may keep to yourself."

"But Lola—if I could only explain—"

"The devil take your explanation!" snaps she, and her Irish was as thick as Paddy's head. "I've no wish to hear it."

So I sat back meekly, with my valise between my feet, and she sat there opposite me, thoughtful and angry.

281

I recognised the mood—it was one step short of her piss-pot flinging tantrum—perhaps that mad walk through the crowd had shaken her, after all, or she was simply fretting about tomorrow. I tried one placatory remark:

"I'm most awfully sorry, Lola—about what has happened, I mean. They seem to have treated you shamefully—"

But she paid no attention, though, so I shut up. It came back to me, all of a sudden, how it was in a coach I had first met her, years ago—and I had been a fugitive then, and she had rescued me. If necessary I might remind her of it, but not now. But thinking of it, I made comparisons; yes, even in my present desperation, I could appreciate that she was as lovely now as she had been then—if I made up to her, carefully, who knew but she might relent her present coldness (that Ranelagh business must have bitten deep). She might even let me accompany her all the way out of Germany—the prospect of another tumble or two presented themselves to my ever-ready imagination, and very delightful thoughts they were.

"Stop leering like that!" she shot at me suddenly.

"I beg your pardon, Lola, I—"

"If I help you—and I say 'if'—you'll behave yourself with suitable humility." She considered me. "Where do you want to go?"

"Anywhere, darling, out of Munich—out of Germany, if possible. Oh, Lola, darling—"

"I'll take you out of Munich, then, tomorrow. After that you can fend for yourself—and it's more than you deserve."

Well, that was something. I'm still, even now, at a loss to know why she was so hard on me that night—I do believe it was not so much dislike of me as that she was distraught at falling from power and having to leave Bavaria in disgrace. And yet, it may have been that she had still not forgiven me for having her hooted off the London stage. At any rate, it seemed that her kindness to me when

I first came to Munich had been all a sham to lull me into easy prey for Rudi. Oh, well, let her dislike me as long as she gave me a lift. It was better here than tramping round Munich, starting at every shadow.

We stayed that night at a house in the suburbs, and I was graciously permitted to share a garret with her servant, Papon, who snored like a horse and had fleas. At least, I *got* fleas, so they must have been his. In the morning word came that the station was closed, as a result of the recent disorders, and we had to wait a day, while Lola fretted and I sat in my attic and nursed my valise. Next day the trains were still uncertain, and Lola vowed she wouldn't stay another night in Munich, which pleased me considerably. The sooner we were off, the better. So she decided that we should drive out of town a day's journey and catch a train at some village station or other—I've forgotten the name now. All these arrangements, of course, were made without any reference to me; Lola determined everything with the people of the house, while poor old Flashy lurked humbly in the background, out of sight, and expecting to be asked to clean the master's boots at any minute.

However, in the wasted day that we spent waiting, Lola did speak to me, and was even civil. She didn't inquire about what had happened to me in the time since she had helped to have me shanghaied out of Munich by Rudi, and when I took advantage of the thaw in her manner to try to tell her, she wouldn't have it.

"There is no profit in harking back," says she. "Whatever has happened, we shall let bygones be bygones." I was quite bucked up at this, and tried to tell her how grateful I was, and how deeply I realised how unworthy I was of her kindness, etc., and she did give me a rather quizzical smile, and said we would not talk about it, but we got no warmer than that. However, when it came time to set out on the day after, I found she had gone to the trouble of getting me a clean shirt from the master of the house, and she was quite charming as we got into the coach, and even called me Harry.

Come, thinks I, this is better and better; at this rate I'll be mounting her again in no time. So I set myself to be as pleasant as I know, and we talked away quite the thing (but not about the past few months). It got better still during the morning; she began to laugh again, and even to rally me in her old Irish style—and when Lola did that, turning on you the full glory of those brilliant eyes—well, unless you were blind or made of wood you were curling round her little finger in no time at all.

I must say I was a little puzzled by this change of mood towards me at first—but, after all, I said to myself, she was always an unpredictable piece—melting one minute, raging the next, cold and proud, or gay and captivating, a queen and a little girl all in one. I must also say again that she had uncanny powers of charming men, far beyond the simple spell of her beauty, and by afternoon we were back on our old best terms again, and her big eyes were taking on that wanton, languorous look that had used to set me twitching and thinking lewdly of beds and sofas.

Altogether, by afternoon it was understood that she would not part company with me as she had intended; we would catch the train together, with Papon, of course, and travel on south. She had still not decided where to go, but she talked gaily of plans for what she might do in Italy, or France, or whatever place might take her fancy. Wherever it was, she would rebuild her fortune, and perhaps even find another kingdom to play with.

"Who cares a snap for Germany?" says she. "Why, we have the whole world before us—the courts, the cities, the theatres, the fun!" She was infectious in her gaiety, and Papon and I grinned like idiots. "I want to live before I die!" She said that more than once; another of her mottoes, I suppose.

So we talked and joked as the coach rattled along, and she sang little Spanish songs—gay, catchy ditties—and coaxed me to sing, too. I gave them "Garryowen", which she liked, being Irish, and "The British Grenadiers", at which she and Papon laughed immoderately. I was in good spirits; it was gradually dawning on me at last that I was going to get away high, wide, and handsome, jewels and all, and I was warm at the thought that all the time the brilliant, lovely Lola never suspected what she was helping me to escape with.

At our village we discovered there was a train south next day, so we put up at the local inn, a decent little place called Der Senfbusch—the Mustard-Pot—I remember Lola laughing over the name. We had a capital dinner, and I must have drunk a fair quantity, for I have only vague memories of the evening, and of going to bed with Lola in a great creaking four-poster which swayed and squealed when we got down to business—she giggled so much at the row we made that I was almost put off my stroke. Then we had a night-cap, and my last memory of her before she blew out the candle is of those great eyes and smiling red lips and the black hair tumbling down over my face as she kissed me.

"Your poor head," says she, stroking my bristling skull. "I do hope it grows curly again—and those lovely whiskers, too. You'll wear them again for me, won't you, Harry?"

Then we went to sleep, and when I woke I was alone in the bed, with the sun streaming bright in at the window, and a most devilish headache to keep me company. I ploughed out, but there was no sign of her; I called for Papon, but no reply. The landlord must have heard me, for he came up the stairs to see what I wanted.

"Madame—where is she?" says I, rubbing my eyes.

"Madame?" He seemed puzzled. "Why—she has gone, sir. With her servant. They went to the station above three hours ago."

I gaped at him, dumbfounded.

"What the devil d'ye mean—gone? We were travelling together, man—she can't have gone without me?"

"I assure you, sir, she has gone." He fumbled beneath his apron. "She left this for your excellency, to be given to you when you woke." And the lout held out a letter, smirking.

I took it from him; sure enough, there was Lola's hand on the cover. And then an awful thought struck me—I sped back into my room; blundering over a chair, and tearing open the cupboard door with a mounting fear in my throat. Sure enough—my valise was gone.

I couldn't believe it for a moment. I hunted under the bed, behind the curtains, everywhere in the room, but of course it was not to be seen. I was shaking with rage, mouthing filthy curses to myself, and then I flung down on the bed, beating at it with my fists. The thieving slut had robbed me—God, and after what I had been through for that swag! I called her every foul name I could think of, futile, helpless curses—for it didn't take an instant's thought to see that there was nothing I could do. I couldn't lay an accusation of theft for stuff I had lifted myself; I couldn't pursue, because I hadn't the means. I had lost it—everything, to a lovely, loving, tender harlot who had charmed me into carelessness—aye, and drugged me, too, by the state of my tongue and stomach—and left me stranded while she went off with my fortune.

I sat there raging, and then I remembered the letter, crumpled in my fist, and tore it open. God! It even had her coat-of-arms on the sheet. I cleared my eyes and read:

My dear Harry,
My need is greater than thine. I cannot begin to guess where you came by such a treasure trove, but I know it must have been dishonestly, so I do not shrink from removing it. After all, you have a rich wife and family to keep you, and I am alone in the world.

You will find a little money in your coat pocket; it should get you out of Germany if you are careful.

Try not to think too hardly of me; after all, *you* would have played *me* false when it suited you. I trust we shall not meet again—and yet I say it with some regret, dear worthless, handsome Harry. You may not believe it, but there will always be a place for you in the heart of

Rosanna.

P.S. Courage! And shuffle the cards.

I sat there, speechless, goggling at it. So help me God, if I could have come at her in that moment, I would have snapped her neck in cold blood, for a lying, canting, thieving, seducing, hypocritical, smooth-tongued, two-faced slut. To think that only yesterday I had been laughing up my sleeve about how she was helping me on my way home with a fortune unsuspected, while she was going to have to go back to regular whoring to earn a living! And now she was away, beyond hope of recovery, and my britches arse was hanging out again, and she would live in the lap of luxury somewhere on my hard-gotten booty. When I thought of the torture and risk I had gone through for that priceless haul, I raved aloud.

Well, it was no wonder I was put out then. Now, after so many years, it doesn't seem to matter much. I have that letter still; it is old and worn and yellow—like me. She never became like that; she died as lovely as she had always been, far away in America—having lived before she died. I suppose I'm maudlin, but I don't think particularly hard of her now—she was in the game for the same things as the rest of us—she got more of them, that's all. I'd rather think of her as the finest romp that ever pressed a pillow—the most beautiful *I* ever knew, anyway. And I still wear my whiskers. One doesn't forget Lola Montez, ever. Conniving bitch.

Of course, when you're old and fairly well pickled in

drink you can forgive most things past, and reserve your spite for the neighbours who keep you awake at night and children who get under your feet. In youth it's different, and my fury that morning was frightful. I rampaged about that room, and hurled the furniture about, and when the landlord came to protest I knocked him down and kicked him. There was a tremendous outcry then, the constable was summoned, and it was a damned near thing that I wasn't hauled before a magistrate and jailed.

In the end, there was nothing for it but to pack up what little I had and make back for Munich. I had a little cash now, thanks to Lola—God, that was the crowning insult—so that at long last I was able to make for home, weary and angry and full of venom. I left Germany poorer than I came in—although of course there was still £250 of Lola's (or Bismarck's) money in the bank at home. I had two sabre cuts and a gash on my arm, a decent grasp of the German language, and several white hairs, I imagine, after what I'd been through. Oh, that was another thing, of course—I had a scalp that looked like a hog's back for bristles, although it grew right in time. And to make my temper even worse, by the time I reached the Channel I heard news that Lola was in Switzerland, fornicating with Viscount Peel, the old prime minister's son—no doubt he was well peeled, too, by the time she had finished with him.

I've only once been back to Germany. Indeed, I don't include it even among the garrulous reminiscences that have made me the curse of half the clubs in London—those that'll have me. Only once did I tell the tale, and that was privately some years ago, to young Hawkins, the lawyer—I must have been well foxed, or he was damned persuasive—and he has used it for the stuff of one of his romances, which sells very well, I'm told.

He made it into a heroic tale, of course, but whether he believed it or not when I told it, I've no idea; probably not. It's a good deal stranger than fiction, and yet not so strange, because such resemblances as mine and Carl Gustaf's do happen. Why, I can think of another case, connected with this very story, and I saw it when the Duchess Irma came to London in the old Queen's diamond year—they were related, as I've said. It's the only time I've seen Irma since—I kept well in the background, of course, but I had a good look at her, and even at seventy she was a damned handsome piece, and set me itching back over the years. She was a widow then, Carl Gustaf having died of a chill on the lungs back in the '60's, but she had her son with her; he was a chap in his forties, I should say, and the point is that he was the living spit of Rudi von Starnberg—well, that can only have been coincidence, of course. It gave me quite a turn, though, and for a moment I was glancing nervously round for a quick retreat.

Rudi I last heard of with the Germans when they marched on Paris; there was a rumour of his death, so he's probably been stoking Lucifer's fires these thirty years and good luck to him. Unlike Mr Rassendyll I did *not* exercise myself daily in arms in expectation of trying another round with him: one was enough to convince me that with fellows like young Rudi the best weapon you can have is a long pair of legs and a good start.

Bismarck—well, all the world knows about him. I suppose he was one of the greatest statesmen of the age, a shaper of destiny and all the rest of it. He got to his feet for me, though, when I looked down my nose at him—I like to think back on that. And it is queer to consider that but for me, the course of history in Europe might have been very different—though who's to know? Bismarck, Lola, Rudi, Irma, and I—the threads come together, and then run very wide, and are all gathered together again, and go into the dark in the end. You see, I can be philosophical—*I'm* still here. [43]

I wasn't feeling so philosophical, though, when I journeyed back from Munich to London, and arrived home at last, soaked and shivering with weariness and our damned

March weather. I seem to have come home to that front door so many times—covered with glory once or twice, and other times limping along with my boots letting in. This was one of the unhappier homecomings, and it wasn't improved by the fact that when I was let into the hall, my dear father-in-law, old Morrison, was just coming downstairs. That was almost the last straw—my bloody Scotch relatives were still on the premises when I had hoped that they might have gone back to their gloomy sewer in Renfrew. The only bright spot I had been able to see was that I would be able to celebrate my return in bed with Elspeth, and here was this curmudgeon welcoming me in true Celtic style.

"Huh!" says he; "it's you. You're hame." And he muttered something about another mouth to feed.

I gripped my temper as I gave my coat to Oswald, bade him good afternoon, and asked if Elspeth was at home.

"Oh, aye," says he, looking me over sourly. "She'll be glad tae see ye, nae doot. Ye're thinner," he added, with some satisfaction. "I take it Germany didnae agree wi' ye—if that's where ye've been."

"Yes, it's where I've been," says I. "Where's Elspeth?"

"Oh, in the drawin'-room—takin' tea wi' her friends, I suppose. We have all the fashionable habits in this hoose—includin' your ain faither's intemperance."

"He's well again?" I asked, and Oswald informed me that he was upstairs, lying down.

"His accustomed position," says old Morrison. "Weel, ye'd better go up, sir, and be reunited wi' the wife ye'll have been yearning for. If ye make haste ye'll be in time for tea, from her fine new silver service—aye, a' the luxuries o' the Saltmarket." And to the sound of his whining I ran upstairs and into the drawing-room, feeling that tightness in my chest that I always felt when I was coming back again to Elspeth.

She gave a little cry at the sight of me, and rose, smiling, from behind the tray from which she had been dispensing tea to the females who were sitting about, all bonnets and gentility. She looked radiantly stupid, as ever, with her blonde hair done a different way, in ringlets that framed her cheeks.

"Oh, Harry!" She came forward, and stopped. "Why—Harry! Whatever have you done to your head?"

I should have expected that, of course, and kept my hat on, or worn a wig, or anything to prevent the repetition of that dam-fool question. Oh, well, I was home again, and in one piece, and Elspeth was holding out her hands and smiling and asking:

"What did you bring me from Germany, Harry?"

(The end of the second packet of The Flashman Papers)

APPENDIX I: *The Prisoner of Zenda*

Whether Flashman's real-life experiences in Germany provided Anthony Hope with the basis of his famous romance, *The Prisoner of Zenda*, is a matter which readers must decide for themselves. Flashman is quite definite in the text in two places—especially where he refers to "Hawkins", which was Hope's real name. There is certainly some similarity in events, and names like Lauengram, Kraftstein, Detchard, de Gautet, Bersonin, and Tarlenheim are common to both stories; Flashman's "Major Sapten" is literary twin brother to Hope's "Colonel Sapt", and no amateur of romantic fiction will fail to identify Rudi von Starnberg with the Count of Hentzau.

APPENDIX II: *Lola Montez*

Although several of the notes following this appendix refer to Lola Montez, she deserves fuller mention than can be conveniently included there. She was, after all, one of the most remarkable adventuresses in history, with an intellect and personality to match her looks; for these gifts, rather than her capacity for scandalous behaviour, she is worth remembering.

Her real name was Marie Dolores Eliza Rosanna Gilbert, and she was born in Limerick in 1818, the daughter of a British Army officer. He was probably Scottish; her mother was part-Spanish, and Lola was brought up in India, in Scotland, and on the continent. When she was 18 she ran off with a Captain James, and after living in India, returned to England in 1841. She seems to have begun on her long succession of lovers while still in her 'teens, and James divorced her in 1842. Her career as a Spanish dancer followed, and after a series of Continental appearances, lovers, and scandals, she became the mistress of Ludwig of Bavaria. It has been suggested that his interest in her was purely intellectual; that is a matter of opinion. What is not to be doubted is that she was the ruler of Bavaria—and there have been worse governors of nations—until the revolution of 1848 forced her to leave the country. She later went to America, where she lectured on such subjects as beauty and fashion, and died in New York in 1861, when she was only 43.

Apart from Captain James she had two other husbands, a young officer named Heald, who died, and a San Francisco editor, Patrick Hall, who divorced her.

This is the briefest outline of her short life; there is no room to include all the lovers, real and reputed (apart from those mentioned by Flashman, gossip included even Lord Palmerston), or the endless catalogue of scandals, scenes, escapes, and triumphs. These can be found in her biographies, of which *The Magnificent Montez*, by Horace Wyndham, is particularly recommended.

Flashman's account of Lola's behaviour, and his assessment of her character, seem both authentic and fair. His enthusiasm for her looks and personality were generally shared (even by his old Indian acquaintance, the Hon. Emily Eden); there is ample evidence of her promiscuity, her optimistic cheerfulness, her sudden furious rages, and her tendency to physical violence—the men she horsewhipped included a Berlin policeman, the boots of a Munich hotel, and the editor of the *Ballarat Times*, Australia. But none of her contemporaries has left such an intimate portrait of her as Flashman has, or come closer to explaining the magnetism she exerted. And in spite of his conduct towards her, he obviously respected her deeply.

NOTES

1. The Minor St James Club may have been new to Flashman in 1842, but it was notorious to fashionable London. Its proprietor, a Mr Bond, was successfully sued in that year by a disgruntled punter who received £3500 in respect of his losses. (See L. J. Ludovici's *The Itch for Play*.)

2. Mr Wilson's performances were a great success all over England, especially with exiled Scots like Mrs Flashman. His repertoire included "A Nicht wi' Burns", and a lecture on the '45 Rebellion, as well as popular songs. He died during a tour of the United States.

3. Horse-drawn omnibuses had been running in London since Flashman was a small boy; possibly he is referring to a new service. Their conductors, or "cads", had a reputation for violence and obscenity which lingers in the word to this day.

4. Raiding of gambling-hells was common after the Police Act of 1839, which permitted forced entry. Flashman's observations on the proprietors' precautions and their right to sue the police are accurate. (See Ludovici.)

5. Hughes' passing reference to Speedicut certainly brackets him with Flashman, and can therefore be taken to be highly uncomplimentary. Flashman shows him in a new light, which prompts the thought that Speedicut may have been one (or both) of the anonymous companions in "Tom Brown" who spared the fags in the blanket-tossing episode and was later in favour of only

295

partially roasting Tom before the fire.

6. The "barbed wire" comparison must have occurred to Flashman at some later date; it was not in common use before the 1870's.

7. Nick Ward claimed the championship of England after beating Deaf James Burke in September, 1840, and Ben Caunt in February, 1841. He lost a return bout with Caunt three months later.

8. The second Marquis of Conyngham was among the victims fleeced at Mr Bond's Minor Club; he lost at least £500 on two occasions in 1842.

9. Flashman's description of Bismarck evokes a different picture from the popular impression of the Iron Chancellor, but it tallies with those details of his early life which biographers seldom dwell on at length. Bismarck's taste for playful violence, his boorish conduct in public places, his whoring, carousing, and riotous behaviour (the habit of firing a pistol into the ceiling to announce his arrival to friends, for example), and his 25 duels in his first term at Göttingen, all testify to a nature not invariably statesmanlike. He appears, in fact, to have been an unpleasant young man, brilliant beyond his years but given to cynicism and arrogance. He was as tall, strong, and handsome as Flashman remembers him, with blond-red hair and aristocratic bearing.

As to his presence in London in 1842, he did indeed travel extensively in Britain that year, and was rebuked for whistling in the streets of Leith on a Sunday. He is said to have liked the British; his affection encompassed at least one beautiful English girl, Laura Russell, with whom he had been infatuated some years earlier, but who had broken their engagement to marry an older man. Possibly this prejudiced him in later life.

10. Peel's introduction in 1842 of an income tax of 7d in the pound on all incomes above £150 was regarded as iniquitous. Lord Brougham argued (with what effect we all know) that "such a tax ought on no account to form a part of the ordinary revenue . . . but should cease with the necessity which alone could justify its imposition".

11. Bismarck was accounted something of a wit, and like most wits he seems to have had a habit of repeating himself. His remark that a gift for languages was a fine talent for a head-waiter is also recorded in Prince von Bülow's "Memoirs", where it is suggested that Bismarck was in the habit of using it on linguistically-gifted young diplomats.

12. John Gully, M.P. (1783-1863) was one of the most popular and respected champions of the bare-knuckle ring. The son of a Bath butcher, he conducted his father's business so unsuccessfully that he was imprisoned for debt, but while in the King's Bench in 1805 he was visited by an acquaintance, Henry "Game Chicken" Pearce, then champion of England. In a friendly spar with the champion in the jail, Gully was so impressive that sporting patrons paid his debts, and he met Pearce for the title at Hailsham, Sussex, a fortnight before Trafalgar. Before a huge crowd which included Beau Brummel and the Duke of Clarence (later William IV), Pearce narrowly beat Gully over 64 rounds; it has since been suggested that Gully outfought the champion, but was reluctant to knock out his benefactor. This seems unlikely. However, Gully won the title two years later with decisive victories over Bob Gregson, "the Lancashire Giant", and then retired, aged only 24. He made a fortune on the turf, where he owned several Classic winners, and by investments in coal and land. He was M.P. for Pontefract

from 1832 to 1837, was twice married, and had 24 children.

Flashman's portrait of Gully accords with other contemporary accounts of the gentle, quiet six-footer who, when roused, was one of the most savage and scientific fighters of boxing's golden age. "At heart," says Nat Fleischer, "his ambition was to belong to the gentry. He had little use for the professional ring and its shady followers." Fleischer is probably right when he suggests that, but for chance, Gully would never have become a pugilist at all.

13. Flashman's reference to a horse called "Running Reins" is most interesting. In May, 1844, a year and a half after the party at Perceval's place, the Derby was won by a horse entered as "Running Rein"; it proved, upon inquiry, to be a four-year-old named Maccabeus, and was disqualified, but not before the scandal had developed into a court case (Wood v. Peel) and become the talk of the sporting world. The principal villain in the case, Abraham Levi Goodman, fled the country; the horse Maccabeus disappeared. But there certainly was a genuine Running Rein, whose performances in the 1843 season had given rise to suspicion. Flashman's mention seems to suggest that Running Rein (his rendering of the name as Reins is obviously a slip) had a reputation earlier still, although not an unsavoury one. Turf records of the day contain no mention of Running Ribbons, however, so Spottswood was probably doing Gully no great favour in offering to sell him.

14. John L. Sullivan won the first recognised world heavyweight title when he knocked out Paddy Ryan in nine rounds at Mississippi City, on Feb. 7, 1882. It is reported that the spectators included Henry Ward Beecher, the Rev. T. De Witt Talmage, and Jesse James.

15. Gents and Mooners. In the 1840's the term Gent was

most particularly applied to the young middle-class idler who aped his superiors and dressed extravagantly; the Mooner was rather older and spent his time "mooning" at shop windows and ambling gently about the town. Flashman would consider both species to be well beneath him.

16. Despite Flashman's enthusiastic notice, it seems probable that Lola Montez was not a particularly good artiste, although the historian Veit Valentin observes that she had "the tigerish vivacity that inspires the Andalusian dance".

17. The account of Lola's disastrous appearance at Her Majesty's Theatre (June 3, 1843) is splendidly accurate, not only in its description of Lord Ranelagh's denunciation, but even in such details as the composition of the audience and the programme notes. (See Wyndham's *Magnificent Montez*.) This is a good, verifiable example of Flashman's ability as a straight reporter, and encourages confidence in those other parts of his story where corroboration is lacking and checking of the facts is impossible.

18. Lola had a passionate affair with Liszt in the year following her departure from London; after their first rapture she appears to have had much the same effect on the famous pianist as she did on Flashman. He tired of her, and did indeed abandon her in a hotel, whereupon she spent several hours smashing the furniture. Typically, Lola bore no grudge; in her high days in Munich she wrote to Liszt offering him Bavarian honours.

19. The coat-of-arms of the Countess of Landsfeld is accurately described; the "fat whale" was a silver dolphin.

20. Stieler's portrait of Lola in Ludwig's gallery is a model of Victorian respectability. A more characteristic Montez is to be seen in Dartiguenave's lithograph; he

has caught not only her striking beauty, but her imperious spirit. (See Mr Barbosa's rendering of Stieler's portrait of Lola on the left side of the front cover of this edition.)

21. "Lola was always vain of her bosom". She was indeed, if the story of her first meeting with Ludwig is to be believed. He is supposed to have expressed doubts about the reality of her figure: her indignant reply was to tear open the top of her dress.

22. There is no supporting evidence that Wagner visited Lola in Munich at this time, but it is not impossible. They met for the first time in 1844, when Liszt took her to a special performance of "Rienzi" at Dresden, and Wagner's impression was of "a painted and jewelled woman with bold, bad eyes". He also described her as "demonic and heartless". Curiously, the great composer gained as much favour from Ludwig II as Lola had done from Ludwig I—so much so that the wits nicknamed him "Lolotte".

23. The American may have been C. G. Leland, a student at Munich University and a friend of Lola's. He claimed that he was the only one of her intimates at whom she had never thrown "a plate or a book, or attacked with a dagger, poker, broom, or other deadly weapon".

24. Schönhausen. Flashman's view of the castle's "medieval ghastliness" was echoed by Bismarck himself; he described it to a friend as an "old haunted castle, with pointed arches and walls four feet thick, (and) thirty rooms of which two are furnished." He also complained about its rats and the wind in the chimneys.

25. Flashman's summary of the Schleswig-Holstein Question is accurate so far as it goes; enthusiasts in diplomatic history who wish greater detail are referred to Dr David

Thomson's *Europe Since Napoleon*, pp. 242-3 and 309-11. German and Danish versions of the problem should not be read in isolation.

26. The *schlager* play of the German students, whereby they could receive superficial head and face wounds which left permanent scars for public admiration, was a unique form of the duel. The equipment is as Flashman describes it; the *schlager* itself was three-and-a-half feet long, with an unusually large guard ("the soup-plate of honour"). The practice of leaving the wounds open to form the largest possible scar is curiously paralleled by the custom of certain primitive African tribes. In the duel itself, thrusting was strictly forbidden, except at the University of Jena, where there were many theological students. These young men would have found facial scars an embarrassment in their careers, so instead of cutting at the head, Jena students were allowed to run each other through the body, thus satisfying honour without causing visible disfigurement.

27. Bismarck liked to picture himself eventually becoming a rustic land-owner; his remark about Stettin wool market occurs again in his recorded conversation, when he spoke of his ambition to "raise a family, and ruin the morals of my peasants with brandy".

28. Bandobast: organisation (Hindustani).

29. In 1847 Germany suffered its second successive failure of the potato crop. In the northern areas wheat had doubled its price in a few years.

30. The emblem of Holstein was, in fact, a nettle-leaf shape.

31. "a plumed helmet, à la Tin-bellies". Flashman is here almost certainly referring to the New Regulation Helmet which had been announced for the British Heavy

301

Dragoons in the previous autumn. Its ridiculously extravagant plumage—popularly supposed to be an inspiration of Prince Albert's—had been the talk of fashionable London in the weeks shortly before Flashman's departure for Munich.

32. Libby Prison, in Richmond, Va., was notorious in the U.S. Civil War. Federal officers were confined there by the Confederates, often in conditions of dreadful overcrowding; it was the scene of a mass escape by tunnel in 1864, and two subsequent Federal cavalry raids to rescue prisoners. Flashman's reference seems to suggest that he was confined there himself; no doubt examination of those packets of his papers as yet unopened will confirm this.

33. Kibroth-Hattaavah—"there they buried the people that lusted" (Numbers 11:34, 35)—seems to have been a popular subject for sermons at public schools. Dr Rowlands preached on this text in *Eric, or Little by Little*, by Dean Farrar.

34. It is just possible that the orator was Karl Marx. The Strackenzian coronation must have taken place before his recorded return to Germany from Brussels, where he had conceived the *Communist Manifesto*, but it is not inconceivable that he visited Strackenz beforehand. The coronation certainly offered a tempting target at a time when European politics generally were in a precarious state. Against the fact that there is no evidence of his ever having visited the duchy, must be balanced Flashman's description of the orator, which is Marx to the life.

35. Eider Danes, a faction who wished to make Schleswig Danish as far as the River Eider. Von Starnberg's concern about pro-Danish militant organisations in Strackenz is understandable, as is his anxiety over Hansen's

unexpected appearance at the wedding. What struck the editor as curious was that none of Bismarck's conspirators seem ever to have been alarmed at the prospect of Danish royalty attending the ceremony; that surely would have led to Flashman's exposure. But obviously none did attend, and this can only be explained by the fact that King Christian of Denmark died on January 20, 1848—shortly before the wedding took place—and that this kept the Danish Court at home, in mourning. A rare stroke of luck for the conspiracy; one does not like to think it was anything else.

36. "Punch" stayed neutral in the checked-or-striped trousers controversy. One of its cartoons suggested that "checks are uncommon superior, but stripes is most nobby". But it was a middle- rather than an upper-class debate.

37. Flashman believes he sang the old nursery rhyme in English, yet it is interesting to note (see Opie's *Oxford Dictionary of Nursery Rhymes*) that it appeared in German, apparently for the first time in that language, in 1848 ("So reiten die Herren auf ihren stolzen Pferden, tripp trapp, tripp trapp, tripp trapp") the year in which he and the Duchess Irma were married. Possibly she had noticed after all.

38. Domenico Angelo Tremamondo (1717-1804), known as Angelo, founded a dynasty of fencing-masters who conducted an academy of arms in London in the eighteenth and nineteenth centuries.

39. Revolution swept across Europe in those early months of 1848. Within the space of a few weeks revolts took place in Sicily, France, Austria, Italy, Germany, and Poland; new constitutions and reforms were adopted in Naples, Tuscany, Piedmont, Rome, Budapest, and

Berlin, and the *Communist Manifesto* appeared. In Britain a Chartist petition was unsuccessful, and John Stuart Mill produced the *Principles of Political Economy*.

40. Presumably Flashman is referring to David's highly romantic painting of Napoleon in the Alps, and confusing it with other works by the same artist in which the Emperor is shown with retinues of suitably respectful subordinates.

41. In fact the telegraph had been in existence for some years, but its use was not sufficiently widespread to have caused Flashman concern.

42. There is some confusion about Lola Montez's movements during her final weeks in Munich; more than once she changed her mind about leaving, and made efforts to re-establish her hold over Ludwig. As to her walk through the hostile crowd, it is mentioned by at least one authority, and there is no doubt that the incident of her appearance on the balcony, splendidly dressed and toasting a raging crowd in champagne, is authentic. Her indifference to physical danger was remarkable.

43. And in the end Bismarck got his way; by waging war on Denmark in 1864 he achieved the occupation of Schleswig by Prussia and Holstein by Austria, thus helping to provoke the Austro–Prussian war of 1866. With Austria defeated as a rival, Bismarck by the Franco–Prussian war of 1870 united Germany minus Austria, and Schleswig and Holstein became part of the German Empire.